Praise for *The Gr*

MW00593648

"David Bluder's novel allows us to see where gambling on sports could lead if we allow it to be unregulated. *The Great Gamble* shows how the game can be destroyed by greed, leaving our children with examples of crime as opposed to appreciation and selflessness."
—Senator Bill Bradley, Three time All-American, Princeton University. 1965 Associated Press Player of the Year. Final Four, Princeton. 10 years with New York Knicks. 1970 and 1973 NBA Champions. NBA Hall of Fame. Olympic Gold Medalist. Rhodes Scholar, Oxford University. Served in US Senate 1979-1997. Former Presidential Candidate. Author of seven books.

"David Bluder takes the reader on an exhilarating, violent journey through the underbelly of sports gambling, made all the more frightening by his page-turning storytelling and the fact that his fictional account may not be so far from the truth."
—Melissa Isaacson, Award-winning sportswriter, ESPN, *Chicago Tribune* and award-winning author of *State: A Team, a Triumph, a Transformation.*

"*The Great Gamble* is a book I couldn't seem to put down. The characters draw you in and the attention to detail makes you feel as though you're in the story right along with them. With plot twists around every corner, this book gives a close up look of when the high stakes of the sports world clashes with the dangers of gambling, fixing, and drug cartels alike. Overall a fantastic read, and I love the tribute to scenes written about Iowa City. Go Hawks!!"
—Megan Gustafson, 2019 Naismith Player of the Year, AP Player of the Year, ESPNW National Player of the Year, First Team All American, Lisa Leslie Award.

"Bluder lays out the road map for how this could happen anywhere! A riveting work of fiction that should open the eyes of all fans to the traps that student athletes could fall into."
—Bobby Hansen, World Champion Chicago Bulls, 9 year NBA career.

"Riveting, what a read! You not only are engulfed in the fictional storyline but also start to think that this is reality. Is this happening more than we suspect? Bluder writes so that as a reader, you become part of each page as if you are experiencing being in the character's life. You can't help but empathize with that person and his situation. You don't have to be a sports' fan to enjoy this book."

—Tim McClelland. Retired as MLB's second most senior umpire. Four-time World Series and three-time All-Star game umpire. Plate umpire during George Brett's "Pine Tar" game, as well as Sammy Sosa's corked bat game. Also, umpired two perfect games.

"The corruption that can accompany sports gambling should have no place in organized sports. In *The Great Gamble*, David Bluder exposes how devastating and far reaching this attack on the integrity and character of those involved can go. I am hopeful his effort to highlight this dark reality of sports will keep others participating."

—Aaron Kampman, former NFL All Pro, Green Bay Packers.

"A novel that could be reality. The research invested into this work is amazing. Throughout my twenty years of officiating football in the Big VIII and XII, I never experienced nor knew anyone who had dealt with this situation—not that someone would readily discuss. After reading this novel I certainly understand and appreciate how entrapment could occur."

—Tom Ahlers, previous chief official of Big Twelve and Big Eight Conferences, football.

"David Bluder takes readers on a fast-paced journey through a sinister side of the sports world that will leave them questioning the integrity of even the most seemingly wholesome local high school basketball games. A sobering vision of a future in which corrupt forces gain a stranglehold on the sports industry through the gambling portal."

—Dan Matheson, former Director of Operations New York Yankees. NCAA Associate Director of Enforcement, University of Iowa Presidential Committee on Athletics.

"*The Great Gamble* comes out at a time when the growth of sports betting is about to expand greatly. When placing a bet is as easy as making a phone call (and is also legal), who knows what can happen. An interesting read and a very relevant topic!"

—Tom Davis, former Head Coach, Boston College, Stanford, Iowa, Drake. AP Coach of the Year, 1987

"David Bluder is a gifted storyteller, and the story he tells in *The Great Gamble* is at once insightful and thrilling. What he discovers at the intersection of college basketball and criminality will make your head spin. 'We can't go under hypnosis anymore?' an FBI agent asks. 'They're afraid we would reveal too many secrets.' This is precisely what makes *The Great Gamble* such a satisfying read. Whether he is posting up or shooting from the perimeter, David Bluder never misses."

—Christopher Merrill, Director of International Writing Program University of Iowa. Prize winning American Poet, essayist, journalist and translator. Appointed by President Obama to National Council of Humanities. Honored knighthood in arts and letters by French government.

"Relentlessly entertaining. Heart pounding. Sometimes when I didn't want it to be. Is everybody making money from sports gambling but me? David Bluder knows a lot about sports and gambling, but he knows even more about is character development. It's about ice cold international financial crimes, but it's also human people sharing human feelings and it's so well written you can feel the weather change. The surprises are stellar. You'll go back and reread a few chapters to see why you didn't see everything coming. The only thing that was a little unsettling was, apparently, I have to figure out what all these guys do next. A great book."

—Tom Arnold, Actor, Comedian, Television Host.

"An intriguing and fascinating look at today's big business of sports gambling. Fact or fiction, the lines become blurred in this gripping tale by newcomer David Bluder."

—Dave Dierks, Chairman, Herbert Hoover Presidential Foundation.

"Instantly captivated by the emotions and depth of the characters and how their lives collide in a modern-day twist in the dark, underground of sports"

—Debbie Antonelli. ESPN Analyst.

"David Bluder weaves a fascinating web of deception, self-interest and manipulation around college basketball and the recruitment processes that take place. *The Great Gamble* meticulously follows Jason Carson along a plausible and exciting pathway while exposing the reader to interesting and despicable characters in pursuit of power, influence and money. This book is a genuine page turner."

—Bob Bowlsby, Commissioner of the Big Twelve.

"Wow! I was overwhelmed with what appeared to be the blurring of fiction and non-fiction on our current American Culture. News headlines and story lines that appear as if I'm watching Sports Center or reading *USA Today*. The descriptive nature of David's writing took me on a journey that stirred up images of *Pulp Fiction* meets *Sicario*. Loved it!"

—Marv Cook, Consensus All American Univ of Iowa 1988, Two Time All Pro TE '91&'92.

"If you enjoy an intense thriller, an international footprint, the truth about sports gambling and a fast paced story then *The Great Gamble* is the perfect book!"

—Terry Reynolds, President Florida State League, Former Special Assistant to General Manager for the Cincinnati Reds. Director of domestic and international scouting for the Los Angeles Dodgers. Minor League Executive of the Year Award winner.

"*The Great Gamble* was hard to put down! Absolutely LOVED it! As it resonates so much on what is happening and what is coming!"

—Ann Meyers Drysdale, only female to sign a contract with NBA team, USA Gold Medalist, Basketball Hall of Fame, Current President and GM of Phoenix Mercury. WNBA analyst.

"*The Great Gamble* is a must read! Growing up on the east coast and hearing stories about the legendary CCNY point shaving scandal of the 1950s, I have always understood how young men could be easily influenced to do something out of necessity and greed. Bluder's character development, his unique storytelling ability and understanding of the recruiting game gives him a deft knowledge of today's athlete. I found it spell binding how he developed a realistic and dynamic adventure into the dark side of sports. I finished this novel in one night, I promise you won't put it down either!"

　　—Anthony DeSanti, Producer: CBS Sports/NBC Sports/ABC Sports/ESPN. Producer of two Olympics for NBC, both receiving Emmys.

"*The Great Gamble* is an amazing book that delves into the pitfalls of stardom and sports gambling. David Bluder does a remarkable job of bringing this story to life. The twists and turns kept me engaged. I couldn't put this explosive book down. A must read!"

　　—Quinn Early, 12 year NFL veteran wide receiver with New Orleans Saints and San Diego Chargers. Hollywood Stuntman and Screenwriter.

"Money has proven to be a main means of exercising power in our society. We have been warned that power corrupts and Dave illustrates the level of dysfunction through his book, *The Great Gamble!*"

　　—Joe Urcavich, former chaplain, Green Bay Packers.

"Remember this a fictional novel...one that I wouldn't want to be actual reality! With this said it is an entertaining and educational piece that brings notice to further good answers and solutions now and in the future."

　　—Dan Gable, two-time NCAA national Champion. Gold Medalist-Olympics, World Championships, Coached the University of Iowa to 15 NCAA titles. United World Wrestling Hall of Fame Legend.

"As a former University of Iowa athlete, and former professional athlete, I can appreciate how one little decision can open up so many other layers of corruption and life altering moments. Truly an in depth view of how sports have now turned into a largely complex business that everyone wants their hands in."

—Robert J. Gallery is a former American football offensive guard who played for eight seasons in the National Football League. He played college football for the University of Iowa, and received unanimous All-American recognition

"Dave Bluder writes of the dangers and temptations of big time intercollegiate athletics with sympathy and intelligence. With the legalization of sports gambling by many states and the NCAA's refusal to evolve, its only a matter of time before the cautionary tale of Jason Carr becomes reality."

—Jim McCoy, Director of University of Iowa Press

"Suspense and intrigue with a twist. *The Great Gamble* is an adventure through the dark underbelly of sport betting. In the end readers will win."

—Andrea Wilson, Executive of The Iowa Writers' House and Author.

The Great Gamble

David L. Bluder

Ice Cube Press, LLC
North Liberty, Iowa, USA

The Great Gamble: At What Price? A Thriller Novel

Copyright ©2020 David L. Bluder

First Edition (4th printing)

Isbn 9781948509138

Library of Congress Control Number: 2019953230

Ice Cube Press, LLC (Est. 1991)
1180 Hauer Drive
North Liberty, Iowa 52317 USA
www.icecubepress.com | steve@icecubepress.com

All rights reserved.

No portion of this book may be reproduced in any way without permission, except for brief quotations for review, or educational work, in which case the publisher shall be provided copies. The views expressed in *The Great Gamble* are solely those of the author, not the Ice Cube Press, LLC.

The paper used in this publication meets the minimum requirements of the American National Standard for Information Sciences—Permanence of Paper for Printed Library Materials, ANSI Z39.48-1992.

Manufactured in USA

Disclaimer: This is a work of fiction. Names, characters, businesses, places, events and incidents are either the products of the author's imagination or used in a fictitious manner. Any resemblance to actual persons, living or dead, or actual events is purely coincidental. Any names or incidents regarding this work or the University of Iowa is purely fictional and not intended to be journalistic or factual.

Photos on previous pages: Numerology; Mexico flag image; Hidden windows at Saint Patrick's; Empty frame following the theft at the Isabella Stewart Gardner Museum. Title page: Kryptos sculpture in front of CIA offices.

Project Assistants: Lauren Chesire, Ameila Johnson, Madalyn Whitaker, and Jennifer Becker.

Dedication:
To my wife Lisa and children Hannah, Emma, and David.
My mother Anne and sister Nancy.

Chapter 1

Only the strum of the fan could be heard in the suffocating heat. Scott Reynolds held his Glock against his chest and waited before he took a step into the bus barn. Reynolds couldn't pick up his partner's location. Something must have gone wrong. An FBI agent never turns off his GPS.

Scanning the ceiling, Reynolds slipped past one of the buses, but at five foot five inches he wasn't tall enough to see over the hood. There were dozens of school buses lined up in the warehouse. Two security lights spread murky shadows along his path, the smell of diesel made his throat sting. His Lilliputian physique topped by a moon-shaped face wore a mosaic of sweat. His clothes always pressed without a wrinkle. The top button of his oxford remained buttoned in the Tucson heat. He touched his phone. Backup was on its way.

Everything had been planned, that's the way Reynolds lived his whole life. This was where they were supposed to find the Diablos drug and weapons ring. He took two more steps and looked both ways. A pigeon cooed as it flew over his head. He continued moving beside the buses. Methodical. The air in the warehouse was dead. Sucked out like his dreams of redeeming himself. His shoulder grazed a mirror. He kept running the whole situation over in his head. A half million dollars of cocaine and heroin just lost in the desert sun—right under his nose they would tell him later. His foot slipped on something green, probably antifreeze. His imagination spinning, he heard a sound. He crept twenty paces, squatted and leaned against a bus. Peeking around the bumper he noticed a battery blinking. When he turned the other way, he saw from the corner of his eye a body crumpled on the cement floor. Instinctively he raced to his partner's side. Kneeling in the blood from the motionless body, Reynolds placed his fingers on Henderson's neck. A pulse could not be found.

Chapter 2

Tucson (CNN)—On Thursday the FBI released a statement asking for the public's cooperation with their investigation into the murder of special agent William Henderson. Henderson, 53, a special agent assigned to Mexican cartels was found dead on Tuesday inside the Tucson school district bus center on the east side of Tucson, across the street from Arizona Electric. Cheryl Kohl, a spokeswoman for the FBI's Arizona's field office, confirms Henderson died of multiple gunshot wounds to the head. Anyone with information is asked to call the FBI at (800) CALL-FBI, Option 5. (1-800-225-5324).

Chapter 3

It was the same old thing: three dribbles, look up at the hoop, flick his wrist and the ball was released—he'd already made one hundred and twenty nine in a row. A routine Jason Carson loved more than anything else, shooting the basketball. Oak Park's open gym was packed today, just as it was packed last week. Seeing all the college coaches sitting in their roped-off area on the east side of the building was entertaining.

Jason glanced over and recognized most of them: Duke, North Carolina, Kansas, Michigan State, Iowa, Virginia, UCLA, Indiana, as well as a bunch of others he didn't know. The gym was filled with shouts, echoes, and the clobbering hammer of basketballs. While Jason's teammate, Dillion Nash, stood underneath the basket, Jason, dribbled the ball behind his back, gave Dillion a wink. "Watch this, bro." Jason pointed to his eyes and mouthed, "Blindfold." He shut his eyes, took three dribbles raised his arms and shot the ball. Nothing but net, fascinated by the sound of snapping nylon as the ball sailed through.

"Quit showin' off Carson." Dillion joked.

"Got to practice dude," Jason snapped.

Nash dribbled between his legs. "Project group meets at 4:30, I need an A."

Jason stepped back behind the three point line as he twirled the ball on his finger. He took a step up to the line, jumped back and let a shot fly then turned to face Nash as the ball floated through the air. "Nobody really cares about Chemistry," he quipped, while the ball sailed through the net.

"Bull-shit. I'm trying to get into an Ivy League."

Jason tried not to look at the visiting coaches again, but he couldn't help himself. They had come from all over the country just to watch him. He reached over at a loose ball, pounded it against the floor, straightened, crouched down—his eyes looking at his size 17 Jordan Jumpman Pros—took two dribbles, slashed to the hoop and elevated into the air while his body twisted 360 degrees and dunked it. Hanging onto the rim he waited until the ball rolled away, then landed like a panther onto the court. He looked around, picked up another ball, dribbled a bit then flipped it to the ball cage and gave a quick wave to the coaches. He knew NCAA rules didn't allow coaches to talk to him during the evaluation period but all those eyes were on him and he adored it.

Chapter 4

Jason pushed the elevator button for the third floor of Oak Park General Hospital just outside Chicago. His head touched the cracked ceiling. The doors closed. Two nurses stared at him. It was the same old thing, the looks. That was what women did around Jason Carson, they stared. He was eighteen with blue eyes deeper than the summer sky and shoulders that must have been handed down by a Greek god. His beardless cheeks and chin scarcely needed a razor and hair the color of the sand after the ocean waters recede. People watched him whether on the court or off.

The elevator rattled to a stop. Doors opened. This was the third time he'd been late today, including his ACT test prep session. He lowered his head and darted out of the elevator and jogged down the hallway towards room 327. Couldn't they just let her come home? Hospitals. He hated them almost as much as he hated school work. The smell, not of disinfectant so much, but the stench of anxiety. His stomach moaned—he was hungry again, always hungry. He slowed down in front of her room, took a deep breath. He squinted, ducked his head, moved in. The overhead light flickered. Jason's mother took a moment before smiling. He tried not to look at the tube in her nose and monitors swallowing her. He hated to see her this way—all flimsy and shallow, like a ghost that could float away with a small breath of wind. A tray of food sat on a table next to her bed, untouched. A silver bed pan sat next to the food. There were flowers stuffed in every available space. Carnations, roses, azaleas, even the seat next to her bed held a yellow mum new since yesterday, another church member no doubt. Jason knelt down next to her.

"How you feelin' Ma?"

"Little weak, but better now you're here." She reached through the metal side bars and placed her hand on his forearm. "How'd you do on the history test?"

"Two NBA scouts at practice today," he replied.

A white-haired woman with milky skin snored and wheezed at the other end of the room.

Her voice was as anxious as the expression on her face. "What about the tutor, Jason,…you call her?"

"I put on a show for 'em, Ma. Scored 38 in the scrimmage, showed 'em my new corkscrew dunk."

She tried to sit up. "You need to work on your studies, son."

He brushed it away with a flick of the hand. "Thought you were getting a single room this time?"

"Medicaid isn't going to pay. We can't afford any luxuries."

"Wait 'til I make it big." You'll have the best room. You'll have the penthouse."

"You're dreaming again."

"I'll talk to the doc, he comes to all my games. His kid Ashton's in my math class."

Her face was as bleached as the pale walls. "Hope I won't be in here long this time. Starting chemo tomorrow, then maybe I can go home." She ran her tongue over her lips. "Bills keep adding up."

He had spent a half hour opening all of them last night. The MRI thing was crazy money. "Don't worry, I'll pay for it. NBA's gonna make us millions."

"Hush that talk, honey. Maybe I'll just die, then the bills'll stop."

No, God wouldn't do that to him. He leaned in toward her. He knew the odds weren't in his favor but she was too young to leave him. "Ma, cut it out." This sort of crazy talk was happening more than he could take lately. He ran both hands through his hair. That haircut would have to wait until next week. Twenty bucks, shit. Standing, he stuck his head outside the room, looked down the hall and saw no one. No way was he talking to the doctor again. He didn't want to hear any more about how the ovarian cancer was back.

He moved back into his seat. Trembling, she patted the top of his hand. He shivered again. "I have a fifty dollar bill inside the family bible, not the one on the coffee table. The one next to my bed. Twenty third Psalm. There's a fifty in there but only for an emergency."

"Last five years have been an emergency."

"Hush," she said as her face calmed. Jason had seen that look before, and it frightened him. "Don't worry son, God always has a way of providing in time of need."

Jason reached over for her sandwich and took a bite. "Problem is, we're always in time of need," he said with a laugh.

"What I love about you is your honesty…you're always telling the truth, but don't lose your faith, son. We've got a lot to be thankful for."

Jason studied the tray of food. "You going to eat any of that Jell-o?"

She shook her head.

"Mind if I have that roll?"

She nodded, then coughed. Spittle oozed down her chin. Jason bent down and wiped it away. "Son, you've been blessed with many gifts… remember to use them wisely."

He stood and looked at her, remembering how beautiful his mother had once been. Now someone must be playing a trick on him. Those gray lips and lifeless eyes. He bent down and kissed her forehead. "I think it's time for me to use some of those gifts. Keep getting better 'til I get back."

Jason walked to the end of the hallway. Pulling out his cell phone he thumbed through the dozens of college coach's numbers, then the agent numbers. Was there any another solution? Where else could he get help? He pressed the number for Ricardo Perez and waited.

Chapter 5

The Starbucks in Oak Park, Illinois, on a Saturday night in March was normally filled with long-haired poets, computer geeks, single mothers looking for a date, and a handful of high school students who had nowhere to go. Jason Carson walked in, took off his gloves and stuffed them into his letter jacket. A short Trekkie sat by the door rolling dice and turning over cards. Another one sat beside him with orange buttons in his earlobes and glasses the size of fists. They were everywhere nowadays, he thought. The Trekkie looked up at Jason and gave him that "shut the damn door, asshole," look.

Jason stomped the snow off his pricey Nike LeBron V2s. Why did he wear these shoes in the snow? He was in a rush. Again. He wasn't thinking straight. The bills in their shitty apartment needed to be paid—Oak Park Electric, Packey Webb Automotive, Dental Associates—Final Notice—stamped in red. Plus, Jason hadn't decided on a school on last November's signing date because his mother was sick. So, the letters and phone calls from coaches never stopped. This week it was UCLA, Duke, Kentucky, Louisville, Syracuse, Arizona, Colorado, Iowa, Florida, and Princeton; where the heck was that even? Every school in the Big Ten and Big Twelve, he couldn't keep them straight. Maybe that's why he never got his homework done. No dad. No money. He looked around. The coffee house was dark, the smell of clove, the glow of copper, ethereal His eyes adjusted. He could barely make out Ricardo Perez in the corner of the room. Perez was holding a white cup and wearing his trademark pair of Versace sunglasses. Versace's would certainly impress the babes, but Jason knew he could probably get two pairs of shoes with the dough it cost for those things. Why does he even wear sunglasses inside he wondered?

Perez was relentless about staying in touch. The guy called him nearly every day. He constantly left messages on Jason's phone, texted him at all hours just to let him know he could help. Could help him by providing a down payment on his NBA signing bonus and, man, he needed the money now.

Jason walked to the back of the room, shook Ricardo's hand, placed his jacket on back of the chair, and sat down. Ricardo's dark hair glared in the weak lighting. Perez was five or six inches shorter than Jason, but his posture made him look taller. The dimple in his chin looked like someone with a big ring had punched him there. A scar on his left cheek made his face slightly off center. Maybe that was what made Jason a little nervous, the scar.

Perez had been after Jason for more than a year now. Ricardo's mantra was: work your ass off and make it big. He had told Jason he was born in Mexico but spent time a majority of his time in the US Said he sported an undergraduate degree from Columbia and an MBA from Harvard, with a stint of investment banking on Wall Street. He was a third place finisher in the bantam division of Mexico's extreme boxing league six years ago. Jason wondered why the guy told him this since he definitely must be a loser—third place? Who cared about third place?.

Perez smiled when they made eye contact and cracked his knuckles. Jason stared at the space between Ricardo's two front teeth. "You've been playing very well lately, Jason. Scouts must be drooling over you these days."

Jason could tell there was still a tad of an accent when the guy talked, kind of like he was chewing on every word. "Thanks, Mr. Perez."

"Please. Call me Ricardo. We're friends, no? " He smiled again. "How's school going?"

He shrugged. "Still not my thing. Born to play ball."

"I know you're an intelligent young man. Someone that will be a big star in the NBA. Someone that knows how to make his own decisions."

"Wish I could play right now, but I need to do the one year college crap."

"Too bad," Perez answered. "I know for a fact the Knicks could use your shooting right now." He paused. "No reason you shouldn't be rich already. I've told you I've worked with hundreds of players and haven't seen your talent in over a decade."

Jason nodded.

Perez tapped his nails on the table. "Had time to see any good movies?"

"Just watched *Hoop Dreams* again."

"Great movie."

Jason scratched the side of his face. "Mr. Perez, I mean Ricardo.... Things are kinda weird right now. I don't know who to talk to." He stopped, cleared his throat. "I just think I might...I might need a little bit of help."

Perez gave him a big smile. "I'd love to help you in any way you need, Jason."

Jason swallowed. He needed to take charge, didn't he? Geez, he tried talking to coach Felter at his high school, but the guy had his own money problems. There was no other place to go. "I need a little money and I know you told me..."

Perez tapped Jason on the forearm. "You're not alone with this, Jason. There are loads of players in your same position. You're just looking for some help. Help with your mother's illness. I can be there for you.... that's what I do best. I'm here for you any time you need help and you've earned it."

As far as Jason was concerned, Ricardo was spot on. He couldn't say anything. Jason nodded.

"Would be happy to have you talk to some of the dozens of clients I've had. Kobe, LeBron, Rose, Curry. Even the international boys use us. They'd let you know we got them more then they'd get anywhere else. World Sports Advisors is second to none and we know talent when we see it."

Jason took a breath. "I do know one thing and that one thing is I can ball. My high school coach told me that there was a scout who said I don't pass. Said I could do everything else except I don't give up the rock. Mr. Perez, I can outscore anyone on any team so why should I give up the ball when I know I can score?"

"You are a lock to be one of the top three picks in the draft after a year in college?"

He knew how to respond to this one. This was a slam dunk. "I'll be number one. Guarantee it."

"Confidence. That's what I like to see. I'll put together a contract for you that'll break records. Can't wait to have a chance to make them name a bank after you. Carson's Bank and Trust. We'll dump wheelbarrows of freshly printed hundred dollar bills to use as mulch in your front lawn."

That's what he wanted to hear. "We could really use some of that right now." He could feel his chest begin to vibrate. "We need some help with bills now my mom's back in the hospital. She can't work right now." His words starting to trail off. He felt his jaw tighten. "My mom just hasn't been able to get any breaks…. She's always wanted the best for me." He wished he could stop his legs from shaking. "The landlord keeps knocking on the door at night and I'm not supposed to answer it. I always try to have answers for him, Mr. Perez." He rubbed his palms together. "I always seem to get things that I need…but I can't seem to work this money thing out…That's why I'm here."

Perez nodded his head, leaned forward. "How 'bout a down payment on your signing bonus. That's an easy accounting entry for us. Rest of high school, one year of college and you pay us back."

"What's somethin' like that cost?"

"We'll come up with some kind of arrangement. In the meantime, we can both count on trust. That's what you're really here for aren't you?" He said as he gave him a slow grin, teeth almost fluorescent, radiant now.

"Guess so."

"How much do you need?"

Jason rubbed his hands together again, a little faster this time. "Don't really know. I'm not the greatest with numbers." He could feel heat rising in his head and neck. "Credit cards, bills and now a new stay at the hospital…probably nine, ten, twelve thousand, who knows. Until my Mom is able to get back to work at the Care Center." His legs were shaking even more.

Perez raised his chin and thought for a moment. "How about twenty-five thousand, Jason?"

Jason straightened in his seat, dizzy. "Whoa…OK…that'd be great. I could finally buy a pair of the Air Force One Jordan's. Sweet. Maybe replace the TV or at least get a remote that works." He ran a hand through his hair. "I'd probably have to talk to my mom and coach about it first. Make sure they'd think it's the right thing."

Perez grabbed his gold chain and rearranged it higher on his neck, looking tall, almost as if he was trying to look down on him. "Jason, this is where you can make the decision. This career, this profession, this deal…it's all up to you now. We don't need an attorney or paperwork. I trust you to pay me back. Think it's time for you to trust." He paused and pushed his sunglasses toward his face with his finger. "Do we have a deal?"

Jason moved back in his seat, cleared his throat. "We don't need to sign something?"

"Just a handshake. You and me."

Jason wanted to rip off fifty pushups while he tried to think about this. It was just one extra thing to think about right now and that's all he was doing lately, thinking. He needed to relax, workout. "What about the other agents?"

"They're not used to these kinds of deals, Jason. We do this all the time. You need something, you can come to me. Couple of years from now you'll laugh at this deal since you'll be making so much coin. Gold watches, gold rings, gold necklaces, you'll be having trouble shooting with all the gold hanging from your body." He laughed showing his big teeth.

Jason tried to breathe, oxygen was gone. The guy was just dangling it out there for him and he wasn't ready for some reason. He was totally worth it, wasn't he? "That's a bunch a dough," he said with a half smile that was gone as quickly as it appeared.

"It's nothin' compared to the big pot at the end of the rainbow. You've already pulled the lever and hit the jackpot, Jason. We're just starting the presses for the dollars that'll be coming your way son."

Jason's knee was jumping up and down, then bounced into the bottom of the table and spilled some of Perez' coffee. "Sorry bout that," gritting his teeth. And his lips...he touched his lips. They had gone numb, like after a big shot of Novocain. "Hmm, I should probably think about...

"Nonsense, Jason. I can have the money to you by tomorrow. Just a small down payment. Small piece of the big treasure. Let's shake on it." He held out his right hand.

It took a moment before Jason's eyes could focus. He looked at the gold watch on Ricardo's wrist. It matched the bulky ring on his finger. That gold just kept coming at him. He was ready for it. He knew he deserved it. "Well." He put his hands under the table and twisted them. Biting down on his cheek he pushed the thought of danger away. Should he take a gamble here? He looked into Ricardo's face and found his own reflection in Perez's sunglasses. This is all up to me he told himself, and he shook Ricardo's hand.

Chapter 6

Everywhere Scott Reynolds looked he saw signs of evil. He'd never gotten used to the suffering and wickedness that he chased every day of his screwed-up life. Reynolds sat in his office in Washington D.C. chewing nails gnarled down so deeply his teeth wouldn't find them for weeks. At 6:10AM the Federal Bureau of Investigation was already running on all cylinders. Reynolds didn't care much about time anymore. He just wanted to clean up his part of the world and spend the rest of his time with a line in the water waiting for the fish to bite. But he was doing his best to show devotion. That was all they wanted around here anymore, complete and unadulterated devotion. No time to piss anymore, too many goddamn things to watch out for. Always guarding, watching, looking, dissecting, investigating, protecting. The crap just kept hitting the wall and those walls just kept leaning in on Scott Reynolds. He looked at his screen with crinkly skin around the sides of eyes that made him forever look as if he was squinting.

His thin, gaunt face winced. Eight men lay on the ground, each with their throat cut. The murders were the third mass killings in Mexico this month. Reynolds didn't mind carnage, he was used to bodies. When he looked at dead bodies lying in front of him, it brought him back to his childhood. Being the son of the town's undertaker made him an oddity. Reynolds Funeral Home was no place any kid in Salem, South Dakota, wanted to play. Friends, and he didn't have many, never wanted to come over. Every time Johnny Curtis walked by him in the school hallway he'd yell, "Ghostbusters." During math class one autumn Johnny asked why he wasn't going to the homecoming dance: "Can't dig up a date this year," he said with a howl.

Scott Reynolds liked everything in its place. Maybe it was because he was short. Short and thin with pouty lips which hardly ever smiled. Hovering over a sloping brow he had gray hair that sometimes gave him an advantage of seniority since he was only thirty-eight. He patted the front of his pants and straightened his shirt. The one thing in life he had mastered was determination. Nothing stopped him. Not even during his early days with the bureau when he forgot to wear steel toe shoes while he counted livestock in western Nebraska, resulting in three broken toes when a Herford stomped on his foot. Or, the time when he was counting cattle and a Holstein pissed all over his new chinos as he fell backward into a fresh layer of manure. But his days counting cattle seemed like a Caribbean cruise compared to trailing child molesters in Baton Rouge. After becoming a senior agent for the FBI, Reynolds spent twenty-four months with the CIA working with the Counter Terrorism Center on cyberattacks to prepare for the FBI reorganization and his new assignment: Senior Agent-Analyst.

The Diablos case was given to him directly from the Director of the FBI, Peter Hamilton. Clearly, things had paid off for Reynolds ever since he captured Jose Topez, one of America's ten most wanted three years ago. He pounded his fingers onto the keyboard as he talked to himself. He was having trouble finding the correct word for his morning report which was making him anxious.

He kept wondering. What the hell went wrong in Arizona? Bill Henderson was tortured and murdered and no one had any answers. Traveling through the night without sleep he found little evidence about the murder and the gone wrong. Who were these guys? There was a knock on the door.

"Enter," he said without lifting his head. The tan suit was faded, double buttoned with the top one so tight it was ready to burst and take out an eye. You'd never believe, looking at Ron Lamb, but he'd been in shape when he was younger; actually great shape when he was wrestling at Oklahoma. He used the term, "wrasslin" when he talked about it. And he loved to talk about it whenever someone would lend a cauliflower ear or two. He sat down and starting talking, "Top o' the morning, shortstop. Finished with the briefing notes?"

Reynolds kept his eyes on the screen. "Just going over it one more time."

"Same shit, different thug, buddy," he said, then sighed.

"Need to get it right. Can't miss anything."

"It's all the same. Nothing new."

"This is different."

"You're always saying that. Give it a rest." Lamb squirmed to sit up higher in the chair.

Reynolds didn't want to head down this road today. He needed someone to be on his side. "Not much sleep again last night. Need to call the doc but I never have the time. Haven't been through emails and have a teleconference with our oh-so-beloved NSA, our suddenly incompetent National Security Agency at ten."

"Find out anything about Henderson?" Lamb asked.

"It doesn't add up. Even NSA has no satellite photos of anyone?"

"Maybe the guy was in there for a day?"

Reynolds shook his head. "Don't have anyone coming out either. We don't have any audio, data intercepts. Nothing."

"NSA guys get too much time off. They're never on top of their game. Third time this month." Lamb was in his late forties and lost his hope for humanity years ago. "Looks like we're headed back to Mexico. Could use another chimichanga and banana margarita. They're the best."

"These cartels keep growing."

"Read yesterday they sawed the heads off of four cops down there with a chain saw. My god, they scooped out their eyeballs with a stiletto and stuffed them in their nostrils. Then they cut out their nipples and shoved them in their eye sockets. Then they hung the damn heads on the overpass of a bridge for all the cars to see when they drove by. Maybe they can win some kind of architectural award or something." He gave him a slight grin. "Same shit used by Jihad."

"Hardcore," Reynolds said.

"I'm more of a softcore man myself," he said with a wink.

"Last night's brief said the Diablos are moving all the way down to the equator. Moving north and south."

"I'm waiting to roll over one night and they'll be next to me playing a little ass grab."

Reynolds let it slide. Rather, he found himself concentrating on the job, nothing else. "These guys are Ivy League smart. Brooks Brother suits, well educated, yoga lessons, speech therapists, hair stylists, manicured nails, the works. Hard to recognize them. New world terrorist, running down our streets, working in our coffee shops."

"Versus the old world, blow things up kind of terrorist."

"Enough. My head wants to explode."

"Been fighting terrorists my whole damn life, Scotty."

"Not this kind. It's not just the drug rings, it's the business extortion, duplicate books, skimming millions to capitalize their distributorships."

"Just like Amway."

"Not exactly."

"Just trying to relieve a little pressure, Scotty. I've seen more killing in my lifetime then butchers at the pork plant. Don't know if I can take it. Retirement's still ten years away, probably more the way my old lady keeps spending it."

"Why don't you just cut her off?"

"Right. Just like that. Then she'll cut me off my hunting trips, and that once in a blue moon slap and tickle."

"Not playing your cards right?"

"I folded a long time ago, Scotty. Old lady's got more cards in her purse than my dealer at the casino."

"Can't control mine either, Ronnie." He studied his screen again. "Mission Centers can't help find these cartels. Don't understand it."

"Kind of like the border." He smiled. "More like tomatoes. Picked south of the border and end up in your kitchen for dinner then go rotten in a few days," Lamb said with a smirk.

Reynolds rubbed his hands and rocked slightly in his seat. He looked out the window and decided to share something with Lamb. "You know, I think someone was following me yesterday."

"Probably just groupies or creditors. You're too anxious buddy."

God, this life was a cold, crazy thing. And yet it was all there was. He kept his eyes on the window. "No, I'm sure someone was tailing. Sad thing though. Don't know how long it's been going on. Think I've seen the face before. Maybe too many times now that I think of it."

"Just the job getting to you."

Reynolds shook his head.

Ron Lamb took a deep breath, crossed his arms. "I've seen so much ugly shit it makes me want to puke. And when I close my eyes, I don't get much sleep either. 'Sweet dreams.' That's what my mamma used to tell me before I went to bed." Lamb looked out the window too. He lowered his voice. "Henderson was a good friend of mine. We went to college together. Went through the academy together." Lamb lowered his eyes and laid back in his seat.

For a moment Reynolds just sat there. He didn't particularly like dealing with emotions. "Sorry. Didn't know you knew him that well. We're not prepared. We never seem to be prepared."

Lamb interrupted. "Yeah, preparation. Life is just a preparation for disaster." He stood up and walked out.

Chapter 7

"Men plan, god laughs." —Yiddish proverb

Jason watched Coach Felter walk into the locker room. Felter was six foot five and had wide shoulders and a beer belly covered by his Property of Oak Park t-shirt. "Not our best practice, Huskies." He rubbed the side of his nose. His mustache weighed down his face, saddened his eyes.

He gargled some phlegm in his throat, nodded his head, looked around the room as his team sat waiting. "Not our best practice I gotta say. Thing is boys, we play defense like that on Tuesday and Fenwick's gonna kick our butts. Be on the floor at three tomorrow. We'll have a short practice and then watch a little tape. Get some rest tonight," When Felter stopped yelling he walked over to Jason. "Can I see you in my office when you're dressed, Carson?"

"Sure, Coach." Jason's ankle was swollen again, hopefully nothing that would slow him down. He'd ice it as soon as he got home, then he'd come back to shoot more free throws after the ice brought down the swelling. For some reason something was always aching, scratched, swollen, or throbbing every day. And yet he fought through, coming back to shoot when there wasn't anyone else in the gym each night. Just time with the ball and everything would be fine. He dressed and hung a towel around his neck and knocked on Coach Felter's door.

'C'mon in…shut the door behind you," Felter said. He was seated behind a tiny scratched up wooden desk, providing an illusion that made Felter look bigger. Jason stepped over a stack of Sports Illustrated magazines and shut the door. A light bulb hung down from a wire; Jason ducked his head as he moved around it. Two cracked plastic chairs stood in front of the desk, Jason sat down. He glanced at the tilted photos hanging on the lime green walls. His favorite was the autographed photo of Felter with his arm around Michael Jordan. Felter didn't have gray hair in that one. What Jason liked best about Felter's office was his display of bobble-head dolls. Spock from Star Trek, Laurel and Hardy, the Three Stooges, along with two Michael Jacksons; the young Michael with dark skin and an Afro. Next to the young Michael stood the late model Jackson with a kind of Caucasian skin and a mop of stringy hair. Next to the Michaels stood Hillary Clinton sporting an Adolph Hitler mustache.

Felter swung his chair around, sat upright. "How's your old lady?"

"Docs won't say much."

"Hmm." Felter put a finger in his ear and twisted it back and forth. "Wondered if that's why you didn't seem to be yourself today."

"Still won the scrimmage."

"Bite me, your team usually dominates."

What was the right word here? What was Felter trying to say? Jason didn't want to talk again. Coach always wanted to talk lately. Almost without realizing what he was doing, he began, "Mostly trouble sleeping."

"Christ, I got to have you in this kid. This is playoff time. Championship time. Once in a lifetime, time."

He stared into Felter's eyes, clenching his hands, driving his fingernails into his palms. He'd learned to live with pain, to keep everything inside. Life was learning to protect oneself. "I'm good, Coach. Everything's good."

"I need you. Need you next game. You can make this all happen, kid," Felter said. He opened the desk drawer, pulled out a bottle and dumped a handful of pills into his palm. He slapped the pills into his mouth and chewed.

"You've been able to work through it in the past. I really need you next game, bro."

"I'll be fine after I get some sleep," he said grabbing his shoulder, rubbing it with his palm.

"How's the knee?"

"Fine. Shoulder and ankle bugging me though."

Felter winced at him, never able to banish suspicion from his face. "Shoulder now? I need a scorecard to keep up with your ailments."

Jason lifted up his arm, stretching it from side to side. "Just need to get some sleep."

"You got a lot on your mind. Your mom. College choice." He rubbed his thighs with his palms. "You can at least do something about one of those," Felter said nodding without stop.

Jason knew needed to make a decision about his college choice, but it never seemed to be the right time. He'd missed all of his campus visits last fall because his mother was taking chemo treatments. His last ACT score was an eleven, and he kept prolonging his retake. Decisions just hung in his mind, swaying, tugging, casting long shadows. "Mom says everything will work out for the best."

Felter was strangely still and staring at him as if he was looking for something.

"Listen kid. I'm sure everything will work out with your old lady. Docs are amazing. You're her most prized possession. Only thing she wants is for you to achieve that big dream." He cracked one of his knuckles on his left hand.

He nodded.

"So that's what you're worryin' about again."

"I never worry. Worryin's for losers."

"Bullshit. You can be worried about your mother. That's normal."

"I'm not normal...I'm special."

"What about all those bills you been worrying about."

"Kinda heavy. Last bill was about a grand just for some x-ray thing. I'll figure a way."

Felter stood and began to pace in the small space behind his desk. "I might be able to help you with it. Let me make a couple of phone calls." He pulled out his cell phone and squinted at it, gazing.

It was the same line as before. Phone calls. He'd make some phone calls and claim everything would be better. A picnic of words coming from a guy that had plenty of money problems himself. Jason heard all about his troubles a year ago when Coach Felter called him after he had been drinking—complained the credit card companies kept chasing him. They chased him so hard he declared bankruptcy after his wife left him, even taking his 1965 red candy apple Mustang convertible, half of his baseball card collection with the Mickey Mantle rookie card, and the house with two mortgages. "I do need to talk to you about agents again. There's this guy..."

Felter sat down. "You need to use the guy I've been telling you about," he reached into his drawer and fumbled around, pulled out a business card. "There are thousands of guys out there kid, but Dougie Evans really knows his stuff." He handed the card to Jason. "But that's not what we need to talk about right now. The agent crap can wait." Almost without knowing what he was doing, Felter began clacking his teeth together. "We need to talk about college. These college coaches keep bugging the piss out a me. I wish you'd tell `em where the hell you're going." He paused and gave him a tiny grin, the quality of the smile was peculiar; frail, troubling. "Have you given anymore thought to UCLA? I've known Coach Johnson for a coon's age and he'd take great care of you and help you with the transition to the bigs."

"Just haven't had the time." There were plenty of awkward moments with Felter, but on the other hand, he was the only male Jason was really close to trusting.

"Christ, you need to listen. You need to spend more time on this, Jason. Mommy's illness can't stop you from making decisions. I've coached you since seventh grade. You should look to me for this, son," Felter said as he fingered a molar in the back of his mouth. "My guy at UCLA will showcase that talent of yours and you'll never have to worry 'bout money the rest of your life."

"I need to figure out the money thing right now, Coach. Promises and coaches aren't payin' the landlord." He looked down at his hands. "I'll figure it out…."

"Wasn't there an Uncle of yours that was going to help you guys?"

"You could say that."

"Charging you big interest?"

"Zero interest. Don't want to owe somebody something again." Jason shook his head. "No strings…"

"Let's get back to making your college decision. Take the pressure off you. Take the pressure off your mom, if you know what I mean. Why don't you text Coach Johnson. Better yet, give him a call." He paced around the room again, pulling his phone from his pocket. He shook his head and sighed. "Hell, he can't call you right now, NCAA bullshit. Let's text him," he said pushing his phone in front of Jason's eyes.

"Not now, not ready."

Felter slapped a hand on his desk. His face leaned into Jason's, "Come on, kid. Let's get this over with. Let's do this."

Jason froze a moment, leaned back, closed his eyes. "Not now coach... not ready...give me a break."

Coach Felter showed him a smile, teeth freckled with sunflower seeds. "OK. OK."

"I'll decide."

"You're a late signee. You don't have any more time kid."

Chapter 8

Twenty minutes later Brian Felter was looking over the Fenwick High School roster. He picked up a newspaper article from a game in November when his team beat Fenwick by twenty-two points. The headline read "Superstar Carson lights it up again."

"Kid didn't even play the fourth quarter," Felter told himself.

"Day-O," shouted from the Grateful Dead on Felter's cell phone. He looked at the screen, "Unlisted." He felt sick again. At first he was totally against the idea but his situation had made him curious. He had too many bills to pay too. So much of Felter's time was guessing, hoping, then praying to get out of his financial mess. He could never remember feeling more ashamed. He took a breath, held it, then pressed the answer button. He waited two seconds, Felter said, "Hello?"

"Congrats on winning the conference," the voice whispered into Felter's ear.

"Thanks."

"This is Bob," the voice said with that machine or whatever it was that made voices unrecognizable, hidden. "Your boy looked good out there. He'll fit well in California."

He felt an itch in his throat. "I love the kid. He had a great game."

"Looks like his vertical has improved. Jumps out of the gym now."

"Yeah, he had a dunk and almost hit his head on the rim."

"Incredible. I was there."

"You were at the game?"

"Of course."

Felter tried to filter this comment in his head. "Anyone know that you…"

The voice interrupted. "Of course not. Just another fan. Bruins could really use him, buddy. How many other coaches were at the game, Friday?"

"The usual bunch of cheaters and liars. Duke sent their assistant."

"Is he getting closer?"

"Carson said 'Mother's back in the hospital. Cancer knockin' on the door again.'"

"Sorry to hear."

"He's been preoccupied." Felter surprised himself by saying this, his voice hoarse with feeling. "But I'll keep workin' on him."

"Beautiful. We'll make sure it's worth your time and effort. Fifty grand wired into the savings account as soon as he signs."

Felter stood. The light bulb began to flicker. He couldn't believe what he said next, "It's not enough. I need more." The words "need more" hanging in the air. "My ex got her hands on everything."

"Thought we had a deal?"

"I help you and that's all I get? What happened to the condo in Naples?"

"Hmm."

"I do something for you. I get the condo?"

"That's pretty expensive. Don't know if we can do that?"

"Bullshit. That's what I want or no deal. Take it or leave it. The one with the two bedrooms." He was now in game mode now. "The kid's a complete scoring machine. He'll listen to me because his old man is still AWOL. Mother still wears rose colored glasses. He doesn't have anyone else. I'm the only one that's guided everything he's done. AAU, personal training, clothing. The kids does everything I say. I'll make it happen Bob...count it done. I'm close to complete control of him right now. Just give him another week or two.

"That's what I like to hear. We can do the condo. Two bedroom. Just remember..." the line was quiet for a moment. "...we're counting on this. It better work or things could get ugly."

Felter stood and looked at the door. "A threat?"

There was a laugh, then, "We play to win."

Chapter 9

Jason walked through an inch of vanilla snow, unblemished and refreshed in the parking lot behind his school. The skin on his neck tightened, cold air evaporating the sweat. He wanted more time to think about the transaction. Ask more questions, but who would he ask? He felt empty, his breath vaporous in front of him. No other place to go for help. He spotted his beat-up Honda van sitting alone, covered with snow. He opened the door and pulled out the ice scraper.

He noticed a car parked behind his without any snow. It was one of those new Corvettes. A red Vet with chrome wheels, dark windows; the perfect vehicle for him. So long his legs would fit. That was what he'd be driving in a year or so but he didn't know if he could wait. He bent over to look at the car. The tinted windows didn't let him see inside. The door opened, he moved back. Out stepped Ricardo Perez. He was wearing a black parka-hooded jacket, his sunglasses beginning to cloud. Sunglasses again, always wearing sunglasses, as the Vet hummed behind him.

"Jason," Perez said, head shivering. "A man of my word. Wanted to keep our arrangement." He reached into his pocket and pulled out an envelope. "This is my side of the bargain." He pushed up the sun glasses with his glove. He looked to his left, then back to Jason. "Cashier's check for the amount we discussed and an extra five hundred in cash for you. A little gift from me."

Jason looked at the envelope in Ricardo's hand. He looked at Ricardo's leather gloves. He could smell Ricardo's cologne. He looked at the envelope again. This didn't take long. This guy must do this every day. He looked at it for several moments as if he was a doctor considering a patient's condition. Was he ready to just take the cash? He casually looked around the parking lot. No cars, only snow. His hands wanted to reach out and grab the envelope. But they didn't move. They stayed hidden inside the pockets of his letter jacket. He knew he deserved that money. Maybe it would be fine? Of course it would. Jason wiped the snow from his eyelids, vision blurring. He did not know what was more strange, never having money or having the money in front of you and not wanting to take it.

Ricardo wiggled the envelope.

Jason wondered—who needs to know about this? Everyone would tell him to do something different. He needed to be the hero here. A shiver moved down his back. "I'll make this up to you Mr.—I mean Ricardo," he said with a small vibration in his voice he hadn't heard before.

"You most certainly will, Jason," Ricardo said, white breath seeping from his mouth.

The air was freezing Jason's lungs, and his stomach was hurting. Been at least an hour since his two protein bars. Ricardo waited in silence. "Haven't told my mother about this yet. Didn't tell my coach, either."

"Too many hands on the treasure make for less gold for everyone. Am I right, Jason?

He felt cleansed somehow, finally able to make things work for him and his mother. "Spose you're right." Almost without realizing what he was doing, he laughed a bit, after all, this was crazy, handing out money. "I make my own decisions, Ricardo. I've been making 'em for a long time. "He wiped snow from his forehead. "I need to take care of the family. This money's not for me, it's for my mom."

"Sounds like the perfect son to me."

His heartbeat filled him. "Maybe I should talk to her before I take it with me?"

"Nonsense, Jason. It'll be a wonderful gift."

Silence. Jason didn't respond. A thin line of snow accumulated on the top of Perez' sunglasses, on top of his head, but there wasn't a sound. Nothing. A plume of white breath escaping in front of Jason's mouth.

Perez pulled out a piece of paper from his coat. "You said you wanted proof. Says you can pay me back at any time. No interest…Doesn't include the gift, no."

Jason said without inflection, "guess there's a need for this."

"No, really. I signed, and you can sign," he said as Perez held out a pen.

Jason gazed at the pen, waived it away.

"No, no, it's what you wanted. Go ahead, read it. It will only take a minute."

He looked at the paper. There was an aching in his shoulder again, his knee, everywhere. The words on the page were scrambled again. Was it Spanish or English? There was a sound in his head like a million zippers zipping shut.

"Read it, Jason, go ahead."

"Now?"

"Whenever you want. Up to you."

Jason jammed it into his pocket. He looked at the Corvette, glanced at the sunglasses again, looked at his car, took his hands from his pockets, slid off his gloves and blew some warm air into his fists. A shiver moved down his spine, into his chest, but his heart felt warm. Must be the right thing then, he told himself. He looked at Ricardo, stared at the envelope. A new pair of Nikes would make him feel better. He reached out his hand and Ricardo slapped the envelope into his palm and Ricardo grinned.

It was all he ever wanted. All he ever wanted to do for his mother. "I'll pay you back Mr. Perez."

"We're partners, mi amigo." He said. "I need one little thing from you, though."

"Sure."

"My partner's son plays for Fenwick. I know you guys will bury them early; don't need you breakin' a sweat in your next game. Don't want things to get too out of hand."

"What'd ya mean?"

He smiled again. "You're supposed to win by thirty-five or so. Like the first time you played them." He leaned in slightly. "But I just need you to keep the win at twenty-five or twenty. Let my friend save a little face. Saving face is very important mi amigo, si?"

Jason looked at the envelope again, squeezing it, hard. "I don't know."

"You can still beat them, yes. It'll still be a big win. Just don't make it a massacre for my sake," he said. "Let's just say the five hundred could cover it."

Jason turned and looked back at the school. The snow was falling harder now, frosty white bits of feathers. The place had taken on a delicious strangeness. He looked into Ricardo's glasses and slid the money into the pocket of his leather jacket. "Guess I can try to help this one-time, Ricardo."

Chapter 10

"Man is the only kind of varmint that sets his own trap, baits it, then steps in it." —John Steinbeck

Alone with these thoughts, Tim McMurray knew this life was all about basic instincts. Not exactly an original thought, but McMurray may have never had an original thought in his entire alpha-male existence. He was some kind of listener though. He'd listen to just about any theory, point of view, vision, thoughts, the newest ideas, even untested notions or concepts. Within the last year, Tim had been caught up in the Pana Wave church which included a bit of Buddhism, a dash of Christianity, and a pinch of New-Age. Their pet cause was raising awareness of the dangers of electromagnetic waves which they believed was the major cause of climate change and a long-term destroyer of the world's economic system. During their last meeting in Sacramento, everyone covered themselves in white, including white masks and discussed the least unpolluted areas of California where they could have their next meeting. Wearing his white, on the way back to his hotel, Tim stopped for gas and was instantly surrounded by a group of thugs who thought he was a member of the KKK. He ran to the bathroom, stuffed the white clothes in the trash can and jumped in his car without paying for the gas and squealed away. But Tim loved to listen.

Six months ago, Tim overheard a discussion in the Dallas Hilton lobby which inspired him to follow a group of men to the main conference room where he learned about the Happy Science religion. First he thought it was some kind of a joke, but after meeting with elders of the group he was encouraged to prepare for the second coming of the Angel Gabriel. An angel who was to appear as a vision in Bangkok the following week. Tim waited, prepared, filled out his will, and spent the week studying their religious beliefs—which was to bring Happiness to Humanity. However, the happiness and the Angel never arrived.

Tim moved on to the Aetherius Society's online chat room forum. That's where he met Cara. They both were taken by the view of evolution controlled by the Cosmic Masters, Cara explained the connection between aliens and yoga; a true balance to humanity.

The first night they spoke, she leaned into the camera and said, "Reverend George King, our Cosmic Master says that we must stand in the valley of decision. What are your favorite yoga poses?"

Tim had done a bit of homework. "Either the downward dog or the Bound Lotus."

"No way? Me too. I also love the Embryo Pose. It's totally universal. I'm in total equilibrium every time.

Seeing Cara in her yoga tights during a skype call drove Tim totally out of balance, a new heavenly angel had appeared. After an LA Clipper's game last year, Cara convinced Tim, over a bottle of Caymus, that she was mastering the various forms of Yoga which enabled her to attain the elevated state of consciousness know as Samdhi, a spiritual energy sphere providing enlightenment and true understanding. Tim listened and his yoga session with Cara was truly enlightening. Her body looked as if Michelangelo had sculpted the perfect woman. But that's what Tim did best, listen to just about anything that would bring him pleasure along with meeting his own needs. That's what males did. That's what all human activities can be traced back to, basic instincts.

But on the court as an NBA referee Tim didn't listen to anyone. The LA Lakers called time out and the music in the Staples Center blared: "Start Me Up," by the Rolling Stones. Lakers coach Rob Larson yelled something at McMurray who shrugged his shoulders, then jogged with his typical swagger to center court to stand next to fellow referee Willie Barton.

"What the hell was that call down there?" Barton asked, "Larson's pissed."

McMurray smirked, patted his stomach. He was also religious about his workouts and six pack abs. "Lost another half inch on the waist this week."

"Come on, man, think you might have missed a couple calls this quarter."

"I had a better angle, Barts," he said patting himself again. "Hardest abs on the planet."

"Larson's been M-f-ing me the last two trips down. You need to talk to him."

Tim was good at talking to coaches.

They'd always get pissed, but Tim could usually control them. He'd try to laugh and smile at them while their veins were popping from their necks, spit blasting from their mouths. Mainly, he had a way of making them feel like they were getting the best of the deal. He would quickly remind them of the last call he made on the opposing team and then, best of all, the game would be moving again. Short memories.

While the kid who brought him Gatorade during time outs handed him his drink, Tim ran a hand over his Redken-For-Men Icy Platinum black dyed hair. At forty-two the thinning and receding was causing him fits. He took two quick gulps, handed the glass back to the kid, nodded. The first buzzer sounded.

"I want to get out of here, Timmy. Stop delaying the game. No more fouls" Barton added.

Tim had to make sure the spread wasn't covered. He needed money again. Lakers 99, Sacramento 99. Money would be wired into his account tomorrow morning. He needed cash for his next installment of hair plugs. Eleven thousand bucks for hair surgery certainly wasn't in Tim's budget but he needed to look good, He spent hours trying to look younger. Moisturized his face six times a day, he even tried growing a beard for awhile when he heard that it revitalized wrinkles around the mouth. Tim still owed his plastic surgeon Dr. Weinbrenner just over six thousand for last year's nose job. He slapped Barton's thigh as the second buzzer sounded. Another quick glance over at the Lakers cheerleaders to see if any of them were looking his way. Lindsay was smiling at him as he straightened his back and winked at her. But something was still bothering him. He studied his palm. Portia, his palm reader, had scared the hell out of him this afternoon. Normally, it was all good news when they met, but not today. She stared at his palm for what seemed minutes before she spoke.

"The Mount of Jupiter, line at the base of the index finger. Reveals ambition, leadership, and love of nature." She looked up at him with eyes shallow, tempting.

Nice to hear, but all this had been told to him before.

But when she continued her face tightened, squinted, her hands even trembled a little, "Your heart line." Her eyes on him again, sad, almost empty. She tried to smile, but couldn't.

"What is it? Tell me."

"Your heart line."

"Yes?"

"Represents your love life."

"Of course."

"I see a negative charge…something very negative. Something that reveals a surprise…not a good surprise. An awful surprise. Danger," she said, nostrils flaring, lips wet. She dropped his hand, stood and left, moving into the back bedroom slamming the door behind her.

Tim had shrugged it off then but now tried to understand it. He slapped the ball with his hands and ran to the Lakers bench to get the game under way. He tapped the back of one of the players to break the huddle. As the team moved back to the court, the Lakers coach gestured to him.

"What the hell was that call at the other end, McMurray?"

The smile fell from his face. "Feet weren't set."

"That's three horrible calls this half…you owe us."

McMurray nodded and ran down the court. Thirty-two seconds left. Lakers inbound the ball, McMurray bites down on his whistle. Fans standing inches from the court as he races by, as he tries to keep up. Twenty seconds. Sacramento Kings player reaches for a ball, ties it up and McMurray calls a travel on the Lakers, Sacramento ball. Fans bellow, "Traveling?" They scream as the Kings bring up the ball and for a last shot. McMurray looks up at the scoreboard. Tied. The Sacramento guard dribbling, looking at the clock. Ten seconds. He begins to drive at seven. Dribbling to his right, screen set, fall away jumper as the horn sounds, backboard lights up as the ball rains through the net. Game over. Sacramento wins. Fans screaming, two players reach for his arm. Lakers coach running over to him, more booing. McMurray sprints through the tunnel hearing a yelling above him. "Go back to

Footlocker dickhead." He feels something wet hit his shoulder and side of his face—beer.

Chapter 11

Minutes later, McMurray finished dressing after a shower. He glared at his teeth in the mirror to see if they were getting whiter. Willie Barton stepped to the locker next to him, toweling his wet hair.

"Hey Tim, what's up with the whistle in the fourth quarter, man?"

"Just wanna make sure everything is called."

"You got something in for LA? You need to keep your feelings to yourself. Could get your ass in trouble."

"I was born with trouble. Where you headed?" Tim asked.

"Beautiful Detroit. How long you off?"

"Four days at home, then head to Dallas. How you getting along?"

"OK" Willie said.

"Divorce ever come through?"

McMurray waited, buttoned his shirt. Everybody always wanted to pry into his life. "Yeah."

"Shit, you're a free man. Nothing's holdin' you back buddy."

"Can't seem to keep the babes away, Willie. Got a young one tonight. Hope I still have a little stamina left," Tim said and whistled.

"Sheeee-it. You the luckiest honky I know, Mighty Mac."

Luck. That's what a guy needed. He looked down at Willie's shoes. "Don't tell me those are real alligators?"

"Yep. Anniversary gift from the wife. Got these kicks from Harry's of London." Willie beamed.

"Didn't you get a new watch last month? Rolex?"

He nodded. "Birthday."

"You're the one with Karma," Tim said.

"Karma my ass. Father-in-law. Owns a bunch of businesses. Buys and sells."

"Yeah, you told me. Must be going well now."

"Damn right. Gifting a bunch of stock next Christmas."

"Nice," Tim said in a faint voice. When was good fortune going to rain down on him? He always needed more scratch.

A few minutes later McMurray walked out of the stadium into the back seat of a car.

"Does it ever get dark around here?" he asked his driver.

The bald driver turned his head. "Always dark round here. Keep the lights on to cover it up. Where to?"

McMurray looked at his palm again, rubbed it on the leather seat. "Nice ride…Need to go to this new night club." He paused for a second. I think the place is called, Womb. Ever heard of it?"

The driver turned his head and stared at McMurray. "You want to go to Womb? The nightclub? You?"

This guy was as critical as an NBA coach. "That's the place."

The driver pulled out as he shook his head. "Hope you got the right club. You may be the oldest guy ever to step foot in that crazy ass place."

"Meeting someone." Tim replied.

"That's a nut house. Heard last week they got in trouble. They were giving back massages to men in the latrine while they were using the urinals, only for a small tip too."

"Maybe I'll like this joint after all." Tim said.

"No offense, but they won't be playing any Beatles in there. Heard it was louder than the coliseum."

Tim didn't answer. He didn't need to be reminded he was in his forties everywhere he went. He knew the place was for the young. They drove bumper to bumper a couple of minutes before Tim started to squirm, face itching. His mind back to racing. What the hell was the cryptic code? Sometimes he wondered if he was paranoid for thinking about secret codes and ancient puzzles too much but he felt them everywhere. Sitting at a red light Tim asked, "Where's the closest candy store round here?"

The driver looked into the rear-view mirror and stared at him for what seemed forever before he replied. He'd been right about this guy. "I'll make a call for you. Someone will meet you at the club. Outside though."

"Perfect."

At 11:40, the car stopped in front of a long line of young adult clubbers. The driver continued to look forward as he spoke. "Contact is across the street with the black Raider's cap. He'll take care of you."

Tim paid the driver added a generous tip, and walked across the street. Even though he had done this dozens of times before, he detested the exchange—probably the relinquishment of supremacy. Nevertheless, he winked at the dude in the black hat. Deal done.

Seconds later he stood in front of two guys, all biceps, yet heads even bigger than their arms, guarding an iron door. Tim pulled out his wallet, showed his I.D. Muscle man one pushed a button on his belt and the door slid up into the ceiling. Tim walked into the foyer, maroon velvet walls. The noise of the bass was crashing through the wall against him, vibrating. He still had time to run for it. A sliding door opened and a rush of light and sound plastered his face. A three hundred pound Asian dressed as a sumo wrestler waddled up to him, flesh jerking from side to side. "Why you here old man?"

Tim handed him a card, waited. Knowing ex-ballplayers came in handy.

At first glance the wrestler didn't recognize the name on the card, but then raised his head, nodded, said. "You're in."

A waitress, or maybe she was a hostess, dressed in a purple tasseled fishnet jumpsuit with orange tattoos on her hips handed him a black mask. "Wear this or you may not enter."

Don't tempt me he thought to himself.

"It's masquerade night. Everyone needs to be disguised," she said turning and walking away, displaying even more tattoos on each of her cheeks.

McMurray stretched the elastic over his head. Hopefully no one knew who he was here. He moved into the main room. The sound thundered into his ears. The ceiling glowed with baseball size colored lights, yellow flashing, blue fading in and then out, green blinking with each beat. Below the lights four woman swung on trapezes. The colors cascaded over their near naked bodies, nipples covered by doilies in the shape of X's. He had never experienced anything like this, but it was something he could learn to like. In the center of the dance floor, bodies rotated, mashed and gyrated to a sound more tribal than the pop or disco at other clubs. To his right was a wall of dirty glass. Puzzled, he walked closer and could see through the smudge. There must have been twenty to thirty people completely covered with mud. Some dancing, some wrestling, others body painting with or without clothes.

He looked back into the crowd. McMurray felt a hand on his right shoulder. He turned and was kissed by Cara Lawrence. There was no disguising Cara. She was tall and slender, probably too slender, even for him. She had corrected pearly white teeth and wore a long lingering smile prompted by something. Something like a promise he would need to uphold. Always waiting for the promise.

For some reason he had filled her head with promises. But this was how it was done, giving her everything she wanted. He thought it was the only way a guy his age could attract a thing so luscious as Cara. That's the way he caught women, fulfilling their needs and then fulfilling his. Quite simple. He was amazed at how easy it was for him. He paid a few hundred bucks to Hackers For Hire, and in less than forty-eight hours he had more personal information on Cara then he ever wanted. She was the third female he had caught this way—knowing personal information. Not just Facebook and Twitter of course, but emails, texts, medical reports, shopping trends, family history, where she ate, where she shopped—the works. At the coffee shop, where he ran into her by complete coincidence, drinking the same chocolate latte as she was, told her his brother was a Hollywood movie producer. By the look on her face he could tell she was waiting to meet a man like him all her life. They did hot yoga together, watched Friends reruns, chatted on-line, even received a daily poem from him in her morning inbox.

Her blonde hair fell thick to her shoulders. On their skype, less than a week ago she was a redhead. She hugged him and kissed him hard, and he felt cleansed somehow. She ran a hand down the sleeve of her maroon leather jacket, exposing her red fingernails. "Do you like my new coat?"

He nodded and wondered if he had paid for it, but already knew the answer.

She grabbed his hand. "Let's dance," she said as she swayed her shoulders from side to side.

"Let's sit for a bit. I bought something for you."

Cara folded her hands, bounced up and down. He had seen this moment of anticipation from her and he had her. "I love surprises," Love hung on her tongue.

He handed her a small blue box with a red ribbon.

She looked at it almost embarrassed, cheeks even more red now. "Is this what I think it is?"

"Just a stepping stone, darling. Plenty more to come."

"Blue box. That means Tiffanys." She twirled around, without missing a beat.

"How'd you know?"

"Blue means Tiffanys. My favorite, silly," she said giggling.

Should she have known better? Fake blue box bought on line. Imitation sterling silver, gold plated from Mexico, "Open it, princess."

She opened it and let out a sigh, a hand covering her mouth. "I love Tiffanys, sweetie. Anything from there. Totally, awesome."

"When my brother hooks you up with your movie career you'll be able to buy a whole store, honey."

"Can't wait to meet him."

Tim raised an eyebrow. She believed everything he told her. "He's the biggest guy in Hollywood, but he's in London working on something really big right now, he says."

She tried the ring on, waiving it in the air, dancing with herself. She kissed him several times; it was her routine. He knew her better then she knew herself.

"I'm ready for a little fun." She moved her hips in a circle as if she was working a hula hoop. Long slow movements. "Are you taking me with you tomorrow?" She asked as she nibbled on his ear lobe and rubbed his thigh with the palm of her hand.

McMurray smiled. Even though Cara was one of his favorites, he told himself that he wasn't quite ready to pay for her lavish lifestyle. It seemed financially impossible after his divorce.

"Can't just yet. I've got some big business opportunities I'm working on. I'll make it up to you…we'll be together soon, baby." He reached for her hand and kissed it.

"I just want to be with you, Timmy. Don't leave me here again." And the way she stood there, eyes pleading he wanted to change his mind.

"My car broke down yesterday and they told me I needed a new pump or something. Said I should look at the new convertibles."

Tim gave her a half smile.

"You know ragtops are my thing, honey. The salesman was really nice too. He had a cool Prada jacket and these totally rad Italian shoes."

"Thought you just got the S350 last spring?"

"Sales guy with the shoes thinks it's time for a flip." She pulled her hair back with both hands. "That's what he called it. A flip, isn't that cute."

"Cute. I need to run to the restroom." He worked his way quickly through the crowd, checked his watch again. Walking to the last of the six sinks in the corner of the bathroom, he washed his hands with soap that smelled like mint. McMurray heard steps moving toward him. A dark set of hands suddenly moved into the sink next to him. Ricardo Perez gazed at the mirror in front of them.

"Finally, did OK tonight," Perez whispered. "But your performance still needs to improve. No more bad mistakes. Tambien, she's too young for you, my friend." Perez looked toward the door, then back at McMurray. He pulled out an envelope from his coat and handed to McMurray. From his other coat pocket he pulled out a sand colored envelope and slipped it into McMurray's hand. "No more mistakes."

McMurray stuffed the two packages into his pocket. He backed into an empty stall, removed one of the packs of paper from his pocket. He needed this again.

Two minutes later he cleared his nostrils, satisfied, left the stall and moved to the mirror. There was a happiness now. Remote, but calm, and it was this by which he lived. He ran a comb through his hair. Looked into the mirror and saw the man he was waiting to see. Waiting all day to see. The man in the mirror had confidence; direction. He was in his zone again.

Chapter 12

Foxnews.com

Atlanta (Fox)—FBI has issued a statement saying they are investigating a weapons/drug ring which has been operating in the US but did not reveal for how long. Atlanta agents disclosed that four members of the police force have been arrested. A Mexican cartel has been trading drugs for powerful guns, including assault rifles. The FBI is not commenting but a high level source who has requested anonymity said that the new evidence is quite troubling. "It's the expansion into new socio-economic areas of the United States which is unprecedented and similar to the days of prohibition." The source believes the Mexican cartel has been expanding through cells in the US

Chapter 13

At first, the bright lights in the lab made Scott Reynolds squint, impairing his vision. As his eyesight improved, Reynolds could see Paul Forester waiting for him in front of his office. Reynolds had been at the FBI's Marine Corps Base Lab twice before but for some reason it seemed brighter today. Forester had his arms folded, legs spread apart and nodded. Reynolds knew the guy never shook hands. He had to be a germ freak which made perfect sense in this business. Everything Forester wore was white, matching his horsetail coarse hair with a slant of pigeon gray at the temples.

They moved into the room and Forester extended his hand to a chair. "Sit down, Agent Reynolds."

Reynolds shook his head. "Why no DNA evidence in the Henderson case?"

"Always takes longer then you guys want. This isn't television's CSI."

Reynolds slid his palms down his pants. "We don't have time. People are dying."

Forester went to his desk and sat on the edge. "DNA profiles are difficult." He picked up a sheet of paper. "DNA evidence contains various, what we call loci, which is the position on the chromosome. The variant of the similar DNA sequence located at locus is called an allele. There are 19-20 thousand estimated…I'll call it protein coding genes that make up the alleles." He raised the paper. "We use what's called Quantitation to determine how much DNA we have and look for profiles. This is an electropherogram." The page displayed gray bars with multiple lines. "We have partial profiles that occur with degradation when more than one person could be involved. This clouds the DNA so to speak."

"I understand the science," Reynolds snapped. He definitely understood it from his upbringing and his interest in forensics but most of all he was irritated with people trying to talk down to him.

"We did come up with something that might be of interest," Forester said.

Reynolds nodded.

Reaching inside a box, Forester exhibited a clear bag and held it in front of Reynolds "We found this toothpick."

"You found a toothpick?"

Forester handed the bag to Reynolds. "I thought you'd be quite interested in it, agent."

"Surprise me."

"We found this in the bus barn about three buses away from where Henderson's body was located."

"Now we know the janitor likes toothpicks?"

"Maybe. But our testing found out that the wood from the toothpick was flavored. We tested for flavor and came up with a hundred dollar bottle of Tequila…Don Julio in fact. And just to add to your sarcasm, Agent Reynolds, we also matched the wood. It came from a Pochote tree. Both the roots and the seeds are known to have healing properties that have been used by generations. The seeds contain sedative properties. And by the way, the most interesting fact is it's known as the sacred tree of the Ancient Mayans."

Chapter 14

The Museum of Modern Art in New York City pulsed with visitors. All to experience the largest collection of Claude Monet's paintings ever assembled under one roof—two hundred and thirty-one pieces. Even from where Ricardo Perez stood in the room he could see seven giant canvases of water lilies shimmering, blending into themselves, alive, moving, portraying a heaven through the eyes of nature. He made his way to one while never taking his eyes off a glimpse into paradise. He had no idea how long he had been there and he had no intention to care. He sometimes dreamed about them. He remained fascinated by the paintings even though he'd seen them dozens of times all over the world: *Musee Orangerie, Musee D'Orsay* in Paris, the Art Institute in Chicago, the National Gallery of Art in Washington D.C., in London, and his favorite, where the feathery plumes of smoke rose near the Gare St. Lazare, oh the clouds of smoke in the train station, so perfect. He made his way through the rest of the exhibit, now looking at his watch, 3:52. He was hungry, but he didn't care. He walked outside, a cold breeze slapping his face, his eyes suddenly tired. A bus rushed past him. He took a minute to adjust. He looked up, then into three parked cars. No flashes of light. No reflection from binoculars or the lens of a camera. All seemed clear. He buttoned his coat up to his neck and made his way down 53rd street. He crossed the street and one block later he crossed back. Three blocks later he stopped in front of a pizza joint, looked back, then walked in. A fat guy with an apron covered with tomato sauce looked up.

"What'll it be, pal?"

Ricardo shook his head, leaned against the wall and stared out the window, waiting. Nothing. He left a five on the counter and walked out. Two doors down he stopped in front of a revolving door. The sign on the glass read, Bank of America. He reached into a coat pocket, patted his chest, looked back, double checked all around then moved inside and stopped. Everything was normal. He walked down a hall, tellers on the right, offices on his left. He looked into the first office on his left. The name plate on the desk read. Chris Locke, Personal Banker. He moved inside as the bank officer looked up from his computer screen.

"Help you," more of a statement than a question.

"Yes." He reached inside his coat and pulled out a single piece of paper. He unfolded it and placed it on the desk. "My name is Tomas Clemente, pleasure to meet you." He reached out his hand, the two men shook.

The bank officer looked at the paper, running a finger as he read. "You want to wire?"

"Yes."

"Two hundred and fifty thousand?" The bank officer looked up, blankness on his face.

"Zurich Cantonal Bank, Switzerland."

The banker's eyes narrowed, slightly. A very slight change and Perez could sense it more than he could see it. He reached into his front pocket, pulled out his wallet. He opened it, placed it on the desk in front of the banker.

The banker studied it, studied the entire wallet from side to side. "Just for your protection sir," he said looking at the left side of the wallet now.

"Certainly."

"See you have a United Way Big Brothers, Big Sister's card here," pointing, but holding his finger from it as if he didn't want to touch it.

"Oh, yes. Favorite charity."

The banker looked at him and said. "I've been a Big Brother for eight years."

Perez did not know if he should be grateful for this or not. "I've been one for ten."

"That's cool."

Perez reached for his wallet, slid it back into his coat pocket, looked at his watch. "Do you need any other information from me?"

The banker looked back at his wire request. Perez could see the emotion move like weather across his face. As the banker looked up at the clock, Perez noticed a photo of the banker with Super Bowl quarterback Joe Namath on his desk, and beside that a Fantasy Football magazine. The banker looked at his computer, "This is your third transaction this month."

A short hesitation, "My business is showing signs of improvement," he said at last.

The banker smiled. "Would you care to open a business account?"

Perez looked at his watch. "Not now. I just want to make the wire today. That's all."

"This transaction won't take place until tomorrow's business. Is that a problem Mr. Clemente?"

Perez shook his head. "That'll be fine."

The banker opened his top drawer, fished out a laminated page, "Overseas wire is a hundred seventy-five."

"Just take it out of my account."

"If you did this from your online account it would only cost forty-five, instead of one seventy-five?"

"I don't have online banking. I'm old school," Perez said with a grin.

He looked at his screen. "I could sign you up, only take a few minutes?"

Of course, the guy was doing his job. Cross sell, add another product. Guy would probably get commission from the thing, but it wasn't going to happen. "No thank you."

"I could set it up for you. Email the instructions, Mr. Clemente."

Perez raised a palm. "Please, no, nada. I don't trust anyone in today's world." Had he said too much? Everything was going his way seconds ago. "Hackers. I don't trust hackers … everything's getting hacked."

The banker shrugged, as if to say, no commission here. "Very well." He stood, no longer interested. "I'll send you an email of the receipt."

Perez shook his head. "I don't have an email account. No need for a receipt. I trust my bank, my banker. Especially a big brother, no?" He smiled, wide now.

There would be no paper trail of the transaction. No possible audit of a transaction from his account on a cloud of the internet. Nothing to trace.

A minute later Perez was done, and stood outside the bank. Was there anyone watching? The bustling noise of the streets stretched in every direction, rush hour. The sidewalks cluttered with foot traffic, a river of people reeling around him. Safety in numbers he told himself. He inhaled the scent of sewage and exhaust. He gazed to his left, then right. He had learned he needed to be careful. The interminable chore of making every move without an error. The wrong move could cost his life. Perez bit down hard on the inside of his left check.

Four blocks later he stopped in front of a windowless building on 57th. He made his way inside where two men with holstered guns stood behind the main desk. He nodded, showed I.D. and placed his palm on the hand reader and waited. He bent down and peered into the retina scanner, green light blinking. The security guy on the left signaled him to follow. He moved to the only elevator within sight where the door slid open. Perez rode to the sixth floor where two more security guards waited for him. "Hello, Mr. Clemente."

He nodded.

They led Perez to a room with high ceilings, no windows, marble floors and a kind of blue light seeping from the ceiling. Soft, like a romantic restaurant, instead of a vault of private safe deposits. His heart began to move faster. Something was filling him, a hunger that had lain dormant since the last time he visited.

"Let me know if you need anything, Mr. Clemente."

He walked into the small room. A wooden chair sat against the far wall behind a desk, His breathing quickened. He loved his private safe deposit rooms in the larger cities. He owned one in Paris as well, but didn't feel it was as secure. The French could never be truly trusted he believed. But the artwork was more plentiful in Europe. The black market much less regulated. He pulled down on a glass door handle and opened it. Another light blinked on. He put velvet gloves on, grabbed a hand carved wooden frame and lifted it slowly. He placed the frame on the desk and sat in the chair. He had been waiting for this without even being aware it. He reached into the desk's drawer and pulled out a magnifying glass, placing it in his lap for now. It was a game of his, a ritual, a concrete comfort, senses soaring. His shoulders began to shake, his thoughts overwhelmed him and his mind went still. He gazed at the painting in front of him. Dark paint covering the edges of the portrait, nothing more beautiful. The face of Rembrandt Van Rijn stared back at Perez as if it wanted to speak to him. There was something undeniable, something mysterious coming from the eyes staring back at Perez. Nothing else could speak to him like this. The most painful part about it was that Perez couldn't look at this face every day of his life. It had to remain hidden. But for how long? He raised the magnifying glass, squinting to admire details in the art. He went through the same process. Again, and again. Putting the paintings back into the vault and pulling out another and placing it on the desk to admire—Renoir, Van Gogh, a pastel from Toulouse Lautrec, a pencil drawing from Leonardo da Vinci. Thirteen in all. There was a knock on the door.

"Fifteen minutes, Mr. Clemente." The time limit he set for himself almost up.

He realized he needed to change this routine as he headed down the elevator. Leaving his love was such a lonely feeling, but it was his only option until he could retire. Would he ever retire? He made his way through the doors and stepped outside. There was a distinct change in the city at night. A voltage, a rhythm shivering through the air. The obese noise threading through the streets.

His eyes worked the streets, watching again. A bus pissed smoke and rattled by him. A black BMW, windows dark, pulled from the curb. He was just tired now, paranoia teasing him. The car shouldered through two lanes towards him. Slowly, Perez began to walk, watching the BMW from the corner of his eyes. It was moving closer. The car's back window lowered. Instinctively, Perez leapt forward, there was a shot. Now, wheels squealing as the BMW vaulted over the curb and around a bus. There was an explosion of screams. He turned his head and saw a woman lying at his feet, blood pulsing from her neck, mouth laboring for air, eyes wild. He pulled a Glock from the inside of his coat, considering what to do. He thought he could reach the car. Instead, he looked down at the lady again. She was already dead. He took his scarf and placed it under her head and gently closed her eyes. The bullet was meant for him.

Chapter 15

Las Vegas (Reuters)—Federal Law enforcement agents stated that Triple Cherry Casino owner Francis Ballard was found dead today in the pool of his hotel. Authorities believe that the private casino owner was tortured and killed before being left in the casino's pool. No other information is available at this time.

Chapter 16

There was hardly ever a day that Jason Carson didn't exercise. His body was a temple for the Holy Spirit. Prayer, push ups, sit ups, chin ups, squats, and lunges. When it came to making his body into a power engine, he could work on the basics for hours. Zero body fat was the goal. But spending time in a weight room, well, that was just a complete waste of time. And yet, that was what Coach Felter wanted him to do. Work in the new weight room. Donors wanted a championship.

Barbells clanged as Jason Carson pushed them from his chest. Coach Felter spotted for him, helped place the weights on the stand. Felter said, "Let's go. You've got two sets to go."

Jason closed his eyes, shook his head. "C'mon coach, this is a waste. Body's already perfect." He lifted his shirt and pointed to his abs. He ran a hand over his chest. "I'm shaving again. Whole body smooth as silk. Ain't it perfect?"

"Isn't."

"The temple. It's perfect, right?"

"Always looking for affirmation? Not everything you do is perfect, Jason. Let's go."

"Just let me shoot a hundred free throws. Call it good."

Felter pointed to the bench. "Sit your ass back down. Guys in the Big Show will push you around the floor. It's gonna be sharks not minnows up there. You need to turn into a shark."

"Feels like studying to me."

."That tutor helping you?"

"Yeah, but it's all work, all the time."

"She helping you with Chemistry?"

Jason didn't answer for a second, irritated by the same questions regarding his incessant troubles. "Yes, but she's a private tutor. Forty-five an hour."

"What about the money you got from Dollars for Scholars?"

"Spent it on some retro Nikes. I don't need to be a scholar."

"Holy shit, kid. What are you thinking," Felter barked, looking half confused and half annoyed. "You need to pass your ACT before anything else, kid."

"Didn't do too good the first time."

"That's too well…not, too good. Adverb buddy."

The talk of school fatigued Jason, as if he was imprisoned by it. God had a plan for him. "Whatever that means coach. Don't like tests," Jason said as he picked up hand weights, began doing curls.

"What are you doing about the dyslexia?" Felter asked.

He tossed the barbells onto the rubber floor making a heavy clanging sound. It was an inheritance from his father, learning difficulties and a surly disposition. He shrugged.

"You're gonna have a shit load of reading in college."

Jason shot right back. "Only going for one year. Can we eat now?"

"That's if we can get ya' in. You need an 18 on the ACT to make it through the clearing house. You got an eleven last time."

"There's a bunch of reading on the test and vocabulary crap has always given me trouble, with my reading ya' know."

"Or lack," Felter toweled himself. He swung his head, looked back. "You've just charmed your way through high school. The way those female teachers look at you. I wish I got some of those looks, kid." He smiled. "I could use some of those looks. But you, you just give 'em that smile. Next thing you know you're on dean's list."

Jason knew most of the teachers loved having him in class; especially Mr. Abrahamson the Social Studies teacher who balled at TCU and always talked basketball with him during study hall. Abrahamson used to give him study worksheets to take home and they ended up being the exact same questions as the tests. And, English teacher Ms. Zelinsky used to stare at him while the rest of the class wrote about a book they all read. Jason would hand in his paper and receive an A along with her cell phone number and the message; reach me any time, day or night for some special tutoring and extra credit.

One of his prayers had yet to be answered. "I know I need to pass. Or else I'll be on some 'Watch List' or maybe some Prop. 48 or whatever it's called. Just need to get some sleep." He rubbed his calf, sighing. "My whole body hurts." He'd been home late twice this week from games and before he could sleep he had to ice his ankles which took another forty-five minutes. His left shoulder had been sore for a month and two fingers on his left hand had never quite recovered from being jammed on a dunk in December. Everything hurt this time of year. How in the heck was he supposed to sleep? "I keep waking up all night. My mom thinks I'll do just fine next time I take the ACT."

"You and your mother are both naïve. That's why you need me to help you with things."

"I fell asleep last time I took it."

"What does the doctor say?"

"Can't really afford that either. I just take some of that P.M. stuff. Works good most of the time."

"Works well for God's sake. You need to come to me. I'll help you."

Felter just kept attacking him, never saying what he wanted to hear. "You just keep making promises and that's it," Jason said in a sharp voice.

"Bull crap, kid. I've been talking to teachers on your behalf nearly four years now. O'Reilly told me there was no way you'd get out of American Lit. and I moved you into Hennigan's class so you could get through it."

"I thought that was because of something to do with too many kids in one class."

"That's what Callison told you, but that's because I made him make the change, or else you were dead meat."

"Hmm."

"Yeah hmm. What about Dr. O'Malley's hundred dollar handshakes."

Jason gave him a look. "What ya' talkin about?"

"What do you mean what am I talkin' about? I've known he's given you cash every now and again. We've been trying to take care of you. Trying my best to get you to reach that big dream."

Jason didn't react right away. "OK."

"Well, I'm the one that set it up with the Doc. I'm the guy, Jason, me. Whatever happened to that money, anyway?"

The question hung in the air, so did that word, money. Strange how everything always came around to that word.

"I spent it."

"Spent it on what?"

"Shoes"

"Shoes...what kind of shoes? Dress shoes?"

It was endless, answering coach's questions. The guy was always asking. Always interfering.

"Nikes."

"Nikes. You spent that money on Nikes? More Nikes. Good god, you've already got hundreds of basketball shoes," he said, voice vibrating.

"Vintage 85 Air Jordan's, High Black Reds. You can't even find those in size 16s."

"Holy shit, kid. You need to get your head outta your ass."

Jason stood up, grabbed his water bottle and threw it against the far wall. The eight foot mirror exploded, shards of glass rifled into the mat floor. There was a sound in his head like a world of chainsaws starting buzzing.

"I never even wanted to take it. I'll pay the guy back someday. Thought you had your own money problems." Spittle exploded from his mouth. "I'll pay you back if it was you."

Felter raised his palms, took a step back. "Slow down here, kid. I know you have a lot going on. You don't need to pay anybody back." He glanced over at the wall and breathed. Turned his head back. "Thing is, you need to listen to me when I tell you what to do. It's just one of the hundred a things I've done for you to make sure you make it out of here on time. It's not all been up to you, as you like to say."

Jason grunted.

"Look, if you don't pass this thing, you'll be bobbing for long johns at Oak Park's Dunkin' Donuts. And those girls that look at you with those, 'He's-gonna-be-a-billionaire,' kind of eyes will be looking for you to fill up their lattes and give 'em change for their twenties."

Jason threw back his shoulders. "I'll be OK. Tutor says so."

"If you'd ever use her. Listen, I know a guy who could make that ACT easy for you. He'll put a camera in a pair of glasses that you'll wear on test day. We'll have an egg head dude read the test from his home and send you the answers into the lens of your glasses. Agent friend of mine told me about it. Be a slam dunk."

Jason thought of the arrangement with Ricardo Perez instead. He took a drink. The most painful thing was letting another team score a couple of extra baskets at the end of a game. Even a game that was already decided. What was the harm? For several seconds he stood silently, his posture beginning to droop. All the pain in his body was joined in a chorus to sing punishment for all his sins. Maybe help with a test would be the same kind of thing. Wouldn't cause much harm to anyone if he just got a little help when he needed it. But, was it honest? "Don't think that would be the right thing to do, coach."

Felter groaned. "Kid, you just don't know how tough it is in the Bigs. Those coaches, agents and general managers don't give a shit about you. The only thing they want out of you is winning. You're just a machine to make their engine go and as soon as you run out of gas or blow a piston, you're sent to the scrap pile. I've been through it. It's something your old man should have told you a long time ago," Felter said as his voice slowed and trailed off. "Sorry kid. I forgot."

Jason arched his back, always in discontent now. "Don't talk to me about my old man again." He walked out.

Chapter 17

Scott Reynolds felt he had lost his bearings. He closed his eyes and opened them. All around him, white light flashed. The room seemed to bulge, to throb; his skull felt brittle, delicate. The Bellagio Casino in Las Vegas, Nevada, on a Tuesday night. The bustling noise of bells and sirens in every direction. He watched the hundred dollar blackjack table for a long time. Two Asian men sat opposite each other on the ends of the table. Glasses of water sat next to piles of chips in front of both. The dealer flipped his card over. "Bust," sliding chips to them. It was hard not to see these two men had the advantage, now. Reynolds was counting the cards from the six decks. Counting and storing them in his head as he did in his early years before joining the Bureau. He loved the game and didn't even have to bluff. His counting and winnings, usually in Atlantic City, had almost cost him his job, until the FBI thought it was a good idea to have him work the casino beat. He had won enough to put a down payment on his first house, but he hadn't played in years. Regardless, the addiction was real, deep. Sure enough the dealer tossed out cards, one player showing an ace. Of course. Twenty-one, more chips moved to the winner. Without much of a change of expression, the dealer looked up at Reynolds. "Good time to get in?"

Reynolds knew he couldn't even think about it, but he did. It was his fault, one of the many faults of thinking about what could have been. He'd figured out pretty quickly the good life on the bureau's salary was impossible. As soon as he realized he wouldn't have that house on the lake, he threw himself into his work. Eradicate evil. His only way to even the score. The dealer was still looking at him, waiting. A set of bells echoed from the ceiling. At times like this he felt his body being seduced into the moment: Pavlov's dog. He reached into his pocket, pulled out his wallet and placed it on the table. The dealer said, "You'll have to go to the window for chips."

Reynolds eyes watered, his mouth and throat dry. More bells pulled him awake and he swiped his wallet off the table. What was he thinking? His ears hummed as he backed away. He collided into a women walking behind him, her glass crashing to the floor, ice cubes scattering like marbles. He turned, apologized twice, and handed her a twenty dollar bill and charged away as quickly as he could..

Reynolds cleared his throat and sniffed, kept walking. He reached into his pocket to pull out a pill box. He popped three Advil into his palm and swallowed. A minute later Reynolds found the sports betting area. He squinted through all the lights from the televisions, the general odor was perspiration. He looked at hundreds of betting options. A risk or a wager for everything. Reynolds stood looking at everyone in the room. Some of the heads down, staring at newspapers or phones. Other heads up; watching games, faces vacant, anguished as if they were waiting for their fate, their summons. Reynolds stepped through an Employees Only door. A stocky man wearing a blue blazer and a Bellagio emblem on his pocket nodded and walked him to an elevator. Up he went until it opened in front of a room with two double doors, and then into a back room with closed circuit televisions being watched by men in white shirts watching the betting. Was everything and everyone being watched?

A man with a swath of red hair and freckles turned his head to Reynolds. "Something of interest at the blackjack table?"

Reynolds shrugged blankly as if to say he wasn't interested. "Just routine."

Twisting his chair around and seated backwards, the freckled man said, "We made the bust last night in Atlantic City."

Reynolds stiffened. "Thought we were going to wait to see if we could catch more?"

"I found out from a source they were all leaving town. We had them all together."

Reynolds stuck a thumb between his teeth, sawing. "What time?"

"About 9:30 eastern."

"Where?"

"They were all playing. We went and arrested eight, pulled the cameras out of the wall."

"What about the wire rooms in Philly? Weren't they watching and handling the bets from there?"

"Sting came at exactly the same time. They didn't know what hit 'em."

Was he the last to know these things? Who was giving the orders? The Bureau always had agents trying to take charge, make a name for themselves. "Next time, I'm making the call," Reynolds said.

"Thought you wanted me to make the call," he said and looked back at the row of screens.

"I want to know. I want the last call, understand?"

The freckled man hesitated, then nodded once.

"How about the hockey coach?" For some reason Reynolds couldn't think of the guys name right now, there were so many. There was so much damn betting going on with the explosion of fantasy sports and the misuse of insider information. Even the owners were buying into sports betting companies. A dense pain was threading into his forehead. "Did we take him in?"

There was a silence. Everything in the room languishing. "Tocchet wasn't there."

Reynolds shook his head for a second. "He wasn't there. Holy shit, what are you telling me?"

"We still might get him, but everyone else was there. All of 'em. Even the cop Rubio."

Reynolds had been chasing Rick Tocchet, an NHL star who played for eighteen years and coached the Arizona Coyotes. His investigation, known as Operation Slapshot, found Tocchet had processed illegal wagers on professional and college sports. Wayne Gretzky's wife, Janet, was even involved in the betting. He had found Wayne Gretzky on a wire-tap discussing how his wife could avoid being implicated.

He wanted to break this wide open with the dozens of NHL players he knew were involved.

"Might get him. Holy shit. He was the big fish, not the cop."

"Also got five of the casino employees who were exchanging cash and chips."

"I don't give a shit about them. I wanted Tocchet. They've made two million in bets in the last forty days. This has been going on for at least five years now. A judge told me he would give him at least ten years in prison. It ties us into the NHL. It's all about the sport, damn it."

Freckles looked slack and pale. He pushed his seat away, glaring at one of the screens. He pointed. "There he is."

Reynolds steps forward, eyes trying to focus. He fumbled for his glasses but couldn't find them. Damn. He pinched his knuckles, squeezing. He stepped forward, squinting. His eyes struggled to see.

"One of 'em has been at the Venetian and Harrah's already. Our new friend was at the MGM Grand an hour ago." He swung his head to look at Reynolds.

He was on his toes now, back arched, straining to see the top screen. "Where? Can you zoom in?"

"Funny thing," Freckles said as if he hiding a secret. "Our man was here last night. Spent some time at the Gold Spike."

"What the hell's that?"

"Tiny little casino, off the radar. We didn't get to listen to his conversation with the owner. They met for forty minutes. Wish we had the tape. Anyway, the owner came out of the room after the meeting with this look on his face. God. The look on the guy's face was like he'd seen a ghost."

"What he say?"

"He ain't talkin."

"What?"

"Like I said. He ain't talkin'."

At that moment Reynolds saw something on one of the screens. He noticed a face he remembered.. He decided it was time to go back down to the main floor.

Reynolds walked up beside Guy Ferguson who was staring at the dozens of large screens in the Bellagio Sports Bar. Numbers scrolled under the games of basketball, hockey, volleyball, and even Jai Lai. It was the first time he had seen Ferguson in over two years. "Long time no see, Guy."

Reynolds began, "Wondered what you've been up to?" Reynolds and the FBI hadn't been in touch with Guy Ferguson since they'd worked in tandem. Ferguson was an informant on one of Wall Street's largest offshore brokerage busts in US history. Before becoming an informant, Ferguson created his own trading website, a Charles Schwab knockoff that collected fees for executing trades and had allowed him to earn four million a year and amass a nice collection of Lamborghini and Ferraris. After his first fortune, Ferguson suckered investors out of more than twenty million by manipulating the market for shares in a Mexican gold mine and a natural gas project in Alabama. He moved to the Bahamas and was arrested for illegal day trading. It was then he decided to become an FBI informant in exchange for his crime. He had reportedly earned about a million for the deal to boot. But since his one and only case as an informant, he had disappeared until Guy called the FBI and told Reynolds he wanted to work again.

Guy loved the chase along with the dough. Reynolds got the OK to hire him again because Guy had dealings in Mexico and was fluent in Spanish. Reynolds noticed that he still had the neatly trimmed stubble of a beard as if it never changed from day to day. His unbuttoned blue oxford shirt shouted with tufts of presumptuous chest hair matching his secluded coffee colored eyes. His hair was moist and slick but not as full as Reynolds had remembered.

Reynolds began. "We found some evidence that suggests the Mexicans probably murdered agent Henderson."

As expected, Ferguson shot him a calculated but confident look. "Do we know what cartel?"

"We think it's one of the three we talked about, but we need your help with this. We're definitely following a guy named Ricardo Perez. We think he's the major player in the gambling syndicate."

"I'm thinking about selling my Mexican gold mine. I'll head down to Mexico City and work my contacts."

Reynolds knew Ferguson had contacts. That's why he made so much damn money doing some of the same things he did. Reynolds said, "I should have been a snitch. Pays a lot better."

Ferguson smiled. "I'm up for it. Last one was a gas. But I'm trying to stay under the radar," he said looking over his shoulder. "Not good for my private businesses if I'm away too long."

Reynolds nodded as he looked at all the games being played in front of him. "Let me know as soon as you have something."

"You know I will," Guy said with a grin.

Chapter 18

This is how Jason dreamed it would be—the final game of his high school year playing for the championship. He had never been a normal eighteen-year-old boy, probably a man now, that's what his mother told him. He never thought about other professions.

He never hung out with the guys, never had a job, never played any other sports except basketball, never wanted to do anything else since he got a new basketball on his fourth birthday. He never thought about anything other than basketball, his mother, and Jesus. Never. He bowed his head and said a prayer. His palms clammy, left eye twitching, he couldn't relax. But he did tire of his pregame ritual; it was almost shameful, especially after talking to the pastor about it. The nauseous pulse in his body. His stomach tightened. Tilted. He knelt in front of the toilet basin, draped an arm around the back of the bowl, ice cold. He felt heat rise in his neck and cheeks. He always knew what was coming next, but sometimes it seemed as if it lasted for hours. But it was only minutes. Maybe nerves were natural? Maybe it would stop as he got older? Maybe someday, but not now. He positioned himself over the top of the bowl, teeth chattering. Ten seconds later he wiped the sweat from his forehead, resting. Then it was over, gone. Tranquil now. He was ready. Hypnotizing. He headed for the basketball floor feeling like a warrior.

Confetti floated down from the top of Assembly Hall in Champaign, Illinois. The Oak Park Huskies band blasted the fight song. Teammates celebrated at center court. A player handed the 6A bronze championship trophy to Jason. He raised it over his head, as if he had done it a thousand times and the funny thing about it, he had. He had raised the trophy in his mind almost daily for years. Jason kissed the trophy and passed in on to a teammate. Beads of sweat ran into Jason eyes as he hugged one of the players. Jason moved into the crowd. He reached down and gently hugged his mother. He felt exhilarated, as if he could finally give her what she deserved. This prayer had been answered for him. Jason gazed into his mother's eyes. Eyes that normally gave him so much comfort looked yellow and tired. And those eyes were filled with tears and he knew those eyes had watched hundreds of his games since he was in third grade. He just hoped those eyes would be around long enough to see him play hundreds more. He smiled faintly.

His mother had been out of the hospital for two days. Jason couldn't help looking at her wig. Something about the wig she was wearing made him feel uncomfortable, made the moment a little less fulfilling. The black silky strands that used to enhance her beautiful face, were now replaced with something artificial, something unwanted like the disease itself. Yet there was nothing more he could do now. He had just given her the only thing he could, his best. He kissed her on the cheek and pressed his arms around her frail body. Stared at her and wondered if she had lost more weight. Confused he tried to give her his best smile but something kept tugging at him.

She wiped a tear away. Her voice trembling. "I'm so happy for you, dear. The good Lord has bestowed his blessing upon you."

He wanted to say he didn't understand. How did he receive the blessing that she deserved? She spent her entire day looking for ways to help others and now this. How did it all fit? He wanted to dispute her but she wouldn't listen anyway. He nodded. "Glad you came. You feeling OK?"

"Just a little dizzy. Maybe it's just all the excitement," she said grabbing onto his arm.

"You're the one responsible for this. Wouldn't have happened without you. I owe all this to you, Ma."

She was shaking now. "I just want everything to work out for you." Her lips had gotten thinner, her smile pulling at wrinkles. "You're the most important thing in my life, and I don't know how much time I have left."

"Stop," he said. "You'll be fine." Hugging her again.

"Shouldn't you be down on the floor celebrating with the rest of your friends, dear?"

He thought maybe he should go back down and join the celebration, but something held him back. He was the big go-to man on the court, but he definitely was the odd man out when it came to hanging out with the team. "I'm fine right here."

She nodded, slowly. "Just glad the Peterson's were able to bring me. Couldn't help pay for gas, though."

"I just put a huge chunk a dough in the checking account." There was a lump in his throat that he couldn't swallow. "We bought the car and paid your hospital bills. The rent...all that stuff?"

She gave him a half smile, patted his arm. "I owed Uncle Paul some cash, owed some money to my lawyer. Also gave $500 to Doctors Without Borders. They're really helping with all the problems in Africa...kids dying every day."

He felt a sudden flutter in his chest. "You mean all the money we had...the money that I brought home is gone?"

She just smiled at him. He could see lipstick on her teeth. "Don't you worry dear. The good Lord will provide. Just like he did last time." She looked so happy, he felt a moment of calmness.

He looked away. Let out a long breath. Shook his head. His eyes moved through the stadium. He recognized the college coaches sitting in the area behind the scorer's table. All schools from last year's Final

Four: North Carolina, Duke, Iowa, and UCLA. He looked at his mother and she was staring at him. How could he ever go too far away from her and play college ball? She needed him. His ankle was starting to ache again. He needed ice. He looked over and saw a familiar face standing next to the tunnel. It was the face of Ricardo Perez.

They weren't alone. In the thirty-third row of the arena, a man sat with a blue Kentucky baseball cap that was partially covered by the hoodie of his sweatshirt. Under the bill of his cap, round brown glasses lodged on a face inconspicuous and unshaven. Hands folded and covering the lower part of his face, Scott Reynolds watched.

Chapter 19

Scott Reynolds stared into his bathroom mirror at 10:20PM. He pulled down on his bottom lip and inspected teeth that look grayer than the last time he had examined them with his wife's magnifying mirror. He liked how everything in the mirror looked so much bigger to him. He even wished for a minute that he could jump into that mirror and finally make his small body into something larger; something that would make others look up to him for once. But his teeth did look darker since he last took the time to study them.

Reynolds knew that he was good at studying things. He raised his top lip and cringed at the yellow covering the front teeth that once had been as bright as a harvest moon. He knew he should set up the appointment with his dentist to make a mouthpiece to sleep with and bring back the white shine, but he didn't think he'd have the time with this new case and he definitely didn't think he could sleep with that thing in his mouth. Hell, he couldn't even sleep through the night now unless he medicated himself with a few drinks to settle him into dreamland. When he was thirteen he had braces for two weeks but the orthodontist had to take them off because Reynolds wasn't able to sleep. Instead, six to seven cups of coffee a day had left his teeth dark.

Reynolds phone vibrated. He thought his wife might be asleep down the hall. After so many nights of Reynolds flopping around, giving her fits, she moved into the other bedroom. Reynolds didn't want to wake her. He hadn't even checked on her after he arrived home. He knew he had awakened her enough for one lifetime.

Reynolds picked up his phone and closed the bathroom door. The call notification indicated "private," nothing new for someone that worked at the FBI. He cleared his throat and sniffed. "Reynolds here."

"Agent Reynolds, this is Attorney General Greg Wolfe. Sorry for calling so late." Reynolds had only spoken to the Attorney General on one other occasion, in the White House after working on a drug case in El Salvador.

Reynolds' Adam's apple was stuck in his throat. He leaned back, widened his feet and studied the wall, focus, "Yes, how can I help, Sir?"

"We're investigating something that's been brought to us by NSA. Possible leaks in the communication system. We're running an expanded audit on all geographic regions in the Northern Hemisphere to try and find the source," Wolfe cleared his throat. "Director Hamilton and I need your help with our investigation in Mexico and Central America. I'm sending two members from the NSA to meet with you tomorrow at 8:00AM They'll brief you. You'll have total access to the NSA Director Jack Phillips. There's a leak in the dam, we can't afford to have our security in breach."

Reynolds wet his lips with his tongue. "I'll do my best Mr. Secretary," and looked in the full-length mirror, straightened his back and wondered if he was getting any taller. Although he knew this call should have made him feel taller and more important.

Chapter 20

Jason was going to have to pick a school. He sat at the end of his bed thumbing through the UCLA media guide. His room smelled musty and of hair gel. Seemed everyone in this apartment complex was just trying to survive. Footfalls hammered from his ceiling, somebody running again up there. A dog barked in one of the apartments. Probably Mrs. Garner who was always trying to hide two cats and a Boston terrier in a complex that didn't permit pets. Jason turned off his iPhone, flipped it onto the pile of cards and letters from colleges stacked on the nightstand; Duke, Arizona, Villanova, Iowa, Syracuse, Michigan State, Georgetown, Kansas, there were dozens. He closed the UCLA media guide and rubbed his eyes. Time to decide. Almost from the beginning, he was terrified of making a decision by himself. He took a bite from an English muffin, licked the peanut butter off of his finger. Not that he wasn't getting advice from everyone. Clearly he had to decide and time was running out. Everything in his life was running out of time and maybe that's why he was always late. He dropped to the floor and pushed away a pile of Nikes. Fifty pushups. While doing pushups he thought he should be studying his Spanish. It was all too much.

His mother stuck her head into the doorway.

"Lots of studying to do?"

He didn't answer.

"Are you hungry?"

"No. I finished the meat loaf Aunt Julie brought over."

Jason's mom walked over in long slow movements and sat at the edge of his bed. Her arms hung from her shoulders like sticks. Her eyes gray, deeper inside sockets, obscured. "You haven't played today. When was the last time you took a day off?" She pulled out a tissue from the sleeve of her sweatshirt. "What's troubling you?"

Where would he start? He remembered how she looked at him the last time he tried to talk about it. She always thought things would just work out for the best.

"I didn't shoot my hundred free throws. First day in about a year I've missed...just don't feel up to it."

"Is it Jessica? You haven't talked to her in over a month."

"Na, not interested anymore."

"I really liked her."

"Too selfish and jealous." He leaned back and dropped into his bed.

"God has his plan."

"And I've been praying about it." His mother looked at him then and he wanted to make her happy. He waited while she waited. "I just wanna get through college, get drafted and play ball every night. That's all I really ever wanted." That was the paradox he was presented. At one end of the spectrum, time couldn't move fast enough. On the other, every day he could be closer to losing his mother. He looked into her eyes. "But I also want to give you things you've never had...buy you a house and..."

"I'll be fine, honey." She dabbed her nose.

Again. Everything was always fine. She was a perpetual fountain of hope.

"We need to make sure you pick the right school and be that number one draft choice everyone's been talking about."

He thought he should tell her about Ricardo Perez but where would he begin? He cracked his knuckles.

"I don't want to disappoint anybody."

"I'll be fine." There it was, same answer as if it was a recorded response, I'll be fine, again and again. "I never want you to stop dreaming. You need to promise me..." she didn't finish, coughing.

"I didn't mean to upset you."

She took the tone she used to have when she was advising him. "You need to be happy. Finally winning the state championship. A grateful heart is a joyful heart." She raised her hands over her mouth and coughed, then took a deep breath. "I thought you'd be happy now?"

He looked into his mother's eyes. The most painful thing about looking at his mother now was the look in her eyes. He felt sick. "Just worried about you. Maybe I should stay close to home so I can get back more often. Iowa went to the final four last year and its three hours away."

She looked as if she was in a trance and not listening. It was that look when she was praying talking with the Lord. She reached out for his hand, squeezed. "We're never to worry, son. There is a master plan."

"I want that plan to include you."

"It will son, it will. Whether I'm here on earth or in heaven. I will always be a part of you."

It was something he had noticed lately, all the talk of heaven. She had the strangest look on her face now.

"You've got to stop talking about dying." He was waiting for a miracle. "Everything's gonna be OK."

"OK."

"Please tell me you're going to be OK"

His mother put her arm around him. "I'll be fine."

Chapter 21

There was a massive hum inside Oak Park High School on Saturday morning. People moved around like bees shaken out of their beehive. Waiting. Anticipating the decision of Jason Carson. For the last ten months it was all he had heard about, texted about, read about, emailed about, phoned about.

Jason tried to pull his collar away from his neck. The full Windsor tie was strangling him, almost suffocating. As long as he could remember he hated to dress up. But his mother was adamant, he would look his best when he made the announcement. So for the first time since his church confirmation, he went to the men's store and bought a gray suit that fit him; thank the good Lord for their big and tall section. He was almost late this morning. For some reason he couldn't figure out how to tie a tie. Dozens of tries watching the dopey looking guy with the gray mustache on You-tube. No one around that could help him either. He was on his own again. But he didn't give up, thirty minutes of trying and he finally got it right.

Jason swung open the locker room door, walked into the hallway. Lights flashed, cameras clicked, shouts, people jostling about. Reporters everywhere. ESPN, Fox Sports, NBC, WGN, NBA TV, Star Sports, there was even a someone from the Golf Channel. Cheerleaders jumping, pumping pom-poms. Only a couple of his teammates sat along the far wall. Where were the rest of them?

He moved down the hallway and he did it as if he had done it a thousand times. A crowd never affected him. Memories flooded him and as he made his way to the end of the hall and moved toward a table full of microphones. Voices went silent, breathes were held, all looking at him.

Waiting for him to uncover the mystery. Jason spotted his mother at the far end of the long table. He forced himself to look around

Coach Felter and Principal Martin were standing next to the table, waiting for him. He shook some hands, bent over and kissed his mother and sat. She looked tired, always tired. The color of her blush was the first thing to catch his eye. A heavy dose of magenta covered her cheeks, covering the pale, the demise. But her eyes, the color of her eyes disturbed him, a crimson red swimming from her lack of sleep. Her pupils full, swollen. Lips overripe from the poisons languishing inside her willowy body. Funny how he never got used to how she looked now. But she smiled at him. A smile that was genuine and real, nothing contrived or artificial and there was no substitute for it. Nothing.

He forced himself to look over at Coach Felter who had moved to the corner in front of the doors that led to the gymnasium. Jason looked away. Principal Mason thanked people for coming and handed Jason the microphone. Jason reached into his front pocket and unfolded a piece of paper. The pressure against his throat was suffocating. He pulled on his collar again. "I would like to thank all of you for coming today and supporting me during my high school career. I want to thank my family and the team for making this possible." He cleared his throat. "I also want to thank my coach, John Felter for helping me during my high school career," Jason looked straight ahead but not at Coach Felter. "After talking with my mother the last two evenings, we've decided…I've decided." He paused to clear his throat. He turned and looked over at his mother. He would remember how she looked at him then, weary, but also saintly. "I've decided to play at the University of Iowa next year," The cameras in the room cracked like gunfire.

After Jason announced his decision, there were words of congratulations, slaps on the backs, a dozen or so interviews and a mood that was nothing less than celebratory. But not now. Not in his coach's office. To put it bluntly, he hardly recognized the man in front of him. "Come in, shut the door."

Jason shut the door and sat down.

"What the hell happened?" Felter barked, glaring.

Jason dropped his head, looked at the stains in the gray carpeting, and slid his hands into his pants pockets. He could feel the heat rising in the small room. If he did not know better, he would've mistaken Coach Felter for not wanting the best for him.

Felter's face beet red. Neck veins popping out like twisted cord. Jason hadn't seen coach look like this since Tommy Halloday spray-painted New Trier's team bus.

After a moment of deep breathing Felter started, "So, just when the hell did you think you wanted to tell me about this change?

"I dunno."

"You don't know," Felter screamed. "Wish at least I wasn't left in the god-damned dark like all those other reporters and idiots out there. Assholes that never spent any time with you." Ruddy streaks bloomed on his cheeks and forehead. "I mean…all of a sudden they're here at my school waiting to get this scoop about where my player is going to college and I don't even have a fuckin' clue about it,"

Jason could only shrug. It was like standing in a windstorm, listening.

"I thought this thing was decided," he said as he shook his head. "I've gone out of my fucking way to arrange things with the coaches at UCLA." He jerked his chair by the handles and jumped closer to his desk, knees crashing into the front. "The promises I've made and favors, for god's sakes…"

"Coach…" he took a deep breath, but couldn't find much air. "I'm sorry," voice quivering. My mother and I had a long talk. She didn't want me to go that far away…Doctor's keep telling me she may not have too much time." He forced himself to look at Felter now, to reach out to him. "I don't know how much time." College is one year. She thought it would be better to stay closer. Iowa is only three hours away."

Felter interrupted, "Your mother said this and your mother said that, shit what did you have to say about it," as he pointed a finger at Jason's face. "All of a sudden your Ma is an expert at big time college athletics and professional basketball?"

Where was the comfort and protection he was looking for? Jason pointed back at Felter. "Listen. My mother is the reason I'm the number one recruit in the country. She's the one that made all the trips. Got me to all the practices." He pounded a fist onto the table, swiped the pile of newspapers from the desk. "And when my old man left." His heartbeat filled him. He shouldered off his new sport coat, wadded it up and threw it into the corner. "It was my mother that pushed me. Found the money for the private lessons, travel, games, everything."

Felter sniffed the air like it might give him strength. "How many of those lessons came from me. Free lessons, huh?"

Suddenly, Jason felt confused: he was probably right. He'd spent hours with him. Took him places when he couldn't find a ride. Jason stood up, looking at him for a long time, pulled the tie from around his neck. "My mother's dying."

But Felter only seemed to be half-listening. Felter cracked the knuckles on his left hand. "Now this whole thing is in the crapper."

Jason stared back. Suffering had formed him: made him confident, determined, made him a warrior.

Felter rubbed his whiskers with his hand. "I'm in a shit load of trouble kid…we had this whole thing worked out." Felter tilted back his head, yelled. "Son of a sweet bitch. What the hell I'm supposed to tell the boys in California now. This whole thing had been planned and now I'm back in the shitter," He kicked the chair.

Jason jumped back. "Settle down, coach."

Felter yanked open a drawer from his desk and pulled out a pile of papers in his fist. "How can I settle down when I got bills to pay. I got creditors breathing down my damn neck every day…I thought we had a deal with you and the Bruins. They were going to let me be a consultant for them in the Midwest. Like a scout, and the money they were paying me would help me get back on my feet. Get outta my sister's shit-smelling basement…maybe find a date again," he groaned, rubbing his eyes with the palm of his hands.

Jason studied him. Did he really just hear that? "Pay you? UCLA was going to pay you?"

Then Felter laughed, "That's the way it works in athletics if you didn't know by now, dumb-ass. People take care of each other. Favors. That's the way the game's played," he screamed. "You don't have a goddamn idea how it works, do you? I deserve something here as well. It's not all just about you," Felter said, the words fat and hanging in the air. Felter kicked his chair, this time with the sole of his shoe, knocking over three of his bobble heads. He spun around, face anguished.

Jason wasn't sure he'd heard right, but that statement chilled the flesh on his arm. And for a moment, he wondered if he was looking at his father. The yelling. He didn't know what else to do now. This was supposed to be his day, yet there was nothing. A sudden tilt factor engaged every space inside his body. He stepped forward.

Felter shook his head. "Now I'll never be able to retire, let alone move into my own place again." His phone rang, he picked it up, glanced at it and fired it against the wall. "My fuckin' life is over."

Face burning. Jason stepped forward, again. Felter smirked. Jason was shaking with anger or hunger, he couldn't tell anymore. He was trying so hard not to lose control.

There was an awful pause, followed by a moment of disbelief. Something about the memory of being yelled at. Listening to that sound, yelling, ridicule, was beginning to work him. He couldn't explain why, just that it was. He closed his eyes and willed his body to be calm, but not this time. Jason took two more steps forward and shoved Felter in the chest. Felter tumbled back, hitting his head against the cabinet. Books cascaded onto his head, bobbleheads jerking everywhere.

"Isn't that what coaches and teachers do. Try and help kids? The only person to help me, to ever be there for me. The only one who cared, was my mother." Pounding another fist into the table, then throwing a chair against the wall, a photo smashing to the ground. They exchanged a long glance, then Jason walked out of the office.

Chapter 22

Nowadays it was just one tough night after another. Sometimes in the morning it was necessary to clear the cobwebs. Mornings weren't his thing anymore. The sky was chalky, brisk air snapping at his face. Referee Tim McMurray jogged through the wet grass as he looked for field number 7. He was late for the 9:30 start and looked for the blue team; or was Conner on the blue team last year?

He found field eight and knew he was close. He saw his ex-wife and daughter bundled in a chair with a Minnesota Vikings blanket draped over them. Tim walked over and kissed the top of his daughter's ski hat.

"Daddy, I miss you," she said as she wrapped her arms around his neck. Tim looked over at Janet who didn't seem to notice he had arrived.

"We brought you a chair," Janet said as she swung a thumb over her shoulder but kept her eyes on the game.

"Thanks," He pulled his daughter's hat down over her ears. "Who's winning?" he asked.

Janet turned her head, rolled her eyes. "They don't keep score at this age, Tim," she said and looked back at the field.

McMurray knew it was cold in Bloomington, Minnesota, in the spring, but the words out of his ex-wife's mouth felt like they had traveled all the way from Siberia just to slap him in the face and give him a little welcome back frost-bite.

"How's Conner been doing?" he asked.

She didn't answer, just shrugged. Janet hadn't taken the divorce well. He'd tried to make it as painless as possible by giving her the house and only asking to see the kids when he was home during his breaks in the NBA. But Janet didn't want to talk him now. Not after she learned from their CPA that Tim was renting an apartment across town. Janet hired a private detective who told her after three days Tim had at least one girlfriend, possibly two or even three, but stopped the investigation because the P.I. wanted to keep her bill to a minimum. And then there was the call about his love child. He didn't even know about that one. Janet took that call. Eventually she'd had enough of him.

Good thing Janet didn't know about the time with his doctor yesterday. He'd never tell her about that. Dr. Zupov wasn't what most would call a fully qualified M.D. in the sense of normal medicine. He was more of a psychometric clairvoyant, clairsentient some called him, others, just fortune teller. Zupov took a sample of blood from Tim. Instead of sending it to the lab, like others, he held the blood up against a yellow light. Examined it for several minutes, swirling the test tube as if it was a decades-old, French Bordeaux. He told Tim that he could scan his blood and extract all of the colors like he was looking at a prism and by the brightness of certain colors, foresee his future. Two months earlier, Dr. Zupov examined Tim's urine sample and told him he was in for a bit of luck. And Tim took him for his word, stopped at the 7-11 on his way home and bought an instant Lotto ticket and won $500 bucks. But, yesterday wasn't so encouraging. Zubov studied Tim's blood sample and went on about his dull erythrocytes, his lack of globulin, his elevated Rh factor, and that something bad would happen to someone he loved.

He didn't sleep much that night and couldn't get the doctor's diagnosis out of his head. Maybe it was the traces of cocaine in his blood that could have thrown off the doc? Something bad was going to happen to someone he loved? He hugged his daughter and looked at his ex-wife starring out at a field of kids playing soccer in ski caps, gloves, and mittens. The official blew his whistle and the teams ran to the sidelines for halftime.

"How's Conner's reading going, honey?"

"Don't call me, honey."

"Sorry."

"Save it for all those princesses. All those princesses you keep in castles all over the country."

"Sorry. Just trying to be nice."

"Sorry's always been your favorite word. Always sorry."

He almost always knew what was coming next, lecture. And for a moment he wondered if he deserved it. But now wasn't the time and place, the ears of neighbors and old friends seemed to hear better under a ski cap. The gossip would fire up again, warming the flesh. All at his expense.

Now he was chained only to the fact that Janet had him right where she wanted him. At her disposal, for all the parents to hear. The neighborhood surrounding the field held onto their coffee mugs, lips even tighter. Cheers and "way to go's" gone quiet. Waiting.

"Can we discuss this later?" he said in a whisper.

Janet sat up in her chair. "Yeah, let's keep everything a secret. That's the way you roll, isn't it?"

He did not know what was stranger, listening to a coach during a game or his wife? Always on the attack. "Did you ever find a handy man to fix the tile in the kitchen?" he asked.

Janet didn't answer for a few moments. Eventually she turned her head and gave him a look. "Now you're interested? The guy said he wouldn't do anymore tile work until we pay our last bill. The spindles on the deck. Remember that one? Guess he never got paid either." She looked back at the field.

Tim had not anticipated this. He leaned in. "Sorry, can we discuss this later?"

Janet became ice as she sat there. "You're never around to talk about this stuff, too busy courting the ladies."

Courting? Who in the hell used that term anymore? He reached over and wiggled the tassel from the top of his daughter's ski hat. "Erin, you need to paint me a few more pictures. I love your artwork."

Erin gave him a wide smile. "I have a folder to give you."

Janet hissed and shook her head slightly. "You missed your last two dates with the kids."

"Had to go to Europe for training."

"Family values training," she fired back.

The game had restarted and there was a whistle on the field, some stoppage of play and Tim felt like they were all waiting for him to respond. He knew better than to say another word, but the quiet was killing him. He clapped his gloves together, cold reaching his extremities. "Erin, what would you like to do for vacation this summer?" It was the only thing that came into his head.

"Mom's new boyfriend, Tony, is taking us to Italy this summer."

Tim sucked in some cold air, lungs tightening. "Taking you where?"

"Italy. They talk different there."

Tim was having his own trouble. "Boyfriend? Tony?"

Janet reached into her purse, pulled out a juice box and gave it to Erin, then added. "Maybe Tony will let you come too. I can ask him today. He's been staying with us. He's nice, always brings me presents."

Janet launched Erin from her lap. "Why don't you go play with Jessica," she said, pointing. Erin yanked up her boots and ran down the sideline.

Tim casually glanced down each sideline, people holding their coffees and hot chocolates next to their chest. It was quiet for a time. He whispered. "Tony? I didn't know."

"There's a lot I wish I would have known myself," she said, voice chilled.

Now, he just wanted to watch the game in silence. It was worse than being on the hardwood working with NBA coaches. "Can we watch the game, Janet?"

She laughed twice. "That's the way it is. You walk in, play nice, cutesy smile, and march out."

He looked down at the grass. "Just thought I'd come see the game."

"You never call first. Just show up. I don't need that."

"How 'bout a truce? Let's not torture the little ears now, Janet."

"You don't have any idea what torture is, Mr. McMurray."

But McMurray did know a little bit about torture. Janet had been frigid after she had learned about the girl friends and that bitterness hadn't melted with the winter snow. It was still as cold as it was when the fighting had begun, and Tim realized that maybe the bitterness wasn't going away anytime soon. The final whistle blew, and the kids ran to the sidelines and waited for the snacks and drinks. Conner ran across the field and hugged Tim who bent over and kissed him on the forehead.

"Nice game out there Con-man. Love to see that hustle in the morning."

Conner nodded and took a bite from his rice crispy bar.

"I know your Mom doesn't really care, but what was the final score?"

Chapter 23

Jason parked behind a line of cars in front of the Iowa Memorial Union and galloped up the stairs. He found the sign that read Athletic Orientation and walked inside. Perhaps time had stopped; perhaps time was just in slow motion, but all eyes now were on Jason. It wasn't because he was late. It was something else. The room went quiet and the heads stayed turned in his direction. There appeared to be a great deal of interest in him. It was the same thing in Oak Park and all the tournaments he attended and the games where he dazzled the fans. The attention was the same. But it probably wasn't real. Never had been before. Just short lived. He was the freak in the circus, the unidentified flying object, Big Foot in the flesh. Everyone always wanted to see him. It was bad enough living in the fish bowl at home. A skinny redheaded kid, probably a track dude, knocked over a chair coming over to shake Jason's hand. Before long, there was a circle around him. Two kids on his left were taking photos with their phones. What followed was the onslaught of questions: how many hours did it take to shoot that many free throws in a row, what's your vertical jump when you knock quarters off the top of the backboard, what grade did you start dunking, how can you spin five balls at once? They peppered him with questions, and he spoke quietly, usually just one or two words answers.

He wasn't even late. The first thirty minutes was a "get to know your fellow athlete" session. Something he could have done without. His stomach rumbled, he patted his abs, three hundreds sit-ups this morning and ten minutes of planks, but he didn't finish his squats and lunges. He spotted three tables of food in the corner. Without answering the last question, he walked over to the table. Enough talking. Where would he start? Greek yogurt, granola bars, boiled eggs, cheese sticks, pistachios, almonds, sandwiches and salads in plastic containers, cut fruit, whole fruit, bagels; oh yeah his weakness, drinks, drinks galore. Protein shakes, Vitaminwater, Hydration Multiplier, Alkaline Water. Jason grabbed a Core Power Pure Protein drink. As he moved down the line someone chest bumped his shoulder. He turned and looked at a tall male with long curly blonde hair.

"Hey Carson, how you be? Brandon Sellers, your new roomie." Brandon gave him a smile that split his face, nothing but teeth. He had a yellow L.A. Lakers jersey, muscles flashing, appearing to be carved from granite. Jason had seen the face before. He had checked the guy out on Facebook and sent a couple of messages to him. Besides he was tall, almost looking Jason in the eye. Not too many non-basketball players in his height range. He had tan cut off shorts and flip flops. His skin was chalky white, an oversized diamond stud in his left ear. But there was something distinctly different about this guy. He could tell, in the first minute, that Brandon thought he ran the show. He had an aura of danger. Brandon showed him a fist and Jason responded by pounding his knuckles, nodding.

Brandon shook his hair from side to side, flocks of blonde curls flapping over his face. "Nice to finally meet you. Read all `bout you on the net and Facebook. You're one big slab of dude I must say," he said and laughed to himself.

This wasn't exactly what he was expecting. "Looks like you could play for the Lakers yourself?"

"Baseball's my game. That, and America's favorite pastime, chasing babes." He swung his head left and scoped out at a group of female athletes standing together next to the window. "Before we can work on that we gotta get through this first, man."

"Anything's better than sitting in a friggin' classroom."

"Never a good day to sit in class, shooter. When you get to town, big boy?"

"Just now."

"Should have been here earlier. We could've hit the links and hit the town."

"Not a golfer. Just stick with the round ball."

"You're athletic. I'll teach you the game. You'll be a big swinger when I'm done with you, if you know what I mean?" he said with a wink.

"Don't even have clubs. Time it takes to play a round, I could take a thousand shots. That way I don't miss... Parents bring you here?"

"Nah, L.A.'s a long way and my old man has a new movie coming out. The old lady had to go to San Fran for some food convention," Brandon said as he bounced up and down.

Jason glanced at the beaded necklace hanging from Brandon's neck, flung some almonds into his mouth.

"When you get to town?"

"Jumped in Monday to spend some time checkin' out the establishments. Got a little drunkicidal last night, ended in bad shape. You know, drove the porcelain bus," Brandon said, squeezing his eyes shut.

Jason knew better than to say another word, when a guy like this got started. He put a sundried tomato bagel on a plate and smothered it with peanut butter, licked his fingertips.

Sellers kept talking. "I checked out the crop round town and I ain't talkin' corn and beans. Didn't see too many babes last night. Saw a couple of dragbeards, mostly a bunch of muffin tops, chicks that look like they're ready for the big McHeart-attack...know what I mean?"

"OK" Jason needed some space and took a step back.

Sellers got even closer now. "Don't get down buddy. I've heard it'll get better. Chicks round here are legend. Heard you have to bring a drool cup to class it's so good."

Jason nodded. "Girls just get in the way of the game, dude. I'm here to play ball. Then move on."

Just then a blonde and brunette approached them. The brunette smelled wonderful up close. They both smiled at Jason and giggled.

"You're Jason Carson, aren't you?" the blonde asked.

Jason nodded and gave her a crooked grin. "Beauty must come in pairs around here. Dueling supermodels."

The blonde looked at her friend, then back at Jason, her pony tail whipping around her face. "I'm Katie, and this is Claire," she said as she pointed to the brunette. "We're on the volleyball team and just wanted to welcome you to campus. Team's having a mixer tomorrow night?"

"Mixer?"

"They told you about it on your recruiting trip, didn't they?"

He shook his head. "Wasn't able to make any official visits to schools. I had too much going on."

"I guess a guy like you with all the offers and stuff." She smiled, "It's a get together for guys and gals to get to know one another. Just help freshmen with the social scene and all."

She handed Jason a yellow piece of paper and then looked at Brandon as if he hadn't been standing there. "Oh, and you're welcome to come, too."

Brandon's eyes narrowed. "Yeah, thanks."

The two girls looked at each other and marched away.

Brandon raised an eyebrow. "I think you're already the main target here, bro."

"Kinda used to it."

"That's somethin I'd never get used to. Less than two minutes in the room and the hotties are circlin' the wagons. Impressive."

Jason started putting bagels and fruit cups into his backpack.

"Glad I finally got invited, bitches didn't even know I existed for a minute. Either way, it'll be big time fun. They'll love me once they get to know me."

Jason nodded. "Not for me, too much to do."

"Whatcha mean. The place will be oozing with babes. Be a nice start for us."

Jason gave him a small shake of the head, even a bit of an eye roll. Brandon was sort of his opposite. "I'll be in the gym. I have a three hour workout, dribbling and shooting, tomorrow night. Three hours of drills in the morning. Exercises and I'm trying the hot yoga after that. Gotta take care of the temple," he said pounding a fist to this chest.

"Kiddin', right?"

"Just part of the routine."

"I ain't used to workin' that hard…just gifted myself."

"You need to put in the time, friend. I'm only a short timer here."

"But you're here for a year. That's what the websites say, and you'll be making that year count." He studied Jason's body from head to toe. "Look at you. You're the Nike poster boy today," he said staring at Jason's shoes.

"Gotta earn it. Only thing I've ever gotten for free," Jason said as he stuffed two protein drinks into his bag. "They give me threads now. Boxes of shoes. When I hit the Show, they'll pay me to wear the stuff."

"Nice. In Cali we don't wear too many clothes if you know what I mean." He kept his eyes on Jason's feet. "Nice kicks."

Jason looked down at his feet. "Retro Jordan's. 91's. Got every pair of the Air Jordan's since 85. Almost a hundred pair. Little fetish of mine"

Brandon smiled. "I've got my own fetishes, dude. As for the footwear." He kicked out his foot. "Nothin' but flip flops."

"Should be fun in the snow."

"Lookin' forward to it. I'm a beach bum, bikini judge."

A female instructor from the front of the room told everyone to take their seats. Jason looked for a seat in the back of the room, sat down. Brandon slid into a seat to his left, groaning. The female instructor began discussing the campus rules for athletes. Two minutes later, Jason looked at Brandon who now seemed asleep in his chair. Jason looked at a colored tattoo on the right calf of his new roommate. He thought it might be an eagle or some type of bird with outstretched wings. It was a blend of red, blue, and green. A black and green barb wired, decal wrapped around his bicep and a small circular marking on Brandon's neck resembled a coin. The instructor turned a page. "It is the goal of the presidential committee on Athletics at the University of Iowa to achieve a drug-free environment. All students are tested through the substance abuse program on a year-round basis. The substances for which you are tested includes, but are not limited to, alcohol, anabolic steroids, central nervous system stimulants, masking agents and drugs of abuse." She had slowed down her talking and walked around the room.

Jason noticed the room had gone quiet. Two tall females in front of him simultaneously sat up in their seats.

The instructor continued, "You are also subject to unannounced testing administered in ways that minimize the chances of any inaccuracy. The test will be administered on campus under the direction of the drug testing supervisor and consist of a chemical analysis of urine specimen." The instructor walked back to her desk and closed her notebook.

Brandon Sellers finally moved and leaned over to Jason and whispered, "I think you'll need to throw a rope for me in a Dixie cup. I'd probably burn a hole in the damn thing." He displayed a wide faced grin like Dr. Seuss's the Grinch.

The instructor sat on the edge of her desk. "All freshmen must take at least fourteen credit hours each semester which includes the fall and spring semester. If you fall below the full-time admission status, you'll be considered ineligible. By looking at this group, you all look appear intelligent to me," she said with a laugh. "Any problems, see your counselor or tutors in the Gerdin Center." Her words had scratched Jason's pride, but he knew he would only be here for one year.

The instructor glanced up at the clock. "You have about an hour to eat, and we'll begin again at one sharp. This isn't high school so make sure you're early for classes, early for practices and in your seats before 1PM, got it?"

Brandon Sellers punched Jason in his chest with the back on his hand. "Love the female Nazis the athletic department hires. Hitler bitch up there has everyone shaking in their swastikas."

Jason was shocked by the way this guy spoke. It was impossible for him to tell what was real and what was not. His mother would have slapped him if he called a woman a bitch. If he mentioned Hitler like that. He didn't know how he was going to live with him. "Most jocks are too soft. We all need a little discipline, now and then. Need to suffer a little." Jason replied.

"I am suffering, watching the babes walk around in front of me without inviting me over to their place yet. You got a steady babe at home?"

"Used to, but no girlfriend right now. Kind of a long story."

Brandon flared that big smile again. "They're all long stories man. Everyone you get to know turns out to be a long story. Yeah, it's better to just brush the horse with these gals and not get too attached. You gotta be careful dude, and I'll be here to help you big man? Let's eat."

"Never miss a free lunch," Jason said and then walked to the food table and put three bananas and two bagels into his backpack before picking out what he'd eat for lunch.

Chapter 24

Fox Sports—A NCAA survey of more than 22,000 college athletes found nearly one-fourth of male athletes had violated NCAA rules by gambling on sports within the previous year. 13 percent of the male athletes who had gambled on sports had wagered on in-game bets, things like whether the next football play will be a run or a pass or if a basketball player will hit the next free throw. "The major concerns are wagering enhancements such as live in-game betting that present increased opportunities to profit from 'spot fixing' a contest as has been uncovered recently in a number of international sports leagues," the study concluded.

Chapter 25

*"Such is the human, often it seems a pity that Noah…
didn't miss the boat."*—Mark Twain

Tim McMurray glanced at the pouring rain outside Orlando's airport while a plane bounced to a landing. A woman with a screaming baby in a stroller ran by him as a voice from a loud speaker called for final boarding at gate G.

He looked into Sandra's brown eyes which were as wet as the outside runway. He hugged her again, checks touching. His cheek was still as smooth as hers after his second shave of the day. He stepped back, wiped her tears and checked his manicure. He pulled on his collar to check the stiffness. Next time he would tell her to use more starch, but now wasn't the time. Putting a finger inside the waist of his pants he realized he had lost another pound or two. One sixty-eight at the age of forty two was the same weight he had carried in college. However, his inky black hair needed more coloring around his temples. The game last night at American Airlines arena was louder than usual and left him with a headache. He glanced at his watch.

"I need to make sure I don't miss my flight, darling." He couldn't remember, but somewhere along the way he started calling her darling. Darling was probably the right word for Sandra. It was astonishing how he could take on different personas as the age of his girlfriends changed. Sandra was in her late thirties, and he needed to use one of those charming voices that women her age would understand. Cara and the others wouldn't want to hear the word darling. They'd think he was talking to their mothers, always trying to come up with the right words, the right slang. Like all womanizers, Tim McMurray was always thinking about the next female he would see; the next female he could catch as if he was loaded with ammo waiting to find the next twelve point buck. He was a master at it—find that trophy female. Two summers ago he visited a clairvoyant convention in Miami after a weekend of deep sea fishing. He visited an eighty-one year old fortune teller named Bea who used the original rod and pendulum technique, which dated back six thousand years. She meditated for a long time and told him that the world was stocked with females and it was up to him to catch as many as he could.

He'd known Sandra for about a year or was it two now, meeting her at the Marriott bar in Orlando after a Magic's game. At the time, she was recently divorced. Her five year marriage over when her husband left her for another man. Childless and lonely, she had been captured by Tim McMurray. Almost without knowing what he was doing, he told her that he was single and that he had never seen dark voluptuous eyes like hers.

But Sandra was just a minor trophy to Tim. The anticipation of the capture was great, but the joy was in the hunting. He never tired of it. He'd begun to tire of all the attention she gave him. Tired of all the perfume she wore. Tired of the constant questions, constant smothering and constant cuddling as if he was her Siamese twin. He wasn't able to take the attention. He was a hunter, and he missed the hunt.

He stepped back, tilted his head slightly and said, "I'll call as soon as I touch down in L.A."

"Hope you can come back before next month?" Sandra said as her bottom lip quivered, her eyes pleading.

"I'll count the hours away from you my darling, minute by minute." He backed away slowly, his eyes never leaving hers. He blew her a kiss, turned and looked up at the screen. His plane was leaving from gate C14. He looked up again, not understanding what he was seeing. His flight number to L.A. was 495. A small vibration moved down the center of his back. 495. It was the same number that Dr Zupov had given him after evaluating his blood sample. What the hell was that number all about? More importantly, what was going to happen to someone he loved and to whom?

He decided he needed to awaken his wife with a phone call.

"The kids are fine," she said and hung up on him, more perturbed than he was used to hearing her.

Five minutes later, McMurray sat in the front row of the DC-9, staring out the window, watching the rain. He tried to conceal his wretchedness. He looked down at his pressed khaki pants with a heavy front crease that Sandra had laundered for him. Hands folded, shoulders perfect. His eyes felt like two burning coals. He tried to hide the sadness with self medication. Truth was, McMurray couldn't stand himself. Of course he would always keep up the image. When he didn't understand, he just got better at playing the part. But lately, more often than not, he felt lonely, not knowing exactly who or what he missed. He was headed to California to see Cara which usually excited him. Her love for old movies and working out with him had really built a true attachment. She loved to surprise him and that usually came with gifts, matching gifts like the Salomon hiking boots which they used to hike up to the 'Hollywood' sign last month. Problem was, the $552 charge showed up on his Visa bill last week. He kept thinking about her massive dress collection which needed at least one pair of matching shoes and sometimes leather pumps. Corinthian leather boots came with a hefty price tag. She had more shoes than he had. Perhaps he could look at his trusty Ouija board again for answers.

Tomorrow he had an appointment with Patricia the Palm reader in Burbank. For five years she had been a trusted friend. Clearly, she had been his favorite, throwing around karma like pixie dust every time he visited. It felt forbidden and dizzying just to think of her name. At times when things had gotten so bad he speed dialed her two or three times a day. The flight attendant turned on the overhead TV's and began the flight instruction procedures. Tim felt sick and buzzed the attendant.

"May I have a glass of ice water and half a lemon?" Tim asked.

The flight attendant pressed her lips together, shook her head. "We'll have to wait till takeoff sir. I'll bring you something as soon as we're in the air and the captain gives us the OK."

He motioned her over. Time for the casual interest to begin; slight smirk, big eye contact, "your earrings are superb…go terrific with those vivacious eyes I might add." He touched her bare forearm with the back of his hand and inched it down her to her wrist. "I'm with the NBA and have a very important meeting. Need to be sharp and was just hoping you could maybe give me a little help," he said in a tone that was more like a sonnet than a sound. A lullaby. A manipulating hypnosis.

She covered her mouth as if she was about to cry. Lips barely moving without any sound. She turned to look down the aisle and then back. He had moved forward slightly now, lips parting. She swallowed and put a hand on his shoulder. "Just this one time, sir," she said wetting her lips. She turned and scampered away. He felt cleansed, somehow, the way things happened with the ladies.

McMurray closed his eyes and thought about his two days with Sandra. He was trying hard to like her, but she was a bit too old school for him. Thing was, she was completely different than all the others. She wasn't like Cara who had lists of demands as long as the tattooed arms in the NBA, didn't come with the demands of his ex-wife and children. The alimony, tied up assets, child support, bills that never stopped hitting him. He wanted his hands on that Ouija. He could feel the plane pulling back from the terminal.

Chapter 25

The baggage terminal at LAX was a mixture of Woodstock and Mary Kay Cosmetics. Gobs of makeup, cheap perfume, or was that incense, surrounded Tim as he hunted for Cara. She was easy to notice with this crowd, probably easy to spot in any crowd if you had a hint of testosterone pumping through your veins. She was wearing black shorts, something Tim's father used to call hot pants on a body that was excessively thin. She wore a jean jacket with sleeves rolled up to her forearms and knee-high black leather boots with colored feathers streaming from the top; normal airport attire Tim told himself. She saw him looking at her and ran to him. He instantly thought of his own daughter who always used to run to him after he returned from one of his trips. Cara wrapped her arms around his neck, curled one of her boots around the inside of his pressed Khakis, and smothered him with pink lipstick. She smelled wonderful up close, but she was chewing gum. Tim didn't like women who chewed gum, and he had tried to talk to her about it on several occasions, but she just wouldn't stop. Smacking lips, mouth always open, churning, the noise made his skin crawl.

"I missed you, honey," she purred into his ear as she ran one of her heels up his calf.

"Missed you all the way to the moon and back," he said. She smiled again, the smile he knew wasn't a smile, just learned behavior, "Pick out a nice place for us to eat tonight?"

Cara bounced up and down and rubbed herself against him. "Dinner at Rudolphs, dancing at the Dynasty Club, then a really big surprise." She snapped her gum.

Tim tried to smile away his irritation. "I read on the plane that chewing gum can cause tooth damage?"

"Sugar free, hun."

"Said sugar free too. Don't want that to get in the way of your modeling?"

She shrugged. "Nothing my orthodontist can't fix. Super excited about tonight."

"How bout we do dinner and then curl up by that fake fireplace of yours with a drink or two?"

"Not tonight, babe. Steven Spielberg's photographer invited me to this party after he saw me modeling at the Polo Club on Rodeo Tuesday.

Keeping it a surprise for you 'til now." He tried to visualize what this thing was going to cost him. "Love surprises. I just thought we could be a little low key this time."

"We'll be low key tomorrow night, buster." She laughed, but it was more of a honking noise. When would she change that he thought to himself. "You think your brother will be there?" She asked, squeezing his arm, blowing a bubble.

A psychic in Portland told him months ago to always tell the truth, but it was hard for him. He winced. Hopefully, it didn't register on his face. His real brother was working in the shoe department at Nordstrom's in Seattle.

"Doubt he'll be there. Been working on a movie in London for the last couple of weeks."

"Thought your brother would make things happen for me but if I can meet Spielberg himself..." Cara said. Tim reached for his suitcase on the carousel and placed it on the ground. "Maybe I'll be his new star," she said with a squeal.

But he was in control here, wasn't he? Always stay in control. He'd met Spielberg's assistant, Bob Hamm at some party a couple years ago and loved to drop his name to babes who were looking for a movie career. "Hmm. That will be great, but Bob says he doesn't like to talk business when he's entertaining. Kind of a big turnoff."

"Well I just want him to notice me. I'll think of something awesome to do," she said giggling through her nose.

Two and a half hours later, Tim slithered through a pack of people on the main floor of the Dynasty Club, blinded by the light and bruised by the thrones of young flesh. The last time he was here he wasn't able to hear for a week. The music vibrated off him. Cara ran her hand over his chest. "Isn't this great?" She yelled, pulling a string of gum from her mouth and wrapping it around her finger.

A grimness plagued his mouth. He didn't want to yell, but it was the only way to communicate.

She grabbed his hand and worked through the crowd. They moved to the dance floor. Cara was lip-syncing, a lingering smile frozen to her face. How long would he have to endure this? Her hair splashed across her face like a wave and then she twirled it into the air. Clubbing was irrational, ridiculous, but here he was.

Cara jumped up and down, face reddening, bouncing as the lighting on the floor went dark. "I love this song," she shouted. Five seconds later she screamed, "Damn!" She looked back, grabbing the back of her bare leg. There was a trace of blood in her palm. Glaring at a woman with a shaved head and short black dress, "What the hell was that?" Cara yelled.

The bald headed woman placed her hands over her mouth. "So sorry, I think my bracelet hit you." The bald woman raised her arm to display her jewelry. She pointed to her bracelet, metal spikes surrounded her wrist. "I'm soooo sorry. Probably shouldn't be dancing with it. Kolo. New designer, Very hot."

"Holy, crap, you gotta be careful, bitch. Hurts like hell," Cara cried, touching the back of her leg, looking at her hand, more blood on her fingers.

Shrugging, the bald woman ran to the back of the club.

Cara's eyes went small. "Think I need to sit down for a minute."

Tim nodded. He put an arm around her back and moved his way through the crowd. Cara let out a low moan. "Crap…that thing really hurt…like a hornet or something."

Tim leaned in, her pupils now twice the normal size. Cara dropped her purse and leaned on the bar. He yelled to the bartender who was serving a customer on his left. "Need your help, buddy."

The bartender gave him an unsympathetic look. "Name is Jake, not buddy, pal."

"Sorry Jake." He always used first names. Clearly he was shaken. "Little lady here just got stabbed in the leg. Have band aids or a first aid kit?"

"Pretty busy here, pal. I'll look for one in a few minutes."

They all needed to be pushed, it never ended. "You'll look for one now, ass-wipe," Tim barked. "She got hurt on your property. Move it or I'll sue your ass." He stepped up and leaned against the bar. "Let's get some help. Buddy."

The bartender folded his towel. "Be right back."

Tim looked back at Cara. Her face was flush, mouth open, tongue out, panting.

"You feeling OK kid?" he wished he hadn't used that term.

"I feel so hot," she said, voice cracking.

Tim wouldn't lose composure. "Rest a minute, you'll be OK."

She just gave him a weak nod as if she hadn't heard him. Her lips were trembling. Breath now shallow.

The bartender handed Tim a first aid kit and a plastic bag of ice.

"Thanks, Jake," Tim said and placed it under Cara's leg. "Looks like the bleeding has stopped."

Tim patted her arm. He stood up from his seat and looked around the club. At first he thought she might be playing this little pin prick to the leg thing to the hilt. He could usually tell when she needed extra attention, as if she didn't get enough anyway, with her hypochondriac bursts of injuries. When he looked back again he saw her breathing faster. Had she experimented with a new drug? She didn't usually do drugs, not unless he was there to buy them for her and even then she didn't usually like the way she felt after she used them. But now the smallest tinge of fear had crept into his mind. What was going on here? People were beginning to notice them. She stared at him, saliva streaming from her mouth. She gripped his hand harder than she ever had before. Unutterable fright filled her face and colored her cheeks. McMurray was hoping her anguish would stop. She had started to sweat.

"Something to drink?" McMurray asked as he inched closer.

She blinked at him. "Cann noot mooove," she slurred, and started to pass out.

Tim reached over, put an arm under her and hoisted her over his shoulder. He turned and moved to the door. The lights were swirling, he felt his head spin.

Tim grabbed a bouncer by the arm. "Call an ambulance."

Eighteen minutes later Tim McMurray paced in the waiting room of L.A. General's hospital. He could hear shouting and groans in all directions. McMurray hated hospitals. Waiting to hear about Cara was driving him crazy. Before he realized how long he had been standing there, a nurse with white clogs and green scrubs walked over to him. "Are you here with Ms. Peyton?" she asked. "Are you related?"

"Just a friend," he said.

"Dr. Shinn would like a word with you."

His heart was flying now. He hoped it was something she ate? The nurse stopped in front of room 495. A familiar weariness invaded his bone. It was that number again. "Mr. McMurray is it?"

"How is she?"

"Cara received a substance, Ricin…maybe about fifty or sixty minutes ago."

"What's that?"

"Ricin is a poison, Mr. McMurray. A toxic strychnine."

Tim didn't answer.

"I'm very sorry. There was nothing we could do."

"What are you saying?"

"She's dead."

Tim didn't respond.

"Please stay here the police will need to talk to you."

"Police?"

"They'll have some questions. What's your name?"

"Bob Brown."

Seconds later Tim McMurray stood in the parking lot of L.A. General in front of a row of cars. People sick or people milling around waiting for something to happen. Either waiting to get better; cured of disease, or the other option, that's the one that had McMurray hating hospitals, that option of waiting to die. Waiting for your time to pass and moving on to a new level of consciousness, maybe reincarnated, was the most logical option he'd decided. Everyone inside just waiting on doctors to tell them their fortune, good or bad.

He ran to his car. His stomach ached as his thoughts moved to what lay ahead. How was he going to explain this? They must be getting close to me? Maybe Perez sold him out, or was it one of the other guys he'd worked with? Was Cara involved in something that he wasn't aware of? Or did this happen to be about him? Of course. What did the Ouija board tell him before he left? There was no such thing as coincidence. For a moment he seemed embarrassed, or was it shame? It couldn't be fear, that was never a possibility. They must be after him. Never lose control. He started the engine and rocketed out of the parking lot.

A minute later he was flying fast on the Santa Monica, darting around cars. His foot punched the accelerator, hands gripped the wheel, knuckles white. He sniffed his shirtsleeve. His clothes smelled of Cara. He wiped his sleeve on the seat beside him. He needed to wash her away. Something was buried in the back of his brain…something, what was it? It was the fortune teller in Miami. The old lady. She was right. "Something bad would happen to someone you love."

It had kept him up for two nights, but he had pushed the thought away this evening; maybe the drugs had pushed it aside. He needed a snort, right now. He needed a hit. All the dead and maybe-dead were coming after him. He hadn't listened. He swerved in front of a truck almost taking out its front bumper. He exhaled audibly through his nostrils. He twisted through two cars and accelerated down the exit ramp. The street was dark, he couldn't see where he was going. He slammed on the brakes, looked at the dashboard, it was dark. He'd never turned on the car lights. "Shit." The steering wheel felt as if someone was trying to drive for him. He was wrestling with it, trying to keep the car straight but something was pulling on it. His stomach was on fire, he was starving. He saw a Hardees ahead. He jolted over the curb and steered down the sidewalk. A woman jumped to the side, screamed at him. He skidded to a stop in front of the drive-through window. He swung open his door and pounded on the window, hands balled, pounding. The window slowly opened. Skinny teenager, acne covering a face that was more confused than scared. "Yeah"

"Get me two of those thick burgers, now," he blasted.

There was a sort of amusement on the kids face. "Spose to order at the window back there, dude," he said flicking a thumb to the side.

McMurray's hands shook. "Get `em now."

Sitting in his car waiting, he wasn't even aware of the car behind him, honking. He needed red meat. He noticed his phone blinking. He reached for it and read the text message. "We've had enough of you." A second later, another ping. "Two of the last three games, we've lost..." Another ping. "Don't let it HAPPEN AGAIN."

Chapter 26

Scott Reynolds stood under a high definition TV in a luxury suite overlooking Cleveland's Jacobs Field. The suite smelled of old grease, old beer, old smoke, nothing fresh.

Reynolds sat next to Ron Lamb in padded seats. "No way to watch a game up here Ronnie. Everything too artificial."

"It's the good life, buddy. Just enjoy it."

"Can't get the real feel up here. That's what the games all about, feel."

"You need to enjoy this, Scotty. You're the baseball fan. I'm usually asleep in the first inning. What do you say we order a beer?"

"We're working."

"Nobody will know."

"Bureau always knows."

Scott had always been a baseball fan, the only sport he enjoyed other than wrestling. Baseball was the only sport that didn't have a clock and he loved the balance to it; everyone gets equal number of outs and innings. Baseball might be the only thing other than fishing that slowed Reynolds heartbeat. It had rules and strategy and order.

Ron Lamb remained silent and watched the game while he listened to information coming from his earpiece. Reynolds looked down, rubbed his eyes. He opened a black notebook and ran a finger over the list of players names that he and Lamb were watching. He turned the page and looked at photos of three umpires that he had not seen before.

Lamb raised an eyebrow. "Eyes hurting you again, buddy?"

Reynolds swallowed hard and shrugged it away. "Same stuff. Not much sleep lately."

"What you doin about it?" Lamb asked.

Reynolds nodded. "Took your advice last week. Tried the new headband you suggested."

"The Zeo thing?"

"Yes. Wore the headband for three nights. Tracks my sleep cycles. It told me I wasn't getting enough REM sleep." He smirked. "Also was supposed to wake me up naturally. My only morning off in the last month and it woke me at 4:30AM Real nice suggestion."

Lamb waived a hand at him. "Did you hear about the CHILLOW? Saw it on TV two nights ago and it's all the rage, buddy."

Reynolds closed his eyes, shook his head.

"Dr. Oz says it keeps your head cool. Lets you sleep your life away."

Reynolds smirked. "I need a life before I can sleep it away."

Scott Reynolds held iPhones in both hands. "Have we seen anything unusual about this umpire, Tata?"

"COMINT tells us that Tata's made two called third strikes on the big hitters in the middle of the Red Sox order, left players stranded in scoring positions. Says that both pitches were very questionable." COMINT was the FBI's communication between individuals, and Lamb loved to get his gossip this way.

As he picked up the Cleveland Indians scorecard, Scott Reynolds began, "What do we know about Mr. Tata?"

Lamb laughed into his fist and rubbed his stomach. "Well, he's an interesting character to say the least. Lives in Charleston, South Carolina, in the off-season. His wife usually hangs around there most of the season unless he's umping in Toronto where she likes to go and brings home a new mink coat from the great White North. Guess she has quite a few. Her favorite is the 'blonde beaver.'"

Reynolds flared a smile. "Is this the guy with the business problems?"

"His family owned a cement business in Charleston which he bought from them. He never thought he would make it to the Bigs because he spent so much time in the minor leagues he thought he could run a business while on the road and his partner robbed him blind."

"Didn't one of our bagmen take down the mayor too?"

"Sure did. Nailed the damn mayor who resigned from office and serving time now."

Reynolds sat forward in his seat. The batter smashed a ball to the third baseman right into a double play. The crowd cheered.

Scott Reynolds looked down at his scorecard and wrote, "6-5-3 double play."

Lamb laughed, "You need help?"

"Shut up. Go on."

"Anyway, Tata has to go bankrupt and needs money to support the wife and her mink collection. Tata also has his own quirky collections. Has this crazy spice collection that he works on when he travels around the country and has nothing to do during the day."

"I could tell he likes his food based on the size of the guy."

"That's just the start of it," Lamb replied, "Tata was actually involved in world wrestling when he graduated from LSU. Guy actually thought the whole thing was legit. His third match was against Jesse 'The Body' Ventura, and as soon as the acting was over 'The Body' turns Tata into a human pretzel. He didn't last long because he didn't usually like the script, and when you're new to the world wrestling actors guild they usually don't let you win, until you pay your dues. So next thing you know the guy tries to take on a grizzly bear in Wyoming at some big carnival event. Ends up in the hospital for two months."

"Athletes are geniuses."

"Well, he needs cash, and we think the Diablos have been helping. Guy also has an incredible knife collection. I was told that he bought the original knife from MGM that Sly Stallone used in the Rambo movies. Guess he never told the wife."

"He's not the only one that collects stuff either.

"Hmm."

"Tata's wife. In addition to the furs, she has an exotic bird collection which may be one of the best in the South. Birders make special trips from all over to come see."

"What kind of birds?"

"She has this massive collection of mockingbirds and macaws that speak. She even teaches them foreign languages. This is where it gets even better. During his off-season he teaches the talking birds to mouth off."

"Polly want a cracker?"

"You need an imagination, Scotty." Lamb smiled, shook his head. "Stay with me here. Robbie Swenson sends me an Eyes Only nugget from PHOTINT. Hilarious. This group of women from Atlanta came to see the special macaws, and as they're sitting having tea, a big green macaw says, 'Look you son of a bitch' then another white cockatoo perks up and chirps, 'Eat shit and die you ass wipe'. A middle-aged Baptist dropped her teacup in her lap and headed for the door. I heard all this on the briefing during the plane ride. Techies actually spliced in the cell phone call of the old lady and Tata after his game in Houston. It's a classic."

Reynolds gave him a crooked grin, looked at his scorecard.

"We have taped SIGINT conversations between him and the Diablos cartel but not enough evidence to prove anything. Not yet."

"When?"

"Little more time?"

"Don't have it."

"Working my ass off here. Give me a break."

Scott Reynolds nodded. "I need to piss. Can you keep score for a batter?"

"You're nuts. How long you known me? Wrong game, buddy."

"If pitcher tackled the hitter, you'd love it."

"Spear him too," Lamb said.

A female usher, twirling her hair with her finger opened the door and asked the two men if they cared for a piece of cake or pie from the dessert cart. Both shook their heads.

"Intelligence thinks the Cleveland pitcher in the bullpen is working with the Diablos," Lamb said. "Guy's name is Roy Rondo, and he's one hundred percent Native American. Kid grew up on a reservation in South Dakota, and the parents managed a casino outside of Rapid City. Roy spent so much time at the casino as a kid he knows his gaming."

"I spent some time chasing livestock in the Black Hills years ago," said Reynolds. "Never could get the smell out of my jeans. Had to burn `em."

"Not enough to keep me away from a nice porter house. No, make it a rib eye instead."

"Get on with it."

"Well, this kid's a natural for the cartel to persuade. He believes gambling is as normal as sleeping and church on Sundays!"

"Church. Maybe if I went to church again, I could sleep?" Reynolds said.

"Just come to St. Paul with me. Pastor will have you baggin' Z's in seconds."

Reynolds looked up from his scorecard. "Damn it. Who made that play? I missed it."

"Get over it. Dumb game. Other wild thing about Roy is his dad. Like a big part of the rest of the natives, he really enjoys hitting the firewater. His old man would get juiced and ride around the reservation on his Bo taco motorcycle at neck breaking speeds and howl at the moon in native Apache war chants."

"And when did you stop being such a racist?"

"I'm no racist, little buddy. Just tell it like I hear it."

"You see everything a lot differently. You're going to get reprimanded again."

"Anyway, after an hour or two, the father would go home and lather himself with war paint, throw on his grand pappy's feathery head dressing and start over. The guy thought he was Evil Knievel, started jumping cars in the back of the casino parking lot until someone called the reservation police."

Reynolds shakes his head. "Can't believe the old dude's still alive. Can intelligence check with the official scorer for me?"

"Since when don't you pay attention?" Lamb drank from his plastic Indian's cup, "Roy's dad wants to go out in a blaze of glory, he's trying to get a waiver that would allow him to jump over that huge Indian monument they're building in the mountain down the road from Rushmore."

"Crazy Horse? They'll never finish the damn thing. They've been working on that for thirty years. No money either."

"The old Injun don't care. Thinks he can beat Evil Knievel's Grand Canyon jump record."

"I'd like to be there for that one," Reynolds looks down at his scorecard and rips it in half. "How'd we find out the Diablos have been working with Rondo?"

"I think we intercepted some smoke signals," Lamb replied in a high tinny voice. "We also had a bug in his tepee."

"Careful," snarled Reynolds. "My wife's half Cherokee. Her mother is full blooded Native American. That's where she gets the nice tan. Good color without any tan lines if you know what I mean."

Lamb raises his eyebrows with a reaction of embarrassment and taps Reynolds on his upper arm. "Sorry about that Scotty, didn't know.

Didn't mean any harm. What'd ya say we go out and I buy you a beer after this game, maybe smoke the peace pipe?"

Chapter 27

Jason Carson sat on a bench on the east side of the Iowa River and watched a pair of scullers lurch down the river in front of him. Behind all of the boats, sunlight flickered on top of the wakes. The temperature was somewhere in the low nineties. A few cotton topped clouds populated the sky. He rummaged through his sack lunch. The humidity had melted his box of raisins and peanut butter into soup. He'd eat it anyway. His love of peanut butter was endless and timeless, some consistency to his life. Comfort, even. Everything tasted better to him with peanut butter; things like pancakes, apples, hotdogs, meatloaf, French fries and his favorite, bagels.

He studied the boats in the water. A coach in a john boat behind the two sculls barked instructions to the rowers with a bull horn. He was mesmerized. Jason loved competition. Everything was a game to him. And if he wasn't playing, he was watching. He'd exercise as he watched soccer, football, baseball and even tennis if there wasn't a basketball game to watch. Crunches and planks during horse racing on Sundays. He'd crank out an extra two hundred and fifty pushups on Thursday Bull Fight Night from Madrid when his mother was working and couldn't pester him about homework. Running with the Bulls was always a must in tandem with squats and lunges. Lawn mower racing, chess boxing, hot dog eating contests, and one of his favorites, Dwarf throwing, it never stopped. If he could get his hands on a system, he'd play Xbox for hours. Sport was competition, and competition was rivalry, and rivalry was wrapped with a surprise that would always motivate. All other times, he'd be shooting hundreds upon hundreds of free throws. Typically he was by himself, that's how he got better. Alone.

Jason finished a second peanut butter and jelly sandwich and licked his fingers. Normally he'd eat a couple more sandwiches, but his head was spinning from today's Economics lecture on the Laffer curve. He stood and threw his lunch bag into the garbage, swish. He moved beside Iowa Ave, sun heating his face. The university Cambus roared past him. He didn't see where it was headed. Which bus did he need to get back to the dorm? But Jason needed more cash in his pocket so that he could hang out with the guys on the team. He wanted to go to Wig and Pen last night for pizza but didn't have enough dough. His high school teammates got tired of him never having any cash when they did ask him out, so he ended up never being asked. Truth was, Jason was broke. He could see the Kum & Go on the next block. If he won that Mega-million, he could hang with the boys. Sooner or later he'd hang with them.

Jason walked into the store. He eyed the florescent sign above the counter; Mega-million jackpot: 388 million. It was already a good day today. Better than the day he had last week when he went to the Iowa Book store. The girl at the register brought out a pile of books and slapped them down on the counter. He couldn't imagine how he would ever read two feet of books. That made him sick to his stomach. There were eleven books in all: pre-Algebra, Economics and Lab, Spanish 1, Sociology, English Composition, and five novels. He stood and looked down at the books while the employee asked him three times if there was anything else he needed. He would have a hard time getting through one or two of these, let alone eleven of them.

She finally cleared her throat, "You're that new basketball star."

He showed her his Athletic ID.

She whistled. "Must be nice, free for athletes. Saved 700 bucks."

Jason walked back to the dorm with a twenty-five pound backpack and a million dollar headache. Luckily, he had found out two weeks ago that he had passed the ACT test with a score of seventeen. He had taken it on his own without anyone's help.

Now Jason walked down an aisle in the convenience store. He looked at the PowerBall sign again, flashing at him. The attendant waited as Jason reached into his Nike shorts and opened up his wallet. Sixteen dollars. How long would that have to last him? One week, two weeks? He would have to set a budget for himself. He took out two dollars closed the tri-fold and slid it back in the front pocket. He bought two tickets and made his way to Clinton Street. He waited for less than a minute as a Cambus ground to a halt in front of him. Stepping onto the bus, he glanced at the driver.

"This going to Burge?" he asked.

"Nope, this is ABW, Studio Arts. Need to read the sign," the kid said pointing to the front window.

"OK."

"Take the Blue Route or the Hawkeye Interdorm."

"Thanks." He backed down, waiting again. He was on his own. They all knew who he was in athletics, but around town, he was somewhat of an unknown at times and that was pleasing to him, adventurous even. It was as if he was invisible for a moment and that feeling calmed him.

Ten minutes later, Jason walked into his dorm room in Burge Hall. The room was fairly small, especially for two oversized young men. The two beds were lofted and under one of the beds an air conditioner hummed and rattled, spitting out an occasional wave of cool air. Brandon Sellers sat at a desk with his knees tapping the bottom. He kept the beat to Led Zeppelin's "Black Dog" as it swelled from the speakers on his desk. Jason sat on his bed and gazed at Brandon.

Brandon's Humanities book sat open on the desk, but he stared at the screen of his Apple laptop.

"Pisser," Brandon whispered to himself as he grimaced. "Let's go baby. My turn now. Come on." He was playing another game of Texas Hold 'Em with an online gambling website in Jamaica. Jason had watched this routine yesterday.

"Hey bro," Jason said.

Brandon swung his head, gave him a quick nod and looked back at the screen. "Didn't hear you come in, man."

"Class today?"

"Hell no, bro. I'll read that crap later. Up a buck forty, twenty minutes ago." He looked at his phone and then back at the screen. "But I'm in a tub a hurt here, down two and a quarter." He wiped the sweat from his chin with the back of his hand. "Got to lift weights today but I do better after I win some big scratch."

Jason stood and moved in behind Brandon to watch over his shoulder. "Saw a show about poker rooms on ESPN."

Brandon grunted.

"Said that vet players just wait for rookies to log in and they soak the crap out of 'em."

"I ain't no rookie."

"They said that you're supposed to fold at least half of the time. If not, the piranhas let the new guys win a few games, then empty their pockets and move to the next freshman. Find new blood."

"Thanks, Mr. Card Shark. I'm doing the devouring now. Watch this. Coming back." He pushed a button, calling the twenty bucks bet by 'Kid Shalene', who showed his cards: two kings. Brandon slammed his back into the chair. "Son of a sweet bitch," he shouted, face twisted with anguish.

Jason unzipped his backpack and fished out three Gatorades, two

G2s, four power bars, and three whole wheat bagels onto his bed. He walked to the refrigerator and unloaded two oranges, three apples, four Yoplait Greek yogurts and a wild berry cream cheese tub into the bottom shelf.

"What's with all the grub you bring home every day, you're the king of dumpster dining, dude?" Brandon said.

"It's free, man. It's my favorite type of food. Free."

"You drag home so many munchies. I'll be baggin' fries next week."

"We'll have a Thanksgiving spread by the end of the month."

"You'll need to steal some colon cleaner if you keep up this crap. Pun intended, dillweed."

"What's a pun?"

"Your head ain't right. Don't have time to explain. How'd you get through high school anyway?"

"Don't be a smart ass. Won't let you sit courtside next to the Laker girls when I'm playing next year."

Brandon laughed. "Little testy these days, homie."

Jason cracked his knuckles and looked at the boxes in the corner. He leaned over and opened the first box and pulled out a high top sneaker. "New sandals are here, baby. Be walkin' on water with these," he said as he tossed a shoe at Brandon.

Brandon paid little attention to it and tossed back the shoe. "Think this is your third delivery this week."

"You know it," Jason said at last as he studied the second pair of shoes.

"Thought you never had any money. How you coming up with the scratch for these?"

For a long time Jason wondered the same thing, but BRUH was spending every dime he got from his athletic stipend on Nikes. Jason held a shoe with both hands, brought it to his face, and kissed it as if it was a prized trophy.

"These are just gifts?"

Brandon stood, grabbed a shoe, and looked at it doubtfully. He closed his laptop and stood. "Better get my ass to the gym." He tossed the shoe back to Jason. "Hmm. Seems like it's your birthday every week."

Never worried about what others thought, Jason said, "Make it to the big show and every day will be my birthday."

NPR—May 15, 2018 -7:18 AM ET. The Supreme Court has ruled that a 25-year-old law that had barred most states from legalizing sports betting is unconstitutional-opening the door to legalized sports gambling across the country.

NINA TOTENBERG: The Supreme Court says the bets are on. Yesterday, the court ruled that a 25-year-old law that had barred most states from legalizing sports betting is unconstitutional.

For the record, the Supreme Court, by a 6-3 vote, struck down the 1992 federal law because the court said that barring state legislatures from legalizing sports betting amounts to an unconstitutional commandeering of the state legislatures. Congress can outlaw sports betting on its own, the court said, but it can't achieve the same result by telling state legislatures what they can and cannot do. The federal law struck down by the court was known as the Bradley Act after its chief sponsor, Senator Bill Bradley of New Jersey, a onetime college and pro basketball great.

BILL BRADLEY: I think the court ignored the impact of their ruling on sport. I think they've turned every baseball player, basketball player, football player into a roulette chip. There's nothing to prevent betting on high school or even grade school games with this ruling.

Chapter 28

"Adam ate the apple, and our teeth still ache."—Hungarian Proverb

But there it was: Scott did not believe it would ever change, that wallowing sense of exhaustion. Reynolds thought about the recent murders by the cartels. Regardless of the number of cups of coffee or amount of caffeine he pumped into his stomach, he couldn't rid his feeling of sluggishness for meetings. It was the eleventh meeting this month. Eyes today a bit more swollen, burning. Dreaming only of sleep. If only he could dream again. Why hadn't his 'light therapy' been working? It had helped him sleep last year. At least that's what worked for him for a few weeks last year, but like everything he had tried, it wasn't working for him now. He was constantly looking for order and perfection but lived in a world of imperfection and danger. Even his life at home was in danger. His wife Elizabeth barely talked to him anymore. But Elizabeth wasn't the one he really loved, it was her sister, Mary, who was the woman Reynolds had lived for. She knew and loved everything about him. Watching her climb a tree, run barefoot in the grass and swim in the creek a mile away from his house. But since she left to work in the Peace Corps he wasn't the same. With Mary he loved to laugh. Yes, Scott Reynolds once used to laugh. Marrying her younger sister, Elizabeth, was the only hope he had to stay close to Mary, but Elizabeth wasn't Mary, it just wasn't the same. That's when Scott's star stopped shining, when Reynold's star faded in the sky.

Straightening the goggles and mask over his face, Reynolds hunched down behind the six foot barricade and pointed the .45 caliber Thompson submachine-gun at the target. He hadn't trained in over a year, and he needed a score of eighty-five to keep his eligibility. He was familiar with Hogan's Alley, a ten-acre training complex thirty miles outside of D.C., because it reminded him of the small town where he was raised—small homes, a bank, a barbershop, and Post Office. Sure it was created by Hollywood, but it gave him the feeling he was back in his hometown, shooting at targets that looked like oversized milk bottles. He zeroed in on a target and squeezed the trigger. The submachine gun vaulted into his shoulder. Five shots in a row, then he moved the gun to his hip and rifled five short bursts. He had twenty-five seconds to remove the first clip and insert the second as the target moved back to fifty yards. He fumbled with the clip for a second and swore. He had passed the test with the .30 caliber rifle and the .38 caliber revolver, but the submachine gun seemed to always give him trouble. He knew the power of it, six hundred shots per minute and excellent range up to one hundred yards but for some reason it felt strange in his small hands. The sound of the bursts chattered against his earmuff protection like rain drops on a metal roof. Sweating, he fired another round, all in less than the allotted time of twenty-five seconds.

Five minutes later he released the tension on the firing mechanism, hammer, and recoil springs and checked for dust residue on the outside of the barrel. Reynolds understood cleaning was a strict rule for all issued firearms and he kept his in pristine condition like everything else he owned. He handed the machine gun to a guard and watched him put it into the vault. He reached for his phone and saw four messages, one from Guy Ferguson which must be urgent, it was the only time he'd ever heard directly from him. He pressed the call back button..

"Agent Reynolds."

"Ferguson, what do you have?"

"Everything's fine with me. Thanks for asking by the way."

"I'm due in a meeting," he said as he shouldered on a coat with his free arm and began to scurry up a flight of stairs.

"I have some information you'll like."

"About time."

"Be nice, Agent Reynolds."

"Running out of time. What'd you have?"

"Found out the Diablos' main connection is a guy that's connected to players, coaches, referees, trainers, the whole gambit."

"Who is it?"

"Guy by the name of Ricardo Perez."

Reynolds went silent.

He jerked as he heard a knock on his office door. Ron Lamb entered.

"Ever tell you how beautiful you look in the morning," Ron Lamb said as he sat.

"Court would probably recognize us as married as much as we cohabitate together."

"I'd tell the court you were a good kisser, ya know."

Reynolds was never much for small talk, but he had to keep Ron Lamb in the game. "What do you have for me today?" he asked folding his hands.

"Want to bring you up to date on the Toledo point shaving," Lamb said.

He nodded.

Ron slapped down a pile of papers on Reynolds desk. "Finally got a sport I like. But we got some bad asses here too. Got a five-page affidavit which includes wiretaps of our friend Tommy 'the Trigger' Tucker."

Reynolds was typing on his computer and didn't look up. "I'm getting ready for a teleconference with NSA and CIA. Remind me again."

"Dickhead's a self-described gambler from Miami," Ron Lamb explained, "who's been at the center of three other investigations."

"What about the affidavit?"

"The document is the transcribed conversations between 'the Trigger', and a former University of Toledo running back by the name of Adam Corso. Love these ESPN names don't you?"

"Continue."

"Corso has admitted he set up the betting scheme aimed at influencing the outcome of both football and men's basketball games. The first document is the complete transcription on the same day as the GMAC bowl game between Toledo and Texas-El Paso. The running back told 'the Trigger' he'd use another teammate to encourage a senior offensive lineman to help shave points, by committing penalties during the game. The Trigger said he would pay the lineman big bucks according to this affidavit."

Reynolds rubbed his forehead, then looked back at him. "Future leaders of America on our football fields, selling out for a few bucks. What happened to the greatest generation? Surprise me. Did we have any penalties during the game? Forgot to watch that one."

Ron Lamb smiled, and Reynolds noticed that Lamb hadn't shaved this morning. "Ninety yards, Toledo didn't beat the spread either." He hesitated and the two just looked at each other.

"The NCAA." Reynolds slowly shook his head. "What a crock a shit. They're just a bunch of academic vigilantes who couldn't even investigate shoplifting at the local mall." Reynolds used his sarcastic voice; one that only showed up when he was tired. He opened his file drawer and pulled out a manila folder that was about an inch thick. Opened it and flipped through two pages. "Toledo's got a reputation."

"They've been down this field before."

He was struck, as he was always struck by what some would do just to make extra bucks. "The cheating never stops. Maybe I should get a bookie?" Reynolds put a finger on the page in front of him. "It's goddamn everywhere. Toledo's men's basketball players were charged last year on felony counts of conspiracy."

Reynolds felt ashamed, gambling was killing sports and he hadn't been able to conquer it. "Everybody is influencing a damn game. It's bribery. It's an epidemic."

"Maybe we can make a vaccine," Lamb replied, already wishing he hadn't.

"Funny."

"We're catching some of it."

Reynolds didn't know what else to do so he pounded his palms on his desk spilling his coffee. "Time to bring their asses in. Then maybe I can get some sleep."

Lamb leaned back in his seat, surprised. "We need more evidence. Get the big hitters. If we wait we get the big players," he responded in a calm, slow voice.

"We still don't have enough?"

"Not yet. Not just yet," Lamb murmured.

"Bingo. Wait, bingo is legal, am I right here? Jackpot then. Oh, that's legal too. Let's just make all gambling and lying and stealing legal in this country, and we'll be out of a job, Agent Lamb."

Lamb didn't answer for a moment. "We're wiring both groups and following every one of them. We're using all the GPS, infra-red listening tools, RAVEN, Surveillance, PHOTINT, the whole shebang. Most of it is probably legal too," he said, waiting a moment, then grinning.

"Touché. A little quid pro quo here for our side, Ronnie."

Lamb glanced at his papers again. "Oh, we also came across," he looked up at him. "The Chicago kid, the one we talked about the other day. Another college kid. The basketball player."

Chapter 29

Jason sprinted to the hoop, flew through the air and dunked the ball as LaMarcus Bellamy tried to undercut him, but Jason hung onto the rim and watched LaMarcus run by and into the pad under the hoop. Jason hopped down and LaMarcus stood and stared at him.

"Next game's mine, bitch," LaMarcus rapped.

"Hope you like your new facial I just gave you. No tip needed."

LaMarcus glared at him as he walked away once the scrimmage had ended.

Jason looked over to see the reporters waiting next to the bench. He wanted to shower and get to class but they always wanted to talk to him. Jason was amazed at the way the media followed him. Just thinking about talking to the group made Jason queasy. They snapped photos, stood waiting for minutes even hours, and showed up in places all over campus to get a new story. Today was no different.

When Jason walked off the court at Carver-Hawkeye Arena, two dozen reporters and cameramen surrounded him. Microphones and digital recorders were thrust into his face; one grazing his left eyelid. This was part of the game that he didn't care for. Why did this have to be part of it? He just wanted to play, shake hands, and go back to his dorm, but reporters were invited to talk to players after practice once a week.

Carson strained to smile while talking, "Jason, what's the difference between high school and college ball?" Someone blurted out.

He wasn't sure he'd heard right, so he nodded instead.

Everyone waited and then it started again. "How long do you plan on staying at the University of Iowa?"

There was that itch in his throat again. "Win. Or make that when we win. A championship," he said. Before he could even make sense of what he said, a gray-haired reporter stepped closer to him. "After you win your national championship and move to the NBA," he looked at the microphone, "What are you going to do with all the money you make?"

He had to admit he was ready for this one. This one wasn't like reading aloud or learning a foreign language or thinking about expressing himself clearly. His mother drilled it into him as often as she could. The good Lord had given him special skills and he needed to give back. He grinned, and for a second he felt almost at ease. "Probably use it to help others, cancer, because of my mom. Help kids who don't have enough money for food. Stuff like that. Buy so many Nikes!"

Everything went silent for a second. "What's the toughest part of college so far, Jason?"

He had never really mastered the white lie, but telling the truth here, probably the whole truth wouldn't be such a good thing. Academics was a sore subject. He sighed, his voice thin and weak. "Sleep. Getting some good sleep." Reporters laughed, but Jason struggled to laugh with them. It felt forbidden and dizzying just to say something. They were crowding him, closer, touching.

"How do you like your new teammates?" Somebody asked from somewhere in the back.

On the court none of these guys liked sharing the ball with him. They gave him looks in the locker room and didn't hang out with him after practice, certainly no love lost here. "Good…real good…nice, yeah." He was only hearing part of the questions now. Strange how he had a hard time concentrating. Everything was quieter, tough to hear.

His eyes were wet, blinking. He wiped them with his palms. "I just like it…the game, you know."

There was a long period of silence, everyone watching him. "Sorry, got to run, need to get to class."

Twenty-five minutes later, Jason walked up a flight of stairs and entered his dorm room which was full of Brandon's buddies. Brandon himself was draped on the couch sipping a Heineken and watching a western on his 60 inch Sony 4k television. The dorm room was beautifully decorated in Early American bachelor. Turquoise walls papered with posters; babes in swimwear, a retro poster of Dodger's Don Drysdale, and a black and white poster of John Belushi wearing a black t-shirt with the word "College" printed across his chest. Most of the furniture looked as if someone had intentionally taken a baseball bat to it; fossils excavated from the 1970's. The only items of value were the Bose speakers wired to Brandon's iPhone stand, the flat screen TV and a nice new six foot General Electric refrigerator. How it all fit in the room remained a surprise.

Jason threw his coat on top of his bed. The maroon lazy-boy with pock marked cigarette burns on the arms had been switched with the desk and chair.

"What's with the change, again?" Jason asked, pointing to the desk.

Brandon slid a hand down the front of his sweatpants and fumbled with his genitals, smiling. "Just rearranging the furniture, champion." They laughed. "That's another pun if you're keeping track fellas."

It was different every time he walked in. A change in the floor plan, new faces that he hadn't seen before, even the music switched from seventies rock to hip hop to country western, "That's like the third time this week."

"Giving you my best Martha Stewart, sunshine." Brandon sat up, leaned over and spit into a copper spittoon. He wiped his bottom lip with the back of his hand. "I spent two hours in the batting cage today.

Hands are a mess." He raised his palms. Jason could see the blisters on both hands. "How was the big Press Day?"

"Just stupid questions, asked by stupid reporters," Jason replied. "Happy hour already for you?"

Brandon raised his bottle, tilted it toward him. "Its Drafternoon big man...help yourself."

"I'm already at the top of my game. Don't need any help."

Jason looked back at wrestler Mike Conway. He was shirtless and wore a pair of camouflaged pants. It was as if he was another species, ears mangled and swollen, a neck that was as thick as his head, patches of whiskers freckled his face.

Conway pointed to the television, "You've been on the ESPN twice already. "

"Naturally," Jason shrugged and patted his chest. It had been three days since he shaved his body, and everything was starting to itch. He needed to get into the shower, one by himself, not in front of his teammates, but no time. For some reason he didn't have time anymore.

Conway leaned over the couch, lowered his head. A wad of brown saliva dropped into the spittoon. "Think we got a new name for you Sellers...Mongo, from now on." Carson and the others in the room nodded their heads. "Reminds us of the guy who punched the horse in Blazing Saddles."

Brandon Sellers strolled over and opened the refrigerator and handed Mike Conway another Heineken.

Sellers talked some more, "Chiefs versus Chargers, closer than I thought this week, Vegas line has Chargers at four and a half." Sellers shoved the refrigerator door, the bottles clanged, "that's a damn lock. Chargers are on fire and they play great at home, K.C.'s running game sucks the big one. How much you want on that one Conway," asked Brandon, as he glanced at Jason. "You want any action this week J.C.?"

Jason shook his head.

Brandon tossed his empty bottle over his shoulder into a large cardboard box, glass splintering. "Baseball season ain't over yet J.C. We could still hook you up with some guaranteed cash flow once the playoffs start."

Jason was confused, "Thought we weren't supposed to gamble?"

Brandon spat, rolled his eyes. "That was just all a bunch of mumbo jumbo. This is all legal and the best way to bank some dough, Bro. Chicks love a guy with some green hanging out of his pockets. Come on?"

"What about your baseball weight-lifting today?" Jason asked.

"Paid a manager to sign me in, but I'm curling twelve ouncers today."

Jason grabbed his knee with both hands. "Any ice in the freezer?" Maybe he was at the point of trying to prove something.

"Don't have any free cash right now."

"Bullshit. You just got two new pairs of shoes yesterday…you have dough for that. We could float you a little IOU until you hit pay dirt."

As Conway tossed his bottle into the cardboard box, he shook his head. "Fact is, you owe us from last week, Mongo."

Jason walked to the refrigerator and pulled out an ice bag and placed it on his knee. Good time to change the subject. "Why the early happy hour today, Mongo?"

Mike Conway laughed. "You didn't hear the news J.C.?"

Jason shook his head.

"Mongo got dumped by his girlfriend. She's livin the good life at USC. Breed of studs must be a lot better in the Sunshine state…eh Mongo?"

Brandon flipped him off. "Listen Einstein. For one thing Florida's the Sunshine state, not California. Second, I wasn't giving her the time a day, she was my eight ball corner pocket gal.

"Yeah right, Mongo. Where's your new replacement?"

"Just started workin on it, butt face. I have my eye set on some new hotties. Been workin' my ass off on my business. I've already devoted my life to slow horses and fast woman."

Chapter 30

"Knowing many, loving none."—Allman Brothers

Tim McMurray sat in a bar in east L.A. next to two Harley bikers. The one closest to Tim had a receding hairline along with a gray fuzzy beard and a beer-belly. The beard was braided at the bottom and held together with a green rubber band. He was setting a record for coughing as he hacked into a wrinkled pine green bandanna. McMurray took his drink and moved down to the other end of the bar. An antique jukebox with a crack down the middle played Johnny Cash's "Ring of Fire." He sat on a ripped stool. The Pabst Blue Ribbon clock on the wall flashed 2:42. It wasn't exactly what he'd hoped for, but he needed a drink. He squinted at himself in the mirror in front of him. His face looked a bit like a ghost—grayish white, with red rings around his eyes. He could feel the constant drip seeping from his nose. Tim McMurray, always superstitious, felt his mind racing. They told him they would mess with his life if he didn't do exactly what they wanted. He never thought they'd mess with his girlfriend. The front door opened and Tim looked over. No cops, just two guys in plaid shirts. He took another bite of his tenderloin, grease sliding down his chin onto his pant leg. Would they be waiting for him at his hotel room? When would this end? He reached for his phone and pressed number one. After the third ring, he heard her voice.

"Hello," Janet said in a slow whisper.

"Everything OK at home?" He was surprised he used the word home.

She sighed. "Why in God's name are you calling here again?"

"I just want to make sure everything." He paused, "is OK. You and the kids?"

"You've been drinking or using drugs again?" she sighed.

"No, no, I'm fine. Sober I swear. I just have this bad feeling something might happen to the kids."

She cleared her throat. "Listen. You've got to quit listening to those witches and warlock friends of yours. It's making you crazy. Maybe you need a good exorcism."

Tim just went on, "Everything is OK, right?"

"Tim, I'm hanging up. Don't listen to those crazy devils in your head any longer and don't call here from now on."

He heard the phone line go dead. He looked back at the mirror behind the bar. His face swollen, eyes glassy. He took another bite of his tenderloin, but he wasn't hungry anymore. His stomach was aching now. Too much food. Francine, the Palm reader, had tried to prepare him for this. She told him that there would be an unexpected surprise in his life: was she talking about Cara? Maybe it was the 1965 Rangoon Red Mustang he rented for Cara while he was in town. He tried to remember the license plate of the car. Did it have the numbers 495 on it? He shook his head. It didn't matter anymore. Cara was dead. It had to be a sign. They would come at him next. Come after his family. He'd be the next one to get poisoned. He looked at his food, then at the bartender who smiled at him.

"Need another, Pops?"

Good god, did he call me that? Was the food safe? Tim pushed the food over the counter and onto the floor. What was happening to him?

The rail thin bartender looked at him through his Roy Orbison glasses. "You OK, Pops?"

Tim pushed his glass away too.

The bartender started cleaning up the floor and didn't look to happy.

Tim looked at his watch. When did he leave the hospital? His head was aching now. He thought about his job in the NBA. Would the police find him? He stood up. The cold seeped into his legs. He gripped the bar to steady himself. Everything moved in slow circles. His breath hesitant and shallow. He thought about going back to see Sandra in Florida? Or, what about calling Crissy in Detroit. He hadn't seen her for awhile, she might still be interested. He would have to come up with a good story to get her interested again and he was good at that. She liked the money and attention and she loved to wear leather but she kept insisting on using the whip on him and he'd been whipped enough for one lifetime; but maybe he'd call her again? But he didn't know if he had enough money. The NBA's union had gone on strike last week and Tim wasn't going to get paid next Friday. What the hell was he going to do? Tim's nose began to run as he ran his hand through his hair. He needed to go hunting again. He was best when he was on the prowl. He'd get back in his car and drive down the streets of L.A. Surely there were still places open where he could find women. That's what he did.

Chapter 31

The Air American black helicopter trip from Langley to Jimmy Island on Chesapeake Bay took twelve minutes. Reynolds followed two secret service officers and Ron Lamb off a short flight of stairs onto the island. A theater of woods flaunted their branches of platinum blonde, crimson, candy apple red, a garish molten of rainbow. Scott's first visit. Birds floated in front of thready streaks of clouds. The odor of rotting wood and skunk reached his face. Reaching for his handkerchief, Reynolds covered his nose, eyes watering.

Reynolds was followed by two computer analysts, two of the CIA's finest. Both men wore black mesh baseball caps that read, "Star Trek". CIA Director Peter Hamilton followed the computer analysts down the stairs. Hamilton was dressed in a navy sport coat with tan pants, no tie. It was the only time Reynolds had seen Hamilton without a tie, including the summer picnics with temperatures in the nineties. The group met two Navy Seals that waited with identical black Range Rovers. Scott Reynolds slid in to the seat next to CIA Director Peter Hamilton. Reynolds could already feel his eyes beginning to itch. His allergies seemed to be worse in the fall. His doctors tried to find something for him to take that wouldn't jeopardize his sleep, but Reynolds was worn out. He knew most antihistamines made him drowsy. He would just tough it out. Clearly that's what had been handed to him, agony one day, misery the next.

Director Hamilton clutched the leather briefcase on his lap. Hamilton reached in and pulled out a cell phone as the Range Rover moved down the dirt road. "Agent Reynolds," he began as he looked at his phone, "this Sanderson is quite the personality. Media dicks call him the Premier Renaissance man."

"So I've heard." Reynold's grabbed the hand rail above his head as the Range Rover bounced from side to side.

Hamilton rolled down his window, took a deep breath, "I need to speak with Sanderson face to face. It's great to get my ass out of the office for a couple of hours. Fall's the best time of year. Love the leaves." The Range Rover climbed onto a gravel road leveling out the ride for its passengers.

Reynolds stayed quiet for a moment. He had never seen Director Hamilton this relaxed. He needed to get back on track. "Isn't Sanderson an artist as well?"

Hamilton rolled down the window and stuck his head outside like a dog. "Absolutely beautiful." He moved back inside, shouldered off his jacket. "Help me here, damn it."

Reynolds held onto his coat as if it was breakable.

"How long has Sanderson lived here?" Reynolds asked.

Hamilton swung his arm out the window, now. "Ever since he created Kryptos."

Every bureau member knew the story behind Kryptos. Reynolds spent two weeks studying the encryption process in the Counter Terrorism Center before he became an Intelligence Analyst and understood the complexity and challenge to break Kryptos. The Pentagon had told him that they received ten million hack attempts per day, and Kryptos still survived. Even the Russians, Chinese and a host of cryptologists using super computers hadn't been able to decode Sanderson's Kryptos.

Reynolds watched the Director unbutton his shirt. "How long have we used his encryption?"

Hamilton crawled over to the other side of the SUV and rolled down the window, the breeze now sweeping through the vehicle. "Ask the statues over there," he said pointing to the computer guys.

One of them said, "Since the late 80's."

Hamilton pounded on the side of the car. "Pull over, pull over, damn it."

Hamilton took off his shoes as the SUV rolled to a stop. He opened the door and jumped outside. Reynolds watched in amazement. Should he follow? He stayed inside. Hamilton walked through the tall grass in his bare feet, mesmerized as if he was sleep walking. Everyone in the SUV just watched. Hamilton unzipped his pants and urinated into the grass. He walked back into the SUV and buttoned up his shirt. No one spoke. Hamilton waved his hand to start the vehicle again. "Marking my territory, boys."

Reynolds never knew what to say to the Director.

"So, Sanderson, yes, he developed the heart of the encryption text," the Director said. "Experts say the guy's a great artist. Sculpture bull shit. I think his stuff looks like he's had brain damage."

Reynolds said, "Kryptos is the Greek word hidden."

"Look at the colors through here. Smells a little nicer than the beltway," Hamilton sighed. "Didn't take Greek at MIT, took Italian, the language of love."

Scott Reynolds tapped his foot into the floor and tried to hide his annoyance of the wind swirling in the truck. Reynolds sneezed twice into his handkerchief. His eyes blurred from tears. "Nobody's been able to penetrate K-4. It's been impossible."

Hamilton turned from the window and glared at him, "That's why we're here Agent Reynolds. Everything depends on it: Militarily, Economically, Governmentally. It's our life blood. I need assurances that's it's safe."

The Rover made a sharp turn to the left and rolled onto a smooth road surface. "I'm going for a walk out here as soon as we're done," Hamilton snapped.

Reynolds wondered if the Director even had a private life.

The two Range Rovers stopped in front of a chalky red barn, surrounded by metal works of art. Metal structures of different shapes, heights, colors; Picasso with a blowtorch glinting amongst the bulging evergreens. As Reynolds walked toward the barn, sunlight flashing from the structures like lasers, a delicious strangeness of light disoriented him.

The barn door was wide open and the team moved into the center of the room. As they waited for Sanderson, Reynolds counted sixteen sculptures of warped shapes, odd colors he didn't even know existed sprawling throughout the inside: an unordered supernatural charm filling the room. If he did not know better, he would have mistaken it for a psychedelic dream. No semblance of order or structure, pure chaos.

Reynolds continued to gaze around the room. A sudden tilt factor fell upon him everywhere he looked. Stones were stacked in a corner, metal piled against a wall. The smell of steel, a tinge of cedar, an ashtray hung in the air. A stuffed moose head with lights dangling from the antlers hung over the front entrance. Drawings and blue prints decorated the wooden walls. In the far corner stood a twelve foot copper desk scattered with smaller sculptures, partially assembled.

Director Hamilton reached out to touch one of the sculptures but pulled his hand away.

A cat jumped down from a workbench behind them. There was no reply. Everyone stood, heads rubbernecking around the room. Ron Lamb laughed and moved toward the workbench. He stopped suddenly, "My god," he yelled," as he took a step backward. The team rushed toward him.

A man was lying on the floor swimming in a puddle of mahogany liquid. The head of the man severed from his body. Only Reynolds moved forward. A shimmer of sweat blanketed his skin. One of the techies was on one knee praying. Reynolds took another step closer. The head of the man had a long gray ponytail covering his face. Reynolds pushed the hair away. The head had a diamond stud in his ear. Reynolds recognized Sanderson from his file. His mouth was wide and all of his teeth were lying around his head like a halo. Scott Reynolds had seen this before. It was the work of evil.

Director Hamilton pulled out his cell phone, his hands shaking. He tried to settle himself and pushed a key. "I need to speak to the Secretary of Defense, now."

Chapter 32

Jason dipped a plastic spoon into a jar of peanut butter and smeared it over half of an apple, licked the spoon clean. It was the only pleasure he was going to experience today. He was still stunned by a practice where he barely touched the ball during a thirty minute scrimmage. How could he score if he never got any touches? Everyone around him seemed to be in it for themselves. The hyperextension of his left thumb with a minute left in practice didn't help things either. No one except the trainer gave him much attention. When he got hurt in high school or in AAU ball, everything would stop, everyone was concerned about his health as if it were their own. But not now. Not everything on campus focused on him. His humanities class had close to two hundred students and the professor didn't even know his name. This wasn't exactly as he imagined it. He took a bite of the apple but knowledge did not follow. Jason changed the position of the ice bag on his thumb. His humanities book was lying on the couch next to him, but instead of reading he was watching the Running of the Bulls from Spain. He couldn't study or go to sleep when someone could get trampled or gorged. The competition would relax him. He was totally geared after two games of Grand Theft Auto on Brandon's Xbox. Jason heard the key in the door and looked at the clock, 11:48.

Brandon barged in followed by two coeds, giggling and holding on to each other's arms. One look at the two, and Jason knew they were identical twins. Brandon took their coats and tossed them into a corner. Both females had red hair, probably dyed, in pony tails. They wore cowboy boots with six-inch heels and fluorescent lime neon tops tight enough to constrict their breathing. They wore dark smoky eye shadow and lipstick coating swollen lips. Leather chokers suffocating willowy necks. One of the females walked over to Jason, placed a hand on his chest. Her perfume smelled like fruitcake and old ladies. "I shaved my legs for you tonight, handsome."

Jason looked over the top of her, glared at Brandon. "I shaved my legs too, but not for you two."

The other redhead was looking at the boxes in front of Jason's closet. "Who's got all the shoes?" she squealed.

Jason took a step back; the hand fell from his chest. He glared at the female in front of him. He definitely didn't want these two here, but he was always told be nice. "What's your major?" he asked.

The redhead pulled a string of gum in her mouth, looked at her fingernails. "Major, I'm not in the army, silly."

Brandon walked over and kissed the twin wearing a nose ring. Then said, "J.C., I want to introduce you to a couple a my new friends." He put his arm around each one and pulled them in. "This is Mandy and this is Bambi. Thought we'd bring the party to you, big man." Brandon slapped both of the girls on their behinds.

Jason's coach had warned him. If he let woman get in his way, he'd never make it in the Bigs. But he wasn't ready for this combination. A voice inside his head rang through him. His mother told him to stay away from temptation, and the Lord only knew this was some great temptation. He waited a moment as he tried to decide. Jason shook his head. "Not tonight. Not here."

The woman stopped and looked at Brandon. "Thought you said he was fun? Big star and all." One of the woman pointed her finger at Jason and opened her mouth slowly. "Thought you'd like to get to know me, big fella."

Jason shook his head, slower this time. "Another time." He picked up their coats walked to the door.

Brandon pushed himself between them. "Hold it J.C. They're my new friends and they're going to stay awhile."

Jason gave them a fake smile, but he wanted them out. "I really need to get my sleep. You guys need to go somewhere else," he said in a polite voice but then stared at Brandon.

Brandon was speechless for the first time. "What the hell are you doing, man?" he said as he pushed Jason in the chest. Doing you a big favor bringing home a little sugar, dude."

Jason pushed him back harder, and Brandon flipped over the back of the couch. "My high school coach told me about all these chicks that want a piece of me. Then they'll go to the cops and tell them I raped 'em, ruin my career." He pointed his finger at Brandon, thumb aching again. "Not happening here, buddy. Plus, this ain't my style."

Brandon sat up and belched. "You might be the cockiest som-bitch I ever met."

"I'm dribbling downhill. Nothing's getting in my way."

Chapter 33

This morning Tim was preparing for the hunt with Danny Krauser. Danny and Tim had been roommates at the University of Minnesota and spent dozens of times together at Danny's A-frame cabin in the woods near McGregor, Iowa. Danny used to marvel at Tim's accuracy and ability to field dress a deer in record time. Danny nicknamed him, "The Assassin," which Tim loved.

Tim laced up his boots as he thought about how he was going to pay rent and alimony this month. Maybe he could call his parents again? He was clothed in tan camouflage, his face hidden behind black paint.

Danny's cabin had been in his family for over sixty years. The pine cabin smelled of kerosene, old beer, and old smoke. Reaching for a can of Mrs. DoePee from his bag, Tim sprayed his entire body. He splashed Tinks 69 onto his boots to disguise human scent. He was a walking doe in heat. Just another way to conceal himself. But he still couldn't hide from his needs. He opened a small cylinder case and placed a rail of coke between his thumb and forefinger, closed his eyes, covered his nostril and inhaled a long slow sniff. He had learned the slow draw would activate the mucous faster giving him a quick blitzkrieg of ecstasy. In seconds he was enchanted by the rapture of his body. Better enjoy it since he didn't get a paycheck this week. Maybe he could pawn one of his watches?

The men stepped outside. An ethereal October breeze was combing through the leaves. Tim's lungs filled with cool air and his nose dripped. Was it the weather or the cocaine?

The two men clomped down the wooden steps of the cabin and into waist-high grass. Tim inhaled the scent of damp earth. A chorus of birds sang out. "You still got a job?" Danny asked.

"Nope. Still on strike."

"Heard the agreement stalled?"

"That's the NBA for you," Tim said.

"Thought the thing was over awhile ago?"

"Thought so too."

"What happened?"

"Should have been over weeks ago. They're now talkin replacement refs. Hope it's just a bluff."

"Didn't work last time."

Tim stopped for a second and pulled his grandfather's single string recurve bow back over his shoulder, tightened the bill of his orange cap. Wiped the drip hanging from his nose. "Complete disaster. Nobody likes the replacements. Hell, we're professionals and no one likes us either. Coaches don't like us. Players don't respect us, and fans abuse us, and now they want to replace us with a bunch of jock sniffers. This is a contract renewal year with television; no way they want games being called by the sales guy at Foot Locker."

The two went quiet. They were in the woods to listen.

Platinum blonde light percolated through the tops of the trees. Crows began calling up the sun. They walked to the top of a knoll and stopped to look at the sunrise. Tim wanted civilization to be this peaceful. No one telling him what to do. No measurements here. They tromped down a hill through a group of ferns.

"I love this spot," Tim said softly. "Ferns remind me of the rainforest in Washington. Amazing."

"How the ladies treating you? Got a main squeeze right now?"

"Still workin on it. I've locked up Abby on the east coast, and Wendy in the Midwest, Sandra in Florida. But the Pacific is wide open.

"What about the one you liked the best, Cara? What's up with her?"

Tim felt an itch in his throat. It was bad enough having to constantly think about her but he didn't want to face it. He was tired of the questions. "Just lost interest. One of her cheerleader friends always was interested in me. Thought I'd take a stab at that," he said feeling cleansed somehow.

"Was never able to keep up with you. Glad to say Brenda and I are still happy."

"If I could meet a gal like Brenda, I would settle down for a long winter's nap myself."

"I'll make sure you won't be napping with Brenda," Danny snapped back.

"No worries there. I'm happy for you. I do miss the kids though," Tim said pulling an arrow from over his shoulder. As Tim was fiddling with his arrow he heard the crack of leaves in the distance. He was an expert and could tell the difference between the sound of a squirrel or the sound of a deer. It was only a squirrel he told himself.

"Let's break up here, and I'll try to push a few big racks your way," Danny said.

Tim didn't answer. He detected something faint. It was that sour, pungent smell he remembered. The scent of a deer that had urinated on its hocks. Tim placed a finger in his mouth, held it in the air to check the direction of the wind. He pointed and began to walk away from Danny. He was on the hunt. As he moved through the trees, he was shaking with excitement. He loved the chase. Danny was always the one to sacrifice, push the deer his way, allow him to search and capture. The old tree stand was a half mile away. He followed the path noting the recent deer droppings. He pulled on the bow string over and over as he walked, his fingers numbing from the tension. He was getting closer. The pulse in his ears echoed against his earflaps. He could see the old tree stand in the distance, surrounded by an ensemble of aspens. There was a noise that he didn't recognize. Quiet was never quiet. Maybe it was a coon or a turkey? No, something much bigger. He waited and listened. Silence. The anticipation was always glorious. Tim took two slow steps forward. He reached for an arrow, placed it against his string and pulled back. Tighter now. Fingers trembling. He heard a rustle. He could feel the heat now in his chest. Damn, he loved the feeling. Cocaine was even second fiddle to this. He took four more steps forward. Stopped.

He squeezed the maple handle of his Eddings bow, the way Papa had taught him. He leaned against a tree and peered around the corner. A giant buck was feeding on a small bush twenty yards in front of him. Tim counted thirty-two points. The largest rack he'd ever seen. This wasn't what he was expecting, not this close to him. In the wake of his realization, he pulled back the strings of his bow, his heart pounding in his ribcage. The deer didn't move, but Tim wasn't able to let go of the strings. His hands were frozen. He was confused. Why did he hunt innocent animals? Was it a learned behavior from his father or was it something that he was born to do? Sweat began to roll down his forehead, stinging his eyes. Things were never clear in Tim's mind. The buck swung his head and looked back at Tim. He blinked the sweat away, winced and released the string. The arrow whistled and pierced the buck above the front shoulder, it was stumbling. The deer was moving quickly, limping through ferns, finally dropping down into a ravine. Tim sprinted after it, his head dizzy. The deer moved up a hill gaining speed for a moment before it began to hobble. Tim's legs thrashing, arms pumping trying to gain ground. It was all about the chase. Thrilling. He was getting closer.

Tim stood in front of a fallen tree. The deer limped to a stop and turned to face him. The deer's nostrils pulsated, eyes lacking any light, dirty, secretive. Tim felt hot and his head drummed, mouth dry. The buck stomped its hooves three times, then stood on its hind legs, ears pinned back against its neck. It snorted through its nostrils, then lowered its head showing the antlers that were as dangerous as knives. He could read it in the buck's eyes. Eyes wild, fur quivering. He was going to charge. There was a connection between them that he didn't like. The woods swayed a bit as Tim ripped off his glove, pulled out a pistol from his coat and fired ten rounds into the deer. The echo of the shots made the entire woods throb. Unexpected tears, stinging and hot, rose in his eyes. His Ouija board and palm readings hadn't prepared him. And what was that number 495. What the hell did it mean?" The holes in the buck oozed and kept growing wider. Tim flinched as he backed away, but he had nowhere to go. As he studied the buck he had no pity on it. His knees bent and quaked as he fell backwards. He took sharp, tiny breathes, eyes staring at the tops of the trees. He closed his eyes until he heard a noise. Danny stood above him.

"What the hell are you doing?" he screamed.

Tim nodded as if it made perfect sense, but he wasn't listening.

"Sweet Jesus, look what you did….what are you thinking, man?"

He sat up and looked at the animal, hide covered with black bloody holes, starring back at him. "I dunno," he said as strength began to leave his muscles. "I don't really know."

Chapter 34

It was one of those dreams where you'd show up to class for an exam and hadn't read the book. Jason Carson didn't have just one of these dreams; he'd had one every night since he started going to classes, and the dream had grown into a nightmare. At first, the dream was simple, the bearded professor scolding Jason for being late. The next sequence of his dream turned into arriving at the classroom and finding the door locked. Once he dreamed he'd handed in blank pages for a midterm exam. The latest nightmare had him showing up twenty minutes late on exam day and finding the test was in Braille. Often, in the most action-packed dreams, the professor couldn't speak a word of English, and when the bell rang to end class, Coach Trammell from Iowa and Coach Felter from Oak Park would walk into the room and stand in front of Jason, holding his high school and college jerseys. The coaches would light the jerseys on fire and toss them at Jason while he sat frozen at his desk. This was always the point when Jason would scream, sit up in bed shaking and quaking. Brandon never heard him because he usually had enough alcohol to place him near the coma stage. Then the dreams became a reality. The D plus he received on his Geometry test proved that this wasn't high school. This was new territory, a cold place.

Jason sent a text message to his basketball tutor, but for some reason the tutor put him off for two days. He was out of peanut butter, so he ate a bag of Cheetos Brandon had left on his desk. He went to practice, barfing into a garbage twenty-five minutes later. Two girls with yellow yoga pants watched him vomit and laughed at him.

"Can't hold your booze, big shot," one said bursting into laughter. Jason was a master at purging his food before a game because of nerves but now the nerves would come upon him without warning almost anytime.

Jason was amazed at how good he felt when he was back on an open basketball court. With practice over he was working with the shooting gun along with one of the managers. The court was quiet now except for the hum of the machine that fired out basketballs to him like a cannon, one every eight seconds, ten balls from each spot on the three point arc on the court. He was in a groove. Only the sound of the hum and the repetitive snap of the net. Part of him wanted to stay with this feeling, but the other part of him knew he had other responsibilities. After the last shot from the corner he reached for a towel. He watched the manager look at the results on the orange screen and then turn off the machine. "How'd I do?" Jason asked.

"Sixty five percent."

"I don't think it counted two of 'em. Thought I beat last week's sixty seven?"

The manager only smiled. "Incredible shooting from the three point line either way."

Jason shook his head. "Improvement. Either getting better or moving backwards."

Ten minutes later he strolled around the Big Ten room looking at the photographs of past athletes. Some kids liked to go to museums, Jason liked to hang around trophy rooms. He wanted to know the history because he wanted to break it. The third photograph on the wall was a name he knew well, Cy Frye. Better known as Mile High Frye because the guy could jump out of the gym. Played at Iowa and then eight years with the Orlando Magic until he beat up his third girlfriend in 3 years. Magic let him go and he never played in the NBA again. A couple of years later the sad son of a bitch ended up in prison for assaulting two more women. Jason knew this would never ever happen to him. Career or no career, he'd never ever assault a woman.

He made his way to the corner of the room. A dozen TVs hanging from the walls. His stomach growled. He moved to a buffet table. After grabbing a bagel along with a G-2, Brandon Sellers moved in next to Jason. Jason took an extra-large bite from his bagel, peanut butter sticking to the sides of his cheeks, worried that he wouldn't keep it down.

"Dumb-bitch, what's taking you so long," Brandon asked bluntly.

"Five or six reporters wanted to talk." Jason grabbed a handful of unsalted almonds packets and jammed them into his pocket. "Celebrities are always busy."

"I shouldn't wait for you to thank me for coming," Brandon said jerking his head. "Let's go."

The two moved out of the room and down the long hallway. Four players walked out of the women's basketball locker room. They waved and smiled. Jason recognized three of the four women. Of course, it was Brandon who broke the ice.

"Hello ladies. Enjoyed watching your squad much more than the men tonight," he said.

"Thanks," said the group in unison. They stopped at the elevator and began to talk basketball; Jason looked at Krista Garrison. Krista was about six foot one, slender and pretty from head to toe. Jason couldn't keep his eyes off her. Long blonde hair, his favorite, with Air Force blue eyes that stared back at him. His stomach lurched.

"Hey," she said dismissively.

"Hey," he answered.

"You boys ever try to play ball without tackling?"

"Huh?"

She snickered. "Too bad you guys don't play ball the way it was meant to be played."

He didn't answer.

"Football should be played on a field, not a court. Basketball's a finesse game not a wrestling match," she said with a conspiratorial wink.

"I can play either way," he said bracing himself. "Doesn't matter to me."

"Doesn't matter?" she asked anxiously.

"It's the way it is in the big show," he said, his voice as rough as sandpaper.

Krista's eyes widened. "OK, sorry."

He fumbled in his pocket for his phone. Took a step back. This isn't the way women usually treated him. "I just can't let it affect my game, that is," he said despondently.

She tilted her head. "Why not?"

"I'm not staying long. One and done," he replied matter-of-factly.

"Oh yeah, men get to skip school. Go right into pro ball?"

By the way she spoke to him he didn't think she knew who he was. It intrigued him. "I try not to get too worked up over it. Can't let it affect my game."

She pressed her lips together. "Hmm."

Jason experienced another pang of stupidity. He knew who she was but wanted to play it cool. "What did you say your name was? Sorry. Got a lot on my mind."

She shrugged, as if to say she wasn't interested in telling him. "Never mind. It was almost nice to meet you," she said and turned away.

He had blown his chance here. The rest of the group was silent and watched them. He looked into those sea water eyes of hers. "Sorry. Didn't mean to come off that way." He waited a beat. "I watched a little bit of your game. Like watching your style of game."

"Thanks, I guess. Sorry we can't be compared to you guys." Her eyes narrowed.

"Look. Uh, sorry. Didn't mean it that way. Just saying that you ladies really play the game with great fundamentals."

She sighed, and he felt defeated.

"Fundamentals, huh? No skill, that's what you're saying?" She said stepping back against the wall of the elevator.

"I didn't say that at all. I just said I enjoy watching."

He heard the anger in her voice. "Maybe we should just wear little tight skirts and cheer you fellas from the sidelines," she said with a smirk.

The doors of the elevator opened. Everyone moved out except Jason and Krista. They stood staring at each other, not talking.

"Well, too bad we can't continue this deep discussion sometime" Jason then added, "Carson." How did she not know his name? Everyone who was an athlete knew who he was.

"I know who you are. Just wanted to let you know how it feels sometimes. I'm Krista Garrison the ball player." She stuck out her hand and squeezed it until one of his knuckles cracked.

The elevator doors started to close. Brandon slapped a hand on one of the sliding doors and they jumped back open.

"Let's go you two love birds. Elevator's no place for dating."

Everyone headed outside into a cold, clammy wind. As they walked, they listened to Brandon tell a story about one of his professors who always mumbled and scratched his balls when he couldn't think of the right word.

Jason glanced at Krista. "Nice to meet you. Hope to see you around."

She didn't look up, staring straight ahead. "Wish I could say the pleasure was all mine," as she said under her breath walking away.

They slid into Brandon's BMW and shut the doors in rhythm, *clump, clump*. Brandon turned on Pearl Jam and looked at Jason who was hunched over in the small seat.

"Babe-ilicious" Brandon yelped as he turned up the volume. "I love BBW's. Big Beautiful Women."

Jason turned his head, looked out the window.

"I think Krista was diggin your chili? That's what I've been telling you the last few weeks dude. You're the international man of mystery," Brandon said, as he slapped Jason's thigh. "I think you're gonna have to take another shower again…cold one this time, skipper. "

Fifteen minutes later, they were back at Burge and their room. Brandon took off his shirt and pants and climbed into bed. Jason rapped out fifty pushups, ate two bananas, and brushed his teeth. He grabbed the four empty Budweiser bottles from the sink and dropped them into the recycling box. A cockroach ran down the side of the same box. Jason shuddered and squeezed his eyes shut. "You gotta empty that thing tomorrow, bro." He turned off the overhead light. The room went dark and was quiet. He crawled into his bed, his pillow hard, crusty.

It went quiet again for a few seconds. "You pissed about the joking in the car?" Jason asked.

"Hell, no. You're just not used to seein' a chick magnet in action.

hotties can't say no to me. I was voted best French kisser in high school. I can sell my body for big mo'."

"Yeah. You're always selling something."

"If you've got it, you need to move it. That's what my old man taught me."

"Wouldn't know much about that."

"You've been pissy lately.

"Paper due in Comp and I'm pulling a D in Psychology."

"I told you. You don't need to spend any time studying."

"Yeah, right."

"You're the king of the jungle, man. No worries, they won't let us flunk. Everybody in athletics passes, dude."

"No worries, my ass. You never even go to class with me. How are you not worried about the test?"

"The T.A. gave me the test from last year. Told me it's the exact same one we'll take. You and I can study thirty minutes and we're bootylicious."

"If I get caught cheating, I'm done, dude." Cheating scared Jason to death. In high school, Coach Felter had found a kid from Chicago who could take the ACT test for Jason in Tinley Park for the unaffordable price of fifteen hundred bucks. Felter was never able to come up with the money, and Lord knows Jason didn't have that kind of dough and it wasn't a Christian thing to do anyway. "No way, man."

"Sure. You and I on farting terms now J.C." He burped. "This ain't cheating…you'll actually know the shit. Think of it more like an open book test."

All of these things just kept coming at him. "I dunno. I didn't cheat in high school."

Brandon grunted. "I had those high school teachers, jock sniffers, they didn't make me do diddly as long as I was 'goin yard,' every afternoon on the field."

Jason knew it was true. There had been times in high school where he didn't even need to turn in that paper. In Spanish class, the twenty-five year-old blonde bomber gave him his final oral test and just had him repeat everything she said. Easiest A in his life. But he always tried to play by the rules. At least in everything except school, when he really didn't have any other way out. But the help was always given to him, a gift. It was something that was offered, a way to help him because of his faith. He was never the one who was deceitful or fraudulent. He was tired again. His head throbbed above his eyes. "I don't know," he said.

"You kiddin' me. It ain't cheating. It's just tutoring. Same blow we get from the tutors. They tell us what's on the test, we learn the material. What's the difference whether we go over the real test or the tutor's study guide?"

Jason recalled his mother's faith in him. It was all she had right now. How much time did she have left? He piped up with a halfhearted, "S'pose, you might be right."

"Damn right I am," Brandon said with a yawn.

This wasn't what Jason had expected. School was real. The air in the room went fat with the smell of gym shoes. Jason was haunted by the possibility of not passing Psych. "Don't know if I could do it. Don't know if it's right?"

"What do you mean it's not right?"

"It's just that I was brought up with stuff at church that said it wasn't right. It's a sin to cheat."

Brandon laughed, spit into the spittoon and wiped his lips with the back of his forearm. "This ain't cheating…it's manna from heaven, loaves of bread. See what I mean? Just give it a shot. You don't need to be an English professor either. Just get in and out and on to the next semester. It's not like if your grades suck, you'll be playing ball in the Y league with ex-cons the rest of your life.

Jason could hear a couple of students walking down the hall. He had felt a helplessness that refused to leave him. Helplessness when his mother told him she was sick again. Helplessness when he needed to call Ricardo Perez. And a big serving of helplessness, when his Dad walked out on his family. He heard the wind pick up outside. "Maybe just this once…we'll see how it works."

Chapter 35

November 16. USA TODAY-Sports
NBA REFEREES COULD BE BACK FOR OPENERS
The NBA and the referee's executive board agreed Thursday to a contract that could have the regular officials back on the court for season-opening games Wednesday, a person close to the negotiations who requested anonymity during the process told USA TODAY. The Associated Press reported the same information from a person familiar with the negotiations. The contract must be ratified by the referees' 57-person union. But this contract—unlike a deal that fell through— has the approval of the executive board, which consists of veteran referees. The refs have been locked out since their contract expired October 1, with retirement benefits the main sticking point. Replacement referees have officiated preseason games to increased grumbling from players and coaches. Fouls called,

free throws attempted, and game times have increased with the replacement referees.
-Sam Smith, ESPN

Chapter 36

Jason dressed quietly while Brandon snored, and noticed that Brandon was wearing the same shirt he had on last night. Jason brushed his teeth and looked at his phone; no messages. His stomach ached. He opened the air freshener on his desk and shot a cloud of Glade Violet over his left shoulder. Jason had a sensitive stomach and his dorm room reeked. He felt worse in the mornings for some reason, maybe because he needed more protein after he went all night without any. Brandon rolled over, raised his head. "What's goin' on? Smells like a fuckin' garden center."

"If you'd quit throwin' air biscuits in here, I might be able to breathe."

"Thought you'd appreciate some of my crop dusting. I think those seven tacos are talkin' back."

Jason glanced at the green air freshener hanging from the bottom of his bunk. He took a long drink of water and wiped his eyes. "How bout I open the window?"

"I'm tryin' to sleep dude. Need to get up by noon. Where you headed?

"Practice, before homecoming game."

"What time's kickoff?" Brandon asked.

"Two thirty. Talked about this last night. My mother is coming."

"Yea, I kinda remember that conversation. I was a little wasted," Brandon said wiping drool from the side of his cheek.

"So you need to clean the crap on your side of the room. Make it look decent in here."

Brandon licked his lips. "Martha Stewart's coming over later. Probably whip up a couple of pies and redecorate."

"I'm taking your scooter."

"No problem," Brandon said lying back down on the bed, putting a pillow over his head. "I got to go to the batting cage in an hour."

Fifteen minutes later, Jason pushed on the revolving door and headed down the long hallway towards the arena. As he walked down the cement floor, he gazed at all of the Big Ten team banners hanging from the ceiling. He was reminded of all the teams that had tried to recruit him over the years. What would it have been like if he went to Michigan State or Indiana? Maybe the players at those schools would have liked him better. What about Felter's team, UCLA? He said the coaches would have taken care of him. Maybe he wouldn't have needed to go to class there. Damn, that would have been nice. But he wouldn't ever get to see his mother, especially in her condition. He was excited because he would get to see her today.

A wiry team manager jogged up to him. "Jason, if you want your ankles taped, you need to get into the training room. They've been waiting for you."

"Thanks, I forgot." He always got his ankles taped before practices and games. There were four other players receiving medical attention. He sniffed the scent of antiseptic, looked at the head trainer standing in front of a padded table rubbing a jelly substance on the knee of senior point guard Calvin Davis. The head trainer was impossibly thin and had a mouth too big for his narrow head, lips stretched over a mouthful of teeth. He glared at Jason as he wiped his hands on a white towel

"Carson, you need to get your ass in here earlier," he said venomously. "You gotta remember that we're responsible for getting you out on the floor on time, son. You can't keep forgetting 'bout this no more."

"Sorry, Tommy. Nothing's been going easy for me."

"You punks get everything and you're still not happy," Tommy said through gritted teeth. "Gotta take care of yourself sooner or later kid. Helicopter parents are killing your generation," he said curtly.

Nothing was easy anymore. Who could he trust with his problems? "I'm trying sir, but…" he trailed off.

Tommy nodded, grabbed a roll of tape and slapped one of the padded tables, "get your butt up here, I'll work some magic."

Tommy tore a piece of tape with teeth that looked like they probably hadn't seen a dentist in years and even though he hardly ever smiled it didn't seem to stop Jason from liking the old boy. Tommy was just one of those fellas who would give it to you straight.

"You come in here late one more time this month, I'll be taping your damn ankles together, Carson. You frosh come in here with noggins the size of Texas and expect everyone to be your damn peasants. It ain't like that in the real world, and somebody needs to teach you hot shots a little respect."

"Yes, sir. Sorry Tommy, I won't let it happen again" he said, voice faltering, even tears prickling his eyes.

Tommy stopped and stared at him, quickly glanced around the room, then stepped forward. "Look kid, I know you got troubles with your mom. How she doin' this week?"

Jason sat up a bit. "She's coming to visit today. Doc said it was OK. A friend from Oak Park is driving her. Mom's too sick to drive right now."

"That chemo is tough shit, kid. You said this is her second go around, yeah?"

Jason nodded, swallowed hard. "One of the docs said the second time isn't good." He blew out a long breath. "But my mom's got big faith. Has big faith in me too."

Tommy Parker actually smiled. The heavy lines in his forehead broke apart. "I got faith in you too, kid." Tommy looked into Jason's eyes. "You doin OK., Kid?"

Jason shrugged. "Not the best." He looked over at the other tables, everyone else had ear buds or headphones covering their ears, no one was listening, typical. "Having trouble sleeping?"

Tommy nodded, didn't look up.

"And I'm not eating much lately either."

"Hmm."

"Last three days I've had diarrhea…stomach's been a mess."

Tommy nodded with a wrinkled brow. "You got a lot on your plate. How's school work?"

Without knowing it, Jason let out a long sigh. "Don't ask, not good.."

"Not well, ya mean. Even a dumb ass like me knows that."

Jason picked at his fingernails, shrugged. "Is there something you can do that'll help me sleep? Keep me from having nasty dreams?"

"What kinda dreams you having kid?"

He stretched his elbow behind his head. "More like nightmares, maybe. Dreams about flunking out, moving back home, getting thrown in jail, stuff like that."

Tommy cracked a knuckle. "Look it's rough here at first. Seen it a million times before. Rookies round here sometimes get left out. Everyone fightin' for their own position and playing time. Dog eat dog world out there, kid."

"I know I can do a lot better though."

Tommy sat down on a stool, pinched Jason's ankles then wiggled them. "Let me tell you sump-in kid. I've seen some great players in my day. Been through a lot sitting at the end of the bench with more coaches then I can count. I keep my eyes and ears open and I know the score round here, son."

Jason sighed again. "I just need to do this college crap thing for a year and then head to the big show. I'll be fine then."

Tommy's squinted his eyes, tightened his long lips. "Bull-shit," he scoffed. He looked up at the ceiling and moaned. "You're just another one of a million kids that told me that big-dick story. Countin' chickens before they hatch. What are you, crazy?"

"Tons a guys told me I'm a top draft pick," Jason said, embarrassed at how stupid it sounded for the first time.

Tommy shook his head, laughed. "I've been around since the beginning of time. I've seen everything. Punks in here telling me the same story. Making it big. Thousands trying to do the same thing. Some get hurt, can't play the same. Some can't handle the pressure. Some don't have the brains. Some make mistakes, beat up wives, get accused of rape even though it never happened, broads looking for some dough…and sometimes it did happen, who knows. Probably both. Some actually do make the bigs and then blow all their money, end up beggin' on the street corner," he said exasperated. "Just playin' ball and making a lot of dough doesn't solve your problems," he said with a sickly smile.

"Would for me."

"That's a crock a shit. Doesn't solve your mom's health. Doesn't make you friends. Doesn't always happen, for god's sakes. You need some wisdom and a good education." Tommy patted knuckles on his forehead, "you got a lot of life to figure out and you need someone to help you with it kid," he said with a desperate cheeriness.

"Dad left years ago. Didn't have anybody except my mom. She's the only one I got."

"What she been telling you?"

He nodded. "Same as you."

"You need to listen for once."

Jason didn't look at his face, didn't study his eyes, he just heard it in his voice. Kindness, the one sensation he would not have expected around here, someone might care.

"I think you need to spend a little more time with the players when you have a chance."

"I've been tryin. Don't get asked too much."

Tommy nodded, stopped, nodded again. "Basketball's a team game and there's been pretty good chemistry round here the last couple a years. Think that's why we've been so damn good."

"Right," Jason said.

"Time for you to listen again. Thing is, if one player gets too much control, all the other parts don't seem to work as good, I mean, well. There needs to be production from everyone if we want the team to work...not just parts of it. You know what I'm sayin', kid?"

"Sound like my high school coach."

"Damn right. Must have been a genius. What I'm trying to tell you is that everyone needs to get involved. Be part of the action."

Jason had grown familiar with people giving him advice, but Tommy seemed to have a bit of sanity.

"OK, but crunch time, I'm the one who's taking the shot. I'm the one whose gonna win the game. That's what champions do."

Tommy nodded. "But before that last shot, you need to make sure everyone else gets involved in the game. One person can't do it all."

"But I need to have a big year. Show big numbers."

Tommy rubbed cheeks with pockmarks the size of nail heads, closed his eyes. "If you don't get your teammates to care for you or give up the rock sometimes you'll never get the ball in the crunch time. Never see any passes come your way...Boys will just shut your ass out, son."

"I've been shooting lights out."

"How many assists, kid?"

160

It was true, Jason knew he probably should pass the ball more often. "I'm the best shooter in the country." Jason looked at his ankles, waited.

"Seen it before. It's a team game. How many assists?"

"Never had too many assists.

"You don't think scouts are looking at that, too?"

"But I can score easier than anyone on the court."

"I know what you can do kid...But if you want teammates to give a damn about you and work hard for you, your gonna need to be a team player. Give up the ball and quit being so damn selfish. See what happens."

"May not be that easy for me, Tommy."

"May get you a few more friends too. College is a great place for friendship, kid."

"Mother always tells me kids are jealous."

Tommy looked him straight in the eye, squinting. "Course they are kid. But you need friendships. You need to be part of the team. You need to hang out with the boys instead of hanging around the locker room playing those stupid video games."

Jason lowered his head. The guy knew everything, didn't he?

Tommy put a hand on Jason's shoulder, squeezed; "I'll be here for you...but next time you forget about us, I'll tape your jock strap over your shoulders." Tommy shook his head. "You don't even know what a jock strap is, punk. Get in here tomorrow early and we'll talk about your classes."

BBC—Fixing and corruption in sport has a long history. If you were to go to the site of the ancient Olympics in Greece you would find, outside the ruins of the stadium, remains of statues to their Gods. The statues were paid for by athletes and coaches who were caught cheating. Sports corruption goes back at least

2,800 years and some type of corruption will be with us for as long as we continue to hold competitive sports. It is simply a part of human nature.

However, we of this generation are facing something almost entirely new. It is a contemporary form of match-fixing, as if someone had taken fixing and injected it with steroids.

Chapter 37

Tim McMurray sat at the new kitchen table he rented from Becker Furniture World in Edina. The store had six locations around the Twin Cities and rented to just about anyone who held a steady job. The kitchen table, beige suede sofa, king size bed and maple chest were rented with the possibility to buy but the eighteen percent interest rate was a killer. There had been a few items that Tim brought from his house after the divorce. His blue Lazy Boy and Pioneer stereo were leftovers from his original bachelor days. His Sony clock radio with an FM/AM tuning dial made the apartment look as if it was a candidate for the Extreme Home Makeover crew. Who was he trying to kid? He wouldn't have any of this crap a year from now. As soon as money rolled into his Cayman Island account he'd buy a six thousand square foot house and fill up the place with top notch goods. But as long as his TV could get Sports Center and the Outdoor channel, Tim wouldn't really care. His iPhone was his second religion, his surrogate spouse; if only the device could wear lipstick with a bra and silk panties, Tim's life would be heavenly.

Tim stared, eyes bloated, directly at the phone, but his mind was far from the screen saver image of him running down the court. He looked at the time on his phone, 9:22AM Sunday. He took a sip from his green tea loaded with Vitamin K. He needed to drink three cups this morning to stop the glycation of human tissue; keep him looking young. It had to be true since he saw it on the Dr. Oz show a month ago while staying at the Marriott in Toronto. But he still felt eerie, ghoulish. The dread of last night's dream would never leave him. Aliens again. He sat in his boxer shorts and Minnesota Twins t-shirt running both hands through his hair. He flipped to the Horoscope section of the *Minneapolis Tribune*. He moved his forefinger down the page. Gemini: "Clear communication is the key to fully understanding most situations. Ideas and thoughts will have greater meaning now. This is a prime time for negotiations. If nothing else, make those phone calls. Someone in your life is not telling the whole story; be careful. Consider breaking bonds and strengthening others." He closed the page and looked into his tea cup. Yesterday's horoscope was damn similar: "The only way to get what you want is to follow the direction of someone you barely know. You don't trust easily, so now's as good a time as any to start". It was freakish how they were always right. A couple hours after Tim killed the deer, he received a text message: DIE or CALL 919-274-0045 Sunday at 10:00AM Central Time. TELL SOMEONE AND YOU WILL DIE. He looked at his watch, 9:55. What would they tell him? He rubbed his eyes. Two weeks ago a fortune teller in San Francisco gave him a book and told him to read it immediately: The Book of Masters of the Secret House. Even though the pages were yellow and some of the words smeared, Tim spent a week reading it in his hotel rooms before last year's games. But nothing made sense. She told him to study the section called, "Ritual of the Dead."

Tim looked at the book again. He sipped his tea, best way to get rid of the old man bags under his eyes. The Book of Masters of the Secret House still hadn't changed. He went to the eighth page. Masters of the Secret House, Egyptian copy, translated into English. He bit his bottom lip, ran his finger down the page. He raced through the table of content, then the appendix. Something jumped out at him, hit him in the forehead like a fist. 'Numerology'. Of course. He stared at the jaundiced page, mouth dry. The Hindu Vedas, the Chinese Circle of the Dead, Egyptian, Book of the Masters of the Secret House, Ritual of the Dead. He should have known all along. Pythagoras. Pythagoras and other philosophers of the time believed mathematical concepts were more practical than physical ones…they had greater actuality, he reminded himself. He had learned this two or three years ago visiting one of his fortune tellers in New Jersey. Everything had numerical relationships and it was up to the mind to seek and investigate the secrets of these relationships or have them revealed by divine grace. When he first learned of this he was excited, but Tim had forgotten to pursue it further because a redhead moved into his life. He flipped through the book; two pages fell out before he found the appendix. He found the list on page 495. There it was again, the number. His stomach flipped. Page 495. "The practice within Jewish tradition of assigning mystical meaning to words based on their numerical values, and on connections between words of equal value, is known as gematria. The Arabic system of numerology is known as Abjad notation or Abjad numerals. In this system each letter of Arabic alphabet has a numerical value.

1=a,j,s
2=b,k,t
3=c,l,u
4=d,m,v
5=e,n,w
6=f,o,x
7=q,p,y
8=h,q,z

9=i,r

His hands shook. 495 ? d,m,v ; then i,r, then e,n,w? 495.

He stared. Then he saw it. He felt tears come to his eyes, but he forced them away. He was told. He should have known. He should have listened to the fortune teller. The number four, nine, five did represent letters with a meaning. They were telling him something all the time. Warning him. 495 spelled "DIE". Pythagoras and the numerologist had to be right. The number was warning him and he hadn't paid attention. Random thoughts and emotions ricocheted through his head. He should have known something was going to happen to Cara. He could have saved her. An icy coldness blasted through him. He pulled on his face, thinking. He slammed his fist into the table; tea launched out of the cup and onto his newspaper. He stood and scrambled over to his hall closet, opened the door and pulled out his 22 and held it against his chest. He needed to make that phone call. He went back to the kitchen table and sat, clutching his gun. He began to dial numbers on his phone with his hands shaking, fingers tingling. He finished the tenth number and waited. He took a deep breath and waited. The phone rang four times. A female voice answered with an eastern European accent. "Vhat cahn I du for you?" the voice asked.

"Hello." He hesitated, pulled on his cheek. "I was told to call,"

Tim waited. He could hear water running in the apartment next to him. He sat up in his chair. He tried to move his feet, but they stuck to the floor. He touched his dripping nose. A small amount of blood leaked through his fingers. He wiped it away.

A voice jolted him to life. "Hello," the voice said darkly.

His eyes blurry, looking at the numbers on his screen again. "Who is this?"

Breathing.

"I was told to call...don't know what this is about."

"We want to know everything," the voice seethed. The voice went quiet for a second.

Tim couldn't speak, couldn't move.

"No more secrets. When games begin we want you to call four hours before each game."

"Who is this?" His legs begin to shake. "What's this about?"

"Shut up and listen."

Pain like scissors twisted in his gut. "I'm usually in pre-game meals and prep for —"

"Shut up. If you want to keep working, if you want to keep living, we need the phone call."

"This is crazy."

"You need to listen asshole."

Tim could hear noises from the street, a police siren, kids laughing, shouting. Normal shit. But inside him the world was ending.

"I don't know what you want. Who are you?" he said trying to make his voice as unthreatening as possible.

The voice snapped back. "No need to know. No more secrets or we'll chop off your dick, ram it down your throat."

The horror was almost too much to bear. Someone wanted to kill him, suck the life out of him.

"Just follow instructions. No more secrets," the voice bellowed.

Tim didn't respond. Sweat popped onto his forehead.

"We want to know every call you get before each game." The sound echoed in his ear. Every point shaved for each player or each team. Do you understand?"

He didn't understand who would be asking this.

"Do you understand, goddamn it?"

The room was white hot, airless despite the open windows. "Yes," he said straining with emotion.

"If you make a mistake, if you forget, if you play with us…you're a dead man."

He heard a click, then a buzz. Tim waited but there was only silence. His refrigerator had stopped humming. His legs were bouncing, now. He wondered if his heart had stopped beating. But then, the pain started seeping into the back of his eyes.

Tim knocked into the table spilling his tea. He reached for a towel. The phone buzzed and he froze. The phone buzzed again. What do they want now? What would he say? He reached down and pushed the button. "Yes?"

"Good morning, this is Craig Joens from the Department of Natural Resources. May I please speak to Tim?"

How did they know about the deer? "Sorry, wrong number," Tim said and hung up.

Chapter 38

Dribbling between his legs, Jason reached for the second ball. He dribbled two balls now around each leg and then behind his back and then back between his legs. No one was left in the arena except the manager putting the extra balls into the cage. No one wanted to stick around. That's the way it was, players leaving him alone for some reason and he learned to live with it.

An hour later, Jason held onto his mother as they moved through the crowd. The Iowa football team had beaten the Michigan Wolverines 24-20. The sun ducked under a cloud, the air was cool and had a little slap to it. Jason inhaled muzzy smells of grilled meat and beer. As they walked at a slow pace, people slithered around them, slowing them even further. There were plastic cups all over the ground. For the next few minutes they plodded along, Jason's mother breathing, coughing. Life was a cold brittle thing.

His mother's hair covered half her face and eyes. Her black sweater hung from her gaunt shoulders. It was the most painful thing he had ever seen.

"You doing OK?" he asked.

She blinked, squeezed his arm. Her smile was frail. "Don't know if I can make it."

"Do you need to rest?" he asked confused.

"I'll just take it a little slower from here," she said gasping for breath.

Jason glanced down at her shoes. He had noticed earlier that she was wearing tennis shoes. She was a lady and never wore tennis shoes, especially not these; cheap shitty Wal-Mart tennis shoes. For a moment he stopped feeling sorry for himself. He actually did have something. He was wearing Platinum Air Jordans and she was wearing crap. He was totally embarrassed, ashamed that he spent money on himself when his mother couldn't pay her bills. He felt pathetic. She deserved better. She was the one that always gave up things for him. Maybe it was his turn?

He studied her. Her cheeks were painted with heavy rouge, cavernous now. "You need to eat more. Get your strength up."

"I don't feel like it anymore. Fasting is a virtue. Good for the spirit."

"How much weight have you lost?"

She shrugged, her sweater wallowing in the wind. "Not to worry, never worry. Seeing the doctor again on Wednesday. Guess they want to check the size of the tumors again," she said and smiled heroically.

"Tumors? As in more than one?" Someone bumped him in the back, but he didn't care.

"They're small. Radiation should take care of them," she said in a voice so soft he could barely recognize her.

"Holy shit."

"Watch your language, son. Everything's going to be OK Have a little faith."

He covered his mouth as if he was about to vomit. He swallowed it back. "When were you going to tell me?"

She gave him a half smile. "None of us understand the plan," she said in hushed trembling tones.

Jason's stomach tightened. He wanted to say he didn't understand, but her beliefs and trusts were her creed. She lived it every day of her life, and he loved her for it. But he was feeling dumb again, asking questions that may have no answers. Maybe it was lack of sleep, his heart was pounding harder. "I thought you said things were getting better?"

"I didn't want to worry you." She blinked three times, lips trembling.

That's the way it was with her, penniless, sick, and she always thought of others first. She was the one at church that made casseroles for families that lost a loved one. She was the one that taught his Sunday school class every year until he was unable to attend because he was playing in a basketball tournament. She was the one that prayed for him every day of her life. She was the one painting houses for the elderly with their church, while their apartment hadn't seen a new coat in years.

He sighed.

"You need to concentrate on your school and playing."

People were moving around them, but Jason didn't give a damn. Everything was moving too fast, moving away from him. He wanted to punch something. What would happen if she didn't live? He hadn't faced the question because she always told him everything would work out for the best. God's plan. But what if it wasn't His plan? He looked around for help, but no one was paying any attention to them. He looked back into her eyes. Eyes that were pure and filled with kindness. He needed to ask more questions. "We need to talk more about this. I need answers. I need to talk to your doctors."

"I don't want to be a bother to you, Jason. If the good Lord calls me home, I won't have to be a worry to you anymore."

Jason felt himself empty out, no breathe, no pain, no thought. "What are you talking about? That's not gonna happen."

She smiled and waved a hand at him. "All things work for a purpose. Gives us time to have more faith."

"We need you better. I need you better."

"The master has his plan." She coughed again, this time it seemed heavier. "You have your life together. Always made good decisions, you have," she said and tugged on his arm again

The streets were filled with noise, but the silence was staggering. He swallowed, not sure what to say. "Nothing's going to happen to you. Coach told me that one of our biggest fans is head of, what is the Cancer thing called?"

"Oncology, and I have an excellent doctor at Oak Park. He's a graduate of University of Chicago."

"What's he say?"

She looked at him with eyes that told him she really didn't want to answer. "Jason, I don't have too much longer on this earth," she said.

Jason's body went rigid. The words floated through his head. He bent down, wrapped his arms around her. He picked her up, put her in his arms and began to march down the sidewalk. "Excuse me, coming through, coming through." He shouted it over and over until people began to pay attention. They moved out of his way. Everyone moved except a group of four shirtless college students who refused to move out of his way. The group swerved and laughed, too much to drink he told himself. He howled at them again, but none of them moved. He wasn't putting up with this bullshit. He swung his body so his mother was facing away from the drunkards. He bent backwards, lifted his leg and leveled a kick square in the back of one of the guys. The dude's body launched forward face planting onto the pavement. Jason stepped over him and started running, yelling again. His mother was weightless, nothing but skin on bone but it cleansed him somehow, carrying her.

Chapter 39

A white BMW pulled up beside the curb and honked. Jason swung his head and saw Brandon waiting for the two of them, his head swaying to the beat of the music pouring out of the car's sunroof. Jason helped his mother to the back seat of the car and closed the door, moved to the passenger seat. Jason was actually calm now. That's how it was with him; furious one minute, relaxed the next. It was basketball that taught him to get back into the moment, taught him to control himself during the battle.

Mrs. Carson rubbed the crème colored leather seat in the back of the BMW. "This is a beautiful car, Brandon. Must be quite expensive," she said.

"My parents gave it to me for high school graduation. They sent it out here this summer with the Honda scooter that Jason likes to race round town with." Mrs. Carson grabbed Jason by the arm. "Aren't those things dangerous, son? Do you boys wear a helmet when you drive that little thing?"

Brandon sighed. "He wears a football helmet Mrs. C. I make sure he wears shoulder pads and his chin strap and most importantly his protective cup. Take care of the jewels. No worries."

Jason pretended not to listen. He leaned over to Brandon. "I got an electric shaver for high school graduation."

Mrs. Carson patted Jason on the shoulder. "Looked like a nice Presbyterian church where we parked the car. Have you had a chance to get to church lately?"

Jason shook his head. "Still haven't had the time with practices and stuff."

Brandon faked a cough.

"What about you Brandon? What denomination are you?" Are you a church goer?"

Brandon adjusted the radio. "Mrs. Carson, I never went to church much growin' up. We usually went on Christmas and Easter though," He turned the stereo to a little heavy metal.

"Have you been baptized, son," asked Mrs. Carson.

"Yes ma'am, I was baptized at Sea World. Shamu gave me the total immersion when I was ten; you could probably call me a Baptist then.

Jason just shook his head. The car was barely moving because of the traffic. "Where you guys want to eat tonight?"

"I thought we were going to your dorm first?" Mrs. Carson said. Mrs. Carson placed a thin hand over her mouth, "I'm not feeling very well."

Brandon grabbed the zebra skin steering wheel with both hands. "I'll take a short cut." The car bounced over the curb and drove on the parkway, cutting through grass, inches from a light post. "We're in there like swimwear," Brandon said and then turned up the radio. Johnny Cash's "Ring of Fire," Two of the car's wheels were now on the sidewalk. Two students jumped out of the way looking for safety. Brandon moved the car back onto the street. "Don't want any accidents in the new leather seats in the back Mrs. C...Learned that last move from a Bond movie," Brandon cracked.

Mrs. Carson unleashed a small whistle. Jason turned. "Do you want to sit in the front, Mom?"

She shook her head, then fished into her gigantic purse for tissues. Her eyes were watering. She blinked, coughed, swallowed, coughed again.

"Could you turn down the music a little?" Jason's mom asked as she patted Jason's shoulder.

"Anything you need." But it was too late. There was a moan from the back, more like a roar and he instantly knew. His mother began to vomit into her tissue and then onto the floor, her head now buried between her legs. Brandon twisted his head to take a peek. His eyes wide, mouth open. Then he turned forward again, slammed on the breaks narrowly missing the Camry in front of him.

Brandon pointed to the middle of the back seat. "Get the towel, Mom. Under the pull out thing," he quipped. Mrs. Carson took a long breath, then retched again. This time louder and longer.

Brandon fumbled with the steering wheel, gripping hard. "Bite me," he mumbled.

Jason put a hand on Brandon. "Stop the car," he said, embarrassed. He slid into the back seat, slipped his arm around his mother and pulled her against his chest. He held her head with his palm and whispered. "Everything's going to be alright momma."

Minutes later they stepped out of the car. "I'll pay for it to be cleaned," Jason's mother said, now smiling as if nothing had happened. "Just another accident, boys."

How many of these crazy accidents had she had? Jason helped his mother to the dorm entrance. The elevator vibrated to the fourth floor of Burge Hall. The door jerked as it opened. Jason looked to his mother. "I need to use the facilities. Be right back.

Mrs. Carson gave a weak smile. "I'm feeling much better now. You can go."

Brandon followed him. "I need to throw a rope too. Wait up. How 'bout a sword fight?"

They moved into the dorm room. Jason watched his mother scan the room. The look on her face told him all he needed to know.

"You boys did a nice job with the beds," she said as she fingered the ragged couch as if it was contagious.

His mother's face now had a bit of color and her eyes were brighter in her narrowed pretty face. She looked transformed, a replica of her previous self. She tipped toed through the room, inspecting every corner, eyeing everything. "Smells a little stuffy in here, men." She reached into her bag and put a mint into her mouth.

Ten minutes ago she was barfing and now she was examining the place, searching for flaws. "I'm feeling much better now. Miracle, I even have a bit of an appetite too. First I'm cleaning the car."

Jason stepped forward. "No way, Mom. I'll take care of it."

She waved hands around like bees disturbed from their hive. "No, no, no. I've got it," she said humming and left the room in a buzz.

Fifteen minutes later, she returned to the room. "Everything's clean. Really wasn't too bad." Jason didn't know how she would react after her episode, but he was delighted to see her energy and movement back to the way he remembered her. She smiled at him and sat down on the edge of the couch.

"Mrs. C, your son is quite the attention getter round here. Reporters, professors, even dopey fans can't seem to get enough of your Boy Wonder," Brandon said as he slapped the back of his Jason. "Every jock sniffer around has tried to meet him."

Without a word Mrs. Carson kept looking around the room as Brandon spoke.

"Young punk was up here two days ago tryin' to deliver a pizza to our room, and we didn't even order one. The home-boy wasn't even old enough to drive, just wanted to get a hairy eyeball on J.C. We did get to keep the pizza though. Only tip we had to give the kid was an autograph from Mr. Big Show here," Brandon cackled.

Mrs. Carson smiled. "Everyone's always wanted to meet Jason. He's such a good boy."

"He's good at bragging about it too. He likes to tell me how good he is," Brandon said with a laugh.

"Well he's perfect in my eyes."

Brandon walked over to the window, pointed and looked out. "I'm looking for the white smoke, Mrs. C. could be making your son Pope any day now," Brandon said teasingly.

Mrs. C paid no attention. She stood up faster than Jason had seen her stand in quite some time. He was relieved to see her moving and reacting like her old self.

"I'm kind of hungry. What do you say we grab something to eat? I'm treating."

Jason was struck, the way he was always struck, by the way this woman kept bouncing back. "I thought you haven't been eating much? No appetite?"

She gave him a wide smile. "Little miracles every day, son. I usually feel well for an hour or two at a time. Need to make the best of it."

Minutes later, Brandon puttered around downtown Iowa City scanning around for a place to park. The streets were thick with cars and people.

"OMG, no place to dock the ship, mates," Brandon, said.

Mrs. Carson leaned forward and whispered in Jason's ear. "What did he say?"

"No place to park," Jason said, but he had another idea. "Drive by the St. Burch Tavern."

Brandon turned the corner. "Everything's jammed, bro."

Jason rolled down his window waived at two of the greeters in front of the restaurant. The two men walked to the car. "Hey boys. Know who I am?"

The two smiled immediately. "Hey Jason Carson. Can we get a pic with you?"

"Sure, but can you park our car first, kinda valet it, dude?"

The two guys smiled, nodded. Brandon was the first one out the door and handed over the keys. A car honked behind them and Brandon just gave them a wave. Everyone else exited and the car was gone in a flash.

Jason smiled and winked at his mother. "See how easy that was?"

Brandon raised his hands in the air. "Like I said Mrs. C. White smoke is here. He'll be parting the Red Sea tomorrow."

The St. Burch Tavern was already humming, filled with football fans and alumni. Twenty-five to thirty people were waiting to be seated. "How much was this going to cost?" Jason asked himself.

"Looks like a long wait, Jason. Maybe we should try somewhere else?" his mother said.

Jason held up a hand. "I'll take care of it." He moved through the crowd and found the hostess. The short black-haired woman barely looked up. "How many in your party?"

"Three."

She glanced down at her clipboard. "It's a thirty to forty minute wait. Can I get your name?"

"Carson…Jason Carson."

The hostess wrote his name on her list. A high school boy tapped Jason on the side of his arm. Jason turned.

"Jason. Jason Carson? Can I have your autograph?" The kid pulled out a pen from his pocket and handed him a notebook. "I'm from Naperville, visiting my sister." He threw his thumb to the back of the room. "You're awesome dude."

"Thanks." This was feeling all too familiar lately. Every kid, every teacher, every fan just wanted to come up to him and say hello. Shake his hand, maybe get a picture. But these people really didn't want to get to know him like a friend; just use him as an idol to show everyone else how cool they were. A dark-haired man with glasses moved next to Jason as he handed the menu back to the boy. "Jason, I'm Jack Hayes, owner here." He reached out his hand. Jason shook it. "Glad you're here. I've got a booth in the corner for the three of you.

Jason looked back at Brandon and waved. He looked back at Jack. "Thank you."

Jack waved the menus, gave a slight shake of the head. "No problem. We take care of our own here."

The three moved into a booth in the corner with windows on both sides. The sidewalks outside the windows were swollen with people roaming the downtown.

Jason's mother sat slightly forward, back perfectly straight as she stared out the window. "This town is lively. Glad you stayed close to home, Jason."

Brandon smiled, slapped his stomach, "I've got the woofies."

A heavy set waitress with tattoos on her wrists delivered water to the table.

"That was easy, right?" Jason said.

"Better get used to it big boy," Brandon said quickly looking over to Mrs C. "When you make it to the Big Show you'll be a celebrity lifer.

Fancy cars, beautiful babes, big houses, the best seats in restaurants. You'll be the Queen"

Mrs. Carson shook her head. "I don't think he'll let a little money corrupt him. He's got his priorities straight."

A group of students stopped in front of the windows knocking and waving to Jason, Brandon raised his eyebrows. "A nice guy moves to L.A. or New York City and they get sucked into the Celeb lifestyle." He threw an elbow into Jason's ribs. "No more college training table. It'll be private chefs, private planes, private massages by blondes and redheads. I'm diggin' redheads this week," he said with a long sniff.

Jason's mother blinked at Brandon; tilted her head. "I don't see that happening to Jason. Do you think they have anything gluten-free on the menu? I can't have any sugar either."

Brandon smiled. "I'll go au natur-al when they start sellin' organic ding dongs and tofu Cheetos."

Jason shook his head. He wondered if his mother had been getting enough help since he left. Hopefully someone was watching her diet. "Anything look good to you, mom?"

Her eyes narrowed, she shook her head. "Not feeling too well all of a sudden."

A waitress approached the table and smiled. "Mr. Hayes would like to buy your meals tonight."

The three looked at each other for a moment. Jason glanced at Brandon. "Don't think we can do that. I think it's an NCAA rule or something. Think they talked about that in one of our meetings?"

Brandon squinted. "Aw, it'll be fine J.C. Just think about it as another training table. We're all among friends here."

Jason moved his eyes to the menu, checked out the prices. Was there anyone here watching? Maybe Brandon was right. This way his Mother didn't have to pay. She couldn't even pay her bills. What would happen if they got caught? He was tired of facing all these decisions. Almost without realizing what he was doing, he nodded to the waitress. "Thank you," he said. He turned and glanced around the room to see if anyone was watching.

Brandon was eyeing a blonde waitress then turned his attention back to the table. "See Mrs. C., it's only just startin'. Everybody's gonna start treating your boy like a rock star. It's Elvis reincarnated. He just needs to tighten it up and grab for the gold."

Mrs. Carson pointed a finger at Jason. "Go thank the owner please," she said as her lips began to tremble again. There was a slight change in her eyes, pupils the size of pencil erasers.

"Mom, you OK?"

A transformation crossed her face like the weather. The exuberance on her face evaporated. She tried to swallow, nodded once. "Please go thank the man," she murmured with crack lips.

Jason wiggled out of the booth. He moved through the crowd. He watched the bartender making drinks. Someone seated at the bar told him 'good luck this year,' as he nodded back to him. He was trying to relax. He was using his positive mental attitude techniques to calm himself. His mother was in town, and he didn't have to worry about the next test, next quiz, the next paper. He was starting to enjoy the attention that he was getting. Maybe some odd mercy had found him, or as his mother would say, another blessing. Was she going to be OK? Then he wanted to look around at all of the people that might be looking at him. He glanced around the bar. Two guys were staring back at him. A couple standing to their left also were watching him. He did not know if he should be grateful for this or not. Did any of these people want to help him?" It sure didn't hurt that the owner recognized him.

A bald man with an incalculable number of freckles covering his face reached out his hand. "Jim Messerschmit. Wanted to say thanks for coming to Iowa." The two men shook hands and Jason felt something in his palm as he pulled it away. A hundred dollar bill. Jim smiled, winked and walked away. What was he supposed to do? Did anyone see this? He put the money in his pocket, glanced around the room again. He froze when he looked to the end of the cherry wood bar. He stood and looked without seeing, aware but not registering what he saw. Gooseflesh rippled up his arms. It was him. Ricardo Perez, sipping on a drink in St. Burch's Tavern. Ricardo calmly nodded his head; gingerly waved his fore finger to Jason to come over. Jason looked over his shoulder but no one from the booth in the corner was paying any attention. Jason stepped around several women and stood behind Ricardo. "What are you doing here," he panted.

Ricardo turned around half way and didn't take his eyes off the bartender who was flying around. "I'll meet you in the bathroom… downstairs…keep walking." Ricardo now was looking at his glass, then moved to his phone.

Jason looked around for the stairs. He saw a sign that read 'Private Party', 6:30. He walked down the stairs and around the corner. A busboy was working on place settings at the other end of the room. He entered the men's restroom, moved over to the mirror. He squinted at himself. Maybe he didn't really feel like looking. But he wished he wasn't there. One surprise after another today. It seemed like five minutes had passed since he walked into the restroom, but his watch told him it was closer to fifty seconds. The door swung open, Ricardo Perez stepped inside.

"Good to see you again, Jason. Long time no see."

Jason wanted to say the same but couldn't bring himself to it. Ricardo was wearing one of those expensive suits again, and the dim overhead lights made his face look even darker than he remembered.

Jason remembered the words Ricardo had said to him again and again: "Just a little arrangement between the two of us."

"What are you doing here? Couldn't you call?"

His voice was quiet now. "I wanted to see your family together. Maybe I could get a chance to finally meet your mom." He smiled and raised his chin.

Jason could smell the cologne as if it was oozing out of his pores. He could always recognize that scent. His stomach started to move up his chest.

"I don't think that would be the best idea right now," Jason said, and the hardness of his voice surprised him.

Ricardo Perez couldn't stop smiling. He folded his arms across his chest. "I thought you cared for your mother?"

"Why didn't you call?"

Ricardo's smile disappeared, he lowered his head. "I just don't want you to forget about me." There was a pause. "I think it is almost time for us to begin our arrangement again."

There was that word again, arrangement. He wished he had never made that arrangement in the first place. Jason's mouth opened but he couldn't come up with the right words.

"I just wanted to spend a little time getting to know you." He smiled again. "And what it would mean if you didn't cooperate with your side of the bargain."

"She doesn't need to be involved in this." Jason rattled. It would break her heart if she knew about this now. "I just needed some money for bills."

"Easy Jason." He slid both of his hands into his front pockets. "I just thought it would be nice to get everyone together, reunion as you say here in America, no?

Jason didn't say anything.

"I just wanted to surprise you, my friend."

And then, suddenly, he was confused. What did the guy want?

Ricardo smiled again, teeth glistening. "Just want you to keep up our part of the bargain."

Jason was feeling dizzy, a grimness plagued his mouth. "I thought the arrangement was over?"

Perez reached down and tightened his belt. "Jason, we went through a lot of trouble to take care of you, mi amigo. This relationship is just starting to blossom." He turned to grab the door handle. "Adios, my friend. Will talk soon".

Reaching inside his shirt, Jason began to scratch himself. He hadn't shaved his body in three days, skin boiled like the time he had chicken pox. He needed time, but time was just a memory. A new dread was now flooding over him. His stomach was constricting. He looked into the urinal, into the sink. He washed his hands again and again, gathered phlegm to spit but couldn't. He tasted an acid in his mouth. He turned, opened a stall door, bent over. Sweat was working its way down his face. He leaned over and vomited, again and again. He didn't wash his hands before he left, just yanked open the door and took the stairs three steps at a time. He reached the top, a crowd of people huddled together watching something. There was a quiet, Jason stood unable to move. He'd have to admit his mind was occupied. He detected something was happening in the back of the room. He stepped to the side so he could see. It was the booth in the corner. People were standing around his booth. He pushed his way through the crowd, not even excusing himself. Reaching the table he could see a man touching his mother as she lay on her back in the booth. For several seconds Jason stood silently, his posture beginning to loosen. Everything moved in slow circles. There was an unearthly silence. He wanted to speak but couldn't. The man took his hands from his mother and eased to his feet, sluggish. He delayed for a second and turned, his face weary, spiritless. "I'm Dr. Ray Simpson. Are you're related?"

Jason yelled without hesitation or thought. "Of course. She's my mother."

"Has she been ill?"

"Cancer," he snapped. "Ovaries…Ovarian, yes."

The doctor nodded as if he knew a secret. "Radiation can cause problems with clotting and blood lipids. If that occurs," he took a breath, "there is a stronger chance of arrhythmia's and heart failure."

"Yeah, yeah….Will she be OK?"

The voice was reasonable but haunting; in the way the news anchor delivered the news. "I'm sorry…Your mother has died."

Chapter 40

A young heart may never grow old enough to mend. Jason Carson sat by himself on a metal folding chair in the basement chapel of Ahern Funeral Home in Oak Park, Illinois, examining the invoice for his mother's funeral. The director with the black pin stripe suit, red tie, and gold cufflinks told him to check it over; get back to him with any questions. He scanned the list; grave marker, hearse rental, death certificate fee, viewing fee, transportation, vault charge, burial shroud, what the heck was a burial shroud anyway? None of it made a lot of sense, and he didn't know what to do. He tugged on his collar. He was wearing a navy blue blazer he bought yesterday a few minutes before the mall closed; it felt two sizes too small. The cold seeped through his sport coat toward bone. The basement of the funeral home reeked of ammonia and metallic copper. Jason hadn't eaten in over three hours, his face so hot and red his skin burned. At that moment the funeral director, with slicked back hair and a face so tight it looked embalmed, glided over to Jason and sat down. The director's face uncomfortably close to Jason's. Smiling with teeth that looked like dentures, the director hummed," I think everything went well today. I'm so sorry for your loss, Jason."

Every time the guy spoke to Jason he used his name as if he was reading from a script. Jason didn't answer, he just watched people coming down the stairs with flowers, one after the other—white lilies, red roses, pink, white, and orange carnations, even a Hawkeye black and gold chrysanthemum.

The director handed Jason a small white box. "These are four gold filled teeth from your mother. We usually save them for the family since gold is a valuable asset."

Jason stared at the box as the air in the room went blue. The suffering had forced him to be silent and deliberate the last few hours. She was gone. She wasn't there anymore. Wasn't there to help him and show him and provide for him and be his best friend and she wouldn't be coming back again. There wasn't really a home to come back to, just that shit-hole of an apartment with its leaks and its sounds from those skeletal walls. But it was safe when she was there with him. Now he was on his own. Vacated. Isolated. Abandoned. He slid back into the seat and tried to breath. "OK."

Do you have any questions about the charges, son?"

He didn't have any idea where to begin, he just shook his head.

"The $8,100 was a nice savings by using the wooden casket and not having the body present during the visitation."

It was all Jason was able to think about the last few days; not having his mother's body present any longer. Just thinking about her being gone was torture enough, and now he had a monstrous bill to pay.

Loneliness could turn on its head instantly and Jason's had been spinning all day.

The director patted him on his shoulder and stood. "I'll give you some time to think. Please let me know if you need anything," his voice faint.

Jason glanced around the room but noticed nothing. He was exhausted. He fumbled in his pocket for his phone, turned it on. He went to his messages and played the last message his mother had left for him. "We'll see you soon. Can't wait to see my boy again. Keep the faith." Jason listened to it over and over. When would he get to see her again?" He peered at the phone as if staring could bring her back. He raised his forefinger to the screen, waited, then erased the message. He swallowed and dialed Ricardo Perez.

Chapter 41

The UH-60 Blackhawk buzzed thirty feet above the dark ground as Scott Reynolds straightened his helmet. Inside the chopper was hot and his goggles were beginning to fog. Just as they touched ground, Reynolds could see a car on fire and Mexican police surrounding the landing area at the ranch in Chihuahua. The light from the fire was a radical assault on his eyesight through his night vision goggles. The cement buildings surrounding the ranch had an unpolished emerald color through the goggles, giving him a feeling he was under water. Instead of landing, a Seal dropped from the chopper onto the ground from a fast rope. A man ran to the Seal and was instantly pulled up into the Blackhawk, which then bolted into the sky like a thunderbolt. Reynolds held on to the arms of his seat as the Blackhawk tilted forward.

After the chopper began to straighten, the new passenger sat down next to Reynolds, ran both hands through his wet hair. Guy Ferguson looked at Reynolds with triumphant eyes. He scratched the stubble on his cheek and finally splintered a tiny smile. "I thought this was going to be easy."

Reynolds shook his head. "You know better than all of us how dangerous the cartels can be."

Ferguson tilted his head and looked out the window. "I guess I just like the thrill of it."

"That and the money. What happened after the Mexican police arrived?"

"All hell broke loose. They shoot first and ask questions later. Probably two dozen dead. I had Guerrero with me the whole time."

"What happened?"

Ferguson looked back out the window and then at Reynolds. "He's dead."

Reynolds should have gone with Ferguson, but he hadn't been able to get there on time. Now he'd never get an answer out of the number two man in the Diablos cartel. "Shit. You didn't happen to get any info out of him?"

Ferguson's eyes got wide. "I tortured the son of bitch for over an hour."

"You were warned about that. You'll get your ass in trouble."

Ferguson grinned, "I broke four of his fingers and cut one of his hamstrings. He didn't like that one. Then I put my rifle down his throat until he confessed. Said they've been taking over casinos and shaving points with athletes, coaches, managers, officials."

"We needed him alive?"

"They would have killed him. They're masters of execution and torture."

"It sounds like you. How did he die?"

"I shot him in the head."

Chapter 42

Jason's mother would have wanted him in church. But Sunday morning's practice was a renewal for his spirit. With little sleep, Jason offered his best. His shot was falling, he was attacking the basket, and no one was able to stop him. He drove down the lane, dribbled behind his back, vaulted into the air, and as he glided he switched the ball from his left to right hand and throttled it through the net. His performance was a sacrament. The whistle blew and practice had ended as everyone walked to the bench.

"Nice take, J.C.," Coach Trammel said.

None of the other players said anything to him. No high fives or chest bumps again today.

Shaking the water off his wet curls, Jason reached for a towel and continued drying his hair. He shouldered on his Nike fleece sweatshirt as Pearl Jam's, "Better Man" pounded inside the locker room. He stepped into his black Jordan Superfly 4s and walked around the giant Hawkeye emblem in the center of the floor. Bad luck to step on the beloved mascot, he was told the first day of practice. He was famished but was apprehensive about eating too much because of the diarrhea that plagued him the last three days. He patted the tiger hawk on the wall, a daily ritual for all players, and slid out the frosted glass door into the hallway. Coach Trammell leaned against the banana colored wall in the tunnel, reading notes from practice.

"Jason, I need a second with you."

Jason stopped and slid his phone into the pocket of his shorts. He hardly ever wore sweats or long pants even when the weather turned cold. "Sure," he said.

Trammel was almost as tall as Jason, but he looked shorter because his shoulders had a permanent hunch and he only stood up straight when he yelled which, to Jason, seemed like every hour of the day. But now his glasses hung halfway down his nose and his eyes looked puffy and small. He scratched his oyster colored hair with swollen hands. "Just wanted to say how sorry I am about your mother again. If there's anything I can do, please don't hesitate to ask me."

Jason had heard the line dozens of times, but this one actually kind of meant something to him. "Thanks, coach."

"One of your best practices, today. Nice to see you bounce back, kid."

Jason had finally felt like he was in control again. "It's nice to be back." He was waiting for more praise.

"Thing is we have a bit of a problem," Coach Trammel said straightening with long slow movements. "Talked to Will Kemper, academic advisor on Friday. Told me that you currently have a D in Algebra. You failed your last test."

A soreness roused in his joints and spread. "I took it before I left. Hard to concentrate." Jason said.

"We're the first to know this stuff," he said in a whisper as a couple of players walked by.

"I've been kinda busy, out of the loop."

"Understandable, kid." He looked down for a second. "I spent an hour talking it over with the Prof. I told him I needed a big favor," he said kind of apprehensively. "After a butt load of pleading and begging, he said he'd let you take it over. Your situation and all." He puffed out his chest. "That and some damn good persuasion."

"OK, good I guess."

"You gotta understand this. This is a huge deal, Jason. Could fuck up our whole season. Your season," coach said bristling at the very thought of it. "Shit." He cracked a knuckle. "I need you to do everything I ask you to do. Everything."

Jason stared back.

"We got a tutor to spend as much time as you need to get this done. Dude'll be with you everywhere. He'll eat with you, sleep with you. You take a shit, this guy goes with you."

He knew what was expected of him, grades and all, but, seriously, he needed a break, his mother just died. He didn't know if he even had enough courage to go to class. "Don't know coach, so much is happening," he said tensely.

Trammell continued, "You don't understand what's riding on this. I mean, everything's riding on this, kid."

There's that kid thing again, Jason thought

"We need you, I need you, your team needs you."

Jason found that last one hard to believe. Nobody on the team seemed to give a damn about him.

Trammell narrowed his eyes. "Jason, you can't be ineligible next semester, you understand? It's that simple."

Jason had hardly dealt with school the last week. The lining of his stomach felt raw. A life long dream could take years to build and seconds to self-destruct. He didn't want to share his problems, but things had changed. "I have a reading problem coach. I really think I'm dyslexic."

"You think? Holy shit. When did you figure this out?"

Jason shrugged. "Don't know. I've never been tested."

Trammell's eyes went wide as he straightened. "Good god. How'd the hell did you get through school?"

"Teachers kind of liked me. Other kids would do my papers. Stuff like that."

"Greatness comes with privileges but heavy burdens as well."

Jason didn't respond.

"Then we'll get you tested ASAP. I'll have someone contact all of your professors so they'll give you more time on tests, more tutors, the whole ball of wax."

Trammell placed a hand on his shoulder, something a male hadn't done this in years. Men were, by his definition, untrustworthy, but Coach Trammell's hand was not an act of aggression; it was thoughtful, honest, awkward and wonderful at the same time.

Jason's jaw tightened and his lips went hard. Emotion began to overtake him. He began to sob and Coach Trammell moved in and hugged him with force. Something inside Jason, something that had been dormant for years shook his body. He hadn't shed a tear since his mother was taken. And now, for a moment he seemed embarrassed, or was it a bit of shame? Whatever it was he was back and he needed to reserve himself and dominate. Take control. The moment of oasis was gone. He backed away from Coach Trammell and wiped his face with his shirtsleeves, laughing a bit now, ashamed even. He cleared his throat.

Trammell gave Jason a faint grin, "You can take the test at the end of the week. I know you'll do better with more time."

Jason forced himself to look at Coach Trammell now. "I'll prove it to you."

A few hours after meeting with Coach Trammel, Jason walked into his dorm room after studying at the Gerdin Learning Center. He was mentally tired after working with his tutor, who resembled E.T. and had a neck the size of a number two pencil. After an hour and a half, E.T made Jason read four pages in his Humanities book and it didn't work out well. Jason mispronounced the words poignant, phenomenon, meticulous, and debris on the first two pages. E.T. told him to take a break, that he was probably tired from his mother's funeral.

His head pounding, Jason headed back to the dorm. When he walked into his room it was like an electronics convention. Matt Conway sat glaring at his iPad, his friend David Frost was working a hand joist as he used the Playstation on his 15 inch portable HD Sony TV. Three laptops, all showing football games were scattered across the desk, the 70 inch curved 4K TV split-screen was showing two games and Lynyrd Skynyrd's "Freebird" was sucking out through four Bose Companion 2 Series 3 speakers.

He took out his ear buds and tossed his backpack on top of his bed. Hoping to clear his head. He dropped to the floor and cranked out fifty pushups. He could smell the rancid odor of the spittoon. He pushed the thing away from him, a vinegary smell, trying not to gag.

As he turned to his side, pressing into a plank he looked up. Mike Conway and Brandon sat on the couch watching the Oakland Raiders vs Kansas City Chiefs football game. All eyes glued to the television.

"Did my shoes get here today?" Jason yelled.

"It's Sunday douche bag, no mail today," Brandon said, without taking his eyes from the screen.

Conway leaned over the couch. "Didn't you get some new kicks last week?"

Jason rolled to his other side, grunted. "Titanium XX3s."

Brandon howled, "I like the triple X myself, baby." Conway and Brandon high fived. Brandon reached over the coffee table and fisted a green Heineken bottle, shook it, noticed it was empty and put it next to three others and grabbed another, took a monster gulp.

"I'm waiting for the Slam 100's. Found them on Ebay." Jason moved to his back, working sit-ups now.

Brandon turned up the sound of the television as he turned down the music. The Oakland Raider's quarterback rifled a thirty yard pass for a completion to the Chiefs ten yard line. "Shit," Brandon yelled, then slapped the couch with his palm.

"Who you betting on in this one?" Jason asked.

"Damn Chiefs are two and a half point faves and they're up two field goals and now this crap," Brandon said as he pointed a bandaged hand at the screen.

Jason looked at the hand. "What happened to you, Mongo?"

Conway laughed and shook his head. Brandon delivered a punch to Conway's chest with his good hand.

Conway twisted his head in Jason's direction. "Mongo had a UDI last night outside of Brothers…Unidentified Drinking Injury. He was—"

Brandon interrupted while he raised his bandaged hand. "Wasn't no drinking injury ass wipe. Some fat tub of goo stepped on my hand after I fell walking out of Brothers."

Jason cracked a smile. He needed a thousand sit-ups today to stay on track. He hadn't done many since the funeral and it bugged him. "Why'd he fall, Mikey? Drink too much silly juice?"

Brandon straightened in his seat. "No way, I got pushed over by a Mr. Man Boobs and then he stampeded me with his elephant feet."

Conway shook his head. "Should have seen the guy's legs. Dumbo's club feet were massive. Thought Barnum and Bailey were in town."

"I watched tape until 10:30 last night," Jason wheezed back. He looked over at the desk in the room. An iPad and laptop had two different football games.

Brandon put his palms over his eyes. "Can't watch this bull-shit any longer." He stood and moved in front of the laptop, blew out air and sighed. "Hope you studied for me, J.C., I got a test on Tuesday. This Paper Dolly is letting me look at her answers for fifty bone. Sweet deal uh?"

Jason didn't respond. He closed his eyes and worked on his crunches as the dirt and sand from the carpet scratched the back of his neck. As he patted his six pack, he could smell sour beer. He hated to work-out on this nasty floor.

Brandon leaned over and spit a long string of brown saliva into the spittoon lying on the green carpeting. His iPhone began to ping. He placed it next to his ear. "I know they're favored, but the Chiefs aren't lookin' great today." He listened. "Yea, yea…you just need to chillax. Take a relaxitive. The Cowgirls are still up ten and we'll probably hit the over under on that one at least." There was a long pause as they listened to the announcer reviewing the one- handed catch in the back of the end zone. "I'll call the boys in Reno and we can cancel our bets for the monday night game. Patriots are a lock I tell ya and I can play both sides of that line." He stood and paced around the room. "OK, I'm out." Brandon shoved the phone into his front pocket.

The room went quiet. Brandon was on top of the world, the happiest man alive, or ready to jump in front of a moving train from all his bets. For some reason, Jason was captivated by the guy. Listening to Brandon tell him how easy he could make money on a game always mesmerized him. The guy could convince anyone the world would end tomorrow or that you should buy a certain car today because there wouldn't be any cars on the planet tomorrow if you waited. He was better than a Sunday morning TV preacher convincing you to send them money. Brandon could convince Eskimos to buy ice cubes.

Jason tried to change the mood in the room though. "Where we eatin'?"

"My pick tonight," Conway answered. "Pizza Ranch, all-you-can-eat sounds like the best deal in town."

"Aren't you supposed to be watchin your weight Mikey?" asked Jason.

Conway paused, crossed his feet on the table in front of the sagging couch. "I didn't make the wrestle-off yesterday. I have to take a red shirt this year because I didn't make the top three," he muttered, then grunted. Not looking pleased or upset.

Jason never understood not being able to make a team. It was up to the individual. He could feel his abdomen tightening, rib cage screaming at him. "Sorry to hear Mikey. You'll be back, come on down here with me," Jason said lifting his legs in the air, "do some leg lifts."

Brandon turned to Jason. "Just more time for Mikey to hang with me J.C., since you ain't been around much. How 'bout tonight J.C.? Two for ones at the Airliner?"

"I got more studyin to do," he answered.

"Holy shit," Brandon snapped. "This ain't M.I.T. Next year you'll have a handful of babes feedin' you grapes, fanin' your ass, and reading to you from sweet smelling candles. You lookin' to make the dean's list and jump school after one year. What's the point?"

"No way babe. Going back to the Gerdin Center tonight for a reason." He glanced around the room, nodding his head, confidence filling him. "Not that I really want to look at books or anything." The three in the room looked at each other. "No boys," he sat up. "I'm studying some female biology. It's gonna be Babe 101 for me tonight...I'm doing a little work with Krista Garrison tonight; listen and weep," Jason said with a big grin.

"Say what," snapped Mike Conway. "THE Krista Garrison? The one we talked to in the Carver elevator? B-Ball player Krista Garrison?"

Jason clasped hands behind his head, pulled knees toward opposite elbows, howling. "You got it."

"How'd that happen?"

Jason didn't want them to know that he asked his tutor to work it out with Krista's tutor. Told him that he would get his parents some good tickets for a Big Ten game. Nonetheless it worked out for him. "Um, just got the touch boys," he piped back.

"That's ass-tastic, J.C. You're the man. She's one great piece of eye candy, you got game my man, way to go."

Brandon threw back his head. "Maybe you'll need to see if she wants to play a little one-on-one?"

Mike Conway stretched. "I wanna know the odds on that one, Mongo."

Chapter 43

The four inches of snow that had fallen in Minneapolis was a common sight for those in the land of ten thousand lakes. Most Minnesotans were happy to see the snow cover the landscape since the state bird, the mosquito, would fly south for the winter. But Tim McMurray was leaving as well. He finished packing his suitcase to travel to Orlando for the Magic vs. Seventy-Sixers game tomorrow evening. Tim was relieved that the official's lockout had been resolved. He'd be getting a check again. His wife would be getting a check again. The new agreement gave Tim and his brethren a five percent increase and a guaranteed pension that would begin at age fifty-nine for any referee that worked five years or longer and paid a higher percentage for every additional year worked. At the moment, Tim wasn't concerned about his retirement. He needed cash in the short term. Retirement felt centuries away. Writing an alimony check to his wife along with child support didn't leave much left for himself. One look at his monthly statement could give anyone a good case of depression. But Tim always seemed to come up with an answer. He stocked his daub kit with his favorite colognes that helped lure the ladies; one of the weapons from his arsenal. But the most powerful weapon was cash, always popular with the opposite sex. He stared at himself in the mirror, ran a hand over his hair that was sticking up on the back of his head. He was one of those guys that looked in the mirror more than your average Joe. Quite a bit more. He had a face that most men just wanted to punch. The puffed cheeks, cocky jaw, and look of entitlement made just about every male on the planet dislike him. It was a great asset for an official. Only thing was, Tim McMurray loved himself. He moved to his bathroom closet where he grabbed a bottle of cologne. McMurray had more bottles of cologne then books. He opened the cap and slathered his chest and neck with Obsession for Men. He couldn't stop. He put some of the fragrance behind his ears and finally spritzed his stomach. He admired himself in the mirror. His cell phone beeped in the bedroom. He jogged over to his card table desk and pushed the green button.

He heard, "Mr. McMurray," recognizing the deep slow voice. Tim could feel the hair on his arms begin to straighten.

"Hace Frio o no hace fio hoy?"

McMurray had taken a year of Spanish at the University of Minnesota. "Hace Frio hoy," Tim replied.

"How do you put up with that cold, McMurray."

"Not really my choice."

"You need to make better choices. Now that you're back to work we need better results."

There was a pause. "I've given you as much as I can," he said.

There was a laugh, but it sounded mysterious, harsh. "We're not happy. Too many mistakes. Too much money lost."

"The circumstances only allow me to do so much, Ricardo."

"Bullshit. We give you the over under, the spread we need, and a player in each game that doesn't' cover. Jefferson from the Pistons played almost the entire game. Yet only 2 fouls?"

196

It was hard for Tim to keep up with all of it. Call the game, watch the score, the total number of points the points per player. "Can't we just work on one thing each game?"

"We need two out of three. That's how it works. That's what we want…or else things will get ugly."

Tim had a feeling what that meant. What happened to Cara certainly was no accident, was it? It was a wakeup call. He glanced at himself in the mirror. It was what he did when he needed confidence, but there was no confidence this time. Puffiness under his eyes, old man bags they called it. A single deep ebony line above the bags that highlighted his baby blues like a cavernous bull's eye. He needed to drink more fluids, use the line eraser eye gel twice a day. "It's not easier when you take away my friends. Police keep asking questions?"

"Maybe it's the company you keep? We need to win. Nothing else matters."

"I'm doing my best."

"Not good enough."

"For some reason I don't seem to believe that," he wished he wouldn't have said that.

"Tsk, tsk Mr. McMurray. Everything may not work out between us. We may need to ask for a trade. Kick your ass to the curb as they say here in Los Estados Unidos."

"For god's sakes, thought I was playing by the rules, those last games I called were tough," he said in a louder voice.

There was a long pause.

Ricardo started again. "The cold in Minnesota must have moved to your heart."

"My kids are here. That's why I stay." That and he couldn't afford a place in the sun. Not yet that is.

"I prefer the beaches and the warm sand myself," he said with that razzle-dazzle voice of his.

There was still the threat, but the tone had changed in his voice. How quickly it could change, but Tim was used to the game as if he was talking to a coach. But he was still startled by the call. The adrenaline mixed badly with the self-pity he was feeling about his bank account, not to mention the death of Cara. The combination of emotions was making him sick to his stomach.

"I've been reading about your new deal. Unions never seem to be able to hold out anymore."

"I'm a Union man."

Ricardo chuckled. "Unions have that threat of cheaper and smarter talent competing from other countries…like Mexico."

At first Tim knew it was demeaning and pathetic to think of belonging to a union; being captive to the direction of someone else. What man would ever let that happen? And he felt a miserable contempt. "Sounds like you're a strong supporter of free trade?

"Everyone wants a piece of that freedom, and capitalism is a big draw for foreigners like us."

McMurray didn't respond. He suddenly felt trapped, confined, again. It happened that quickly.

"We think Americans have gotten too fat and happy and don't want to work too hard anymore." He paused, "but we can't let that happen to you, Señor."

"Don't worry 'bout me. I'll be working until the next millennium."

"Maybe we can help you with that."

"Hmm."

"I also see you're going to Orlando and Miami this week, amigo," said Ricardo.

How did he know where he was going? Referee names were confidential for upcoming games. The NBA and department officials were the only ones holding that information. "Yes, Ricardo…I'm looking forward to a little sun on my pale body," McMurray said as he looked at the color of his arm; he hadn't been to the tanning booth in over two weeks.

"I think you're just interested in looking at the leetle bikinis my friend."

McMurray tried not to smile. Honestly, he adored all types of bikinis. He loved the original string, g-string, and classic halter-top; however, the lure of the micro, mini-micro and teardrop would also get his Minnesota blood moving. But the bikinis that would always bring tears to the eyes of Tim McMurray were the Tankini, Bandini, and the famous no-top, Monokini.

McMurray fired, "Once I told one of my buddies during my divorce proceedings, that the only woman I would now consider marrying was a woman who could pull her bikini through her wedding ring." McMurray could almost picture Ricardo smiling over the phone. "I prefer the nude beaches in Miami, Ricardo."

"Sounds like a nice plan. But those beaches are quite expensive. We have a proposition for you Timmy." His voice suddenly changed, now a bit sharper, even deeper. "The Miami game is intriguing to us right now. We think this would work easily for you and make both of us a pretty peso?"

Tim stood from the edge of his bed and sauntered around his makeshift desk. Fear began to seep in, but he knew he could use the money. "The peso doesn't go very far lately. Maybe we could work out a better exchange rate?"

"Same arrangement as before, until you perform."

Tim had been waiting for a better cut, more take on the big wins. "No more pesos I hope."

"We handle it any way you want now. Cash, checks, money orders, direct deposit, frequent flyer miles. We own banks. It helps doing the many loads of laundering we do, amigo."

"OK," he said, trying his best to stay rational.

"Bien…we will talk closer to game time. We'll wait for the injury report. I'll call then."

"Fine."

"Hope you pack your Speedo, Mr. McMurray."

Chapter 44

"Hope is a waking dream."—Aristotle

Jason took a few dribbles, a breath, flipped his wrist, held the follow through, and watched the ball sail through the net. He pointed to the heavens. Same routine every time. Repetition. Fifty in a row. Routine was a drug to him. He tossed the ball in the basket at Carver-Hawkeye Arena and jogged off the court.

"What up, Lo-Dog," Jason whispered as he walked past Nick Logan, a guard on the basketball team. Logan was seated at a round table on the lower level of the Gerdin Learning Center, looking like he should be studying. Logan's head bounced up with every new person entering the room. He looked at his phone. Athletic representatives made the rounds in the learning center to see how many athletes were in attendance. They also charted the number of hours that athletes were in the building. Nick Logan pointed to the Sport Illustrated that he was reading. "You see where they have us dude? Ranked third."

Jason didn't have time to talk, he was in a hurry. He gave Logan a thumbs up and jogged up the stairs taking two steps at a time. The arch on his left foot was inflamed. Dr. Fox had made him a new set of orthotics; hopefully it would help. He was late again. His mother always told him it was rude to be late. Etiquette was big in the Carson family: be on time, say please and thank you, treat others with respect, don't scratch your privates in public; the list was endless. He reached the top of the stairs. The second level was quiet. He could hear the faint sound of a copy machine running nearby. He slowed his walk, searching. His heart started to move faster, not from the run up the stairs, but from the anticipation. It was the way he felt before a game. He hadn't made a good first impression, but now he had a second chance. Jason's previous relationships with women hadn't lasted long. Perhaps that's what happened in relationships after awhile. They burned like a fire. Produced waves of heat and energy. Then after the flames subsided, the coals just burned themselves out; extinguished, up in smoke. He spotted Krista in one of the study rooms on the other side of the floor. His mouth went dry. He cracked the knuckles on his left hand. He moved slowly. He tapped on the door frame.

She glanced up from her book. "Come on in," she said," with a perplexed look on her face.

"Hey," he said shouldering off his backpack, placing it on one of the chairs. The entire table was already covered with books, three ring binders, note pads, a calculator, pencils, and a water bottle. What the heck was all of this? "Hope I'm not late."

"No worries. I needed to work on my accounting, so I got here a couple of hours ago." She pointed to a thick Cost Accounting book on the other end of the table.

Jason stared. "That thing's gynormous."

Krista gave him a crooked smile. "Just part of it, ya know."

But he didn't really know.

Krista fiddled with her pencil as she seemed to be reaching for the right words. "How you getting along?"

Jason didn't know if he remembered the question. Krista's low raspy voice had already lulled him. "Um…it's different than high school. Didn't do much studyin' `til now," he said, looking away, afraid he might get lost in those blue eyes.

She nodded. "I know the scenario. Big time player, teachers let him slide when the heavy class lifting had to be done. Teachers love having the big jock in their classrooms and they just about do your homework…am I right?" she asked and punched his arm.

He shrugged. "Maybe some of us didn't need to study too much," he said and gave her a half smile. His foot fidgeted under the table.

"Cockiness again."

It was the way he attacked everything. Confidence. "Just a positive attitude."

"Bit of an ego." She raised an eyebrow. "Heard that about you."

"I appreciate you checking up on me."

"Don't break your arm patting yourself on the back. We ladies have to check up on all men these days. We can't trust `em half the time."

He nodded. "Sorry, must have had some bad experiences?"

She shot back. "I'm sure yours have all been good."

He wondered for a moment if this was such a good idea after all. "Nice one."

They looked at each other for a few moments. She batted her colossal eyelashes at him, a tranquilizing narcotic. "Have you thought about a major?"

"I'm not declaring. Going pro after a year."

"You are full of the confidence, aren't you?"

"It's just the plan, that's all. Need to stick to the plan."

She nodded. " She reached over and wrenched out her sociology book out of her backpack. "So my plan is to do a little studying so I can get good grades and find a great job…The WNBA jobs don't pay as well as the men.

He sat back in his seat. "I guess."

"I guess? That's it? So this is a little weird for you…going to school and not having to be too serious about it?"

Jason pulled out his book and notebook from his backpack and placed it next to Krista's. "My mother wanted me to get a college degree, so I want to remember her. Remember her wishes."

Krista tilted her head back and widened her eyes. She studied him for a moment. "Remember. Did something happen to her?" Krista asked.

Jason felt a tug in his chest, a deeper shift of angst working through him. "She passed away last week," he whispered.

Krista sat back in her seat not knowing what to do. A tenderness transposed across her face, indigo blue eyes radiant and warming. She pushed away a strand of blonde hair. She reached out her hand to touch him but pulled it back. For the next few seconds they sat quietly.

Realizing her uneasiness, Jason moved slightly closer. "Sorry for bringing it up. Seems like I talk about it too much," he murmured, even though he had hardly spoken of it since he returned.

"Wow. Sorry. I'm so sorry. I didn't mean, I didn't know."

"You wouldn't. I asked coaches to make sure it wasn't on social media. Keep it as private as possible. That's the way I want it. Private, that is."

Krista rubbed the drip from her nose with the back of her hand. "OK, I won't talk about it then. Sorry."

A librarian pushed a squawky book cart by the study room's glass door. A siren howled in the distance. Jason pulled out his Gatorade water bottle from his backpack and took a drink. He reached back into his bag and pulled out his Sociology book.

"So how do you plan on graduating if you leave after a year?"

"Summer classes. Something like that. She made me promise."

"What are you going to study?"

"Brain surgery," he replied.

The two of them laughed, breaking the tension. They both took another drink and opened their books.

Krista ran her tongue over her front teeth. "That's very noble of you. Most guys aren't interested in learning and making themselves better. They're usually just in it for the almighty dollar."

"Not my experience...sounds more like a female trait to me?"

"Cute, let the battle of the sexes begin. We'll see who gets the highest grade in Sociology," she answered without hesitation. Blinking her eyes as she thumbed through the pages, "Can you read the study questions at the end of Chapter 2?"

He leaned back in his seat and frowned. "Thought you were going to help with this?"

"My contacts are killing me," she said squinting at him. "Page 32, go ahead."

Jason looked out the window. He could feel the heat ramping up inside the room. His feet jiggled under the table as he leaned toward the open book. He was quiet for a moment as he placed his finger on the page, the words scrambled. He took a long breath through his mouth. "Number 1. Stanley Milgran used the word con...conform... conformity to mean?"

"Going along with peers." His voice moving softer, "Comp. Complee. Comply. Compliance with Authors." He gave a quick shake of the head. "Authorities in a Higher...High-arch," he had a chilled numbness run over his skin. He stared at the word, all the words twitched in front of him. He pressed his finger harder on the page. He closed his eyes for a moment wishing the words would come to him. "Hierarchical. A hierarchical structure." Without hesitation or thought, he grabbed his water bottle and squeezed it. A gust sprayed from the top of the bottle splattering onto Krista's face. Blinking, she wiped the liquid from her forehead and shook her head as if she was a wet dog.

Jason paid no attention, glared at the page in front of him, complete concentration.

"Teach. Technical...Techniques for preventing dev..." He lowered himself in his seat, felt himself vanish, get so small he wanted to disappear.

Krista leaned over and looked at the book, still blinking. She read, "Deviant human behavior in any society." She raised her head, fascinated with him. "You're probably stressed. Sorry. I'll take over," she said as she twisted the book around so she could read it. "I'm sure you're struggling with everything that's happened to you. I can read them."

Jason had held out hope that something would save him. There was a helplessness that refused to leave him but it wasn't just his reading. Over the years he was able to read two or three words in a sentence and still comprehend the entire sentence, but he hated to read out loud. He always had to wait for someone to bail him out. He pinched his eyes with his thumb and forefinger, slumped in his seat. "I haven't slept in days, haven't been doing extra workouts, I'm behind in class work, my shot's off." He rubbed his wrist on his thigh, scratched the side of his face as he tapped his foot. He picked up the water bottle, strangling it with two hands as he took a long drink, repeated it again. He looked at Krista and let the silence grow. What was happening to him? He needed his life back, but things were definitely different now.

Krista stared at him, but it was soothing just the same, the quality of her smile was peculiar: it reminded him of his mother for an instant. She was barely touching the sides of her cheeks, her wet lips separated. Her face frail in her hands. She took the book from him and straightened. "We need to get you back on track. Let's start with studies."

It wasn't what he usually wanted to hear, but he needed help and he listened. They spent the next ninety minutes reviewing as if nothing had happened. But worry began to invade his bones. Jason's eyes began to glaze over after Krista asked him if he was up for another thirty minutes. It was almost as if he enjoyed the punishment of going over information he would never use again. But it occurred to him, sometime during the evening, that he just liked being around her. He never had anyone that he could talk to, at least no one his own age. Most kids growing up just played on their Playstations or texted their girlfriends about where they'd be eating pizza on Saturday night. He didn't live the life of a normal high school student, and now, college kid. He was expected to perform. He was expected to bring a national championship to the University of Iowa. He was expected, at the tender age of nineteen, to make commercials, be a role model for thousands of kids and handle all of it even though most nineteen year olds were still mooching off their parents and trying to decide what type of phone they should buy.

Jason checked his watch; 9:55PM He rubbed his eyes with the palms of his hands. "This is normally the time when I go to the gym and get in my two hundred free throws, then do my ball handing drills."

Krista lifted her eyes from her book, nodded at Jason. "I love shooting free throws." She straightened in her chair. "Didn't think guys ever really learned how to shoot…thought it was just a muscle game for you boys. Should call it men's wrestling now, instead of basketball," she said as she let the words slowly trail off.

Jason found he was watching her more as the evening progressed. "Why don't we go over to the practice gym and see about that," he said.

"Test isn't until 10:00 tomorrow, guess we have time. Like to see if you can keep up with me at the charity stripe, J.C. …that's what the boys call you, isn't it?"

His lips got caught between a hopeless smile and a ray of confusion. Only a few people knew his new college name. Maybe Krista Garrison was interested in him; more interested than just a study partner. "Yeah. My roommate started that." He placed both of his hands on the table as if trying to hold it from floating off the ground. His mouth went dry, he swallowed hard. "As for the test, I really don't like tests too much."

"Maybe I can help you focus a little better. I'll start with those free throws…you can watch and learn," she smiled and stood, stuffing books into her backpack.

"You don't seem to understand, I don't miss free throws."

She tapped her fingers together. "Good, I don't miss 'em either.

Fifteen minutes later, Jason slipped his hand over the entry pad at Carver-Hawkeye Arena's practice gym. He opened the door for Krista. It was dark. Jason turned on the four light switches; two ceiling fans began to swat stale air around the two practice courts. The giant fluorescents slowly began to glow, throwing light upon the two athletes like a sunrise. It was quiet except for a small exhaust fan that hummed overhead. Each had stopped at their locker rooms to get their shoes. Krista looked at Jason cradling his shoes with both hands. "You boys treat your shoes like they're babies. I bet some of you guys even sleep with them."

He kissed his shoes and cradled them. "My shoes and I have a great love affair. It's a romance made in heaven."

Krista giggled. "I hope I get invited to the wedding."

"It'll be a Mormon wedding. Long ceremony since I have over a hundred pairs. Jason loosened the laces and sat down, took his coat and sweatshirt off. He petted his shoes, gave her a big grin. "These precious wonders help me soar through the air and play astronaut. Nikes play a big part in Jordan's slam dunk portfolio…need to take good care of em."

Krista sat down on the bench next to him and tossed her shoes on the floor, slipped off her jacket. "You boys always think it's the equipment that helps make you better. All guys do is watch commercials all day and think they need the new shoe or the sports drink and it'll make them better." She took off her sweatpants slowly and Jason found his eyes back on her again. Oh she was striking, certainly not in the way of other women, but the firmness of her quads, the contour of her hamstrings. Athletic. Designed and constructed with pleasure in mind. But he needed to stay in control. "Shoes make the man, I like to say."

She laughed. "Must revert back to the caveman days when the new club could kill more animals." She giggled to herself. "I see it now. Provide more food for the family with the new and Improved Nike Cave-Club...bet the swoosh was on all the walls back then.

"Lots a chatter. Sounds like you're tryin' to waste time here. Delaying our contest." Jason stood, grabbed a ball from the closet and dribbled it to the free throw line.

Krista picked up a ball. "Men can't just play for the fun of it...always a competition. But it doesn't mean I'm not up for it, big fella."

"I just want action...maybe a little less talk." He fired a shot from the line and rattled the back and then front of the rim, then it dropped in. "Looks like I'm one for one."

"Shoot your twenty five then I'll take over," she said as she dribbled twice between her legs and tucked it under her arm.

Jason shot twenty four more, making twenty three of them. He usually didn't miss, but number seventeen didn't come out of his hand just right, probably because he wasn't able to concentrate. He reached for the ball and sat down on the bench under the basket to watch Krista. "I normally never miss. Give you a big chance, sister," he said.

"Thanks for the chivalry, Mr. Carson. Didn't you ever learn that ladies go first? But no worries, best is yet to come." She walked over to the line and Jason couldn't hear a thing. Of course, even in a tight game with fans screaming at him as he stood at the free throw line he never heard anything. Just the sound of the ball splashing through the net. He now just watched. He watched as she drained one after another; never missing, twenty five in a row. He sat on the edge of the bench in disbelief. He had never been beaten by a female. He normally shot hundreds of free throws without missing but this time something had gotten into his way. "Gave you that one to get your confidence up… now lets have a 3-point contest. I'll let you start this time so I know how hard to try."

"Nice sportsmanship, I might add. Hope you do better than I do on the test tomorrow," she grinned, widening her eyes. "Or are you going to need to sit by me for that one too? Show you how it's done."

"I'll do the schoolin' here, showtime now," he said as he took off his shirt and threw it to the sidelines.

To his surprise Krista followed suit. She walked over to the end line and took off her yellow t-shirt; now only wearing a fluorescent pineapple sports bra with black shorts. Jason stopped dribbling the ball for a moment. He watched as she pulled out her iPhone, walked over and placed it into a cradle on the scorer's table and turned up the volume. "Ready For It" by Taylor Swift, pumped through the overhead speakers. Jason tried to keep his bearings as Krista walked up to him, put a hand on his stomach. "How 'bout a little one on one? We already know who the best shooter is here."

Jason was a bit startled, took a long time to answer. "You want to play one on one with me?" he asked, bewildered.

"I most certainly do big boy. You're not going to tell me you need to get home now are you? Specially after you already took a lickin'," she said slowly licking her lips.

He always had a craving to play one on one with the boys, but he hadn't played against a female since he was in junior high. He looked up at the ceiling. The blades whirling from the big ass fans looked as if they were moving faster but his body wasn't cooling down. He looked into her eyes, they were a bawdy blue. She had a look as if she knew a secret. Looking into her eyes was like unwrapping a present. He ran his fingertips lightly over the ridges of the ball, the rough small bumps of the leather tickling his fingertips. He began to dribble the ball, move his feet. Krista moved her feet in tune with his, now pushing harder against his six pack abs. He wanted to keep playing. He lowered his shoulder and moved left then flashed to the right. Krista guarded like a cat, staying up with every move. She pressed her body hard against his bicep. He usually liked a physical game but this just puzzled him. He swung his back to the basket, continued the dribble. She leaned in and he felt the nylon of her sports bra slide along his back. He swung his head and looked at her. He was infatuated by her, by her decisiveness, let alone her aggressiveness. He wasn't exactly surprised to see her face looking completely serious, her electric blue eyes intense. She moved closer; thrust her hips into his thigh, let out a purr. His lips were parched, his eyes soggy, a bit blurred. He blinked it away. He had watched Krista practicing in the gym as he waited to begin practice, but he had never seen her looking so beautiful. With the beat of his heart skipping in his neck, he slowly moved forward with a hop step. Krista leaned harder against him now and moved her hand up his chest. He was perspiring. He took his free hand and pushed back on her shoulder. He spun his body quickly and headed for the hoop, one of his favorite moves. He laid the ball off the glass for two. The ball bounced on the floor as the two just looked at each other for a moment. Krista nodded, clapped, and grabbed the ball from the floor. He was watching her again. Krista pranced to the top of the key and began to dribble from one hand to the other. She bent at the waist and waited, looking like a bull ready to charge. "Let's go…my turn now." He jogged over and stood in front of her. He waited. She continued to dribble and swayed her shoulders from side to side.

"That's how you're going to guard me?"

A litany of options ran through his head. He let out a deep breath.

"Always heard men didn't play any defense." Her tongue wiggled in the corner of her mouth, lips swollen and succulent. "I learned from John Wooden, belly button defense."

Jason could tell, she really wanted to play. "I've got you covered, let's go."

She sneered at him, took two steps forward, then a step back and fired a shot over his head. The ball flapped through the net. "Boom. Nice D, J.C."

"Nice step back," he said.

She jogged to the ball and threw it at him, harder than usual.

He whipped the ball around his waist, twice. Krista scurried up to him instantly, this time two hands on him. One on his stomach, the other on his right hip. He started to dribble. He felt her left hand tighten on his hip, her other slid up his chest, then back down. He kept dribbling but didn't move. Krista leaned forward, pressing hard against his side. He heard her growl. Her head was now directly under his chin, her hair a clump of strawberry balm. He slowed his dribble and slowly leaned into her. Krista raised her head and stared back into his eyes. His vision clouded for a second. Her eyes flaming with desire They breathed in and out in rhythm together. She slid her hand to the back of his shorts, then back to his hip. She ran a finger inside his waistband and jabbed a fingernail into his lower back and dragged it to the top of his buttocks. He stopped dribbling, as the ball slowly bounced away. Jason didn't know how to react, a litany of possibilities hung over him. His mother and the pastor told him these types of feelings were sinful.

He needed to be careful, but instinct now tugging at him. He reached down, grabbed her chin, lowered his head and put his mouth on hers, her lips moving, his fingers journeyed through her thick hair. He pulled away for a moment, then kissed her again, this time harder.

Krista squinted at him, then lightly pushed away. She took a slow step back and lowered her eyes. Jason stood and watched, confused. "What's the problem?" he asked.

She shook her head, looked up at him. "Just not ready for this... sorry." Her chest gave a slight hitch. She wiped her nose with her forearm. He could see tears beginning to swell in her eyes. "I can't have things happen this quickly." She shook her head again, patted her cheeks.

Jason took a step forward. Krista raised a hand.

Perplexed he said, "Didn't look like you wanted things to move slowly a minute ago?"

She was breathing faster now. She nodded quickly. "I get really intense at everything I do. Like the competition, gets me worked up. Sometimes can't handle the emotions." Some of what she said was blurred by tears but he thought he understood most of it.

"I shouldn't have.....'spose to control myself. You just don't understand...I want to..." Her face now scarlet, she was holding her breath.

Jason hadn't been able to control himself and she was the one to call things off. "Listen...I'd like to try this again. Try it again soon. Next time we'll take it slower."

She shrugged her shoulders. "Maybe. I don't know." She said biting her top lip.

They looked at each other for a moment. Damn, he liked her. He liked smelling her; sure liked the way she stood up for herself and she was beautiful to beat. With his confidence waning, a wave of anxiety spread through him as he tried to come up with his next move. But he wouldn't have a chance. Krista ran to the bench, heaved on her shirt, grabbed her iPhone, threw her pack over her shoulder and ran out of the gym.

Ten minutes later, Jason quietly opened the door to his dorm room, not wanting to awaken his roommate. The television was on, but the room was dark. Brandon was lying in his lofted bed, watching SportsCenter. "What up, Bro?" Brandon asked, his voice deep and soft.

"Studying."

"12:40 in the morning. What were you studyin' this late?" His words ran together, slowly. "Let me guess…my favorite subject, anatomy?" He laughed to himself, then burped.

"Krista Garrison's making me work my butt off for this class. Probably good for me."

"Ha, only thing good for you is that bootylicious Krista. She's one sweet piece of hottie…you lucky bastard, you." Jason could barely understand the words sliding around Brandon's mouth.

"Sounds like you had a big time tonight? Too bad I missed out."

"Boys and I ruled tonight. Had to come back a little early to check on some games though.

"Can we turn off the tube now? Got a test tomorrow."

Brandon lifted the remote, turned off the TV

"Just do one thing for me, J.C."

"What's that, Mongo," he said as he shouldered off his shirt.

"Next time you see that Krista babe…I'd make sure I'd bite her in the ass and then pray for lockjaw." Seconds later he began to snore.

Chapter 45

The November sky in Washington D.C. was heaped with bland clouds. The temperature was forty-one degrees. Cherry trees waited in hibernation. A white Yukon SUV moved past the entrance to the Ronald Reagan National Airport and traveled a mile and a half east to a double gated entrance to the United States Air Force base. The driver rolled down the dark window, waved a palm in front of a security box. Two marines dressed in camouflage approached the vehicle. Each Marine had a Heckler and Koch MP5 9 mm sub-machine gun draped over his shoulder. One of the men spoke to the driver and nodded. The two iron gates slid open and the Yukon drove through and turned towards the third hanger on the right. The door instantly opened, and the Yukon pulled inside, doors closing behind it. All doors of the Yukon opened. Scott Reynolds grabbed his briefcase, black bag, and waited for Ron Lamb to follow him out of the vehicle. Lamb crawled out, pinching his nose, then began to cough into a balled-up handkerchief. Scott Reynolds looked at the white floor and pulled a heel back trying to make a mark but couldn't. He raised his eyes and looked throughout the large space. Metal fans on the ceiling, but everything else was white. Not only white, Reynolds noticed, but almost a sterile white he told himself. Hell, this place could put a hospital to shame. Disinfected and decontaminated. This is the way people ought to live he told himself. Germs, viruses, bacteria sent away to Guantanamo Bay. Reynolds loved the smell of antiseptic perfuming the air. Ron Lamb walked over to him. "Bet you love this joint, Mr. Germ Freak."

"I wish my office was in here. I wouldn't need to keep sanitizing every other week."

"You'd find somethin' to pester yourself with in here, Scotty." Lamb coughed into the sleeve of his jacket.

Reynolds shook his head and took two steps back. "You're a two-hundred-pound germ factory. Thanks for the contamination."

Lamb nodded. "My pleasure. Wish I was two hundy again."

Reynolds pinched his cheek.

"Sleep meds not working again?"

"Tried that Valerian tea last two nights," he said gnawing on a hangnail. "Think it's keeping me up instead."

"Jesus…you need to take a shot a Wild Turkey and slip into Neverland like I do."

"You could sleep standing up if you had to."

"Was that a joke…Did you just tell a joke? He laughed and then coughed.

Scott Reynolds trailed off, smiled wanly. Arguably, Ron Lamb was one of only a few people he knew that could make him smile; not laugh, but at least grin from time to time. He was trying so hard not to be tense.

Scott Reynolds pulled out his phone, glanced at it, let out a breath. "When we land, we'll be met by Estaban Cruz." Reynolds said. "You met him before?"

Lamb shook his head.

"Cruz and the Mexican FBI are working together. An unclassified covert mission arranged by the US National Security Agency. They've been monitoring the drug cartels and Cruz's staff is independent of the Mexican Secret Police.

Ron Lamb slid his hands in his front pockets, scratching his genitals. "Corruption's always in the water, buddy."

Reynolds eyes were everywhere, stopping on Lamb. "We may put handcuffs on you if you don't stop that," he said looking down at Lamb's midsection.

Lamb pinched his nose and wiggled. "These Mexicanos and their drug-gangs are what you might call your one stop shop. They'll deliver your marijuana, cocaine, meth, and now with no additional shipping and handling, heroin, right to your mailbox."

Scott Reynolds looked at his phone and nodded. "What's interesting, if you remember, is we spent millions closing the shores in Colombia and choking the coke trade. Now the lords have diverted to the next lowest-cost rout."

"Bingo," murmured Lamb.

It was like working with the child he never had. Patience never came easy to Reynolds. His lips constricted into a small circle. "HUMINT just reported that illegal drugs are the most successful Mexican, multi-national enterprise, employing about a half a million Mexicans. They're generating over twenty billion in sales. The drug business in Mexico is second only behind the country's oil industry in exports."

Lamb smirked. "Who said free trade and NAFTA hasn't done wonders for our country?" Lamb dabbed his nose with a handkerchief.

The two men moved into the aircraft which wasn't the Nightstalker or Cessna the Bureau normally used to shuttle them around. Reynold's leg began to twitch, and he felt a need for caffeine. He pulled out three manila folders he was planning on reading on the trip. A tall man with a pilot's cap ducked into the passenger area. He had yellow razor-like teeth with too much space in between. He folded his arms and straightened.

"Hello crew. I'm Captain Phil Donaldson and I'll be taking you to Mexico City. They tell me we need to move ASAP so I'll give you a quick rundown." He circled his hand in the air. "This is a US Navy EP-

E3 spy plane. This beauty is a Department of Defense plane which is more sophisticated than those typically flown by the FBI."

Ron Lamb whispered. "Hope we still get the snacks and hot towels."

The Captain didn't respond. "This machine's equipped with long-range cameras, radar and hyperspecral sensors. The EP-E3 contains a forward looking Infra-red, 'flip' for short, imaging device. You can see everything from up there."

Ron Lamb rubbed his eyes. "So long as I can check to see if my wife is sleeping in her own bed tonight."

The agents moved to their seats. Scott Reynolds cursed under his breath as he tried to untangle his seatbelt as the plane moved out of the hanger and onto the single runway. Lamb looked over at Scott Reynolds and laughed. "You need to do somethin' about your sleep little buddy."

Reynolds wrestled with the belt latch and popped the two metal pieces together and grunted. He didn't look up, "I don't think I'll ever get a good night's sleep again," as he slid his back into the seat and lowered his shoulders trying his best to relax.

"Ever try hypnosis? I used it to quit smoking a few years back."

Now there was a depressing thought, Reynolds rolled his eyes. "I've seen how people act when they're under…under the hypnotic state and it turns them into fools. And having to do it under the supervision of the Bureau also makes me want to barf. Like I'm really going to reveal some top secret info"

Lamb cleared his throat. His voice now sounded like he was chewing on gravel. "What are you really scared of Scotty, old girlfriends? Afraid you might unleash some of your private life or private thoughts…that got your pecker nervous?"

It hung in the air, the word nervous. Of course, everything Reynolds tried to do in his life made him nervous. His motto had always been;

go big or go home. He felt guilty for just about everything in his life. It all started when he got his first B+ in seventh grade Art class. Sharing personal information with anyone, even Ron Lamb was for the weak. If he didn't figure out how to open up to others, he'd end up alone. Detached and isolated; he used to believe it was best for him but now his exclusion was leaving him guilty and joyless and lonely. He glanced around the plane. There were gadgets and electronics everywhere. He hadn't been trained on any of them. Never enough time to prepare. The plane jerked to the left and his head was suddenly dizzy. He hadn't had time to stop at his safe deposit box and pick up his meds from Canada. He didn't want the Bureau to know. They probably knew too much. He picked at his eyelash. He hadn't done that in months. Picking eyelashes, plucking out hair, pinching off bits of skin. Reynolds snorted, felt his abs flinch as if he'd been punched. He tried to take a deep breath.

Lamb tightened his lips trying to hold back a smile. "Maybe you think you'll lose control, think they'll make you take all your clothes off and bark like a dog, walk like a chicken? Probably show up on YouTube and the whole department will send it around for viewing during the Christmas party or somethin'."

Reynolds nodded, clenched his teeth so hard he could feel the fillings in the back of his mouth. The air pressure in the plane felt as if it was crushing his head. The screens in front of him turned on. He jumped in his seat. "We can't go under hypnosis anymore. Even with the company shrink supervising. They're afraid we would reveal too many secrets."

"Must not have gotten the memo, sorry." Lamb closed his eyes as if he was waiting to sneeze. "Guess I was put to sleep before the department changed the rules."

Reynolds started to breathe faster now. He tried not to think about his sleeping problem. Once he did he knew he wouldn't be able to stop.

Funny thing, was Lamb was right. He was apprehensive about what might happen if he were hypnotized.

Scott Reynolds frowned and looked at his shoes. Something was wrong. The shoe on his left foot was brown and the shoe on his right foot was black. He tapped his feet together, couldn't believe what he was seeing. He once had the wrong colored socks because he dressed in the dark, but never this. His shoulders slumped. He'd spent so many long days and longer nights making sure things like this wouldn't happen. Pouting, he looked out the window as the plane dashed into an aerosol of white mist. He thought he should be used to being teased. After all the years of abuse, he should now be accustomed to the vilification. In high school, Scott Reynolds used to swallow insults as if they were soda pop. Drink it down and burp it back up without saying a word. He wanted to attack, but he never did. Never did until Bobby Tanner asked him if he ever played with those dead corpses in the basement of his house. Asked him if he ever snuck down to the basement and undressed any of those chicks. He asked during a study hall on a snow covered February afternoon if he ever explored the bodies of the dead women, "Ever check to see what kind of panties they were wearing.' Bobby asked him if his Daddy taught him how to check the woman's private parts. Reynolds felt the blood in his body begin to percolate. Bobby told him the only private parts of a woman he'd ever get to see was one of those corpses. One of those stone cold, never talk back, lifeless, mannequins. And even though they'd been dead for a day or two, they still probably wouldn't let Scotty cop a feel, Bobby told the group at the table. Scott didn't have time to think about it. This time he'd heard enough. He was the guy who always thought about something before he acted. Nevertheless, this time he got up; face hot, fully aware of blood blasting through his circulatory system like a race car, took his fist and ran it through Bobby Tanner's nose as if it were made of paper mache. Blood smattered onto the three kids sitting at the table. It was one of those times that he didn't have control. Scott was suspended for three days of school and his father didn't want to hear his explanation, didn't want to listen to his side of the story, but Scott Reynolds was tired of the punks and pranksters that always made fun of him. That's one of the reasons he went into law enforcement

Reynolds twisted in his seat, looked down. Ron Lamb snapped his fingers. "You alright over there buddy?"

Reynolds massaged the back of his neck with his fingers, digging in hard, his fingers climbed up the back of his skull. He plucked out a small patch of hair and winced. "My sweet wife says I've never been loose my whole damn life. She says I'm wound as tight as a turkey's neck in November."

"What'da say we get a little work done, pilgrim? Normally helps to take your mind off things."

"OK. Let's get to work." He moved a fifteen inch surveillance console to his lap, straightened up in his seat and swung the monitor around enabling Lamb to see. He ran a finger over the screen and pushed the on button. "I'll play back a recording of a master wiretap file that we just picked up on a digital recording translator. We have a rough location of the targets in real time using Global cell information. We've got a mobile surveillance van which is streaming intercepts to us as we watch," Reynolds said with a sudden sense of cheeriness.

The plane banked to the right and the two passengers reached for something to grab. Seconds later a man, who was too thin to be healthy, walked from the rear of the plane and sat behind them. Jim Halliday had inky black hair, branched up in spikes. He wore a bacon collared rusty t-shirt with Frank Zappa printed across his chest. His long arms looked as if they should have been attached to a much taller man. Halliday gripped two hand-held devices that resembled television remotes. He tossed the devices on a table in front of Reynolds and Lamb.

"Nice to see you again Halliday," Ron Lamb murmured.

Halliday gave him a two finger salute. "We've been monitoring your cartel group for the last forty-eight hours. Think it's the Diablos who've been trying to follow asswipe Estaban Cruz and his band of Mexican Secret Police." Halliday grabbed one of the remotes and pressed three buttons. The screen zoomed and focused onto a white Lexus with a gold hood ornament of a bull.

Ron Lamb shook his head. "For god's sakes, look at the resolution. Couple of years ago I couldn't even get the nightly news with my rabbit ears."

Halliday increased the volume with his control. Seconds later the agents could hear the conversation inside the vehicle which had even been translated into English.

"Great technology, Halliday," said Reynolds.

Halliday cocked his head, his hair solid as a statue. "We can bug just about anything now. Ever since the 9/11 attacks we can practically watch you take a shower Agent Reynolds."

Lamb jumped in. "I'm sure Agent Reynolds scrubs every square inch of his body; who you tryin' to kid here, he probably washes behind his ears every time he brushes his teeth."

Reynolds stared at his shoes again. Thoughts of embarrassment: the loneliest sound he knew.

Halliday didn't react to any of it. "We can monitor everything from the air now. With DCSNET, think we got about eighty birds in the sky at all times; playing spy games, occasionally playing paparazzi on a celebrity or two." Halliday pointed to the screen with his remote. "The Cartel found two of Cruz' agents who were following his group. We think they're the Diablos, or possibly have an association with them." Scott Reynolds straightened and leaned forward.

"DCS-6000 also known as Digital Storm, captures and collects the content of all phone calls and text messages." Halliday raised his eyebrows, placed his right hand on his cheek, fingered his temple. "We need to get on the ground and match up the handprints and fingerprints of these matadors to make sure we know who they are."

"Stay on top of this," Reynolds said.

"They're talkin' about what they'll do to Cruz' boys and it ain't pretty. These dudes are nasty." Halliday squeezed his eyes shut.

Scott Reynolds peeked at his shoes and now he didn't care. Every day he was confronted with decisions and consistently did the right thing, his intentions were good and they kept his compass headed in the right direction. The scope of his territory was expanding but his magnetic needle never strayed from due North. He shot out of his chair and stood looking out the window as the plane vibrated with a tinge of turbulence. He turned and faced everyone, voice heavy. "War games, we no longer play by any rules."

United States EP-E# bounced to a landing in Mexico City's International Airport. At 12:15PM the temperature was eighty-three degrees. The metropolitan area exceeded nineteen million people, making it the third largest on the globe. Reynolds hated crowds. This place was crowded with heat, crowded with sweat that flowed from the pores of a nation of people that loved to work hard. The benefits, however, were only given to the wealthy, the corrupt, and now the gangs.

Agent Reynolds and Lamb shook hands with Jim Halliday at the top of the iron elevated stairs outside the aircraft.

The agents moved to three black Chevy Tahoe's lined up in single file. Four military men wearing fatigues splashed with tan and brown waited for them. "Air Force 60th Security Forces Squadron SWAT team just landed twenty minutes ago," Reynolds said. "Came in from

California. Let's go." They moved into the back seat, doors closed and moved forward. The driver never turned his head to the back seat, just stared forward as they swerved onto the street and steamrolled ahead. A man with leathered skin, gray hair, and a grayer mustache swiveled his upper body toward them, his face frozen with a smile, large dark spaces between his teeth. "Buenos dias. My name is Juan Torrez."

Reynolds tried to get his ears to pop, squeezing his nose with two fingers, blowing. Mexico City's high elevation and subtropical climate were already hell on him. His head pulsed and he gathered phlegm but couldn't spit.

"You OK Mr. Reynolds?" asked Torrez.

"Fine…need to get used to the elevation and humidity," he answered as he scratched his forehead with his palm. Reynolds wasn't fine. He hated the travel. He hated the long rides in airplanes. He couldn't take the pounding on his head from the pressure. The pressure at lift-off and landing felt like it would split his head open like a watermelon when it hit the pavement. Sometimes Scott Reynolds thought jumping out of one some high rise would be best for him. But most of all he was just plain tired. Tired of taking pills—pills for his head, his lack of sleep, and his unhappiness. When this was over, he'd be happy, he kept telling himself. The next job and the next case would make him happy again. He rubbed his temples with both hands and cranked his mouth open again to relieve the pressure in his head. He stared out the window and thought about the Diablos. He wanted to nail the Diablos. Nail their asses to the wall and cut into the drugs, the weapons, the gambling. He heard words and knew he needed to listen.

"We've set up the sting for the Diablos," Torrez said. Torrez held up a photo, "this is Areno Coliseo. They're headed for a meeting with a major supplier from Los Estados Unidos, o, United States…por favor,"

The three Tahoe's roared past a building with columns, topped with a gold dome.

"Good," Reynolds said as he stared straight ahead.

The SUV's took a sharp turn left almost hitting an old man carrying a paper bag clutched to his chest. The SUV turned right at the next stop light. The vehicle shot up the entry ramp onto Eje 2 Sur. The elevated highway had four different levels. It looked like a bowl of spaghetti to Reynolds. He needed to keep his mind focused. He cleared his throat. "Keep going Mr. Torrez?" He bristled as he made a circular motion with his hand.

Torrez unrolled his papers and swung his body around further to look at Reynolds. "The Diablos are trading a load of drugs for weapons brought in from the US. We have our secret policia and your SWAT team on the way."

"We know all of this…Where did the information originate," Scott Reynolds snapped.

"We got our informacion from a willing cartel member, Mr. Reynolds."

Lamb looked at Reynolds. "Must be a little like Hatfield versus the McCoy's down here," Lamb said muffling a cough.

Torrez stared back. "The gangs and cartels never end here. You think our bull fighting is violent." He shook his head, face pained. "Cartel fighting is gruesome."

The SUVs shot down the ramp of the elevated highway and dodged a set of pot holes by the exit. The passengers lurched from side to side. Reynolds closed his eyes. About two minutes later the SUVs slowed and drove through what must have been the factory district. Scott Reynolds tried not to look at the hundreds of people on each side of the street selling their wares under tents. Tents, a prism of colors bombarded every centimeter of space. Sunlight spiraling off metal poles from the tents.

But Reynolds paid little attention. His scope again narrowed, boundaries set. Deep inside his soul he was anticipating a capture, a conclusion. The vehicles turned down a street and drove five more blocks. The SUV jerked into a parking lot. The lot reminded Reynolds of the parking spots for football games in the US Games that he had watched trying to determine if sports gambling was being influenced by outsiders. They pulled into the Arena Coliseo, the edifice that held the popular Lucha Libre (wrestling) on a weekly basis; but now the giant parking lot was empty. Only a dented green Volvo missing all its hubcaps sat alone in the deep sea of asphalt. Asphalt the color of a silvery battleship reminded Reynolds of dirty polluted cartels and dirty decrepit games. Juan Torrez rolled down his window. A wave of air rushed into the vehicle and it felt to Reynolds like a steam room with a hint of farm smell gushed in.

"The sauna might be good for my cold," Lamb said breaking the silence.

Scott Reynolds gave his companion a scowl. "What's the problem here, Juan?"

Torrez looked around the parking lot. "The deal was to be made inside. Cash delivered in luxury boxes upstairs."

"Where are the drugs? The weapons?" Reynolds snapped.

"Our men were to break the sting right here, at the entrance to the Luxury Skyboxes," Torrez answered deep in thought.

"So, where are your people?" Reynolds asked excitedly.

"We have a dozen vehicles surrounding the area, all about a kilometer away." Torrez looked out the back window, then glanced at his phone. He moved his head from side to side as his eyes narrowed. He scratched the side of his left cheek and squinted at his phone again. No one in the vehicle made a sound. Torrez pushed his phone and brought it to his ear. The muscles in his jaw tightened. "Que pasa?" he shouted. The back seat was quiet, watching Torrez in the front seat.

"What's he saying," Reynolds whispered to Lamb. "What's going on?"

Lamb raised a hand, tried to listen. "I think everyone's at a loss—," he tilted his head again trying to listen. "Sounds like no one knows where Cruz is headed with his team."

Torrez whacked his phone on the console between the seats, turned to face the back seat. He took a tittering breath, "Cruz' team was following the cartel. All the surveillance, how you say, bugs were with them." He paused, shook his head and ran a hand over the back of his neck. "One of our team members, it appears, was not one of us." He shook his head, suddenly his phone began to vibrate. He looked at it for a moment and then looked out the window.

Reynolds sat forward. He pounded his fists into the seat in front of him. Today was the day it was all going to pay off. "So what's that mean, Torrez?" Reynolds glanced at Lamb, who gave him one of those, What the hell is going on down here looks.

Reynolds phone vibrated. He stared at the screen. "Our surveillance from one of the planes and satellites are transferring the information… here it is." He was reading. "All the cars are on Calle Texcoco." He continued to read, the SUV had again gone silent. "They're parked in front of El-Panian Market on Texcoco."

Torrez clapped the driver's chest with his palm, "Ahora!"

The SUV's tires screamed, lurched forward, and cantered over a curb. Scott Reynolds' breathing increased and his jaw tightened, the pain behind his eyes was wretched.

Reynolds could feel the black star in his chest begin to percolate. He hated the Diablos. He hated everything about them. He hated the cartels and their power and drugs and guns and dark fucking suits with smiles. Their smiles hiding the soiled secrets and evil that sat just beneath their skin, lay in their bones like shark teeth. Ready to bite. Always ready to devour. Always looking for blood and then the smile.

Torrez turned and looked directly at Reynolds, his eyes revealing confusion and a blade of fear.

"We've lost them," he fingered an earpiece in his right ear and waited, immobilized.

Scott Reynolds eyed his phone. "SWAT team's just behind us," as he looked up at Lamb.

Torrez turned to face the back seat. "We can't bring in your forces. Your team, they don't know the area and the situation."

Reynolds shot back. "We're taking over this situation, Señor," as his eyes went wide, spittle flashing out of his mouth. "You've had your chances. You assholes keep making mistakes and keep making us look like idiots."

Reynolds paused, then there was a moment of silence. Much longer than the one when they pulled into the Arena. The SUV raced past the Iztaplapa, vendors selling fruit from their wooden carts fled to safety. A tomato bludgeoned onto the window next to Ron Lamb's head. He turned and glanced at Reynolds. His expression was one of alarm, yet excitement building in his eyes. The vehicles slowed as dozens of people walked across the street. Their SUV's back end took a deep thud. Reynolds reached into his coat and found his holster with his Glock holding his hand over the handle. "This vehicle's bullet proof, Señor?"

Torrez nodded.

"Don't know who I believe around here," Ron Lamb said with annoyance. The driver wailed the horn, pedestrians scattered in all directions. Reynolds phone buzzed. His fingers went to work receiving a new message. His head flicked back. "Two blocks straight ahead and then one block right."

Whisking down the street, they pulled in front of an old excuse for a warehouse. Reynolds cracked his window. A train of dust whipped past his face. He coughed. The sound of a child screaming in the background clawed at his head. "Think we have a problem here," Reynolds said with a gaze fixed on Torrez's face as if he was looking right through him.

Their vehicles idled in front of four warehouse garage doors. Doors that all looked like eyes staring back, watching him, waiting for Reynolds. No pain in his head or his eyes now, even though he lacked back-up and police protection, he opened his door. Lamb and Torrez followed. Reynolds looked both ways, slid his hand into his coat to feel his holster again. The Glock was still unbuttoned. He spent dozens of hours practicing with it, but still had times when he was clumsy. That's what his wife Elizabeth told him. Reynolds straightened his spine. He glanced at Lamb, then Torrez.

"SWAT team's on its way," Lamb said tensely as he pulled out his Browning semi-automatic, released the safety and slid it back inside his coat. Scott Reynolds took three steps toward the building. Lamb stopped him as he reached out his hand, grabbing his shoulder. "Let's wait for the SWAT—" Lamb started to say, but Reynolds shook his hand away.

"Not letting these bastards get away this time," Reynolds said as his heart began to race. His head felt like it wanted to punch that high school kid again, end the frustration. His eyes narrowed so tight he could barely see through them. "I don't want to lose 'em...we're too close." He moved toward the garage door, the scolding sun flogging the back of his neck. He reached for the handle and pulled. The garage door squawked as it slid open. The three of them ducked past the door and into the warehouse. The room stretched the length of half of a football field. Reynolds smelled rubber, grease, and gasoline. Two dim lights glowed from the back of the room. Reynolds waited for his eyes to adjust. Rows of old tires squatted against the right side wall. The cab of a Volvo semi parked in the middle. Reynolds moved in, saw something twitch by his left eye. A screech shot out as wings flapped and a pigeon fluttered and swooped out the garage door. He looked at Lamb and let the silence grow. He could see Lamb holding his Browning by his right leg. Curiosity gathered force in him. Reynolds glanced at a set of metal chairs half-way down the room on the left.

"I'll take the stairs," Reynolds whispered through gritted teeth.

He reached the bottom stair which was dented in the middle. He ran his sole over the metal, slowly stood, listened to a sharp creak, but it seemed safe. The buzz of an air conditioner crept into his ears as he edged up the stairs, tightly gripping the handrail. The stairway swayed from side to side. Reynolds could see what he thought were four floors to the building. There must be another way up in the rear he decided. As the stairs swayed, Reynolds stopped. He thought about going back down but he was already half way up. The next stair moaned as he stepped on it, rails wobbled. He pushed back the vertigo. Keep moving. He came to the top step. Something like a boiler was humming. A long dimly lit hall stood in front him. The only noise now was the beating of his heart as he slowly moved down the hall. No sound and only a trace of light but he kept moving. He was close to the end of the hall, no motion, no sound. He wished he had waited. Waited for the SWAT. Where the hell were they? He moved up more stairs to another floor. He was drenched with sweat. He walked down the hallway and it looked identical to the one below it. He heard a sharp click behind him, swung his head back, and saw nothing. He reached a closed door at the end of the hallway. When he moved in front of it the air felt cold. How could something in this building be cold? He turned the door knob and slowly pushed, the room was partly lit by an overhead fluorescent light. Reynolds peered at the old suede couches against the wall, tables and a hulking wooden desk in the center of the room. Perspiration dripped into his eyes. He wiped his forehead. His eyes froze. The moisture in his mouth was gone, he felt hypnotized. He needed to message Lamb, but he couldn't move. Reynolds sucked the stale air into his nostrils, his stomach tightened. He found his phone, lifted it to his face. Reynolds perspiring had stopped, he was now shivering. He pulled his lips apart and air pushed between his teeth.

"Got a situation…third floor…," he breathed through his mouth, "Need help."

His eyes tried to analyze the situation. There were three bodies. Bodies that looked like they were suspended in air. Blood. Gallons of blood. Blood splattered over the entire back wall. A wall that looked something like modern art on steroids. He was unable to think. Unable to analyze. He was trained to analyze a situation, but he'd never seen anything like this. What he saw was twisted. The smell of rotten fish and uric acid streamed into his nostrils. He covered his nose and mouth with his forearm. Three Hispanic men, his first thought was Mexican FBI, hung against the wall with railroad stakes driven into their stomachs. Their bodies hung like fish. Someone wanted him to see. See the catch. But his eyes didn't sympathize with his brain. The bodies didn't look right. His brain didn't understand. When he saw that the three heads of these three men were lying on the floor in front of their bodies, he became sick. He couldn't stop looking and an inkling of fear threaded into his mind. Where the hell are they? Where was the SWAT team? Reynolds slipped out of the room, placed his back up against the wall and side stepped toward the stairs. He heard footsteps approaching him and he froze, his breath stopped. Two seconds later a bolt of light sprayed onto his face and he heard a voice.

"SWAT team, Agent Reynolds?"

Reynolds dove onto his stomach and rolled. He stretched his arms pointing his Glock toward the light. The spot light moved off his face onto two men in fatigues standing in front of him with M-16 rifles, bullet proof vests, and what he recognized at SWAT helmets.

"Agent Reynolds, please put the gun down."

Reynolds slid his gun on the floor, slowly rose to his feet. His legs trembled as he placed a palm to the wall. "Where the hell are they?" he screamed.

"We're still looking," a voice answered.

Minutes later Scott Reynolds stood next to the three SUVs. Five SWAT team members stood in a circle next to him. Lamb shut the garage door, turned to look for Reynolds, but Reynolds didn't want to look at Lamb. He just stood there in deep remorse. An icy coldness wrenched in his stomach. Lamb walked past two guys with helmets and put his arm on Reynolds' shoulder. Reynolds didn't move.

"You OK Scotty?"

Reynolds replied, "We just got word from our eyes in the sky." He swallowed hard. "Also talked to Torrez. They just captured four cartel members, along with the leader."

Lamb's eyebrows jumped. "That's more like it."

"One big problem, Ronny, they aren't the Diablos. These are the Gallo Grande Cartel."

"We still caught a big fish today. That's what we wanted."

Reynolds did not reply right away. "But not what we're looking for."

"It'll slow 'em down...let us reel them in next time."

"The big one got away. They wanted us to find their adversary." He tilted his head back, peered into the sky. "It was all planned."

"We're making headway, Scotty."

Reynolds shook his head. "They put us onto the path of their biggest enemy, Gallo Grande. They wanted us to think that the killings are from them."

"So?"

"So, the Diablos are still free."

Lamb looked at Torrez. A cough caught in his throat. "At least we nailed the Gallo Grande leaders. That's a good thing, ain't it, or am I missing something here?"

Reynolds stared at the warehouse as if it had answers. He wiped his brow with his palm. "I think Mexico is happy except for the undercover agents stapled to the wall upstairs," as he jerked a thumb at the warehouse. "I'm just wondering if this is going to make the Diablos stronger…one less group trying to slow 'em down?"

Again, eyes fell on Torrez. "Aren't you doing anything here?"

Torrez' face took on the look of a child who couldn't come up with an answer. He peered at his phone, then raised his head. "We followed the leader back to his home, he's under arrest with six others. We have two members of the teams at the cartel leader's house right now…name is Raul Cortez." Torrez fumbled with his phone, looked up again. "The house is in the Lomas neighborhood six kilometers from here."

Reynolds nodded. "Let's go."

Torrez shrugged. "You want to go to the house, Señor?"

Reynolds nodded again. "You bet your ass I do."

Chapter 46

USA TODAY

Verizon Communications has signed an exclusive content and marketing partnership with the National Basketball Association that will bring daily league highlights, new original series and access to some live games to its new mobile video streaming service Team99.

The deal establishes Verizon as the official wireless provider of the NBA As part of the agreement, Verizon will become the title partner of the NBA All-Star Slam Dunk contest and partner of the NBA Draft. The deal is valued at more than $800 million and runs for three years, according to a person familiar with the terms who was not authorized to speak publicly. The non-exclusive arrangement frees the NBA to shop content to other streaming outlets.

Chapter 47

All women become like their mothers. That is their tragedy. No man does. That's his." —Oscar Wilde

Jason slid off his stool and stepped into his Nike sweat pants. The air inside the Carver-Hawkeye locker room was stale and hot. The scent of deodorant and sweaty shoes swelled.

"Pretty nice game, Carson," said Coach Bobby Trammel who slid in behind him.

He swung his head, as water dripped down his forehead. "Thanks, Coach."

"You did some nice things in your first game."

Jason nodded.

"I liked the scoring tonight, but the best thing I liked was the rebounding...that's what wins games."

"I love to clean the glass."

Trammel thought about it for a moment, then lowered his voice.

"You can score…just remember to make that extra pass. It's best for the team."

Jason swallowed. No one had ever criticized his basketball skills before. He didn't know what to say. Silence.

"Teams win championships. That's why you're here."

Jason couldn't really believe what he was hearing. He'd scored twenty-seven points and had thirteen rebounds. He couldn't find words. "Yes, sir."

Trammel patted his shoulder and walked away. Jason stared at him as he walked away. He turned his head slowly, looked back into his locker, glared at his book bag. He mumbled to himself. This was the time that he usually cherished; the exhaustion after a game, the thoughts of all the great plays, the winning, the conquering. But his stomach wasn't ready for food now. It was inflamed. He had vomited before the game, it was his ritual, but now he usually was ravished. He looked back at his book bag. It looked swollen, bloated like his head. He hadn't had time to study much yesterday. He had spent forty-five minutes with his algebra professor going over coefficients and variables and he didn't have time for his pencil-neck tutor because he was watching film from practice.

Teammate power forward Dwight Simmons patted his naked chest and gave Jason a whistle. "Looks like you gettin' the big love from coach." He puckered his lips and squealed a kiss into his palm and slapped his butt with it. "Keep kissin' bootie boy, and you'll be in good graces with da man…mmm…mmm…mmm, oh yeah. You da new Big Man on Campus now."

Jason shook his head. "That's why I'm here."

"Oh-yea," he said with a big smile and nodded continuously. Simmons eyes narrowed. "I think you just want an MVP hangin' round your neck. That's all you think about, bro."

Tommy the trainer had told him that some of the players were feeling this way. He didn't know if he should listen. He was competitive, that's what got him here. But if he didn't listen he may end up on the bench or never get the ball. "OK Simmons. I'll set you up for your favorite alley-oop next game."

"Dat's what I need to hear. You also owe me fifty bones for beatin' yo ass in Madden 25."

"Don't have it right now."

"Come-on now, bro. Don't give me dat. I don't have the scratch."

"Seriously, don't have a cent to my name."

"You kiddin' me. Everybody on this team is flush with dough. Ask John O'Malley."

"Who?"

"Big-ass booster. He fills our pockets with dead presidents." Simmons fished a hand into his backpack, pulled out a clump of cash. He fingered through the wad, then squeezed it together, scrunching it, crumpling, then kissing it. "I worked at O'Malley's ranch this summer and made fifteen hundy a week. Spose to shoe horses for the ol boy." He shook his head slowly, laughing to himself. "Thing is, I got paid for six, seven weeks while I fished in his pond...Never saw a damn horse all summer," he said jerking his body back and forth laughing so hard.

Jason scanned the room and then back at Simmons. "Nice, I guess."

"You guess. Dat's the way it works. You can also call Mama Norris too. Anytime any of us needs bread we call her and she helps us out. Las year I got four hundy for taking down her Christmas tree from her attic. Johnson got seven bills for cleaning her floors...sweet."

"Coaches know this stuff?"

"Hell no. Don't want to ruin a good thing. We just keep it inside the family. That's what we do. We help each other." He smiled wide. "Look bro, trust us. We take care of each other.." He shook his head, eyes went small. They bumped fists.

Jason could feel his mother working through him; he always wanted, always needed to do the right thing. But maybe this was the right way He never knew for sure? He looked over at Simmons, studied his eyes.

"Maybe. Let me think about it." But his head was filled: too many confrontations to compete with now. He was on his own. He brushed his hand over the wallet in his sweat pants, glanced around the room. The piles of shoes in the lockers were amazing. Four, five, six pairs of new kicks in just about every locker. He watched Demarre Campbell lazily pull a shirt over his head. He was moving in slow motion as if he had all the time in the world. Demarre put long corded gold necklaces over his head, eyes closing as he straightened them over his chest. The first, the number 3 which was his jersey number, studded with colored stones: blue, yellow, crimson, a jaded green. The next was a cross etched with twisted black lines strangling the silver beneath it. He fumbled in his pocket for the third necklace. It resembled a chain link fence, like a mountain climber's carabiner. At the end, a pearly white pendant outlined in brass hung in front of the others. It resembled a castle with spires made of beads that glistened from the overhead lights. Jason glanced across the locker room at Ky Simpson who was jamming to music from his head phones. Jason knew the type. They were the Ultrasonic Signature DJ Headphones like players in the NBA wore. Ky was wearing a gold watch the size of a man hole cover on his wrist, diamond colored rings on both hands. Jason slid his hands into his pockets. He fiddled with his wallet again, rubbed two quarters together.

"Maybe I should try to get some cash to pay you back. I could really use some dough."

Simmons nodded twice. "Good. Easiest way to get skin you ever seen."

Jason glanced around the room. He didn't want to do it, but it wouldn't be his fault. His jaw tightened. "You get me some phone numbers of people that need some work done, or what?."

Simmons shook his head. "No, no…No numbers. I'll just have somebody call you. They take good care of you," he said.

Brandon Sellers rubbed his eyes. His stomach gurgled, he'd missed lunch today; one dependency outweighing the next. He only spent an hour in the batting cage and couldn't hit the fastball today. He now sat in his room glued to a screen. His eyes blurry, transfixed, stuck on the twelve inch game of craps from the Virgin Islands. Sellers sat mesmerized with each roll of the dice. His white ear plugs filled with cheers as he peered at a man with a visor and white jacket roll a seven. Two women with low cut dresses jumped up and down and looked for someone to kiss. Brandon watched the winning round for the patrons and the loss for the house. Brandon squinted as the shrieks in his ears ran through his head. But the shrieks were what he was waiting for. His conclusion, his necessity. He was back in the game now. But he wasn't exactly back, he was still down $585 over the last seventy-five minutes. Playing with the online casino from one of the Virgin Island hotels, he couldn't remember which off-shore gambling site he was using today; they all looked the same, except for the Ocean Bay casino from the Bahamas that constantly interrupted his play with pop-ups blocking his screen. Pop-ups of girls he could meet in his area, gambling techniques he could buy and his favorite, the white stallion who could talk and tried to convince him that he needed to try Viagra. He could feel a change of luck coming his way. He began to wonder if his time was coming, because he knew that every gambler had streaks, hot spells, waves of luck that came and he hoped the last roll of seven was the beginning of that streak. He touched his keyboard, the eve of expectation. His heart began to move faster; thirty bucks on the "pass line" and fifteen on "the field." A black haired man with a waist the size of two slot machines grabbed the dice with hands that looked like small pillows. Sellers moved up in his seat and placed his elbows on the table, resting his chin on his hands. The aftermath of suspense always his duty. The dorm room door opened as Jason Carson walked in and tossed his gym bag in the corner in front of the open closet.

"What up, dog?" Jason said.

Brandon Sellers eyes never left the screen. "Yeah…what up J.C.?" The round man on the screen bent forward. Everyone around the table swung their heads as the dice flew, bounced and landed. Brandon Sellers held his breath, waiting. "Seven," chirped from the dealer in a high tinny voice, "house wins…sorry folks."

"Holy shit," Brandon screamed as he kicked the bottom of the desk. Brandon's phone rang. He closed the lap top and answered, listened for a moment. "We'll take the Lakers and the over. That game will be a scoring marathon. Yeah. Also want in on the Sacramento Phoenix game. I've been pushin' the Suns, Sacramento has a couple of injuries that will limit some play. Don't think the boys in Vegas know the full scoop."

He listened.

"I just know these things, ass-wipe. I got a buddy who knows the Kings' trainer. We're in there, like swimwear."

Listened again.

"This time it's gonna work out. I'll pay you back. Should get a big haul this weekend," he said and touched the screen of the phone and tossed it on the couch.

Jason stood watching. He shut the door and stared at Brandon. "At it again, I see."

"Just waiting to get hot again. Things should be shiftin' my way any time now."

"You shouldn't be betting on games?"

He waved a hand at him. "Just a little hobby that keeps me occupado. Otherwise I'd be chasing babes 24/7."

"Yeah, you need to go easy."

"Look, smoke. You got to see how the real world works. I'm a walking good luck charm. You can call me the Wizard of Wagering."

Jason shook his head. The couch creaked as he sat down. "Your luck's run out." He gave him a sour pitiful look. "The horse you bet on last week is still running."

"Speaking of running, you haven't paid me that seventy five bucks that you owe me from the World Series. You owe me for some gas and, listen, I'm due for a big streak. It's comin' my way…I feel it dude."

Jason knew he shouldn't have bet on the Series, but Brandon kept telling him it was a sure thing. Everything was always a sure thing except for the outcome these days. "Maybe you should spend a little more time on school, a little less time throwing your dough away."

"Listen, I don't pitch a bitch when I lose because I know its comin' back, and comin back big." Brandon leaned forward and the two front legs of the chair crashed to the ground. "And the other thing is, I don't tell you what to do; how to spend money that you never seem to have anyway. How come you never seem to have any money anymore?

Jason raised the TV remote and turned on ESPN news. "Dried up."

Brandon didn't respond. The only noise came from the TV "Maybe it's because you spend all your scratch on shoes? You're worse than a chick."

Jason walked over and looked at the boxes of shoes in his closet, "I can't find those Air Yeezy 2's I got last week."

"Those god-awful blue ones."

Suspicion ran through him. "Couldn't find them this morning."

"Hope you didn't pay for those."

"It was a great deal. Forty percent off."

"Listen dickweed, you need to pay off your debts before you buy any more high heels and moccasins for yourself."

"And you need to loosen that vice around your balls."

"Look who's talking. Won't drink with us. Won't let me bring home the cute little tomatoes with the big racks. When do you have any fun?"

Hardship had formed him: made him silent and deliberant. He felt extraordinarily empty the last few days. He remembered how his mother would encourage him, give him hope.

"Give me a break. The funeral cost over eight grand."

Brandon hadn't anticipated the response. He stood without moving for a moment. He slowly moved his head to look at Jason. "How do you know how much it cost?"

Jason shook his head. "Because I have to pay for it and I don't know how."

And for another moment, Brandon looked confused again. "What about insurance?"

"We don't have insurance."

"Didn't your mom have any dough?"

It wasn't what he was ever allowed to do, sharing in the suffering like Job from the Old Testament. He was always to be thankful. He looked into the cloudy eyes of his roommate, a misunderstood look crossing over his face. "I've always been strapped for cash. Mom did all she could to put food on the table."

Brandon sat down on the couch, looked to his lap, rubbed his hands together. "Wow. I didn't know the whole story."

"Nobody knows the whole story," Jason said in a soft voice. "I'm just an orphan now," he replied. And he was beginning to realize it now. The pain of grief; a desolation that only one can share alone.

The sink dripped in the corner. A couple of kids laughed as they walked by the door.

Brandon lingered. Looked up at the TV "What'd you say we go out? Get you feeling a little better? I'm buying."

Jason shook his head. "No thanks. I need to write a composition paper. I didn't pass my first one and coach talked the prof. into letting me write it again," he said as he looked behind the couch. He walked to the closet again and started opening the Nike boxes. "I need to find those Yeezy 2's. Cost me two and a quarter."

Brandon leaned over and spit into the spittoon, wiped his lower lip with the back of his hand. "You tellin' me you bought shoes when you owe eight grand?"

Jason kept opening boxes, faster now. "It was the best deal I've seen on them. I can make money if I sell em."

"But you never sell the sons a bitches."

"Holy shit," he shouted. They're gone," he said as he stood up and kicked the green chair over, empty beer bottles smashing.

"Whoa. Let's not go psycho here."

Jason picked up the chair as if he was going to throw it. He then dropped it to the floor and grabbed his back. "Shit." He clenched his teeth. "My back." He felt like crying but wouldn't. He was taught not to cry. Never let the opponent show signs of weakness. The entire world was in competition with one another. Survival. That's all he ever knew. He tried to straighten, aching in his spine, his legs, his everywhere.

There was a flash across the TV screen: "Breaking News." Both men waited. An ESPN news anchor dressed in a black suit and red tie sat at a desk. "We are interrupting programming with some breaking news to report." The anchor looked down at his papers, then looked into the camera. "Police in Lexington have just made a statement." Anchor looked at his papers in disbelief. "Kentucky basketball player, Jarrod Perkins, was found dead one hour ago in the Ohio River. No other information is available at this time. A press conference is scheduled at the University of Kentucky in approximately 25 minutes.

Jason blinked. His head couldn't process what he just heard. Jarrod Perkins played with him on an AAU All-Star team in Orlando two years ago. Jason remembered Jarrod loved peanut butter almost as much as he did. Jarrod would keep a jar in his backpack and eat it with a spoon during halftimes. Who would want to kill him? Brandon reached into his pocket and pulled out a round container of chewing tobacco, took a pinch and stuffed it into his lower lip. He looked at Jason and rolled his eyes. "Kid at Kentucky. Probably thought he could walk on water," he said with a wink.

Jason shook his head. "I know him."

Brandon spit. "What?"

"We played together for a couple of days, All-Star team."

Brandon chirped. "Mean you knew him. He's been scratched from the team. Bad swimmer."

"Not funny."

"Sorry. Shouldn't make jokes about death. My bad."

Jason's phone rang. He glanced at the TV then looked at his phone. Unavailable. He wasn't ready to talk; questions jostled around his head with unreachable answers.

He hesitated. A bitter swarm of pain stabbed at his back. He rubbed the whiskers on his chest and leaned forward, tilting and grimacing as he pushed the button.

For a moment he felt like he was unable to speak. He held his breath for a beat.

"Carson," Jason murmured.

Finally, a sound surprised him on the other end of the phone but he knew the voice. "First game must have made coaches hoppy. We need to keep coaches hoppy and smilin', Jason, and then, everybody hoppy," the voice swelled.

He didn't know how to respond. "Felt pretty good today," he paused, started again. "The coaches are never happy." Jason walked out of the room and into the hallway, closed the door behind him.

"I'm sure they were berry hoppy Jason, o', J.C. as they call you...It's now time to make us hoppy."

"Thanks for taking care of the funeral thing. Should have called."

"I'm here to help. We are partners, no?"

Jason's neck burned and the blue flames had moved into his temples. "Guess so. I'll pay you back, soon. With interest."

"Let's not wait. We can trade for it. What do you say?"

His voice was low and sounded unused. "Can we wait until next year? Give me some time to impress the scouts?"

"Better to pay off debts as early as possible."

"I'll be more valuable if I do good in college. I'll be a higher draft choice. Then—"

Perez interrupted. "Easy, easy Jason. We are going to go easy here. You need to trust me."

Jason didn't want to answer. He began to hear laughter behind him. Should he say anything to Perez about Jarrod Perkins? "Just give me some time. Please."

"You still don't understand, Jason. We can be quite dangerous to those that stand in our way. You listen to your coaches, but you listen to us first."

There was a lump in his throat that he couldn't swallow. It suddenly struck home to him that he wasn't in control.

"I will call before next game." And Jason heard a click.

AP News/Westgate Las Vegas SuperBook: Proposition bets in Sports betting are more commonly known as a "prop bet." This kind of betting is very popular overseas. It is now one of the fastest growing segments of the sports betting industry in the United States. The growth of prop betting in Nevada sportsbooks is evolving and constantly changing and Westgate SuperBook is always the first to open up to new opportunities.

A prop bet is a wager on an individual player or specific event during a game. Today, Westgate is proud to offer hundreds of expanded prop bets. We have added thousands of new prop bets that can be found on our mobile sports wagering app menu.

Chapter 48

Tim McMurray sat on a stool in the Officials' locker room in Washington D.C. The room was tiny. Tim pulled the bag of ice off his knee, stood and put on his knee sleeves and calf sleeves. The smell of liniment made his eyes water. He applied a slab of Crew styling cream in his hair and sat on the ground. As he worked on his abdomen crunches, he heard the sound of the exercise bike being wheeled into the room. He stood, massaged his quad, ran both hands through his slick hair and climbed onto the bike. After he felt warm on the bike, he climbed off and tied his black shoes. He placed his palms against the wall, leaned forward and stretched his Achilles. His planter fasciitis on the bottom of his foot was giving him trouble again. The room smelled of sweat and dust. The blousy banter of sportcasters blared from a TV in the corner of the cramped room. Tim leaned over to touch his toes, he was stiff tonight. Perhaps he needed to stretch more after games he told himself. He flexed his bicep and wrapped his hand around it. Need to do more curls tomorrow, he thought. He ran a hand over his stomach, patted it twice. His phone rang. He picked it up, looked at the screen. Janet. He hadn't talked to her in about a week. He answered. Her voice was quick and breathy. "Tim, where are you?"

"Getting ready for a game."

As he listened he could hear the tempo of her breath. "You need to come back. Need to figure this out. Don't know what's going on here. Something's happening."

As she rambled on, Tim stepped out of the locker room into a holding area in front of a tunnel that led to the arena. He was alone. "Janet, what's going on? You need to slow down."

"Well I got home from work and when I reached the front…"

"Wait a minute, work?"

"Yeah. Working at the designer shop part time. You never send money on time."

"That what's this is about. I don't have time for a lecture."

"No, listen to me. You need to listen," she blared. "I get home from work, ten minutes before the kids get off the bus." Her words breathy and breaking. "I get home and open the screen door. Dad hasn't been able to put the storm on yet."

"Get to the point, Janet."

"I'm getting to it."

She was blubbering now. "You need to make time. Make time to listen for once in your goddamn life. Listen, you prick." She hiccuped. "The envelope had pictures of the kids."

She probably wanted to know if he wanted 5X7's or 8X 10s?

"Pictures of the kids. Someone left them there. Pictures at soccer. Pictures of Emma and Conner waiting for the bus. Three pictures of Conner in the back yard playing with Ringo. I have no idea who's taking these. Someone is watching our kids. What the hell's going on? I don't know what to do."

And all at once it hit him. He tried to reason, the litany of possibilities scrambled around in his brain, shadows within shadows now in his consciousness. "OK," he said trying to reason. "Where are they now?"

"They're up in their rooms."

"Is this the first time?"

"Of course this is the first time. What the hell do you think?"

"OK Hmm."

"That's it? O.k? I'm calling the police."

"Wait a minute." This one might be his fault though he would never admit to it. "Let's think about this," he said searching. "Maybe it's a prank."

"It's no prank. Who in their right mind would do that you idiot?"

"Can your parents come over?"

"They're in Florida, stupid."

Tim's legs turned into ice as he stood. His phone buzzed and he stared at it. The text message read, "Taking the Wizards under 8 points."

Chapter 49

"Thanks for seeing me, Tommy," Jason said.

"No problem, kid. I live here, call me any time," Tommy said as he planted his cold hands on Jason's back.

Jason lay on a sticky table in the trainer's room, his whiskered chest hairs bristling. The room was shivering cold. "I don't know what happened. Just wrenched it or something." Jason tried to point to the spot, but he let out a "aaaaagggh," before he could get to it.

Tommy put Jason's arm down by his side. "I'll find it, kid. First time this happened?" he mumbled through nasal hair.

"Yeah, never had a back problem before."

"How are the ankles?"

"OK."

"What about the shoulder."

"Good." In basketball everything revolved around your health. Take care of the temple was his motto.

"You and the ladies working on gymnastics back in the room?"

"Funny. No. Just moved and it tightened."

Tommy stuck a gnarled finger into his ear and wheezed. "Doc Simms will be here to take a look."

"It's probably not that bad," Jason said. He tried to roll over, but Tommy held him down. "Let's just get a look-see first." The hands on Jason's back were finally warm, fingers kneading around his spine.

"How you doing?" Tommy hesitated. "Since your Mom passed?"

This guy loved to ask questions. "OK," Jason said trying to avoid lying.

"Hmm. Doubt you're tellin' me the whole story. It's gonna take some time to get over that, kid. Parts of your life may suffer for a while."

"I don't have time," Jason replied.

Tommy sat on the edge of the table, worked his way down Jason's back. "Grief's a tough deal. You need to talk about it."

"I just need to get back on the court. Everything's OK when I'm playing."

Tommy ran his fingers over his bushy eyebrows and shook his head. "But you need to take the time. Time to get over things. It's normal to grieve."

Jason would admit his mind was occupied. Nothing was making sense to him since the funeral. "I'll be fine," he said curtly.

"What about basketball?

"It's everything."

"That's what every dumbass kid says when they come in here. You need to branch out."

"Well, it's true with me. I'm still gonna be the best. Nothin' will change that." But something had changed and he was now faced with a cloud of confusion.

Tommy cracked a knuckle and cleared his throat with a hacking noise. "Teammates may be trying to tell you somethin'. Like today when you tried to take it down the lane."

How in the heck did he know about this? "Got hammered by Tyrone and Mikey," he said spontaneously any time someone corrected him. "I made both free throws, used to getting fouled."

Tommy gives a quick hard laugh. "I heard they tried to give you a little lesson. What they say to you when they fouled you?"

"Just talkin' smack," he crowed. "Been hearing trash talk for years."

"But these are your teammates."

"It's in my blood. It's me against the world now."

Tommy leaned back. "But you're a teammate first. Remember no I in team."

"I'm in this all alone now, Tommy."

The room goes silent. Jason strains to look at Tommy who is giving him that look again. Tommy's voice was reasonable and kind, in a way that his mother used to speak to him.

"What would you do if you couldn't play?"

Jason listened to the whir of the ice machine. This was one of the worst questions he'd ever heard. Funny, or sadly, he couldn't think of anything at all.

Dr. Simms walked through the door, flipping off his stocking cap and jacket on the table next to Jason. Simms had a scar on his top lip which gave him a bit of a hare-lip but the guy hid it well. His head was freshly shaven and one of his ears was disfigured from his college wrestling days. "Howdy boys," he said as he washed his hands in the chrome sink that had a pile of white towels next to it.

"Appreciate you coming," said Tommy.

"I think we may get a couple inches tonight," Simms said.

"Hate the white shit," Tommy griped.

Simms took a few minutes examining Jason, then sat down on a backless chair with wheels. He slapped his palm on his thighs. Tommy helped Jason sit up and handed him his shirt. "Put it on. Need to keep muscles warm." Tommy glanced at Dr. Simms, "Disc bulge, MRI?"

By now, Dr. Simms was moving around the table as he rubbed his hands together. This followed with a long glance at Tommy. Simms gave a quick shake of the head. "Don't think we need an MRI." He considered carefully how to answer. "Looks more like a classic case of TMS," he said in a whisper. Tommy and Simms shared another look. Tommy nodded.

Unexpected silence followed. Jason looked at both men. "What? What's that mean?" His stomach asserted its primal need and growled. Maybe they weren't going to let him play? Perhaps that's why Tommy asked him what he'd do if he wasn't able to play basketball.

Dr. Simms starts. "Tension Myositis Syndrome, otherwise known as TMS. Typical response to stress. Shows up after a large amount of stressors attack someone; anxiety, depression and muscles contraction in your case. New school, new team, death of a loved one. A large number of pressures on the neurological system."

And for a moment, Jason was confused, and he was beginning to realize what he needed to do all along. Take charge. He was actually listening to the doctor and better yet, understood what he was saying. "Should be able to play then I hope," as if he was giving himself his own prognosis, his own orders. He would need to discover the world on his own now.

Dr. Simms shrugged. "Up to you."

He stared at Doc Simms for awhile. "So this PMS."

Simms interrupted with a sly grin, "TMS."

"Yeah, this TMS is caused by stress?"

"I've seen it dozens a times. Millions suffer from it."

"So it's my reaction to losing my mother? An anxiety thing, you're saying?"

"That's my professional opinion."

"Anxiousness, depression. All part of the grieving, huh?"

"All connected."

"So I should go to that counselor coach was telling me about?"

"That would be my suggestion."

Jason pulled his knees to his chest and let out a long breath. "No disc bulge?"

Simms waited a moment, shook his head slowly.

"No MRI?"

Another shake.

"Prognosis, shrink. I mean Psychologist?"

Simms nodded and smiled.

Jason thought imagined his mother in the stands, all smiles and winks, saw her give him the thumbs up and wave frantically. A blitz of agonizing love rushed over him. The glorious face of motherhood appeared to him. She would someday make everything up to him. She would never let him suffer again. She would watch over him every moment of his life. She told him to be grateful. Grateful no matter what happened to him because it was all a blessing. He looked at Dr. Simms and then at Tommy and Jason felt a craving of devotion rise in him, the heaviness of the world felt huddled and hushed. He began to weep.

Chapter 50

The SUV's pulled onto a circular drive and stopped behind six other vehicles on the south side of Mexico City. Reynolds opened his door and jumped down from the Tahoe. He took off his sunglasses. Cashmere clouds moved in front of the sun. The other doors opened, and people rolled out of the vehicles. All heads looked up at the three story house that seemed to Reynolds like Hansel and Gretel met Pablo Escobar. The house sat two hundred feet back from the street and Reynolds studied the gingerbread-like carving featuring Christian and Buddhist figures; goats, fish, lions, and other animals. He turned and looked for Ron Lamb. Lamb was peering into a pond in the front lawn which was fed by a waterfall. The water clucked, shards of sunlight glinted from the cascade. The grounds were surrounded by an eight foot hedge with garden trails intermingled throughout the lawn. The air coming up from the ground was radiant, succulent. Ron Lamb looked up from the pond and eyed Reynolds.

"Hey Scotty," he cleared his throat. "You should see the size of these damn carp."

Reynolds' grunted.

"If I'd brought my fishing gear I'd be able to mount the son of a bitch over my fireplace," Lamb cackled, laughed and coughed, cringing.

Juan Torrez walked over and pointed to the house. "Raul Cortez. Cartel leader lives here. Our evidence."

"You mean the evidence that you were given?"

Torrez looked at his shoes, then his eyes moved to the house. "Sí, yes, correcto. I think we need to wait to go inside."

Reynolds tilted his head and peered at Torrez. "I've been granted full access here. Let's go."

The group worked their way up the long flight of stairs past two guards holding machine guns against their chests and entered through double wooden doors. Lamb touched one of the ivory tusk door knobs. "We're goin' on safari," Lamb muttered as his eyes moved to the animal heads ambushing the inside walls.

Reynolds moved onto the marble floor in the raised foyer. The marble flooring was covered by at least a dozen animal skin rugs: zebra, giraffe, tiger, leopard, black bear, and polar bears with heads. Two rugs on the fringes that he didn't immediately recognize but were probably a rhino and an ostrich. Smells of sweat soaked leather competed with the urine odor of a pet store. The whole space reminded Reynolds of his love for National Geographic's African Expeditions. Ceilings that reached to the sky, walls covered with the garland of animal heads. Furry chasms of unsheltered faces stared at him; caped buffalo, kudus, sables, elk, moose, African elephant, wildebeest, blesbok, nostrils flared, eyes primitive and barbaric. The entire place replicating the role of the hunter and the exhibitionist. Reynolds' adrenaline began to sing in his head. It was nature's way. Even the couches, chairs, and ottomans covered with animals.

"The animal kingdom, right here in the middle of Mexico City." Lamb hissed. He patted the head of an African tiger with four-inch fangs. Reynolds watched as Lamb touched each animal maybe wondering if they would come to life. Lamb turned to Reynolds

Reynolds rubbed his eyes. "I want every computer, every cell phone, every piece of technology from this house immediately." He looked over at Lamb who didn't seem to be paying any attention. "We can find out about the Diablos from their files and communication. Names, businesses, leads, everything. We can use all of it."

Lamb shook his head. "This is a taxidermist's dream."

Reynolds marched over to the couch next to a giraffe. "Let's analyze their encryption. All of their records," he said looking at Torrez. "If you find shredded documents grab them, we can put them back together. Don't waste anything, understand?"

Torrez nodded.

Reynolds heard the clacking of footsteps and turned to see ten or twelve men with green military coats file into the room. They began to open dresser drawers, crawled under tables, looked under rugs. One man pushed at a bookcase. Perhaps, the bookshelf would move, open like a door into an entire new room; that's what Reynolds considered in this culture of unending facades.

Torrez shouted for Reynolds and Lamb from across the room. In the corner, next to him, stood a man that might have been from Madame Tussaud's house of wax. The only difference was that this body wasn't made of wax, it was genuine, bona fide, human flesh. There was nothing Reynolds could compare this to. The thing was a human body. Real, but dead. Perplexed, Reynolds asked himself again, how the hell could this happen? Reason had nothing to do with this. The man was standing with a smile, or maybe more of a smirk on his face. Slicked back black hair, a thin mustache, a black shirt with tan pants, and black snake skin boots. The four of them looked at each other.

"Would you call it a man or a mannequin?" said Lamb.

Reynolds took a half step forward and touched the man's chin. "It is real."

"No way Jose. Sorry Juan," Lamb said after some consideration.

"No, I've read about this," Reynolds snipped. "Chinese have been doing this for some time. Germany has just started and tried to turn it into science."

Lamb broke in, "Don't they drain the fluids and replace the tissue with a plastic substance? Dr. Frankenstein probably knows," he said straining not to laugh.

Reynolds nodded and walked around to the back of the man. "That's plastination, but this is the real McCoy."

Lamb looked perplexed. "What are you saying?"

Reynolds put a hand on the dead man's shoulder. "This is real. I grew up in a mortuary. My old man worked on this stuff every day. I know what I'm looking at here."

Lamb hacked a laugh. "Lenin is probably going to be in the next room. Stuffed Hitler will be next to him. Wonder what pose he'll have. Or should I say *Heil* have," Lamb said forming air quotes beside his head.

Reynolds didn't laugh. For as long as he could remember, dead bodies were no laughing matter. Especially stuffed ones. The workmanship here was incredible. "This guy's been filled with about ten gallons of formaldehyde. They take out the inner organs and fill it with hemp fiber."

"Don't know where you'd find any of that 'round here," Lambed snorted.

Reynolds moved a few inches from the face, studying the eyes. "They must have gotten these eyes from an ophthalmologist. They're made out of glass."

Ron Lamb shook his head. "That guy's too big to be Sammy Davis Jr.?"

Torrez gave the two a quizzical look.

"Torrez doesn't even know who Sammy is."

Torrez shrugged. Lamb wiggled his head, "You gotta know who the 'Candy Man' was? Part of the original Rat Pack, my old man was a huge fan, met him once."

Reynolds stepped back and stared at Torrez. "You seen anything like this before?

Torrez gave him a slight shake of the head. "No sir. All new to me."

Lamb piped in, "Everything's new in this haunted house."

Bristling with excitement, Scott Reynolds couldn't take his eyes off the dead man. "I wonder how old this is? Whoever did this is quite a master pathologist."

Juan Torrez said, "I think it's about eight or nine months old."

Reynolds smirked. "How in the hell would you know that?"

"Because his name is Manuel Clemente. Once the second in command of the Diablos cartel."

"So this is what they do to the enemy down here, gut 'em like fish," Lamb said

"I'd actually like to spend more time with this. This thing is fascinating...heard this would happen someday," Reynolds said, not knowing where to look next.

Reynolds turned toward the door and saw men moving into the house. He grabbed Torrez by the arm. "What the hell's going on?" Reynolds ripped.

"They're from the Asset Administration and Disposal Service," Torrez replied apprehensively now.

Reynolds watched a man on his hands and knees rifling through a walnut desk with drawers large enough to fit one of the two pumas in the room.

Torrez said, "the S.A.E. known for short in Spanish, is well accustomed, as you say, to looking for items that we will confiscate. Things that will help us break the rest of the cartel."

Reynolds dug deep into his pockets looking for a couple of maximum strength Advils for his throbbing head, no luck. "Bullshit. The NSA doesn't want any of this out. We want absolutely no media, no news, not one fucking thing that the terrorist cartels can get their squirrel-dicks on." Reynolds watched the members of the S.A.E. ravage through the house like worker bees gathering pollen. After ten minutes of search, the marble floor in the foyer was covered with items: piles of pesos, boxes of dinnerware that read Versace. Baccarat wine glasses and Lalique Champagne flutes sat next to the dishes. Five Rolex watches, two with bands customized with jewels to resemble leopard's skin. On a stool in the corner sat a pair of gold pistol grips with raised eagle busts adorned with diamonds and emeralds. Piles of jewelry, many with religious themes, such as a palm-sized gold and diamond necklace ornaments depicting St. Jude, the patron saint of hopeless causes all over the floor now.

Two men in camo walked past them, out the front door, and between them were two women adorned in silk robes, faces congealed with makeup; botox lips, ocher, eyelashes the size of tarantulas, checks flushed. Fishnet stockings, twisting legs passed in front of them. They hustled away as if they were never there.

Lamb looked surprised, then amused all over again. "Damn, this joint's got everything. I could help counting that inventory."

"You need to see what we've found in the back," Torrez announced.

Lamb lumbered over to the tiger and touched one of the tiger's teeth, then caught up with the others as they started to move. As they walked to the back of the house, Reynolds picked at his eyebrow hoping the twitch in his eye would calm down. And it was a recurring nightmare, Reynolds understood the hunt would continue. For as long as he could remember, he was the one that always took the bait; this was a big catch, but Moby Dick was still at large. His mantra, "cry me a river," kept swimming through his veins. He deserved more. Torrez was called away as Reynolds and Lamb slithered through an opening almost too small for Lamb's Budweiser belly. The room was the size of a small closet filled with bookshelves. Each shelf was crammed with US currency. Bagged and neat. Every available space, every centimeter packed with dollars. Probably millions of good old Uncle Sam greenbacks held hostage. Ron Lamb touched a taped up bag and grunted. "Lord Almighty, looks like Mexico's Fort Knox. How many shekels you think they've hidden here?"

Reynolds didn't respond. Typically he'd have the last word, but he was preoccupied with the bags on the floor. Six swollen white canvas bags filled with coins up to his knees. Not just any coins. No, these were gold Krugerrands; over a thousand dollars a pop and there were hundreds, no make that, thousands. It was the paydirt of precious metal. He spent his whole life trying to discover the atomic number 79. His wife called him a penny pincher since he'd never given her an ounce. Never thought it was wise to spend money on something so frivolous. He took a handful of coins, as if a dream come true, and dropped them into his briefcase. Another, and then another. Like a prospector. He felt a hand on his shoulder.

"What the hell you doin' partner?" Lamb asked. "This ain't the wild west."

Reynolds wasn't responding, his mind reeling from the catch. He placed one of the coins in his mouth and bit down on it; hard and real and not one of those candy coins, no way this was one of those crazy dreams of his that turned into a nightmare. He jammed more coins into his other pocket.

Lamb grabbed his shoulders and turned him around. "What are you doing? You know better than this," he clipped.

Reynolds looked at Lamb with blurry eyes. The room wobbled as he stood. "This shit is ours, Agent Lamb. I goddamn well know how this shit works. If we don't grab the goods here, the guys behind us will be taking it. That's how things work around here."

"This isn't your style, shorty. You're the most honest sheriff in town."

There was a quake in Reynolds' chest. So perplexed and tempted by his new circumstances, his decisions distorted. 'What about the mortgage?' Then again, 'What the hell am I thinking?'" The intoxication of the moment wasn't going to ruin him. "You're right," he said emptying his brief case.

Lamb growled for awhile. "What's up with you? You're so damn straight, you're the poster boy for Viagra. I mean, you've never stolen anything as long as I've known you...not even a paper clip. You're the only guy that pays full price for everything, never bought a damn thing on sale in your life.

"Things change."

"Yeah, but not you. You're the rock. You're the Bureau's Statue of Liberty with a penis.

"Just a penis to most."

Reynolds was confused. All around him the sight of green was suffocating. Green like chlorophyll filling his mind. "Let's get the hell out of here."

The men caught up with Torrez who took them to the back of the house. They marched down a flight of marble stairs that reminded Reynolds of his trip to Florence, Italy, while visiting the Statue of David. Reynolds held onto the iron railing not wanting to stumble; fear of falling always part of his subconscious thinking, probably from some of those nasty nightmares of his. At the base of the stairs Reynolds spotted horse stables and four or five heads peeking out through open windows. He counted twelve doors and one horse stood in front of one on the far right. Torrez flicked his head. "This way please," and followed him across pristine bent grass, just like polo grounds. Two hundred feet in front of him was an ornamental twelve-foot cement wall decorated with images and statues of Greek goddesses.

On they went, through more doors, down a stairwell lit by Italian candles. Reynolds could smell damp air. A wooden door creaked opened. They walked inside. Humidity blanketed Reynolds' forehead. He was standing in a cave. There were four hot tubs and an Olympic-sized pool. Even stalactites draped from the ceiling like a Salvador Dali painting. The clap and bang of a ten foot fireplace echoed throughout the room. Torrez pointed to the ceiling. Reynolds looked up, his brain buzzed. He felt like he was losing his balance. He grabbed Ron Lamb's shoulder, reset his feet. The ceiling in the center of the room was made of glass. Even through the steam and condensation, Reynolds could make out objects moving overhead. Two tigers pacing across a pair of gorillas.

"Holy shit," Reynolds blared. "Feels like I'm in a science fiction movie."

Lamb took a deep breath. "This place is great for my cold. Hope there aren't any gators in the water though. Think I've had enough of the Animal Kingdom for one day."

Torrez faced the two of them. "Already, we've made major discoveries. The artwork, jewels, gold plated pistols and dozens of machine guns upstairs. We're just starting, and we've found well over a million in US dollars."

"Problem is," Reynolds said, looking back toward the ceiling, "half the stuff never makes it back to the police station. We can't make any goddamn headway around here. You can't even trust your own people, law enforcement included. The police, the judges, your friends, the neighbors, even the wives."

Lamb felt every person he looked at in Mexico was crooked, a cheater from birth. Was it nature or nurture or just living in this crazy jungle of humanity?

Lamb cleared his throat, made the sound of kettle drums. "Reports have always told us how seized assets have a way of disappearing from the government." A crooked smile moved onto his face. "These cartel pricks with fancy lawyers, get off, Scott free. Pardon the expression, little buddy. Next thing ya know they're buying back the same gold Rolex with the leopard skin that was confiscated in an earlier raid."

Frustration percolated in Reynolds' head. "Exactly, we're taking control of the evidence and we're taking it back to the States with us… enough of this bullshit justice system. The US needs to take control of this country pronto, starting right now."

Juan Torrez stepped forward. "You don't have the authority to take assets and evidence."

"Bullshit I don't. Most of this is stolen from the US" He could feel his cheeks reddening. He jabbed a finger into the chest of Torrez. "You need to start taking orders. Back upstairs, now."

Reynolds didn't know who was telling the truth. He spun on the damp floor and stormed back to the house. The others followed. As they reached the top of the stairs, Reynolds saw another dozen intruders with their faces covered with masks, buzzing in different directions throughout the house. He stopped and waited for Torrez. "What the hell's with the ski masks?" He saw four men with bullet-proof vests and black masks on ladders running their hands over crown molding near the ceiling.

Torrez rubbed his hands together. "They're federal cops. They wear masks to hide their identities. Try to work on keeping things secret."

Lamb said. "Looks like trick or treat down here. The problem is, you never know who's gonna soap your windows, smash your pumpkins."

The three of them moved into the family room and saw a man with "US Customs" printed in yellow on his back. The man was photographing everything in the room. Two US Customs' men walked by with a cart filled with computers and laptops.

"Good. Nice to see our people showed up," Reynolds shot out.

The photographer lowered the camera away from his face. "Agent Reynolds, they want you in the master bedroom right away."

"Which way?"

The photographer pointed down the hall.

Without waiting for the others, Reynolds made his way down the hallway. The master bedroom's double doors were both open. Reynolds went inside and found himself on a Spanish red rug. The room was the size of a small house, pillars pigmented in gold, the ceiling painted with a rainbow of colors. In the far end of the room was a round bed with dozens of red and white pillows. It was a menagerie of psychedelic hues, an acid flashback. Lamb and Torrez followed him inside.

And right there in front of him was one of the greatest mysteries facing the FBI over the years. Reynolds gazed at the far wall and looked at a row of paintings, each with a single silhouetted light above it. He made his way to the paintings. It was an odd sensation, as if Ahab had finally captured Moby. He craned his neck to look closer. He had seen the face before, dozens of times and there it was, lavishing, yearning, staring right back at him. An oil painting of a boat that was in a storm, a seascape. He had seen it as a child on The Alfred Hitchcock hour. The black and white television show predicted the future as it portrayed a man stealing this painting from an art museum. It was a violent scene of Jesus calming the storm on the Sea of Galilee, The Storm; Rembrandt, the only seascape the master ever painted. Reynolds love of Alfred Hitchcock made him curious when the piece was stolen from the Isabella Stewart Gardner Museum in Boston in March of 1990. It was the largest art heist in US history and here it was in front of him. Two thieves dressed as Boston police officers persuaded a guard to let them inside the private museum and they walked out with a half a billion in stolen art work. He had followed the unsolved case for years, especially since it had a $5 million dollar reward; early retirement he told himself as he spent weekends trying to solve the case. Reynolds flew to Boston twice following the museum's security guard around town trying to get a new statement, some kind of information. And there it was, hidden for over a quarter of a century.

The next painting was a portrait of a man with a dark top hat, Manet no doubt. The next, a self-portrait etching of Rembrandt followed by a Degas-Jockeys on a horse. There were five of the thirteen pieces stolen over twenty-five years ago and one of the Bureau's most intriguing cases of all time. Right here in front of him. His calmness disappeared and he feared he might faint.

Lamb crept in behind him. "Well kiss my ass."

"Yeah."

"Good god. We've been looking for this stuff forever. Who'd a thought it would be found here?"

"Not I."

"Can't see Mr. Sombrero taking a liking to this cultured stuff."

Reynolds bent down, studying the Vermeer. "This is what we're dealing with. What I've been trying to tell top brass. These guys aren't punks. They're sophisticated and have total access to anything they want. Unbelievable."

"Biggest art heist since King Tut," Lamb heckled. "This shit real?"

A Navy Seal spoke up. "We've sent photos to the NSA, and they've already confirmed them."

Scott Reynolds' phone buzzed. He stepped over to a corner of the room, listened for a minute and returned. "Intelligence was right," he said in a low tone, placed his phone in his front pocket, picked at his eyebrow. "This was an ambush. God damn Diablos caught us with our pants down. This is their competition, the Gallos Grandes. Diablos set the hook, and we chomped at it."

"So they wanted us to take out their enemy?"

"Damn right. I don't know how the hell they're getting their information."

Torrez placed the palm of his hands together in front of his belt buckle. Shame shadowed his face like a lesson in humility. "Well at least we captured the leader of the Gallos Grande. This should help us with our fight against the drug trade."

Scott Reynolds had a spasm of grief so intense that he kicked the back of a chair and bit his lip "It's the old adage in foreign espionage." He raised his head. "Take away one leader and find yourself with something worse in return. That something is a hell of a lot worse... The Diablos." The artwork already all but forgotten.

Chapter 51

"If you're going through hell, keep going."—Winston Churchill

Jason Carson sat across from Krista Garrison at the Gerdin Learning Center on a Tuesday evening. They sat in a study room with a window that looked out at Kinnick Stadium. The door was closed but glass allowed coaches to monitor the studies of the athletes. There were scads of students tonight sitting around tables, heads buried in textbooks and laptops. Jason rubbed the swollen knuckle on his left hand. It still ached after he'd jammed it two days ago. His mouth was parched, lips bloated. He could easily get dehydrated, and that certainly never helped him study. Even after practices he seemed to be perspiring more these days. Pains without exertion sat within him now, a new unfamiliar drudgery. He took a healthy drink from his Camelback. Krista looked up from her book. She took the band out of her hair. Her blonde hair dropped over her shoulders. She swung her head from side to side, pushed it away from her face. Jason watched. There were no distractions when he looked at Krista. She put him in that zone. Something was different about her. She was self-assured, almost as much as he was. But the thing that drew him to her was the way she had of humbling herself. Shy but bold. Outgoing but introverted, in some kind of attractive way that mystified him. The best of both worlds.

"How bout we go shoot in a little while? Need to get my free throws in?"

"That didn't work out so well last time," she said as she looked down at her Cost Accounting book.

Since that night, things had been different with Krista. She was distant but still interested somehow. "What about Friday night? I've got Wake Forest Wednesday and you play...umh.

"Kansas State," she replied, not lifting her eyes.

"Sorry, it's hard to keep up with all this sometimes." He watched her. He inhaled the citrus aroma from her hair. "Friday night we could go to a movie at the Union? Might even buy you some popcorn."

"I really don't think I'm available."

"What about Sunday night after your game? No training table that night. Pizza somewhere?"

She turned the page of her book, still looking down. "I'm going out with the team that night."

He was silent for a moment, charged ahead. "Well what if you pick a night that works. I can make—"

"I think we should just keep things between us as friends right now."

Jason's belly filled with the pain of his pregame jitters. Was this about to end like all the other relationships he'd had over the years? "What about that night we were in the practice center? You seemed to be pretty interested then?"

She lifted her head out of her book and glared at him with cadet blue eyes. Her lips bridled, the skin around her cheeks constricted. "I don't think this is going to work between us, and I don't want to take it any further, especially with your situation and all."

Jason's eyes narrowed. "My situation. You mean because I'm only a freshman and you're a junior?"

"No, you idiot. It has nothing to do with your age. But it does have something to do with you being around a short time." She bit down on her lower lip. "I mean, in a half a year you'll be leaving, moving on to some city, hours from here, and I'll never see you again. You said yourself, that you're only going to be here for a year and then if I get attached to you, I'll be the one left behind." He could see wet droplets blooming from the edges of her eyes, now more of a Caribbean blue. "And that night at the gym, I got myself in a predicament. I am very competitive, probably as competitive as you, but since you're a guy you don't understand sometimes. When my adrenaline gets pumping, I sometimes do things that I regret later."

Jason tried to swallow, but his Adam's apple wouldn't move.

Her face was pained. "I had some bad things happen to me when I was younger."

Jason thought about it for a moment. It couldn't have been as bad as his situation. He nodded. "Anything you'd share.?"

Krista closed her book and wiped her nose. She looked up at him. "I don't talk about it...it's pretty ugly," she said as she swallowed and sighed.

Most of this talk was new to Jason. Heck just about any personal talk was new to him other than his talks with his mother. "I had it pretty bad as a kid. Probably heard it all."

Krista laughed and then sniffed. "That's what I mean. I thought you might be different, but you're just another guy who always looks out for themselves first."

It was probably a true statement when he thought about it. Maybe it was time to be more like his mother? He had prayed when she passed away to take on her wonderful qualities. "I'm sorry," he said as the words sounded strange coming out of his mouth. "I'd really like you to tell me."

Krista wiped her nose with her forearm and took a long breath and shrugged her shoulders. "It was a really bad experience for me, and it's changed the way I've felt around guys. I can't seem to have a normal relationship," she murmured. "When I was in eighth grade I traveled with an AAU team that went all over the country during summers. You know how it is?"

Jason nodded.

"Well my coach was a man and kept pressuring me into his room and forcing me to..." She made fists and clutched herself. Her cheeks were blooming red. "Made me do things, and I was a total mess for awhile until I finally told my parents about it. They took me off the team, and then I thought my basketball career was over, that's how powerful this guy seemed. Well it finally came out that this guy had assaulted other girls, and I had to go to trial, and it was just this long horrible mess," she said gaining a bit of confidence somehow. She sat up straight. "The jerk is in prison…I found another team with a great woman coach."

"Thank God."

She nodded. "But I think I still have some issues….my relationships with guys, are, hard. Especially with someone that's not going to be around for long." She reached into her bag, and pulled out a tissue and wiped her nose.

Jason didn't move. He had thought things were progressing here. In fact, he was hoping this relationship might be a long one; maybe he'd finally found someone he could talk to, share things with and he thought he was doing everything right this time. But suddenly he felt as if Krista had switched teams on him. He felt melancholy and agitated all at once. "I'm sad to hear about that. It must have been hard."

"Still is."

It was a new feeling for him. This feeling of compassion. "I thought I had a tough childhood, but it can't even begin to understand what you had to go through."

She nodded.

"But I thought we had a nice connection. More of a relationship then I've had with other girls. I mean, someone that just didn't like me because I was some kind of circus freak."

Krista sniffed twice, raised her knees to her chest and wrapped her arms around them. She shook her head. "I can't afford to get drawn in with someone that isn't going to be around."

Jason rubbed his cheeks with his palms. There was a tingling sensation in every inch of his body. He couldn't lose someone else. "But I need you," he said without thinking. Did he really say that? He dismissed the question quickly. They were both, to certain degrees, confused by each other. "I need someone to talk to and you're the only one I can really trust."

Krista lowered her legs and sat back in her chair. She laughed. "I just don't want this to be a physical relationship right now. I've got too many things I'm trying to work out."

"I just want to be around you. Talk to you. Laugh. Stuff like that."

Krista gave him a quick smile and widened her eyes. "Yeah, we do seem to think the same things are funny, specially that kid snoring on the table tonight." She giggled, wiped her nose. "I can't wait to see his coach when he finds him."

The two gazed at each other, then laughed. A laugh that turned into a giggle and then into a slapstick kind of bullroar. Jason cleared his throat, turned his head slowly and looked into Krista's eyes. He hesitated and all at once he dreaded what he wanted to say. And he hadn't told her because he didn't want to feel like a fool. He didn't dare let someone get close to him. It definitely was not in his nature. "Um..." No way he'd ever say this to somebody before, but things were different now, heck, different forever. "I could really use," he chewed on his chapped lips, "somebody that I can trust..."

"Someone."

"What?"

"The correct English would be someone, not somebody."

He thought of the times he would fight back, compete with every word someone would say, especially if they were correcting him. His voice was low and sounded unused. "I've had some bad crap happen to me too." Some special force was working through him now. Perhaps his mother's prayers were beginning to be answered. A serendipitous sign of the spirit. For some reason he was less careful about sharing. "I don't really know how to deal with it." He looked out the window, then back into eyes that were straining, watching him.

"You mean losing your mother?"

Oh the things that he'd say if he could. If he could muster the courage. "No, nothing like that. Losing my mom is a problem but I've brought on a few problems on my own."

She stared at him, moved forward, eyes softening. He wanted to tell someone, and Krista seemed like the only one he could trust. He was disgusted with himself. He had lost sight of his target. His only goal in college was to prove he was the number one pick in the draft. But his feelings were taking over here. And God only knows he wanted to release that feeling of imprisonment that kept closing in on him. "Krista…I need to tell you something. I haven't told anyone else about this." He rubbed his chest and gritted his teeth so hard, he thought he was going to crack them. Was he sure this was the right thing? "I got hooked up with an agent in high school that I wished I wouldn't have."

She gave him a stern coaxing glance. "Why don't you just get a new one? There are tons of those guys around. At least that's what I've heard."

He rubbed the back of his neck. Went silent. "This guy wasn't the right guy for me…making me do things I don't want to do…things that may not be right?"

"Why don't you just find a new one. I'm sure coach Trammel could—"

He shook his head furiously. "No, no, I can't. I don't want this to get out." His pulse took off. "I shouldn't even be telling you. I didn't even tell my mother about it." He didn't know if he should go further. Right now he thought maybe if he barfed, he'd probably feel better. He had already said too much.

She gave a quizzical look, twirled her hair with her finger. "I don't think I follow?"

He was showing teeth, but it was the farthest thing in the world from a smile. "I come from a bad situation, Krista. You don't know how bad it was, hell, still is… Geez, we didn't even have a house, we lived in an apartment and didn't even have enough money to live there. My old man left us when I was a kid. Ran off with some bimbo, a lot younger,

I guess." He was nodding fast. "Then my mother got cancer. She went through chemo and that radiation crap. We thought everything was OK. That's what those quacky doctors told us." He unleashed a low whistle. "We couldn't pay for it...had to go bankrupt." His voice sounded wobbly. "So this agent, this guy that had been around a lot. Coming to my games, even a practice or two, told me he could help me. Give my family a little advance on my draft money. To pay for the apartment, bills, especially from the hospital and our car was a complete piece a shit. The guy said he was just giving me an advance."

Krista reached out, put a hand on his arm. "I don't think that's legal."

"I don't think so, now. I didn't know. I didn't have a choice. I needed it to help my mom," he confessed. "It was just between the two of us."

Krista gave him a slight nod. Nothing more.

"But it's gotten a lot worse now."

"You mean you still need money."

Jason shook his head. He told himself he probably said way too much already. He looked at Krista. Let the silence grow. "So that's kinda what I'm dealing with. You're not the only one that's been part of bad situations."

She gave him a tiny nod, rubbed his forearm.

He felt grateful at the way she didn't judge him, fall away from him.

"Well, taking the money was probably your only answer." She glanced at the ceiling, then into Jason's eyes. "But no one will ever find out about it and if they did, I think people would understand."

He was ready to go further, tell her more; felt a bit like it was his turn to lose control. But he waited, took a long breath, felt he was at the free throw line with the game on the line. He wasn't ready to tell her about his current arrangement. "I hope everything works out, that's all." He laughed, feeling confident now. "I'm working out my arrangement with him, I'll fill you in later. That's if there still is a 'later' between us...

You say friends, that's good enough for me, for now, that is." He placed his giant hand over hers. Gave her a soft squeeze and didn't release it. "Let me earn your trust. We can go slow if that's good enough for you."

She blinked at him and he could see a film of moisture sweeping over her eyes.

"Trust is all I'm looking for…just, someone, I, can, trust," he said.

Chapter 52

The New York Times: Americas | World Briefing
Gunman ambushed a Jalisco State police convoy, killing twenty officers in one of the deadliest attacks on security forces in ten years of the drug war, state officials said Tuesday. The convoy was attacked as the police units were traveling though the remote western mountains of Jalisco toward Guadalajara. The gunmen are believed to belong to a powerful gang called the Diablos Cartel, Jalisco's security commissioner, Alejandro Cardenas, said Tuesday in a radio interview. The Diablos Cartel is now one of the most powerful and dangerous drug cartels in the country. They are definitely on the rise, Cardenas commented. Four days earlier, eleven people were killed when a federal police convoy was attacked in Mexico City.

Chapter 53

Jason quietly turned the knob at 12:45 early Friday morning. He was trying to be considerate of his roommate after beating Virginia Tech in a road win. Brandon was hunched over the desk staring at his laptop, a dim light cast onto his face. Jason's eyes adjusted as he moved in and placed his gym bag in front of his closet and shouldered off his coat. Muzzy smells of wintergreen and worms filled the room. Brandon needed to be reminded to empty the spittoon again. Jason's right ankle felt tender, bruised, but it was too late for ice. Rigor mortis would probably set in by morning, but he was exhausted. Brandon remained quiet and didn't acknowledge the presence of his roommate; just remained slouched at his desk like a statue waiting for a pigeon. Jason looked at the Miller bottles lined up on the back of Brandon's desk. A brief flash of grief ran through him.

"What-up, Mongo?"

Brandon didn't move, eyes seemed glued to his screen. Jason moved behind Brandon to see the screen. He saw a poker table with cards being dealt by an automated character resembling a dealer. Jason was baffled. Brandon was a kid that came from money. He always babbled on about how much money he had. But Brandon Sellers was a player. In fact, if he won a game of poker, won a bet on a football game, he would be flying high, but Jason couldn't help but wonder what happened tonight. He'd seen it too many times lately.

"Stayin' up late studyin', Mongo?" he teased.

Brandon inched up in his chair. He looked puzzled for a moment, punched a button, his laptop and screen went black. Brandon turned his head, tried to look up at him but made it halfway, then back down. The pockets under his eyes came in layers. He gave a whattaya-gonna-do shrug. "Had pocket rockets tonight bro…right out of the shoot… first game…pair a aces, my man, and one a the boys pulls a fricken flush on me," Brandon said as if he had a mouth full of liquid. Brandon pointed to the line of bottles lined on his desk.

"Had a few too many tonight." He laughed, then hissed, grabbed his nose with his fingers, wiggling it back and forth. "I'm showing a few signs of technical difficulties, J.C.," as he snapped his head back and forth, finally finding Jason's face. "Your game was beau-ti-ous tonight. Lots of ESPN Facebook close-ups for you tonight, bro. Hope you win an Espy and make sure you thank me when you stand up there with your nice new $5,000 suit and all," he said as he swayed back and forth.

He knew there was no right answer to that one. "Thanks Mongo… love playin' ball." Jason peeled a banana, ate half of it in one bite. "Hope I can keep playing. School sucks, man."

"Don't it?" he said in a slushy murmur.

"Don't get at least a B on my test tomorrow and I'm toast."

"I coulda got the test for ya, if you'd told me asswipe."

"Doing it by myself. No cheating anymore," he said exasperated, "let's hit the hay."

"Don't worry 'bout it. I'll give the T.A. a little lovin' and you'll be settin' the curve on this one…that's after I set straight all her curves or she straightens my curve or sump'in like that…you know what I mean don't you buddy?"

"Come on. Get to bed."

"'Sposed to go out tonight. Didn't make it, even took a disco nap earlier," Brandon babbled as he tried to stand, but his hand grabbed the desk as he settled back into his chair again.

Jason put a clump of toothpaste on his toothbrush.

"My game tonight has been totally," Brandon took a deep breath and gargled his mucous. "Totally, craptacular," he bellowed, then tried to stand again. Steadying himself with his chair and desk. "Just circling the drain all night, J.C." Brandon straightened up to his full height. Jason watched Brandon's body sway from side to side like he was riding out a storm in the middle of the ocean. He wanted to throw Brandon a life line, pull him to safety; at least get him into a life boat. Jason finished brushing. He looked at Brandon and saw blankness in his face, confusion. He glanced at the dresser, and Brandon's wallet was lying next to a stack of plastic cards. He flipped through them; two green cards, Bank of America, Wells Fargo. Blue, red, maroon, purple, orange; all the colors of the rainbow. Jason didn't even own a credit card, but his roommate seemed to be making up for him. How could an eighteen year old accumulate so many credit cards? How much did Brandon owe on these? Sad thing about it, he knew he owed Ricardo twenty five thousand dollars. So strange he thought, everyone looking for money, for all different reasons.

"Think it's time to get you some beauty sleep, Mongo," Jason said as he schlepped Brandon toward his bunk.

"Thanks for bein' sooo nice to me J.C.," Brandon stammered. Brandon climbed up the wooden ladder to his bed, one rung at a time while Jason stood beneath him. Brandon slinked head first into his pillow and groaned.

"Let's not wake up all the neighbors."

Jason crawled into bed.

He mumbled something about the game. "How many rebounds tonight, bro?"

"Eleven. And twenty-nine points but who's counting."

"All those scouts, who you tryin to fool." Brandon let out a long belch. "Double-double for you...double-bubble for me." Brandon giggled.

"Let's get some sleep I got a test tomorrow, remember."

"OK, OK, but you did look good on TV dude. Damn announcers tonight...givin' you frequent flyer miles as many times as they be talkin' bout you, boy. Conway says you get more face-time than anybody he's ever seen. Said everybody else on the team looks like they got voted off the island, 'cept you, bro." Brandon blew out a long breath mixed with some phlegm.

"Yea, nobody else seems to like it. Cold shoulder. Nobody talks to me."

"Jealous bunch of squirrel-dicks. I need to talk to those scum dogs."

"Don't need to get into now. Test tomorrow."

"I wanna be yo' advertising agent when you get into the big show. I be makin' you some real cash if you let me work your commercials and marketing deals, dude," said Brandon as his voice began to quicken. "I be makin' you some real coin with your advertisements on everything bro. No lunch money, J.C....real coin, dude."

Jason felt exhausted; he hadn't been able to sleep on the plane, a tinge of motion. He wasn't even able to study. Now, he just needed to sleep. "OK Mongo, only if you let me go to sleep now."

"Beautiful. Brandon Sellers, Marketing Director." There was a chewiness in his words. "We'll have TV commercials, parts in movies, a line of cologne, hair care products, even a line of clothing with some funky underwear for the hotties. Yes siree, even a book or two with speaking engagements and some stand-in shit on some game shows in the off season. It'll be beautiful, you just wait and see."

Jason pulled up an extra blanket over the top of him, his feet looking for warmth. He was amazed at the way everyone thought things would work out for him. And yet as he lay shivering he knew things were headed in the wrong direction. "Let's wait and see if you can stay away from the crap tables first?"

"OK J.C. I hope you'll respect me in the morning?

"I'll respect you if you shut up. Test tomorrow."

"You'll be fine. Trust me."

Twelve hours later Jason walked out of class and knew that he wasn't going to be fine. He was sure he'd just flunked a test.

Chapter 54

Lamb opened the front door for Reynolds at the Java House in Iowa City, Iowa, on December 6th. Reynolds took off his leather gloves pulling one finger at a time. He folded them twice and placed them into his black wool coat. He tapped the snow and salt off his Italian leather shoes, grimacing. He inhaled the scent of Colombia coffee, and he knew he had come to the right place. Reynolds stood, back straight, shoulders erect as he listened to the espresso machine. With lips damp, he turned and looked at Lamb and proceeded to the back of the room. Smells of sweat soaked furniture filled him. He walked past potato-sack couches, bloated chairs and impostor tiffany lamps to a table in the corner. He shouldered off his jacket and neatly placed it on his lap. He pulled his starched collar away from his neck. Lamb walked over two minutes later with two white cups and placed them on the table.

"Got you a large dark somethin' or other. Hope that was OK?"

Reynolds was sure he'd told him to order the Colombian, but he ignored it. Reynolds combed the room with his eyes and checked his watch. Most of the tables were empty. An old man that looked like a pan-handler sat with his head on a table not too far from them.

Lamb studied the pan-handler for a moment. "Should we buy the poor guy a cup?"

"Just another guy looking for a hand out. Look at the way he's dressed."

"You can't always judge a book, Scotty. You have a tendency to judge others by the way they're dressed."

Reynolds scoffed.

"I don't ever judge by the way someone dresses"

"Come on, guy's a bum."

Lamb shook his head, his eyes skitzy and quivery with Reynolds' response. "When the kids were little I tried to give the old lady a little time to take a nap one day. Stopped in a 7-11 with my new used Chevy Tahoe to get myself a slurpee...you know I love the things."

"Coke or Cherry?"

"I think it was Coke that day." Lamb tried to take a sip of coffee but changed his mind after it hit his lips. "We needed something bigger to drive when Jenny came along. So, I go inside, leave the rig running since both girls were finally sleeping. I serve up my slurpee, get it just the way I like it and head outside, but damn if the car isn't locked."

Reynolds nodded as if he knew all along. "Keys inside?"

"You're in the right business Sherlock. So my ass is stuck outside, can't get in. Started to freak out, knocked on the windows, girls sleeping better than they do all night. Phone was in the car, people walkin' in and out of the store, don't even know I'm there." Lamb flaps his hands, finding a passion he hadn't showed in some time. "Guy with a suit strolls right by me as I'm trying to yell at the girls...wake `em up. I'm starting to get nervous, people just ignoring me like I'm invisible. I'm pounding on the windows, yelling. Then this guy with long hair, braided, clothes like he bought `em in the 60's and hadn't changed `em since, tools up on a rusted old Schwinn with one of those metal baskets in the front to carry all of his shit. Well guess what Sherlock?"

Reynolds shrugged, rolled his eyes.

"Well this guy, he sees my predicament and doesn't even waver. Comes right over, asks me what the problem was, his smile is missing half his teeth, but he starts rocking the car back and forth. I help him and Carrie wakes up and opens the door for me. Guy wouldn't even take any money when I offered it to him. Amazing."

Reynolds' expression didn't change. As far as he was concerned, he'd never ask anybody for help. Take care of yourself first. Personal responsibility. Reynolds glanced over at the guy with his head buried on the table top. "No time for sympathy. Let's get down to business here. Time is short."

"Just trying to explain can't judge a guy by how he looks, plenty of real assholes wear ties."

There wasn't a thing Reynolds could say or do. There probably wasn't anything he could do about anything, not the corruption, murder, or shit that surrounded him every damn day. "Let's just talk about the game. What do we expect out of this kid tonight?"

"Should be a good game…what've you found out about this Johnny Carson kid?" Lamb asked with a crooked grin.

"Our informant Gregory Scarpa found out about him. His name is Jason Carson."

"Scarpa's been doing nice work, huh?"

"Shit, for what we pay the guy. Thought he'd be more help in Mexico City, but he had other business they tell me."

Lamb's smile disappeared. "Wow, extra tight today Scotty?"

It scratched his pride, the never ending deprecation. You say a few words, ridicule follows. Something had to happen soon. "Diablos are killing us," He chewed on his thumb. "We're losing 'em."

"What about Carson?"

"Another dirt bag reeled in by the dirty Diablos."

Reynolds gave him a quick shake of the head. From what he'd read about Jason, it sounded like he had a decent heart. Maybe he didn't have an option? "This one's strange. Everything that I've found about this kid seems to be contradictory to his association with the cartel."

Lamb shook his head, "Bullshit. This kid's no different. He took money. He's a chameleon like all the rest."

"Who's judging now?" The two men surveyed each other for a moment. Reynolds was showing some favor here. He had not anticipated this, but this reminded him of his own situation as a kid. "A Company

Floater told me that he's a decent kid. An HBO (High Bureau Official) said one of his teachers said the kid could be a boy scout. They told us that his mother made him miss games to go to Sunday school." He looked down at his coffee.

"Then we should keep him away from the priests. Come on. No way. You can't trust anyone anymore and these young punks have no morals. They take the money and run."

"Well, we'll need more proof. Maybe the kid just made a bad mistake?"

"Come on Scotty, I've been watchin' others 'drug horses for fun and money' for years now and this kid's no different.

"I don't think so. Kid's got everything going for him. Have you seen him play? Unbelievable."

"Since when'd you get a soft side?"

Some odd mercy had found him, he did not know if he should be grateful for this or not. The kid's story resonated in him. When he was a Cub Scout in fourth grade he took Paul Poppovich's Swiss army knife without thinking. His Cub Scout Leader caught him and had a long talk without telling his parents or kicking him out of the troop. Reynolds knew his Scout leader could have banished him from scouting and he'd never have made Eagle Scout. One bad decision could have changed the direction of his life but he was given a second chance. Reynold's didn't respond

"Yeah, yeah. Youngest star to come around in years. Heard the talk, he wears Superman clothes under his jersey."

"This is so much bigger. So much larger, god damn it." His hands were clenched tight, "It's not just another case. It's what's happening to sports," his voice zooming. "This young kid is the future of the game… the future of sports, everything is fucked. You can't trust any sport if a kid like this is crooked."

"You know it's all been moving that way for years, Scotty."

"But if this kid is on the take. This good kid. There's no hope," Reynolds insisted.

There was a slight change in Lamb's eyes. "Can't trust anybody when there's money involved. Can't blame the kid. It's just the system. Looking at a big contract in the NBA, like you said. Cinderella story. Kid was so poor growing up in the winter he had to wear a coat to the bathroom," Lamb said.

Reynolds paused, gathered himself. "Maybe. Maybe that's why he isn't such a bad kid. He knows he has a big-pay and wouldn't jeopardize it."

Lamb bumped out his bottom lip and tilted his head to the side. "That's exactly why the kid takes the money. He needed it for the family. You saw it, surveillance said the kid was so poor he couldn't even afford to take a piss with a toilet that flushes."

Scott Reynolds looked to his side. "The Diablos."

Lamb grunted. "You keep telling us how brilliant they are?"

"Infiltrate every sport in the US and run their operations by exporting millions from casinos around the globe."

"Do we have a Soundman on this kid?"

"We do now. I had to pull teeth."

"Hmm. We'll see if the kid is just another scumbag."

"No, damn it, I want to believe this Carson kid is decent. I want to prove it's the cartels, the Diablos, the damn Mexicans that trapped him in all this." Reynolds clenched his teeth so hard that he could hear his fillings scrape against the enamel.

Lamb gave him a serious look. "I'm afraid you're wrong, partner. I think our kids are waiting for the money, same as the damn drug trade, no difference. Americans love their drugs, love their money."

"Well, we know the Diablos' Ricardo Perez was in Iowa City last weekend. Surveillance tells us he wants Jason Carson to fake a pulled hamstring in the first half. Carson will let his player go around him for a lay-up and fake the hammy injury," Reynolds said.

Lamb scratched his forehead with his fingertips. "What about the money on the game?"

"Three large offshore bets have been taken and they've all sold off the big money to Vegas. Covered their exposure."

"Hmm."

There was a snort from the bum who had been sleeping. He raised his head and leered around the room as if he'd never seen it before. His gnarled gray and white hair bloomed in all directions. He wiped away a puddle of saliva with the sleeve of his polluted army jacket. His lips were swollen and wet and he made a spiritless growling sound. Reynolds watched as he turned toward him. He was squinting lazily, an estranged flatness in his eyes. A sense of melancholy filled Reynolds. He was beginning to notice that the man's face had a tinge of helplessness, radiating as if it was pulling him closer, taunting him. Reynolds own face was now hot and red, his skin burned. Somehow along the way he never learned empathy. He wondered if it could be caught like a virus. He was beginning, just beginning to notice the man for the first time. His rancid cigarette smell, his unshaven patchy beard, his hands that were knotty and too big for his body, and his movements were timid and brisk and totally fearful. But the unfamiliar emotion and sensibility was refreshing for some reason. Manna from Heaven you could say. It was the same feeling he had for Jason Carson. Maybe he needed to rethink things? Give others a chance? He watched the man who was now whispering to himself fiddling with his tattered bacon collar. And without seeing it before, Reynolds noticed that the man had a smile on his face. The real McCoy smile. Not the phony imitation counterfeit smile worn by TV anchors or hotel clerks, but a genuine rapturous smile and Reynolds had no way of knowing where the hell it was coming from. But it was right there. Right in front for him to see. Reynolds kept watching him and the man's grin was now some sort of beacon. A radiant glow, a lighthouse. Reynolds eyes found their way back to Lamb's. Reynolds nodded to the door. As he stood, he fished into his pocket, pulled out a fifty dollar bill. He waited until Lamb took a few steps toward the door and followed. Without looking at the man's face directly, Reynolds drifted by his table that smelled of urine. He folded the bill as he stepped around a backpack on the floor. He caught a glimpse of the man who looked in his direction. Without breaking stride, Reynolds slid the bill onto the man's table and didn't look back.

Chapter 55

The band pounded out the Iowa fight song. Reynolds and Lamb stood among the Iowa faithful waiting for the team to run out of the tunnel and onto the court. A flash mob of fans waved yellow towels. High voltage music clobbered Scott Reynolds' eardrums, exhilarating and claustrophobic all the same. A pain shot behind his eyes. He nudged Ron Lamb in the ribs. Two overgrown bodies stood in front of them. Both wore black shirts for the Hawkeye Black-out promotion. He leaned toward Lamb and yelled into his left ear. "Nice seats, huh? Won't be able to see a thing." Reynolds screamed.

Lamb leaned down, shouted back, "Don't think you'll be sitting much. Crowd stands for most of 'em buddy," as he looked up into the ocean of black shirts. "Best thing is you get to look at the back of Sasquatch and Bigfoot all night."

Reynolds looked at Lamb, then up at the scoreboard. "I'll watch it on the big screen"

A gaggle of boos followed the team's entrance onto the court. The booing was for a banner of Herky the Hawkeye behind a row of bars; Herky the prisoner. Reynolds looked up at the jumbo screen, then over to Lamb giving him a what's-going-on gesture.

Lamb leaned over as the noise subsided. "Didn't you see the YouTube clip sent to us by the techies?"

Reynolds shook his head.

Smiling, Lamb pointed toward the court. "Herky got thrown out of the last game. Guess he bumped a ref after a few bad calls. Iowa coach got teed-up and the place went nuts." Reynolds gave him a slight nod, squinting. A wake of thunder bellowed through the crowd.

"Security had to come out and pull the bird off with his claw-feet dragging on the parquet floor. Absolutely hilarious. Students in the Hawks Nest were goin' crazy. Kept chanting, "Her-Key, Her-Key" for the rest of the game."

Reynolds watched a fan to his left peel off his shirt. A yellow bird was painted on his chest wrapping around on his back. He turned to Lamb. "So what's with the banner?"

Lamb placed his hand on Reynolds' shoulder. "Fans want their mascot back. Guess Herky got a 3-game suspension. The headlines in the local fish wrap yesterday read: Herky's no Pterodactyl…folks are pretty passionate about their pet bird 'round here."

Reynolds actually smiled. For the last two to three minutes he hadn't thought about the Diablos. The smile erased from his face as quickly as it had appeared, and his thoughts flickered back to Jason Carson. He looked around the arena as the teams were being introduced, fans continued to stand; sound deafening again. He was looking for Ricardo. Would he take the chance to be here? He felt a vibration in his front pocket. He reached for his phone, a message blinked on and off. Reynolds couldn't take his eyes off the screen. Umbra. He'd never received one of these messages before. The message kept blinking Umbra, signaled the highest level of sensitive information. His chest tightened up and began to flutter. The muscles in his face tensed up. He threw a forearm into the chest of Ron Lamb. Lamb swung his head, gave Reynolds a disgusted look. He pointed to his handheld screen. The two men shuffled through the standing fans. They scuttled up a long flight of stairs and headed to a display case of team photos. Reynolds slid his back against the glass and stared at his phone. The message was coming from the office of the Director of the Bureau. Lamb gave him a look as if he could read his partner's body language.

"What is it?" Lamb put a hand in his pocket to reach for his phone.

Reynolds' face was burning. A platoon of screams riffled through the arena.

"Umbra," he said pulling his shoulders back, looking down at the floor. He entered his twelve digit pin number and waited. The wait reminded him of the dead bodies that hung on the walls in Mexico City. Reminded him of the things that someday would drive him away from this job. He looked at the message, then looked into the eyes of Ron Lamb. He felt a knot in his stomach. "Shit. Director of Surveillance sent the message," he said as he let out a breath. "Kryptos encryption has been broken. Somebody's been reading all of the Bureau's messages and encrypted communication, and we don't know for how long. Biggest hack of the century." He tightened his lips, mouth dried up and he took a few seconds to continue reading his message. "Pentagon and the White House want answers. Kryptos has been around for twenty years; now it's all over. They're trying to switch formats."

"Jesus." Lamb's eyes were wide and perplexed. "Russians? Chinese? Middle East? Who?"

Reynolds sucked air. He rocked his head from side to side. "Wasn't a superpower," he said as he clenched his teeth. "Believe it or not," he closed his eyes and stayed silent for awhile listening to a crowd that went quiet in front of him. "Our favorite assholes from the South."

"We knew those son-of-a bitches were smart, but—"

Reynolds thumbed the 'off' button on his phone. They walked over from the concourse to the back railing of the stadium seats to see why the crowd had gone quiet. Reynolds stared at the court and watched as the Iowa coach and trainer attended to a player lying on the foul line.

"Damn. Looks like it's Carson."

The two men looked at each other without speaking. Scott Reynolds's phone buzzed again, but he looked at the floor. He closed his eyes then looked at his phone again. 'Red Alert'.

"Shit," Reynolds muttered, pressing the button. He pulled the phone closer to his face, held his breath. He couldn't believe what he was reading but it wasn't classified information. He looked up at Lamb. "We just got a report that sixteen tennis players were reported fixing games."

Chapter 56

BBC — A new report by the BBC charges "widespread match-fixing by players at the upper level of world tennis." The report charges that a collection of 16 players, all of whom have reached the world Top 50, have participated in match-fixing. The report did not name names but charged that the sport's governing bodies have repeatedly ignored evidence of match-fixing. The BBC report relies on leaked internal documents as well as independent analysis of betting patterns around 26,000 matches and found what the publications consider compelling evidence of match-fixing connected to gambling crime syndicates. The investigation follows the 2016 revelation of alleged match-fixing at matches all over the world, a revelation that ultimately ended without any real resolution.

Chapter 57

Heavy flakes of snow parachuted on top of Tim McMurray's head as he stepped out of the cab on Post Street on the north end of Boston. Last night's post game celebration had found him posting NBA all-star numbers on the breathalyzer. Good thing for him last night's game needed little work from McMurray. Any extra basket or extra bump or hand check or rebound seemed to happen naturally. McMurray just made sure the favored home team to beat the spread and in the end he was back on top of the world. Returned to good graces with Ricardo Perez and back in the money again. An extra shot of cash dunked right into his checking account via wire transfer. Post Street in Boston was home to The Madame Coppola, one of the world's most renowned Spiritualists. Not only was she known for identifying the 'Poltergeist Phenomena', over sixty authenticated cases of poltergeist operations, she was an acclaimed ectoplasmist, reviving corporeal apparitions of departed souls. She had studied the work of Alfred R. Wallace, the originator of the origin of the species while writing her thesis, The Scientific Conclusion of the Supernatural.

Muzzy clouds shrouded the tops of the brownstones. McMurray took two steps up the stairs, his alligator shoes partly covered in snow. He looked at the doorbell and waited, watching the snow. A perfect snow meant he was on the right path. Of course it did; that perfect snow that he'd only seen in movies, soft and falling straight from the sky. Not the type of snow that falls in Minnesota. The Minnesota snow wouldn't be a good sign for him. That snow in Minnesota doesn't fall; it attacks the ground in waves. He eyed the round black doorbell. He studied his fingernails, perfectly polished as he pressed the knob. The wooden door belched as it opened. A woman in her seventies stood waiting. She had ash white hair pulled to a bun on the top of her head. Her face boney and gaunt, red glasses curved upward to a point on each end, lilac lipstick veiling linguine lips.

"Madame Coppola has been waiting for you."

McMurray moved onto a rectangular rug with black diamonds, tapped his feet. The foyer had a gloomy tightness about it, crimson wallpaper which gave the appearance of deceased cemetery plot flowers in white vases. It took him a moment; then he followed the old lady into the parlor. A dozen candles were scattered around the room, casting sulfured shadows on the walls. To Tim McMurray the air was dead again, thick and sullen. He inhaled the scent of dusty wool. The furniture was bizarre: dark, hand-carved statuettes covered with velvet and doilies. He recognized a grandfather clock, a glass barometer, a copper bed pan, a tarnished sterling silver tea set along with curtains; dozens of satin curtains and murals hung on wasted walls. While awaiting the Madame he placed his hands on the back of a Victorian chair, touching the carved wood outlining the top. Tim moved around to the front of the chair, stared at it for a second, then sat down. The room was too warm for the middle of winter. The collar of his starched Brooks Brothers' shirt was damp. He saw the round table in the center of the room where Madame conducted her business. A white sheet covered the table with a raised lump in the center. He knew it was Madame's crystal ball. Despite the deranged composition of the room, that is what he came to see. Without a sound, a white light emanated from the outer edge of the room like a sunrise. The shadows on the walls from the candles jittered. Madame Coppola moved toward the center table. She began a low methodic chanting. Wearing an ivory headdress decorated with precious stones the size of half-dollars, Madame Coppola entered into the room. He could hear her breathing laboriously, almost wheezing like an old accordion. She stopped in front of him and held out a hand, her arm as thin as a twig. He reached out and held her hand for a moment. Her fingers had a bitter iciness to them, shivery, as if petrified bones, almost numbing his hands.

"Sit down Mr. McMurray, the spirits are waiting."

He moved to his seat, light began to drain from the room, then the ball on the center of the table illuminated Madame's face. She closed her eyes, the table flickered. Her lips moved but she did not make a sound, meditating, then such light whispering McMurray could not make out the words.

"We are now moving into another dimension." She hummed, and a rush of cool air swept over the back of his neck. Madame's eyelids fluttered. "Tell us... Tell us why Mr. McMurray is troubled." Her voice was a smooth and continuous low pitch. "They are telling me not to speak to you." Her lip quivered.

McMurray thought she might be hypnotized. Should he speak? He could tell that she was struggling to contact the 'sitter', the intermediary.

Madame closed her eyes. He knew she was channeling now, waiting and listening. A small pink light kindled around the back of her shoulders. "You have been warned... The spirits have spoken to you." Her eyes widened, looking, then, closing. "You haven't listened." Her voice louder now, moving to a higher octave.

Her eyes moved to the ceiling as if she was looking for someone. "You have initiated your own problems. People have suffered because of you." She raised her palms, looked to the ceiling. "Listen, we must listen." There was knocking, one, two, three, four. Then it stopped. She yelled, "four."

Then it started again. Stopped. She said, "nine."

Again, this time five knocks.

"495".

"What —"

"Quiet," she requested. "I am in the Roman Coliseum. There is a crowd. Wild tigers and leopards are parading about. Men wearing armor, with swords. They are chasing the animals. The crowd." She swallowed. "They're mesmerized, drunk, screaming. They want blood, more blood. Wait…everything is changing now," her eye lids flickering, "It's the Emperor standing in his box, waving his arm. It's Nero. I see the year 49AD. There are five Gladiators in the center. Five. With spears and swords. They are waiting. Waiting for someone to come out and fight," , her teeth even clicking together for a moment. "Nero, 49. Five Gladiators pacing around the arena. 495. It's the Roman numeral 495 I see….CDXCV. Of course. That is what you are looking for," she panted.

McMurray could hear laughter in the background. His heart quickened. "What are you—"

"Quiet." She breathed deeply, starting to whisper, "Don't like what they are telling me…someone else will be hurt, murdered."

He waited.

"495. It's a Roman numeral. CDXCV." Her face hardened. She rocked back and forth. It. Is. A. Child," she warned.

He didn't want to believe her. Adrenaline was racing around in his head like a power saw running full speed. CDXCV. Conner David X Chloe Vanessa. The children. His children. McMurray stood right up, moved out of the room, flung open the front door, plunged through it and ran down the street, between cars disguised with snow; there was honking, swerving, others slamming on brakes, chaos everywhere..

Finally, his breath heaving, he stopped. How long had he been running? His feet hurt, knees aching but he didn't stop moving, he just slowed to walk. It was all too much to handle. He felt everyone watching every move that he made. There was no way out. His fingers numb, his face anesthetized, his eyes swelling with water. He saw a lit building and skittered inside. The name Talisker and Sons was printed on the wall above a fish tank, but it didn't matter where he was He just needed to stop, anywhere.

A women with glasses and inflated blonde hair stared at him. "May I help you, sir?"

McMurray shook his head as he stomped snow from his feet, his legs rigid. His hands fluttered, he concentrated, tried to steady them, pressed the name Roger McMurray on his phone. He waited. There was a pause, two rings, waiting.

A voice jolted him. "What's up?"

He couldn't speak.

"Timmy, that you?"

As if his jaw was bolted shut he worked it with his hand. "Bro."

"Walking into tennis center. Call you back."

"No. Listen. No. I need you."

"How bout in an hour, I'm late."

"Roger, listen to me. It's an emergency."

"Dude, everything's always an emergency. Don't have any dough. I'm broke myself."

"Goddamn it. Listen to me," he shouted checking the buffed-up blonde who was watching him, lower in her chair now. "You need to get to my house. How soon can you be there?"

There was a pause. "Look, I got shit I got to do. I'm working at 8:00 tonight."

"I need you now, right away."

"Look, I finally got hired and I'm not risking it, man."

"I'm in trouble. No, no, not me. The kids. Big trouble. I need you."

"Tell your ex to do something. I got a tough match here."

McMurray watched as the blonde inched away from her desk, back against the wall. "Roger, you to need to get into your car and go to my house. Chloe and Conner are in trouble. Somebody wants to hurt them. Maybe kill them."

No response.

"You need to get to my house. My basement. Get my 22. It's in the safe. Password is DUCKHUNTER. Get it out and stay with the kids. You need to stay with them, in their rooms. Don't let Conner and Chloe out of your sight. You hear me, goddamn it?"

"Man." A long sigh. "You know I hate guns. You NRA knuckleheads. Listen to what you're saying. You're paranoid, dude."

"Listen Roger," he wailed. "For once in your fucked-upped life you need to listen. Get to my house. My kids are in danger," he said as he heard sirens approaching. "Get to my house, get the gun, and please don't let the kids out of your sight. Call you back soon," he blurted as he made his way to the door. A moment later he was on the run again.

ESPN—For years NHL commissioner Gary Bettman was staunchly against sports gambling publicly and privately. "It is my judgment that in terms of what we try to create, what we want to present, the atmosphere that we want people to feel part of, is inconsistent with sports betting," Bettman said in a deposition in 2012. Recently, Bettman said that the Supreme Court decision in 2018 made him change his opinion. Today, the NHL announced that MGM will be an official betting partner. Last month, the Vegas Golden Knights announced a non-exclusive sportsbook sponsorship with William Hill, which has 108 sportsbooks in the state.

NHL teams are now free to do their own sponsorship deals with sportbooks.

Chapter 58

Jason pushed the Playstation joystick up and then down, up then down, again and again. Gran Turismo Sport was his new go-to. Seventy-five minutes and he was really getting the hang of it. He put the console on the couch, picked up his phone and couldn't believe what he saw. NBAdraft.com had him now at number 4 with an arrow pointing down. Projections had him at number 3 last week. Crap, no way? He slung the ice bag onto the coffee table in his room. He'd been told by the trainers and team doctor to ice his hamstring for fifteen minutes each hour, and he needed to play the part. The fact was, he hadn't played the deception game before, but he instantly knew he didn't like it. Guilt traumatized his stomach, he had no appetite. Brandon jaunted into the dorm room, leaned his head over the spittoon and dropped a string of saliva onto the edge of the copper bowl. His normal pale face now flushed, blonde curls hung over his eyebrows, blue eyes permissive. "How's that hammy feelin'?" he asked as he twisted off the top of a can of chewing tobacco.

"Better."

Brandon gorged a pinch of tobacco behind his lower lip, his tongue arranging it along his teeth. "Without you in there last night, the

Hawks couldn't give the visitors their normal whoop-ass. You guys only won by eight, line in Vegas, fourteen. Damn glad I didn't bet on it."

"Keep things clean, man. Don't get your ass in a jam."

"Long as it brings in the cash flow baby, I'm usually in." He opened the refrigerator and grabbed a beer. "Goin' out with us tonight?" Brandon pleaded as he snapped the twist off cap into the garbage can.

Jason shook his head. "Studying with Krista."

"Holy shit J.C., the two a you are like wombmates." Brandon pushed the spittoon with his foot, "you better give this place a little fling cleaning."

Jason shook his head, "I flunked the Humanities test."

"Ouch."

"Coach talked to prof and said I could write a makeup paper."

"Since when is that legal?"

"If I'm injured or something, guess I can make it up."

"Yeah, right," he scoffed. "You and you only, numbnuts. Separate rules I guess."

"Still got to write it bro."

"For 100 bone you can have somebody write it for you."

Jason didn't respond.

"Well? What'd ya think?"

"One of the assistant coaches found somebody to write it for me."

"What? A Coach? You kidding me? No cost either?"

"Guess Dajuan's done it a bunch."

"How come I ain't heard about this," he razzed. "Just the ballers I guess."

"Still need to study with Krista."

"Studying your new foreplay these days. Be careful, don't want you livin' in sin with a safety pin, know what I mean."

He was ashamed but he replied anyway. "Won't even let me kiss her."

"After all that time together and you're just singing a Disney song." He made a face as if he'd sucked on a lemon. "Dump her and start trolling with me big boy. Look, I'm celebrating my anniversary." He gave Jason a fat grin showing teeth that looked as dingy as an old dried newspaper. "It's asstastic I'm tellin you, not bein' held down by one babe."

"I'll keep that in mind."

"Next thing you know, you'll be asking me to be your best man. You're given me post fartum depression." Brandon said as he slapped his shoulder and circled the back of the couch.

Looking wearily at him he added. "Listen, Mongo, I need decent grades. You keep telling me you're going to help with this test or that quiz, then it never happens? Same thing everywhere I go, school and grades. I'm in deep shit. I could be ineligible next semester. My career could be over."

"You'll be fine, buddy. You got it made," he said encouragingly.

Jason had heard the praise before. He normally thrived on it but now a thread of doubt needled his soul. He had to resist the urge to hit something, his heartbeat filled him.

"How 'bout your grades Mongo? You haven't been goin' to class and you haven't even been working out with baseball for over a week. What's up with that?"

For a moment he looked uncertain and concave. "Everything's sweet," he said tilting his beer bottle and looking at it as if it had just appeared in his hand.

"Don't think that's the whole story?"

Brandon looked away, scratched his head and took a breath. His voice was soft, almost unrecognizable. "Don't know, J.C., my bettin' hasn't been goin' too good this semester," he glanced at the ceiling, then found the floor. "My bookie service was red hot last year. Had five home boys workin' for me and payin' 'em lunch money." Brandon leaned over and spit into the spittoon, then inhaled and cleared his throat. "Now I got my shit in a bit a trouble, I'm ridin' the girl bike right now." He shook his head. "But I'll get myself back on track. Need to get some coin to buy me some grades at finals."

Jason didn't respond. He just stared at Brandon.

There was a slight change in Brandon's eyes. "But you're the one with your nuts in a vice. No kissy from Krista. Sounds more like friends with penalties to me. Have it your way. I'm going to pick up Conway and Frosty. I'll make up some story 'bout you and Miss Centerfold getting ready for some test or somethin'."

There was a knock at the door even though it was half open. Krista Garrison stood there as she sometimes did, carrying herself in a manner that suggested elegance. She gave the two a smile she must have used in her favor before; a smile that told men to pay attention. She had a loaded backpack hanging over her shoulder.

"Hello, boys. Am I interrupting?"

"Just headin' out, Sunshine. Got to do some studyin' myself." Mongo turned to Jason, winked and stepped for the door.

"Don't forget your backpack, Mongo," Jason said.

"Don't worry, I think Frosty and Conway have all the study material tonight." He closed the door behind him.

Krista waited for a few seconds. She shook her head. "He's quite the character."

He began to fidget. Suddenly he grabbed the ice bag and put it under his leg. "He'd make great reality TV. I'm betting on him having his own show some day."

She sat down next to him and placed a hand on his knee. "How's the leg today?" Her touch rang on his flesh. He looked down at his leg and waved a hand at it. He wasn't able to lie again, not to Krista.

He reached for his book. "Biggest problem right now is this next test. Need to get it right this time, or I'm in huge trouble. Driving me crazy. Can't even sleep. Even missed two free throws today."

She pulled out her water bottle and reached for his book on the coffee table. "Let's get at it then."

"I'll go over my notes, while you read the highlighted areas in the three chapters."

She nodded. "I took this two years ago and aced it. "You'll be OK but it will probably take a good two-three hours."

Several times before Jason had wanted to tell her but his back was definitely against the wall here. "I've never been able to read too well." He cleared his throat, moved the ice back a few inches. "I'm kind of dyslexic. At least not totally, but I have a hard time reading." He paused. "I have trouble studyin' when there's a ton of reading material. I go to class and remember every fricken thing the professor says, but reading tons of pages, gives me big trouble." He had never ventured down this road with anyone before now. He waited.

She stared at him with big alluring eyes. She looked puzzled for a minute. A tiny smile grew on her face. "It's definitely high school superstar syndrome." She nodded. "Not your fault, handsome. We're studying this in Psych right now. Culture overlooks problems with celebs and people of wealth or power." She pulled her hair back. "You've been coddled and babied because you're a celebrity. No one wanted to be the bad guy and stand in your way…been going on for centuries."

"Sure, whatever you say."

"Thing is, folks like you are very bright and can fool people about their learning disability."

"I don't have a disability," he said."

She tilted her head towards him, her look was intoxicating. "I'm just here to help," as she inched forward.

He clenched his teeth.

She looked surprised and amused all at the same time. The room went quite. Jason could hear music pounding at the end of the hallway.

Krista took a deep breath, bit down on her lip. "I did tell you a little bit about my situation, remember?"

His eyes widened. She worked her fingernails. He studied her face.

"I can't have anyone touch me right now, not yet," she said as she straightened her shoulders and raised her chin. Confidence moving back in. "You haven't said anything?"

Jason hadn't expected this, but it was still a relief. More like a bit of confession; good for the soul. Cleansing. She was waiting for him, looking for a response. "I don't know what to say," he murmured.

She twisted her face and forced a laughed. "Guess that's what I get for opening up. It's why I was first interested in you. Handsome, sure, but thought we were alike in some way…could share with each other, but—"

He sat up. "I didn't mean it that way…I'm just not very good at giving advice."

"It's not what I've seen," she said hastily.

He was searching. "I just haven't had talks about this stuff."

She looked away. "I just thought you'd understand…Maybe not understand completely, no one can, but at least try to get what I'm going through."

He snapped a knuckle on his forefinger. "Thing is Krista, I haven't had much practice talking about personal stuff. I keep everything inside. The only time I ever shared things, was with my mother." This time it was his turn to look away. The pain of bereavement tortured him every day since the passing of his mother. Anguish and gloom saturated his soul. He longed for the smell of her, the safety of her smile, the sound of her laugh, the touch of her hand. His faith and security now an inquisition. What can he rely upon? He yearned for a divine messenger. The pain in his stomach never ceased.

"I couldn't trust anyone else…Old man left us. Kids my age, jealous of me. Don't really know why, since I never had the things they had growin' up. Never got to go on vacations. Never got new clothes. Old cars. Never ate at restaurants." He cracked more knuckles and ran his hands down his thighs, back and forth. "I just wanted kids to like me but it's tough when they don't like you because you can do something a lot better than they can." He took a long breath, studied Krista's face. No judging, no interrupting; just listening. The atmosphere in the room was almost serene, perhaps mysterious. Peace swept over him. He wanted to know how far he should go with this. It sounded rational on one level and ludicrous on the other. He looked up at her and saw those big blues just staring at him. No moisture this time, just the look of jubilation, flickering, shining. But it wasn't going to solve any of his problems.

He reached down and pulled the ice bag from the back of his leg. He raised it above his head and shot it about eight feet across the room and made a slapping sound as it landed perfectly in the sink.

"You even practice in your room, I see. Never take a minute off."

He wanted to smile but now wasn't the time. He felt a sudden tightness in his chest. He sighed and looked directly into her eyes. "I really didn't get hurt last night."

She gave him a half grin. "I know you guys were up at the end of the game, but there other ways to get your teammates into the game. You could have told the coaches—"

He interrupted. "You need to listen…I heard what you had to say. What you wanted to get out in the open. Now it's my turn."

"Well, you did tell me about your reading challenges and I think that was sweet—"

He raised a hand and shook his head. "It's your turn to listen and my turn to explain, or try to."

She blinked at him with eyelashes as big as Monarchs. She sat back a few inches. "I'm all ears."

He looked up at the ceiling as if he was looking for direction. "I don't have an injury and I didn't fake it because I wanted to give my teammates more playing time." He paused for a moment. "I was instructed to do it from a man that helped me when my family needed money. A man that lent cash to my family or else we wouldn't have a place to live or medicine for my mother. Medicine to help her beat that damn cancer that kept coming back." His chest began to hitch, but he remained in control. He let a breath through his nostrils. "I wish I could pay back the son of a bitch, some way. Some different way than faking an injury or not playing defense in the last few minutes of a game. A game that's already decided."

He turned back toward her. The look on her face told him all that he needed to know. He leaned back and crossed his legs. "Now you know more about me and the crap I've been going through since I showed up here. Crap that's might screw up the rest of my career, rest of my life."

"OK" she said, dragging it out so it became an "Oooooh, Kaaaaay." She looked surprised now, then amused all over again. But her eyes stayed on him and they were gentle, perfectly soft as she studied his face.

"This could be really scary."

He had a lump in his throat the size of a golf ball. It was infuriating what he had done. "I can't eat. Can't sleep. Can't pass my classes. I'm a dead man," he shrieked.

After a moment she placed her hand on his knee and moved forward. She leaned toward him in slow motion, never taking her eyes off his and pressed her soft lips onto his and kissed him. Kissed him long and hard and brave.

Chapter 59

As a trainer it was like a tornado the way Tommy's hands propelled around Jason's ankles, taping and tearing. "How's the back, kid?"

"Not bad."

"Shoulder?"

"Same."

"See the psychologist lately?"

"Just once. I'm done. That stuff's for wackos."

"Don't give up on him."

"Nah. I can work it out myself."

"Think you should go back. He can help."

His mother never had any help he told himself. As he watched Tommy finish his second ankle he surprised himself, candid, "Guy can't help me get better grades. School really sucks."

Tommy snorted air through his nostril hair. "You're not alone kid. You eligible?"

"Advisor's all over my butt. Calls me all the time."

"That's not good kid. You look thin, lost weight."

"If I do force myself to eat I can't keep it down most of the time," he admitted with a sense of remorse, shame creeping in.

"Maybe a redshirt. Till you figure everything out, kid."

"You're kidding…I got to get the hell out a here," he whined.

"You've got a lot on your plate, young man. Maybe the best is you get another year?"

It was like a bomb fell into his lap. He didn't want to listen. "No way Tommy. I can't…

"Seen it before. Wouldn't hurt you, ya know."

Jason sat up, pulled up on his shorts, kneading his knuckles into his prickly thighs. When was the last time he shaved? "I'm outta here. Need to pass a class and write a paper."

"Need to grieve your mom's passing," Tommy scolded.

"It's not what she would have wanted. She wanted me to fight. She was a fighter. Best fighter I've ever known. Told me to live the dream."

"Sometimes we have nightmares before we can dream. You've had a rough go of things. Death is cruel. Lost my wife five years ago."

Jason withdrew into silence. "Oh. Really," he stopped. "I didn't know. Sorry. Must have been tough."

"Still is kid," he said as he squeezed white liquid into his palm, rubbed his hands together and proceeded to lotion his forearms with stuff that smelled a bit like menthol and a lot more like his mother's hospital room. "Things just ain't the same. Never will be I guess." His eyes looking away. "Thing is, though, you need to adapt and that takes time. You need to give yourself some time, Jason."

"Don't have it. Lot's a expectations, ya know."

"Hmm. Things don't always work out the way you plan 'em, just sayin'."

He shook his head. "Can't afford not to keep going. No dough coming in….So, no shrink, doc. No getting weak here. Staying strong." He pounded his chest. "Just need to pass some tests, write some stupid papers and get my life started."

Chapter 60

Jason watched a basketball manager as he tossed balls into a large cage next to the supply room of Carver-Hawkeye arena. Two players walked by him in the tunnel, neither one spoke. With the other players all departed, the arena was now silent, lifeless again. The manager clicked off lights. Jason pulled on his jammed middle finger as he rotated his aching shoulder. His hips were stiff, he needed an ice bath. Though being a big man, it seemed that comfort was always just out of his reach. The lights of the arena continued to dim as he waited. He heard footsteps from the tunnel. Without a word, assistant coach Brian Granger stood in front of him. Granger was shorter than all the other coaches and had a shaved head that he constantly massaged. He lightly drummed his fingers over his dome as he held a brown folder in front of his chest. He wiggled the folder from side to side. "It's a B plus guarantee."

Jason stared at him.

"A perfect 'A' paper may spark too many questions. This should work out perfectly," he said, gesturing for Jason to take it.

Jason fixated on the envelope, trying to focus, evaluating.

Granger bristled as he stretched out his arm and whacked the envelope onto Jason's chest. "You should be thankful Carson." There was something harsh in his tone. "Not easy getting this done for you, shit."

Jason's sweat evaporated. The cold seeped through his practice uniform toward bone. He had been through this before. The gift, the envelope, the broken promises all compounding his regret and sinfulness. His innocence had been taken from him and his liability never left. May never leave him. What else could he do? The conquest to conquer was conflicting. For some reason, he thought of his mother sitting on the end of his bed when he was a child, maybe when he was ten or twelve. It was one of those nightly bible stories that she read to him each night without failing. This one was the one that he had heard a few times before. It was the story from Matthew that told of Jesus who spent forty days and forty nights in the wilderness without food. Jason remembered this one because he couldn't go two hours without eating. Jason always got scared at the part when the devil showed up to lure him to play for his team. The devil took Jesus to a very high mountain and showed him the Kingdoms of the world and told him that all of it would be given to him if he bowed down and worshiped him. Jesus responded by telling him to get away, that he should worship only the Lord and to serve him only. Then, like superheroes, the angels would arrive and take the devil away. His mother would always smile when she was done with that story. In fact, she smiled after she finished all of the Bible stories she read to him, that radiant joy glowing from her face.

Jason had grabbed the envelope from Granger's hands. The past was a shaky proposition, but there was redemption before him. Extending his arms, he brushed the chest on Coach Granger's Nike sweat-top. He tore the envelope down the center, ripping it completely in half and dropping it to the floor. "No thanks. Not this time." And then was gone.

Chapter 61

The doors snapped closed behind Reynolds. The room was dark. Reynolds saw four men but didn't immediately recognize any of them. Reynolds' contacts needed a fresh cleaning; the fuzziness on his retina never seemed to go away. Reynolds moved into the empty seat at the table and felt the glare of eyes. He was five minutes late. Director Hamilton's eyes looked shallow, almost swollen.

Hamilton cleared his throat. "I just came from the White House." There was definitely harshness in his tone. "I met with the President, Secretary of Defense, Homeland Security, NSA, and one of our favorite four-star generals from the Pentagon." He tapped his fingers on the table, looked around the room. "NSA is monitoring global internet traffic." He squeezed his forehead, looking at a heavy-set man with a long beard. "Clark Perkins is paying us a visit to inform us about the possibility of a security breach." He took a long breath and waved a hand at him. "Go ahead Mr. Perkins."

"Thank you, Director." Perkins ran a hand over a belly so large he looked like he was about to give birth. "Two weeks ago, the Pentagon expanded its worldwide communication network, known as the Global Information Grid, which allows them to handle yottabytes; that's ten to the twenty-fourth power bytes of data, or a septillion if you please."

Hamilton snapped his head back. "Get on with it." Reynolds was familiar with the tightness in his tone.

Perkins nodded, pushed his glasses up his nose with a pudgy finger. "We're storing a mammoth amount of data. Private emails, cell phone calls, and Google searches along with personal data trails, parking receipts, travel itineraries, bookstore purchases, and what they call pocket litter. Our supercomputer works with almost unimaginable speed." He smiled, but Hamilton now stared at the table. "Speed to look for patterns and unscramble codes."

Hamilton reared backward, eyed the ceiling. "Perkins, please tell my staff what they need to hear. Goddamn bureaucrats never get to the point," he said aggravated.

Perkins looked disheveled. He fingered his glasses again. Thankfully,

Reynolds was at the far end of the table, because he had seen the way the Director would take people apart.

"Very well…we've been battling hackers since the Towers went down and the consequences are now much more severe. We—"

Hamilton cut him off. "OK, enough," he barked. "The Pentagon's issued a code Umbra. Our personal and business comm which we have been assured," he inhaled and held his breath for a few seconds, "Was heavily encrypted, is now in peril. Four hours ago, the pricks from NSA determined that our unfathomably complex encryption system is now at risk. Our Kryptos encryption system, which developer James Sanderson told us was 'unpenetratable,' has been lost, unscrambled, decoded, whatever intelligence wants to call it." He waved a hand in the air. "The worst part is that this might have been going on for some time"

Reynolds couldn't believe what he was hearing. How long could someone access data without intelligence knowing? Better yet, who and why he asked himself?

"The brass all have their titties in a ringer and they want us to find out who's responsible." There was a buzz on a screen that sat in front of Director Hamilton's seat. Hamilton took the glasses from the top of his head and glanced at the screen. Silence for a few moments.

"NSA believes the decoding has come from hackers in Mexico." Again, silence,

Reynolds was freaked by the void. "What are the consequences here?"

Hamilton's eyes twitched and quivered. "It's an Umbra, Agent Reynolds."

Reynolds nodded once. He wanted more detail.

"National Security and the Pentagon have gone so far to think this could interrupt all of our comm. They've installed security procedures to watch over our ballistic missiles for Christ sake. Everybody out." Hamilton squawked, People stood and left.

Hamilton paced in circles. "Reynolds, don't leave."

This was one of those times Reynolds wished he was invisible. Alone with Hamilton for god-sakes. Dread filled him.

Hamilton still seemed dumb struck. "They think it might be coming from the south. From a cartel, god-damn it. I need you and—" He looked down at his screen again, "and Gregory Scarpa to find out.

"Scarpa sir?"

Hamilton's face was blank. "I can't have this shit, god-damn it. This might be jeopardizing our country, Reynolds. The sooner we can get indictments the quicker we can get answers. We need to be sure."

There was a quick, hard sink of depression in his gut. He hadn't expected this. The beating of his heart thundered against his chest. "We're ready, Director," he said as he gritted his teeth so hard his metal fillings clanked. "We have a group; NBA referees, umpires, hockey referees, baseball, college basketball players. We're ready to indict." He breathed out a breath through his nostrils.

"That's what I've been waiting to hear." He slid his glasses into his coat pocket. "Let's have it on my desk tomorrow if not sooner."

Minutes later Reynolds was back in his office. He gnawed the fingernails of his hand and bit off a hangnail, spit it to the floor. A sharp pain attacked the space behind his eye, he needed sleep but knew he would get none. He picked up his cell phone, had trouble seeing the numbers now. He reached into his front pocket for his glasses and dropped them. He grunted as he picked them up and found the name he was looking for.

After the second ring, Lamb answered his phone.

"What's the news, Scotty?" he asked.

"Hamilton wants arrests, convictions to see if there's a connection with the communication breach. White House is on high alert." He reached for his coffee, sloshing some on his desk. "Don't know."

"Sure. The Director's been able to handle Pennsylvania Avenue before. We just need more time."

"Not happening Ron. I'll be out of a job by end of the week. NSA is telling us that comm has been jeopardized. Hacked as you like to say."

He waited; no answer. Finally he heard a, "Hmm."

"We need to be ready to make arrests, immediately. Then these guys will start talking."

"Yeah, right," Lamb snorted.

"We can make this happen, Ronnie. We'll make contact with these guys and scare the hell out of 'em."

Lamb grunted. "How we gonna scare these dudes more than the Diablos. Those assholes got our guys peeing down their legs."

Reynolds cheeks tightened. "Listen, Ron, working on the convictions is the easy thing here." He didn't know exactly how to say what was on his mind. He slowed down, "There's something else goin' on here that's even bigger." His tongue felt like sandpaper. "Something big, definitely can't talk about it now, not here, but soon"

Chapter 62

Jason Carson gripped the seat handles, his back frozen trying to keep his mind off the flight. He had only flown four times before coming to the University of Iowa, and two of those times had been harrowing. He was sitting by himself, last seat of the plane, trying his best to stay calm. His chin was stiff from a hard foul, a forearm he took to the face in the second half against Minnesota. Gloomy light overshadowed other players, opened text books, some dozing. He needed to relax somehow. There was a tap on his shoulder. He opened his eyes; Coach Trammel hovered over him. He sat down next to Jason, waited a moment as he rubbed his temples.

"Listen kid," Trammel said. "I know you think there's a ton a pressure on you here, but you need to work on your emotions during the game."

Jason wasn't exactly ready for more criticism, especially during a plane ride.

"You're doing a lot right for us, but I sat you down in the second half because of your actions, not your play."

He had heard some of this in the huddle after the third quarter but couldn't remember all of it. He would always tune out the criticism. Coach Trammel had been in his face, veins rising in trails on his neck.

"I yanked your ass because you were taunting." There was an awful pause, his face eclipsing disbelief. "You utterly pissed off the other team. Almost lost the game for us. Never seen that out of you before, kid."

Jason tried listening but didn't want to hear the truth. Something had squelched his temperament. Now he was chained to the fact that he'd let down his team, his pillar of character ejected.

Trammel went on telling him that he had pointed to the back of his jersey after he hit his fourth three pointer. He was disgusted by the way he pointed to his jersey name and then pointed up at the scoreboard. It was no wonder the ref teed him up for it. And then as his face reddened, he listened to Trammel explain that he'd heard Jason had flipped off the band as he ran onto the floor after halftime.

"Did you actually do that?" Trammell asked in a low voice.

Jason didn't want to answer. He didn't know what was happening to him.

"I've never seen any of that out of you before, kid."

"Don't know Coach...I really don't know what happened out there tonight. I mean my mother would be ashamed of me. I know better."

Trammell nodded, his eyes pained. "I know you're still grieving. Can't imagine what you're going through."

"Can't explain it. First time I've lost control in a game. I'm really sorry."

"I'm worried about you."

Jason watched him nod slowly as if he didn't understand completely but thought he felt the shadow of understanding.

"I want you to talk to Dr. Culver tomorrow. Psychiatrist can help you with this."

Jason thought about his mother and how she told him he needed to handle every situation that came his way. "Whatever you say coach. I'll do whatever you want me to do and it won't happen again," he renounced.

Trammell stood and skidded back to the front.

For a long time now Jason felt the world was delivering him cold brittle surprises. The smell of jet fuel invaded his lungs. Arrival time in Cedar Rapids was 11:52PM, and every minute over the scheduled time would torture him. He reached for the white bag stuffed in the seat in front of his knees. He had tossed his cookies an hour before game time in a tiny bathroom next to the visitor's locker room. He'd tried to be discreet, never wanting his teammates to see the NBA's top prospect, Mr. Cool, as he was called by ESPN magazine, blowing chunks before his second Big Ten game of the year. But his anxiety level kept racing. He rolled up the sleeves of his sweatshirt. Warmness percolated in his stomach. A bit of half-digested liquid leaked into the back of his throat. He leaned over and put his mouth inside the bag. His eyes stung. He took three long deep breaths. He had scored twenty-six points and grabbed thirteen rebounds tonight against Minnesota. Minnesota Golden Rodents is what Brandon Sellers called them, and that brought a weak smile to his face. Maybe he could get through this. He reached for a bottle of water in the empty seat next to him, but found Gatorade. He closed his eyes and counted.

Fifteen minutes later, the wheels bounced three times on the runway in Cedar Rapids. Jason's watch read 11:49. Thirty-five minutes later Jason slid out of the back seat of the Pathfinder and slapped Tyrcke Simpson a high five. He sloshed up the snowy steps towards Burge Hall and noticed one of the lights above the main door was out. His vision blurred as he watched his breath. He reached for the door. A wave of exhaustion climbed through his body, he was ready for sleep. It was early Thursday morning. He had Pre-Algebra at 9:00AM and he needed to keep his C minus grade. It had started to feel like every waking moment he was thinking about eligibility. He felt a slight wave of paranoia run though his head. He thought about Ricardo Perez, and he asked himself why he hadn't heard from him in the last week, or had it been two now? Perez always wanted to surprise Jason but now it felt more like a punch in the nuts, every conversation a threat, every meeting intimidation, another stick of dynamite. He waited, peering at the elevator lights, numbers descending, he surveyed the stairs. But the stairs were empty. The only noise in the dorm was the drone of a fluorescent light above his head. He looked to the light, then at the stairwell. The elevator jerked open, he looked inside, empty. His lungs shrank with expectation. He stepped into the elevator and pressed the third floor. As he shuffled down the hallway, he walked by a room with a door ajar. He could hear the sound of a television and a couple of guys talking. He walked to the end of the hall and reached for his keys in his gym bag. He unlocked the door and slid into his room. He was surprised to see there was still a light on. He walked over to the desk and saw Brandon Sellers' laptop open, flashing. He reached down and pressed a key. Barbados Casino flashed onto the screen. His eyes began to adjust to the dim light and he walked over to the closet shouldering off his bag when he suddenly froze. His legs didn't feel like moving; his eyes gone wild open. His brain engaged. His heart stopped, blood evaporated. He took a step back, found the light switch and turned it on. Eyes on the closet. He swallowed. He looked again at the closet and vomited. He wanted to scream. A rope hung from the top of the closet and it wrapped around the neck of Brandon Sellers, whose eyes looked as if they'd pop out of his head. Brandon's body just floated there, suspended like a coat, lifeless. His chalky face ghostly vacant, mouth open but no animation. A sickly venereal purple color outlined the rope that gouged into his neck.

For a moment he flashed to Brandon, the guy who laughed and played, never worrying about a thing. But now that face was gray, the color of ash and those eyes just staring, just looking, just ready to explode out of that head Jason's knees buckled. He took a deep breath, suddenly the room smelled awful. He grabbed his coat and found his phone, dialing 911. The voice on his phone sounded distant. He couldn't tell what she said, couldn't take his eyes off the closet. He closed his eyes and said, "We need an ambulance..."

The paramedics covered the body and wheeled it from the room. Within a matter of seconds the place was flooded with people. Everyone asking questions he had no answers for. He looked around, feeling a fog of unreality thicken around him. What went wrong? A broad shouldered policeman, with a pissed off look on his face, elbowed his way over to Jason. He was chewing gum and flipping it around with his tongue.

"Scuse me, you Jason Carson. Brandon's roommate?" he asked taking off his hat revealing a bald head.

Jason nodded.

"Any idea why Mr. Sellers would want to do somethin' like this?"

Jason shook his head, "No, sir."

The cop looked at his pad. At last he looked up. "Any enemies? Any major problems?"

"Brandon didn't have any enemies. Everybody liked him." He paused a second. "He was having a bit of trouble with grades I guess."

The cop raised an eyebrow that gave more of a tired look then an interested one.

"Said he was having a little bit of money problems, but he comes from a wealthy family."

The cop chewed on the gum a little faster. "I just read about this kid, says he was a gambler."

Jason shrugged. He didn't know what to do. Brandon was one of his only friends, should he protect him? "Sort of."

The cop looked at a piece of paper that had been rolled up a few seconds earlier. "We have reason to believe that Mr. Sellers was running a bookmaker service, illegal betting—quite a large one—unusual for a kid his age. Worked with a large amount of dough, with a lot of customers. Says here that he even had a couple of celebrities on his list of private clients."

Jason didn't know how much he should share with Mr. Hawaii Five-O here. He had his own secrets to worry about. Could this connect him to Perez? He nodded and ran a forearm across his brow. "News to me on that one. Never mentioned any Hollywood heroes to me…but I'm not around much. Usually in the gym or the Learning Center."

He nodded. "Spose so."

The cop's phone buzzed, and he pulled it off his belt. "Need to take this, son." He turned his body and faced the wall.

What was going on? His roommate had just died and been carried away. How could he explain Brandon taking his own life? Brandon was carefree and happy just about every minute he was around him. If anyone had problems, it was him. He didn't know Brandon had so many problems he'd be suicidal. Something still didn't feel right here. He thought about his own problems. He felt helpless. Ricardo had threatened him before and even threatened his family. Was it possible there some connection here?

The cop turned back to him, tilted his hat back on his head. "Guess someone else is taking over the investigation," he said, rolling up his papers again.

"Investigation?"

He nodded. "Someone from the Fibbies will be contactin' you tomorrow." He glanced at his watch. "Make that, later today."

"What's a Fibbie?" Jason asked.

"Sorry kid. Law enforcement lingo for the FBI."

A shiver ran up his back. "What does the FBI want to talk to me about?"

The cop gave an exaggerated shrug of the shoulders. "They never tell us, son, but when they come in, we keep our asses out of the way." He raised his voice, "OK people, let's clear out...give this kid his room back."

Chapter 63

Tim McMurray sat on a bar stool with one leg too short and wobbled back and forth every time he shifted. He sipped on tequila that would kill a mob of white worms. The place had a rancid jalapeño pepper smell and the floor looked like it hadn't been swept in weeks. No single malt scotch or any scotch of that matter was tilting McMurray into an even more irritable state. The bartender of Casa Vista knew only a smattering of English, probably didn't even have a green card, illegal S.O.B. He told McMurray, only "Español o Mexican Cerveza" and shook his head and raised his shoulders when Tim asked him about scotch. The place reeked of burnt tortillas and onions, along with wet leather. The music was loud and tinny; heavily accented with trumpets and horns. The clientele were all Hispanic. McMurray had never visited this war-torn, north end of Philadelphia but it was the only spot Ricardo Perez would meet him. McMurray had called Perez in a panic. He was paying for a full-time private detective for his children and telling his ex-wife it was just the paparazzi taking photos of the kids. He knew he had to come up with something else soon, or she was calling the police, especially after his brother had stayed two days and left the house in a mess.

Tim had stayed boiling after the photos and the meeting with Madame Coppola. He felt he had to call and started leaving messages with Perez. The Spurs-Sixers game was tomorrow night, and he needed answers. He arrived at Casa Vista fifteen minutes early because he hadn't stopped at any stop signs in the neighborhood. Gruesome homes, dilapidated cars, exhausted appliances languished in lawns like gravestones: crumbling and decrepit. So here he sat waiting in this shithole. He needed to rework his deal with the Diablos. Especially after his horoscope told him he was in for some unexpected trouble. Trouble he was part of after every arrangement he made with the Diablos. He was being watched and running out of time. Tim ran a hand over the top of his head and looked at a clump of hair in his palm. What the hell was he going to do if he kept losing hair?

There was a tap on his shoulder; he turned. Standing inches away was Ricardo, dressed in a leather jacket with black pants and plenty of gel to hold back his thick midnight blue hair. Perez gave Tim a half smile, his black coffee sunglasses, reflecting gloom as he sat in the stool next to him, then looked at the bartender.

"Dos Equis por favor." Perez said, returning his gaze to Tim.

"What was so urgent? Why the meeting, Señor?" Perez twisted one of his gold rings around his finger. "I'm quite a busy man and don't like to be seen in public…with my clients."

"Needed to talk to you face-to-face, Ricardo."

"Glad we're finally on a first name basis, Señor McMurray, o make dat Tim, o no, make dat Timmy," he whispered. Funny how it almost sounded a bit like his wife after the divorce.

Nothing stealthy about it. Just plain talk, no B.S. "My family is off limits. Our relationship is between you and me. If you're not happy, and you never seem to ever be happy, you come to me and me alone, you understand," he hissed.

Perez took a moment to take it in, then suddenly amused by it all. "Mr. McMurray," he touched the sides of his glasses with both hands. "You must understand that our arrangement is serious. A great deal of money is at stake. Numbers of points, halftime scores, players scores, these all are what make us money, what keeps us wealthy."

"I'm not very wealthy, Perez," he ranted.

"Tsk, tsk, tsk," he said wagging a finger. "Your lifestyle has led to that, no? You are quite the big spender. Either way, the more we win, the more you win?"

The jukebox noise falls away, replaced by an airy, infinite quiet. "My family is off limits…you understand me?" He chanted in a furious monotone.

"You've been only adequate, Señor. Sometimes better than others."

"You've got to be kidding?"

"It's time to increase the ante, amigo," he said as he rubbed the tips of his fingers with his thumb. "Time to become a high-roller, bigger bonuses, double-down as we say."

His face now hot, aware what was at stake here. He hated to be told what to do. He had to risk it and now was the time to be convincing.

Staying up for hours last night he had rehearsed it over in over hoping it would sound authentic. He forced himself to look into Perez' glasses. "The head of the NBA Officials has given me a warning, Ricardo," he said emphasizing his name again.

Perez tilted his chin upwards, which brought a chuckle. "Go on."

He paused and waited as the bartender took his fat fingers off Perez' beer and teetered away. He gave Perez a tiny shake of his head, "I've been warned by the Commissioner himself to cut down on the number of calls I make." He detected the flush in his cheeks now deepening. "They're watching me, Perez. Probation would be next and then," he snapped his fingers next to his face, "and then I'm done." The stool rocked beneath him.

Perez ran his tongue over his top teeth, reached for his beer, took a long pull. He looked around gazing at the room. "Mr. McMurray." He shook his head and looked away. "Tim," he looked back at him, so cool, and smugly. "If you were being watched by the NBA," he sighed, "we would be aware of that fact."

Holy shit. Was anyone being honest? He was taking a monumental risk here. "How would you know, Per...Ricardo?"

"We have sources...connections my friend."

Almost without thinking, McMurray fired back. "The Commissioner spoke to me himself, Perez." He knew he needed to be careful., The psychic and his kids still fresh in his mind.

Perez gave him an impatient, I'm-trying-to-listen look.

"These things are very confidential in the NBA office...this isn't your typical water cooler topic, Ricardo. It's serious shit and the League never wants any leaks...it could kill the game, kill the sport," he said in a loud voice that startled Perez who looked around the room again.

The look on Perez' face told him all he needed to know. He put a hand in the pocket of his coat and turned. "Maybe we take a break for a few games…let us do a leetle more investigating ourselves," as he reached for his beer.

A waft of cigarette smoke attacked Tim's nostrils, his eyes burned. What kind of investigating is he talking about? "A few doesn't work, Ricardo." Stay aggressive now, keep attacking he told himself. "They're watching me for God's sakes. They're paying attention…reviewing every call."

Perez slid a hand to his face and pulled the sunglasses off his nose. McMurray saw his eyes, focusing on nothing and yet everything. He looked at him, silence now. "I'm going to talk to my people, Mr. McMurray. We'll come back for you. Meantime," he placed the glasses back on his nose and slowly pushed them to his forehead. "In the meantime, you can play it straight and enjoy those lovely ladies of yours." He grinned and then nodded. "Don't remember if you have a chica here in Philly Mr. McMurray. I must not be watching as well as I should. But that will change Mr. McMurray. We've had a nice trustful relationship so far haven't we?"

He tried not to make a face. He let that one go. How much did this guy know? He loved the money but he needed to straightened things out. "I do have a couple of old friends in this town."

"But not in this neighborhood, I'm betting?" He laughed, almost waiting for McMurray to join him. "Let's just remember what happened to the leetle lady at the night club. We need to remember consequences here, am I right?"

Tim felt a sudden lightness in his chest. "You taking responsibility for that, Ricardo?" And, there it was, he did not believe he asked the question, but he was exhausted from the manipulation. "If you haven't been telling me the truth, I definitely—"

Perez interrupted. "Now, now. I just wanted to remind you dat accidents happen and we must be prepared. We must watch how we live our lives."

Tim looked away, caught the back of the bartender's body, then looked back into Perez' eyes and saw his own reflection off the glasses. Who really was to blame here? No one spoke. Tim had nightmares about that night and each nightmare was different. Each one more intense. One night after a game in Portland, he woke up soaked in sweat, heart racing. He had a recurring dream about rushing to the hospital and waiting for the doctors to explain what had happened. But this time it wasn't Cara they were treating and trying to save. He had to wait to see who was under that sheet in that frozen hospital room In his dream he had to identify body after body, again and again. But this last time was different, this time it was his daughter. His young daughter was in that hospital room and they told him she wouldn't survive, wouldn't make it back home again. He wouldn't let it happen again. If they wanted to kill him he would let them but no more death, no more 495s to people he loved. If he didn't put a stop to the madness, there would be no one left for him to love.

His voice iron-willed and unbending. "My family is off limits," All was still. Stark arrogant blood ran through his veins. "Keep away from my kids. Do you understand?" He stood up, the stool thundered to the ground. If you hurt anyone, anyone I know or love. If there's any more accidents to people I care about, I'll, I'll come after you and every single person that you know, that you care about." The adrenaline was dense and dazzling, saliva was running down his chin, "If anyone puts a finger on my children or even scares them, I'll come after you." He felt his joints unlatch, loosen, "I'll cut your balls out and feed them to pigs while you watch. And I will never stop. I'll make life so ugly for you—"

Perez threw up his hands, smiling as if he thought this was a silly joke. As if he'd seen this a thousand times before. He rolled his head, continued to smile, his palms together as if in prayer. "Mr. McMurray, you need to settle down, take it easy, rest a momento, por favor," he begged with a cadence that was almost hypnotizing.

And then he eased slightly, "I'm just trying to protect you, Perez... along with myself. NBA finds out about us and you're finished. We're both finished and I don't' think you want that to happen."

"Very well, Mr. McMurray. I'll be in touch." He moved off his stool, turned and was gone.

He was struck, as he was always struck, by the way he handled things with power and strength. He knew he'd done the right thing. He knew he was supposed to stand up to Ricardo. He just knew it. He laughed to himself as a slight tremble moved through his body. He picked up the stool and sat back down. He had told part of the truth. He just hoped Ricardo wouldn't find out he hadn't told him the entire story, not all of it. He didn't want to imagine the consequences; as Ricardo would say. The consequences of someone that he loved dearly. What about that phone call that he made every time he had an arrangement with Ricardo? For some reason, he thought more about his children during these times and there had been more of these times showing up the last few weeks, days. He believed the world was once a beautiful place. He'd had hopes and loves and a heart that seemed as big as the sun, but now his heart seemed to be fading, darkening, eclipsing, and making his world colder.

Chapter 64

The New York Times/ Americas
Mexico City- The death toll in the crash of a Mexican military

helicopter shot down Friday by members of a drug gang climbed Monday after tests of remains at the scene determined that they were of three soldiers initially reported as missing. The helicopter, a Eurocopter EC725 Cougar, was participating in a sweep to weaken the gang, the Francisco New Generation, which has emerged as a serious threat in southwestern Mexico. Members of the gang fired a rocket-propelled grenade, a testament to the firepower the group has attained, bringing down the helicopter, according to Roberto Chanez, the federal security commissioner. In total, the authorities said, 15 people died on Friday, including the soldiers, in a series of attacks by the gang and confrontations with the police that left dozens of buildings ablaze and roads blocked by flaming vehicles.

Chapter 65

Reynolds jaunted down the stairs from the Cessna aircraft at Baltimore/Washington International Thurgood Marshall Airport. Jogging across the tarmac he found the gray Tahoe waiting for him, a military driver wearing camo, holding open the back door. Reynolds saluted the driver, jumped into the back seat and began to look over the newest updates and emails from his iPad. In the seventeen minute drive to the National Security Agency, Reynolds scanned a new report from Ron Lamb that identified two tennis players that had been suspected of throwing games in exchange for ownership in overseas real estate and an undisclosed amount of cash.

After arriving, the Tahoe bolted from the second set of security entrances and pulled next to a building made of mirrored black glass.

The light from the sun echoed a brilliant sheer of phosphorescent rays catapulting in all directions like slender flashes of silver. The NSA building still amazed Reynolds with its gathering of data from satellites, phones, computers, wiretappings, and more. Minutes later he walked through the bowels of the building, computer screens covering the blue fluorescent walls and lights so dim it was dreamlike. An incessant hum in the place quickly had Reynolds irritated and he knew that within hours it would turn grievous and harassing. How could these people become accustom to this? Waiting for Reynolds in an oval room that was layered in oversized computer screens, was chalky skinned, milky-haired sixty year old NSA Chief, Keith Anderson. The two shook hands. Behind them sat about a dozen individuals hunched in front of computer screens like school children.

Anderson began, "Agent Reynolds, I wanted to explain to you our newest threats."

Reynolds nodded.

"The protection of our communication is of utmost importance and the Cyber Extortion campaign continues."

Reynolds nodded again, "Thank you for taking the time."

Anderson scanned the room and looked back at Reynolds. "I agreed to meet with you because you may be able to add something to our investigation. As you may be aware, the attacks of Ransomware through a cyber extortion campaign is quite serious."

Reynolds frowned. "I haven't totally been brought up to speed."

"There is reason for that. A group of hackers, known as Shadowbrokers, hack into computers, software, phones, and the like. They have done it by backdooring into security programs such as Kaspersky or Symantec; any type of security system that fronts a computer software system but then allows them to infect the basic software and thus use the infected computer in any way that they wish."

"Ransomware," Reynolds added.

"Hackers over the years have been trying to extort businesses but now they are moving onto a new venue, individual computers. That's why I asked to speak with you."

Reynolds wasn't yet understanding. This was his first meeting alone with Anderson and he couldn't decide if he should have answered.

Anderson quickly interrupted the pause with a sigh. "The newest threat is what we call the WannaCry attack. It encrypts a user's data and demands a ransom."

"OK."

"This is usually small fish to us but we wonder if there is a connection between this smaller group and the big players; ones going after our banks, political parties, government, air traffic, maybe even our nuclear bombs."

"Excuse my ignorance, but what does that have to do with me?"

Anderson wet his lips and patted the computer next to him. "We've found this Ransomware on thousands of computers, but we've also found a few dozen on computers that you may be investigating." He handed Reynolds a folder of papers. "These are referees, umpires, coaches, players that have received these threats. The Shadowbrokers find dirt on these folks based on what the user looks at on their computers, if they're struggling with finances, sleeping with someone, hiding anything, and they sweep in like hawks. Anything they might be hiding on the Shadowbrokers algorithms and then they ransom them."

Reynolds understood this as another avenue into the point shaving and gambling. He nodded. "They identify weakness and trouble, then attack with bribes and ransoms?"

"Precisely," Anderson said as he lowered his shoulders and smirked. "I'm trying to protect the country from major disasters and have no idea if there's a connection. I'm looking at every angle I can find right now, Agent Reynolds."

"So do you believe that any of this is coming from Mexico?"

Anderson did his best to think about the question for a bit. "If it is I'm not aware. The attacks all have been coming from the US, Russia, China, and Korea." He looked back at a giant screen that must have been eight feet long. It showed a map of the US with dozens of circles around cities that must be hit by cyberattacks with lines to cities throughout the world. Anderson lifted a hand towards the screen. "This is our Norse hacking map that currently shows attacks around the world. The lines are vectors trying to identify HTTPs, SSHs, computer jargon."

"I'm an analyst."

"Very well. As you can see the hotspots today are Seattle, the Silicon Valley, New York, Chicago…we identify five thousand attacks per hour. I'm concerned with other business I cannot even show you, Agent Reynolds. For example they attempt ten million hacks on the Pentagon each day." He shuffled his feet and straightened his wavy hair. "So I wanted you to become aware of the attacks and would like you to let me know about anything you may find."

"What about Cryptology and the communication system?"

Anderson shook his head once. "I'm unable say anything at the moment. Keep me informed Agent Reynolds."

Chapter 66

Jason Carson parked Brandon Sellers' BMW on a side street two blocks from the Graduate in downtown Iowa City. He stepped out of the car, his Nike Crusaders hitting two inches of snow. The slap of the ten degree wind peppered his face as he winced and caught his breath. The sidewalks were snow covered, the ground almost perfectly smooth except for the indentations in the street. Jason stiffened, lowered his head and moved forward. He was light-headed; maybe it was because of the lack of sleep? Perhaps it was his fear of Ricardo Perez. He thought about the odds of passing his classes, but everything was swirling around in his head, just like the snow. He'd been sick before, nervous before, but he always played through it. He played in every kind of condition. Sick, banged-up, bruised, big test upcoming; nothing held him back from playing. Playing was something that Jason always counted on, all he really had. But his meeting this morning was something he would love to miss. A howling gale whipped up a pile of snow like a wild corkscrew and spun it around his face. He stiffened and kept moving forward. He hoped this meeting with the FBI would be short. He needed to get his free throws in before practice since he missed shooting last night. He felt cold all over. He couldn't believe Brandon was dead. Maybe he really wasn't dead, just takin' one of those disco naps he liked to say. Maybe he would wake up and go out to party tonight like usual. But Brandon wasn't having any more of his goofy juice, no more pirate juice in the afternoon with the buddies. He wouldn't be "knuckling-up" during the tough times. Wouldn't be able to "jump the couch," "chase the home girls" any longer. Crazy. Jason thought about Brandon's body floating in the closet. He must have run into "technical difficulties," "voted off the island," now "off the grid." At least that's what Brandon would say. Why didn't he tell Jason how bad it was? Why didn't he tell him about his "no worries" before it was too late? Maybe if he did? He wouldn't have to go talk to the FBI and answer questions. He stepped in front of the hotel's sliding glass doors, opening with a thump. Warm air brushed by him. He stood and waited. He could have easily turned and run back out to the warmth and music of the BMW, that's what his old man would have done. But he had to stay. His mother's voice inside him calm and speaking reason.

A man dressed in a black shirt and pants smiled at him. "May I be of help to you sir?"

He shook his head. "No, thanks," as he unbuttoned the top two buttons of his winter coat. He moved to the elevator, entered and pushed floor three. Moments later he walked off and headed down the hall looking for room 323. He knocked on the door and heard voices from behind it. The door swung open.

"Come on in, Jason," Lamb said, backing away. Jason stepped forward, saw two open laptops on a round table and caught the faint whiff of stale cigar smoke and fresh paint. The man at the table rose and took three steps toward him, extended his hand. Jason shook it.

"Hi, Scott Reynolds, FBI Special Agent."

Jason looked down at the man; what Brandon would call, "an ankle biter," maybe a "gumby," definitely short. Maybe this wouldn't be too tough, he thought to himself. Agent Reynolds swung an arm at Ron Lamb.

"This is agent Ron Lamb."

Lamb nodded.

Someone closer to his own size.

"Nice to meet both of you."

Reynolds grabbed the back of a chair. "Please, have a seat, Mr. Carson."

Jason moved to the chair. He gazed at Reynolds shoes. Polished perfectly but something didn't look quite right. He looked again and noticed the heels. The guy had two or three inch heels on the bottom of those beauties. He raised his head to find Reynolds' eyes. Reynolds raised his chin, gave Jason a military strength smile, gone as quickly as it came.

"Mr. Carson, we have reason to believe Brandon Sellers was in trouble." Reynolds said matter-of-factly.

Enough of the small talk here; they moved right to the questions. Jason decided it might be best to listen. He narrowed his eyes, made a confused face.

"Let me put this another way, Jason. How much do you know about Brandon's troubles?" Reynolds asked, an officer's harshness to his voice.

Jason placed his hands in his lap. Keep it simple here. "I knew he was havin' a bit of school problems. Didn't always like to go to class. Kind of a free spirit, I'd say."

Reynolds' eyes narrowed. "We know he didn't pass two of his classes, didn't even show for one of his finals. One professor told us he knew he was cheating," said Reynolds, his face camouflaged, no expression.

"I just know he didn't go to class a lot. Didn't do too much studying either. Liked 'livin' the good life,' is how he used to put it," Jason said as he looked at Lamb, trying to get away from Reynolds' stare.

"How about his gambling, Mr. Carson? What do you know about the gambling?" Reynolds fired back.

Reynolds leaned toward Jason, staring. He'd seen that look on people's faces a lot lately. The heat in the room suddenly seemed to ramp up ten degrees. "I knew he liked to do a little wagering from time to time…maybe he played a little too much on the computer."

Reynolds began to put a hand to his mouth, then pulled it away.

Jason went on, "Sometimes he liked to do that off-shore stuff… poker or twenty-one or somethin' like that." He straightened. "I don't know very much about gambling stuff."

Reynolds didn't respond. Jason was amazed at the posture on this military dude. Back so straight he must exercise or train for this? He had the impression this guy never relaxed. A harsh stiffness invaded every cell in that miniature body of his. Regardless, he was possibly the antithesis of Brandon.

"How 'bout his bookie service? What can you tell us about that?"

"I knew he had some bets on games. He had a group of people he'd talk to on his phone. Said it made the games more fun to watch." How much do these guys know? Suddenly, something didn't feel right here. Jason wondered, was Perez involved?

Scott Reynolds folded his arms across his chest. "Were you aware of Brandon's money problems?" Reynolds then looked over at Lamb.

Jason shot Reynolds his favorite I-didn't-foul-anybody look. "All I know is that he wasn't drinking his favorite beer anymore. Went with the cheap stuff, every normal college kid drinks." Maybe that's part of this too. "Underage drinking that a big problem now?" he asked acting puzzled.

Reynolds didn't stop. The missiles kept firing. "We think he owed about $120,000 to a long list of creditors. That's what we've found so far," Reynolds said.

Jason sighed, looked over at Lamb, then back at Reynolds. "Whoa, I didn't know he was in that kind of trouble." He ran a hand over his head. "But his old man was a movie producer. Guess he was super loaded…he could probably write a check in a minute for that." He shook his head fiercely. "Doesn't make sense he'd take his life for that."

Lamb looked down, shook his head, and said, "That's what he told you? Dad was a Hollywood movie producer?"

You could tell by the way Reynolds' eyes blinked he was processing the thought. "Well, that wasn't the exact truth Jason. Brandon's father was a food broker for a small company in a small town south of L.A. His mother works in a flower shop. They've been divorced now about four years. Your roommate went a little haywire after the divorce. Some juvenile crimes, a couple of DWIs. His old man told him to go to Iowa, straighten up his act. Learn a normal lifestyle. But we think the old man was playing a nice little bookie service on the side, as well. You know, like father, like son, but didn't want the kid to follow in his path. Could be one of the problems with the marriage, we don't really know, and don't really care here." He paused, looked at his laptop. "The old man told the kid not to come back until he graduated. 'Make something of yourself,' he told the kid. Brandon did build quite an extensive bookie service, probably bigger than his old man's. Using some new technology he bought in Asia."

Jason didn't know what to say.

"Brandon was a walking casino. But a few bad bets and some unpaid bills left the kid in some deep shit, with big debts, and then the flunking out of school. Kid had nowhere else to turn."

Jason glanced over at the laptop and noticed it was recording something. He bit down on his lower lip. The disbelief in his voice was faint. "I had no idea."

There was a pause. Reynolds adjusted his collar with his finger. Jason had heard enough, he wanted to get out now.

"Just a few more questions, Mr. Carson, if you please," said Lamb, smiling but his eyes didn't laugh. He cleared his throat, steepled his fingers.

Lamb and Reynold's exchanged a look. Both nodded. Reynolds opened his mouth, closed it, then began. "Do you know a man named Ricardo Perez?" he asked, jaw tightening.

Jason felt dizzy, truce was over, someone had tossed a bomb into his lap, that pre-game nausea landed right in his stomach. For a moment part of him tried to consider how all of this fit. He gave a slight nod. "He was a guy I met in Chicago. He wanted to be my agent," he said as a chill shivered its way up his back.

Reynolds lowered his head, took a deep breath. "Are you still working with Mr. Perez? When was the last contact you had with him?"

His eyes moved to the laptop. Time to keep the answers simple. "He keeps trying to contact me. I have a bunch of guys that want to be my agent. They all hound me, normal I guess." He shrugged his shoulders.

Reynolds pulled out a pen from his shirt pocket, rolled it between his fingers, studied it as if it was made of solid gold. "We know everything about you and Ricardo Perez. We've been following him—following the Diablos mexican cartel for quite some time now."

Jason didn't move.

"We have piles of evidence against this crime syndicate group and we're ready to go after them," Reynolds said and swallowed hard. "This cartel is responsible for drugs, weapons, and more murders than you have ever heard of." Reynolds paused for a second. "We're nailing these bastards and we need your help."

Jason couldn't move. "What do you want from me?" he whispered.

Reynolds placed the pen on the table and slid it in front of him. "Your career's in jeopardy, Mr. Carson. This agreement with Perez could lead you to some hard time in a penitentiary."

Lamb piped in, "Soap on a rope for a tall handsome guy like you would be a great Christmas gift if I say so myself."

Jason was lost, but he nodded as if it made perfect sense. "What do you want? I didn't mean to get involved in this." The strength left his muscles. "I trusted the guy...he just, like, latched on to me, guess he lied to me and then threatens me. I just wanted to—"

Reynolds interrupted, raised the palms of his hands. "Slow down, big guy. We know how these people work. They're very smart and have quite an arsenal of brilliant minds working for them. If it makes you feel any better, these ass wipes are so dangerous they have the attention of the President."

Jason's eyes got large. He leaned back in his chair, the only thing that he could lean on right now. He closed his eyes for a moment, wishing he could talk to his mother. The two men seated across from him could instantly wipe out his career. He looked up and found Scott Reynolds' eyes. He kept staring because that's what you do when you're looking for help. Reynolds' eyes now displayed a glimpse of compassion, a bit of sympathy he thought. Most people never really wanted to give him a break, but the look in Reynolds' eyes showed a hint of forgiveness. Jason had only seen that look a few times. For no real reason he peeked at his watch. He began nodding, a bit of relief oozing into his head.

Jason started talking, "I'm actually glad you guys showed up." He pinched his forehead with his fingers. "I didn't know what to do and I didn't know who to talk to." He let out a long sigh.

Reynolds nodded.

"I know my career is over. I made a really stupid mistake." A long litany of possibilities hung over him. "I don't want any more deaths, like Brandon." He closed his eyes again and took a long breath. The air felt heavy and sticky. Jason was actually happy now, which scared the hell out of him. He lowered his shoulders. His lying and running from the truth would be over. He opened his eyes, vision adjusted. He gazed at Lamb, then at Reynolds. No one spoke. "You gonna take me to jail. Read me my rights or something like that. Ask me if I want a lawyer. That's what they say on the cop shows. You'll have to find me one, I don't have any money. Don't know if you guys know that too?" He nodded violently. "Bet this will make a great lead story on ESPN."

Reynolds looked down at the pen on the table, picked it up and rolled it with his fingers again. "We've got another option for you, Mr. Carson; one that we think could work to your advantage." Reynolds paused, cleared his throat. "You do what we ask, follow what we say.

Help us take down Perez and his cartel," he ran his tongue over his bottom teeth, started to put a finger in his mouth. "We keep you safe." He swung his head and looked at Lamb.

Lamb gave Jason a crooked smile.

Reynolds started again. "You even get to keep your career, NBA even."

"Can keep the whole she-bang," Lamb railed.

Reynolds went on, "Nobody ever knows anything about this, except us. How does that sound to you, Mr. Carson?"

Jason tried to keep his bearings. It sounded rational on one hand and unbelievable on the other. He unleashed a low whistle. "Sounds too good to be true," he said with a half smile.

"Well, I don't think your other options look very appealing, Mr. Carson. I don't do this often but you might get a second chance. That's if you help us nail this guy. It's the best option, get protection and keep playing ball. That's what you want isn't it?"

Jason straightened his arms, then tilted his neck until he heard a crack. It was certainly the answer to one prayer. "Do I have time to think about this?" he asked.

Reynolds' kind of smirked, "How 'bout one minute, Mr. Carson?"

Chapter 67

Reynolds and Lamb stood waiting in a wide corridor inside Salt Lake City's Utah Jazz Stadium. They watched colossal sized men, proportions magnified, even monumental, walk past them. A six-foot-ten Jazz player with a shaved head and Bing headphones didn't look up, unconcerned, as he strode by Reynolds. His hands were stuffed in his jacket. He looked as if he'd punch anyone that asked him a question.

Lamb winked at Reynolds. "Fee, Fi, Fo, Fum, I smelled the blood of a pissed-off Center."

Reynolds shook his head decisively. "These egomaniacs make way too much damn money."

Lamb snorted. "Big boy didn't look too happy, Scotty. Must a been the whipping boy tonight. Four losses in a row for the Jazz and the Mormons are all runnin' to the Tabernacle for answers."

"Got that right."

"Best thing the Utes can do is get outta this slump, maybe a special session with the Mormon Tabernacle Choir. Sing 'Bringin' in the Sheaves' or something," Lamb wise cracked. "Hope our boys brought beer. Driest town in the nation, buddy. Heard the Jazz players have a tough time drowning out their sorrows around here."

"Tell me about it. I had to hide my beer under my bed."

"I forgot you worked here in the Emerald City years ago."

Reynolds nodded. "Yeah, criminals stand out around here like a sore thumb. If you're not in the choir, you're doing time in a state pen, my friend," Reynolds said, even surprising himself with a bit of humor. The two men laughed but their smiles disappeared as they saw Tim McMurray making his way down the hall towards them. Reynolds looked at Lamb, straightened and leaned back against the cement wall. Reynolds ran the back of his fingers over his mouth, ran the palms of his hands down the chest of his blue blazer and waited. Tim McMurray walked with his head down. Reynolds noticed that his hair was wet, and he wore an unbuttoned black leather jacket and some expensive leather shoes, maybe from Italy since he wasn't used to seeing pointed toes in the US. McMurray checked to see where he was headed, then stared down to the cement floor again.

Ron Lamb cleared his throat. "Mr. McMurray," he said in a soft voice barely moving his lips. "May we have a minute of your time this evening?"

McMurray gave him a look of dismay. "Kinda in a hurry tonight, fellas."

"We'd just like a few minutes of your time, Mr. McMurray. I think you'll be very interested in what we have to say," said Scott Reynolds, staring at him with huge eyes.

McMurray scratched his forehead. He looked like a sulky child. "Can't this wait until another time guys?"

No one spoke for a moment. Reynolds peeked down the hall. He saw two security men in yellow jackets laughing. He turned back, found McMurray's eyes. "We've come all the way from Washington, D.C., to see you tonight, Tim." He raised his chin, his eyes narrowing. "You might have heard of us—we're from the Federal Bureau of Investigation and we will only take a few minutes of your time this evening," Reynolds said, his eyes almost daring him to make something of it.

Tim McMurray let out a sigh. He was showing teeth, but nothing close to a smile. "OK, guys, how long this gonna take?"

"This probably isn't a good place to talk. We've got a vehicle outside."

Another referee walked past the three men and smiled as he looked back. "You workin on a big night for yourself again, Timmy?"

"Leavin' town early tomorrow, but I'll see you in a couple weeks." He winked as his partner nodded, gave a quick hand salute and left.

Ron Lamb sauntered over to the door and waved. "Let's head out here." The three men walked outside and moved into a black limousine that was parked next to the exit. McMurray moved inside and the two men entered behind him and sat immediately across from him.

"Nice ride guys," McMurray said as his hand ran over the leather seat coverings. "No wonder our country has a big deficit with wheels like this. I usually get a driver in a Chevy missin' a couple of hubcaps."

The two agents didn't answer.

"This luxury is a little unexpected," McMurray said. "Most people are looking at crucifying me after a game."

Reynolds gave him a dead smile. "What makes you think we don't want that as well?"

"What can I help you with fellas? Thought I paid my taxes last year—even though the old lady took most of it," McMurray said as he glanced at his watch.

Reynolds looked out the window as the limo groaned. "We know you've been looking for a little excess cash...a little part-time job. You might just call it moonlighting." He glanced at Lamb, then back at McMurray. Reynolds eyes were dark now, maybe a suggestion of arrogance. A touch of I'm ready to kick your ass. "We know all about your connection with the Mexicans...The Diablos and Mr. Ricardo Perez. We've been paying close attention to it for some time," His lower lip crept into his mouth. "No bull shit games here now, McMurray."

McMurray gave a 'what are you gonna do', shrug. "You guys have been watching this for a couple of weeks," he said with a sarcastic, almost sticky smile. He patted the seats with both hands again. "I've been doing what you've asked me to do...make the calls after each deal with Perez. I need to get out of this mess. At least that's what my Spiritual advisors have been tellin' me. Damn, that's all they've been tellin' me."

Reynolds drew back in his seat, as if someone struck him in the face. He wasn't interested in taking the bait here. He knew McMurray liked to play games. Redirect coaches when they came screaming at him. He could just play along with him. "So your Spiritual advisors, palm reading witches, and 900 number fortune tellers have been filling you in about us, huh?"

"They've been telling me all along that I needed to get away from the evil...move away from danger."

Reynolds sounded bored. "Yeah, those Cracker Jack fortune tellers are really full of surprises."

A whisper of exhaust rustled through the limo. McMurray suppressed a slight cough. "I don't know why you guys want the phone calls after I talk to Perez? Hell, its cost me a lot of money with my spiritual advisors to try to figure this shit out."

Reynolds and Lamb listened.

"I know I'm in trouble. Maybe at least I can save my life and keep my kids and ex-wife safe," he said, his voice moving faster. "Gotta get out of this mess, out of this imprisonment with the Diablos."

Reynolds looked at Lamb for a second. Quick enough to see if he was understanding this.

McMurray ran his hands down his thighs. "I'm ready to plea bargain against these guys if you protect me and my family, even though my family doesn't care too much for me."

Reynolds was considering where this whole thing was going. He was actually surprised by McMurray's instant regret and guilt. He had no idea what was going on, but McMurray seemed prepared. His confession was playing out like some community theater act. But McMurray was much better than a third rate actor. This act was more like an Academy Award performance. How did McMurray know that the Bureau and the CIA were watching him? Did the Diablos know what was going on, tip him off? Or did one of these hocus pocus psychics really know what was going on? He thought McMurray would play his defense and show his resistance. He looked over at Lamb for some help.

"So you've had this feeling like you're been watched," said Lamb as he played with his giant ring with his thumb. "One of your witchy-poo friends or some ghost give us away?" As a smile crept onto Lamb's face.

"They're telling me I have a big problem and have to face it. Quit running all the time."

Lamb nodded. "That's genius. I'd pay big money for info like that. Now, let's get back to this phone call B.S. you've been giving us. What's with this line of crap?"

"Look guys, I've been living up to my end of the bargain…I've been making that phone call to you after I talk to the Diablos, now I'm looking for a little slack. Maybe I deserve what I'm going to get but I've been giving you all the information before each game like you've asked me." His face giving them that confession look again.

"Do the Diablos know anything about your other contact? Your other arrangement that is?" Lamb said in such a slow voice it seemed as if it took a light year to deliver.

McMurray jerked his head back. "Who you tryin' to kid here fellas? I've been straight with you guys. Giving you all the info straight up. Now I'm looking for some protection and you're giving me this, 'I don't know what you're talking about' bullshit?" McMurray's face tightened, and his hands turned to fists on his knees. "What kind of protection can I get, and what's our next step?" McMurray's face went all loose and narrow.

Reynolds gnawed on the pinky of his left hand. Seconds passed. He guessed it was seconds.

"Let's just get this over with and then maybe I can at least sleep at night," McMurray murmured. "A minimum security prison can't be anything like living with the constant fear and danger that's hanging over my head every damn day. A room with ESPN and the Outdoor channel would work. Do my twelve, eighteen months and I'm out, right? For god's sakes, people are dying here." McMurray lowered his shoulders and sat back in his seat.

McMurray seemed to be waiting for a response, but Reynolds was still trying to think. He wanted order here. He hadn't expected this.

"Give me a few days, Mr. McMurray," Reynolds murmured.

"A few days?" McMurray slapped his thighs. "You guys must be trying out for a coaching position. First, you're my friend and seconds later you don't like my whistle and you're kickin' me in the ass?"

Reynolds' lips twisted. He looked out the window, scratched his temple, "Hmm."

"That's it? A 'hmm.' Why haven't you guys been able to stop the killing? Perez and his boys are nasty SOBs. I've done my part here. Now it's time for you guys to jump in and save the day," McMurray said, tilting his head to one side.

Reynolds looked over at Lamb, studied his face. No response. He swallowed and sat back. "We have one more item we need to work out before we solidify our plan with you." He looked back out the window, took a breath and tapped on the glass window behind his head to get the driver's attention. The vehicle began to lurch forward. They drove two blocks and pulled next to a line of taxis. Reynolds leaned over and sucked his lip, considering: "We'll drop you off here. Take a cab so nothing looks out of the ordinary."

"Just drop me off at the hotel, will ya?"

"This is safer."

McMurray coiled a bit. "Being with you clowns is the safest place on the planet. I barely have enough dough left for a cab ride. Come on."

Reynolds phone buzzed. He studied the message and felt a rushing in his head and not much else. His voice ramped up, "Get the hell out, McMurray. We'll be in touch."

The door opened and McMurray was out without a word. Lamb nudged Reynolds, "What's with the look, what's up?"

"NSA wants us on a plane ASAP. They've got new information."

Chapter 68

Ten-thirty Wednesday morning Jason Carson stepped into Brandon Sellers' BMW after shoot around at Carver-Hawkeye Arena. He had taken a quick shower and headed for the Gerdin Learning Center to meet Krista for a study session, his only time to study before his three o'clock pre-game meal with the team and then seven o'clock game against the ninth ranked Michigan State Spartans. Jason had been driving Brandon's car since his death since neither his father, who was in prison, or his mother could be located. He pulled out onto Elliot Drive in front of the arena and turned on satellite radio. It had been three days since his meeting with the two FBI agents. The music floated into his head. There had been a glimmer, a trickle of optimism wetting his ambitions since meeting with Lamb and Reynolds. He hadn't heard from Ricardo after he left him a voice message asking him if he had anything to do with Brandon. That image of Brandon suspended in the closet would never leave him, but finally he wasn't thinking about it every hour. He turned onto Melrose Avenue. Minutes later he scrambled up to the second floor of the Learning Center looking for Krista in one of the study rooms. He walked by the third glass door and spotted her pink Nike tennis shoes resting on top of the table. He tapped on the glass, moved into the room and shut the door.

"Hey J.C.," she said putting her feet on the floor, and a palm against his chest. She pushed him up against the far wall, away from outside onlookers and planted a we-need-to-spend-more-time-together kiss right on his lips. She moved her arms to his ribs and kissed him again, pressing her lips harder this time, he tasted strawberry chapstick.

"Whoa," he said, his eyeballs watering, a sudden bloom of warmth flooding his body.

"Just wanted to heat up those bones a yours, big boy," she said, running her tongue over her top lip.

"Feel like I'm standing in front of a fire," he said smiling, chest fluttering. He removed his jacket. "Like to put a little more kindling in that fireplace." He stepped closer to Krista again.

Krista raised a hand. "You've got a huge game tonight, Fire Chief, and we also have a test tomorrow. Keep the pilot light on and sit your butt down so we can get to work." She laughed.

After a moment, his neck began to cool. He reached into his backpack for his book and sighed. "Can't we forget about this? I think I know it good enough to do OK."

She gave him a blank stare. "Well enough. Not good enough, come on."

"Never liked English."

"You better. Don't want to sound like one of those dopes on ESPN. Plus, you need to keep studying."

"Just can't stop thinking about the game. We need to win it bad."

"It's badly, you goof. We'll have to get you a tutor ASAP."

"Just so long as she's blonde and wears a bikini during homework sessions."

She gave him a half punch to the arm with the back of her fist. And in that instant, if such a thing were possible, he felt as if his prayers were answered, or perhaps his mother's prayers that is. He broke out in laughter. They smiled at each other, big wide grins.

Krista pushed a button on her Macbook and reached for her water. "Anything new with the Brandon thing?"

"Well, no one has asked about the car, if that's what you mean. Cops haven't said anything about it either."

She swung her head and looked at him. "You've been talking with the police?"

He hesitated. "Kind of." He glanced at his watch, calmness slipping away. He could tell instantly she didn't like that answer. "Thought we had to start working here?"

Her face narrowed. "What do you mean, 'kind of?' What are the police asking you about?"

He arched his back. He didn't know what to do with his hands. "Well, I'm not supposed to be discussing this with anyone. Let's study, OK?"

"Thought we had this discussion awhile back. No secrets anymore. Am I missing something now?"

For relief, he looked sideways, where should he go with this? "Not a big deal."

She closed her book. "Not a big deal about the cops, or not a big deal about that you can't share with me?"

He didn't answer quickly enough.

"That's what I've been telling you. If we're going any further, we need to be open. No surprises," she waved a hand in front of her face.

"It's too damn important. Deal breaker, damn, you just don't get it." He wanted to tell her, but he felt a shadow of misunderstanding creeping back in. "The cops wanted to meet with me a few days ago and ask some questions."

"And you decided not to tell me about this?"

"It wasn't really a big deal…they want me to keep it quiet so I didn't think I should be telling anyone."

"And I'm just anyone, now?"

"Course not."

"That's it? Course not? Your roommate dies and the police want to talk about it because something is up and you don't want to tell me?" There was a slight change in her eyes. "And I'm supposed to trust you? Depend on you? I've shared some of my deepest secrets with you because I thought you'd understand but you just turn up here and let me down again."

"Again?" His mouth was dry. "Whatdya mean?"

"Well you didn't even come to my last game. Couldn't even show up for that I guess?"

"I had to meet with the doc."

"At night? What the hell kind of doctor is he?" He heard the anger in her voice.

There may have been a kind of truth to it; something infuriating telling someone that he was seeing a shrink. But he had no choice. "He's a psychologist."

"What? You're seeing a therapist? Can't you just talk to me about things?"

Seeing how unhappy this was making her crushed him. "I do."

"Yeah right. The only time we talk now is when you need help with homework or when you want me to pick up some food for you…I'm kind of your slave now, huh?"

"No way. I stayed up watching your game on the DVR. Give me a break?"

"We never go anywhere either."

"I've been short of cash. I need to get that contract."

"That's all you think about it seems. Everything is me, me, me, all of a sudden." She laughs. "Or maybe it's always been that way."

"Look, it's been crazy. Everything's crazy. I do need you."

"Oh my god, I just don't know where all this is going," more whispering to herself than to him.

The room moved closer in, swallowing him. "I do need you…more then you know. Ever since my mother died," he murmured. A pittance of his pride, maybe in his ability to share his feelings was succumbing after all. "Just lots of pressure…lots of things not working out." He told himself this wasn't defeat, he wasn't forfeiting here. Without thinking he reached out, waited a second, then placed his hand on top of hers.

"I hope you know how I feel about you." He pitched his voice lower. "They told me stuff like Brandon's father wasn't really a movie producer after all. His mom and dad were divorced and the mother doesn't have an address. Dad is in prison."

"Cops shouldn't be giving you that information," raising her eyebrows.

His strong dislike for dishonesty was working on his head. "They had a bunch of questions. Wanted to know about his gambling problems." He looked around the room as if he was going to see a camera in one of the corners. "That's how he got the car. Dad was a gambler too."

"OK."

"He got himself in trouble with a big bookie business and they knew his grades were bad and parents really didn't care about him. I don't know, they wanted to know more about it, I guess." He pulled his book closer, thumbed through some pages.

She studied him for a moment and reached for her book and started to open it, then closed it again. "How do local cops know about Brandon's mother and father?"

Jason didn't reply, kept his head down in his book, turned two pages.

"And how do they know about his bookie business if he was living in California the last couple of years?"

Jason tapped the table with his fingers. "We've got a test tomorrow."

"You're right. Let's talk about this later. But don't you have some questions about all of this?"

He glanced off toward the window, then looked back into her eyes. He was feeling ashamed of himself. "It wasn't just normal cops, Krista." He took a deep breath. "It was the FBI. They asked questions about Brandon and about me...Brandon and Ricardo Perez."

Krista reached out and grabbed his forearms and squeezed. "They asked you about Ricardo Perez?" She took the tone she had when she was tutoring him. "The guy that gave you money? The guy that asked you to change the outcome of a few games? That Ricardo Perez? They know about him too?"

He thought for a moment until he found words. "But it's not what you think Krista. I wish I could tell you the whole story, but I can't. You just have to trust me a little here. They said they're going to help me."

"If you would have let me know earlier, I could have helped you. I'm afraid you're in deep trouble here, big fella." She said as she closed her eyes, shook her head.

It was time to play the sorrow card. "Look, Krista. My mom died, Brandon just died, and I'm trying to pass some finals so I can keep the dream alive." He sucked in a long breath. Had he said too much? "And these guys show up and tell me they're going to help me, so I just need to listen to them…Give them a chance. What else can I do?"

Her face softened. Her beauty surfaced even higher now, cobalt blue eyes gleaming, almost surprising him. "I'm on your side, J.C. You can let me know more when it's the right time."

"I could really use someone on my side."

Chapter 69

The Gulf Stream taxied down the runway, and Scott Reynolds buckled his seat belt, looked out the window and squinted at the slab of a moon still hanging over the snowcapped mountains in Utah. His sleeping meds hadn't worked last night. He rubbed his eyes. He fumbled through his briefcase and pulled out a bottle of Visine. He squeezed two drops in each eye. He grabbed a half dozen Advil and swallowed them without liquid. Ron Lamb sat across from him and grinned.

"You need some water with that buddy?"

Reynolds shook his head. "I'll get another cup of coffee as soon as we get up in the air." He looked out the window and peered into the chivalrous rays of sunlight stretched over the horizon. The plane propelled down the runway and rocketed into the air. Reynolds opened his mouth for a few seconds then swallowed hard.

Lamb crossed his legs at the ankles. "Tough night, again?"

"Gambling has infiltrated our lives, buddy. Throwing gambling into American sports has been like watching ants attacking a dropped piece of candy during a July picnic. Too many ants for us to stop."

"Don't care."

"Look, we got dozens of athletes, referees, umpires, coaches in almost every sport now that are crooked and helping the gaming industry to explode," he said.

"Outrageous."

"It's moved from the days of horse racing and boxing to everything now. Every fucking game could be cooked."

"This shit is growing like weeds and you think we can just spray the whole industry like a damn herbicide. Pick out a big thistle, a giant foxtail, a cocklebur and corn-bore or two and the whole illegal gaming industry swivels up. It's too late."

Reynolds shook his head and looked out the window. He realized he was chained to the fact he was actually worried about where this was all headed. It was him against this bullshit world and he wasn't going to ask for more help.

"The whole harvest here has already been taken over and has chocked the entire sporting industry." The aircraft banked to the right. The two men went silent. Lamb handed Reynolds a cup of coffee. He wrapped his hands around it like it was newborn baby, he took a long drink from the cup. He was tired of chasing, but he knew he had to keep going. He glanced back at Lamb, who just gave him a 'I don't really give a damn, anymore', look.

"We're not giving up now." he fired back. "We've got enough evidence we can make a big dent in this thing. Maybe, start a big fire that'll clear out all of the weeds you talk about. Then it would set a new standard, with new regulations, new rules, new enforcement that could clean all of this up."

"Your eyes must be red this morning because you've been wearin' rose colored glasses again, boy."

"Don't think so."

Lamb still seemed unfazed. He popped open his mouth, stout tongue oily with arrogance, and said, "This shit's been going on since the cave man. Every sport, every team, never stops." His eyes blooming, radiant. "Every team's looking for an edge. Nothin's new here. Baseball's been stealing signs from each other, keeping baseballs in freezers so they won't be hit them out of the park. Pitchers throwing spitters, scuff the ball to make it move more. Look at Gaylord Perry, guy admitted throwing spitballs and he's in the Hall of Fame. And what about the steroids? I mean the Commissioner even knew it was going on and let it happen. Basketball. Look even Phil Jackson, winningest coach in NBA history and Senator Bill Bradley admitted to deflating basketballs to gain an edge when they played on the Knicks' championship. Football is just as bad. The Patriots videotaping hand signals from the other team, deflating footballs. And how 'bout Mr. Clean himself, Lance Armstrong." A blast of air trumpeted from his mouth as if he was playing a wind instrument. "Asswipe goes on Oprah to tell the world he'd been lying for years. Doping in cycling is the same as brushing your teeth, every Tom, Dick, and Lance doin' it."

Reynolds managed not to roll his eyes.

Ron Lamb glanced around the plane, then back at Reynolds. His voice now more of a whimper. "It's in the culture, buddy. Cheating is part of the human fabric. I mean, that Little League World Series team from Illinois...they recruited kids. Recruited from outside their geographical area. Teaching the kids to cheat Scotty, that's the new American way."

Reynolds looked dazed. He wasn't done though. He looked at his iPad. "We just talked to the Carson kid and then McMurray last night." He ran his thumb over his screen. "We've got three NFL referees, four umpires, two NBA refs, and eleven athletes now that we know are cheating."

"It's the tip of the iceberg buddy and you've just boarded the Titanic."

"I thought you'd feel good about all of this Ron? Finally got enough evidence to blow this thing wide open?"

"I know this has been your baby, Scotty. You've been after these Taco Kings for some time." He sighed. "If you really think we're ready to make our move, I guess I'm right there with you, let's do it."

Reynolds looked down at his knees, shook his head. "Somethin' else just isn't right here. Somethin' smells funny and it ain't the refried beans."

Lamb picked at his ear. "Now you're the racist. You've always got somethin' crawling under your skin. The list of things keepin' you up at night is longer than my penis." He laughed. "You're just wound so tight that you can't even be happy when we got a nice victory in front of us, as you seem to think. Hey we're on way to DC, maybe we'll get your answer there?"

"Something McMurray threw is wrong; he caught me off guard. There's something there I can't seem to get my arms around."

Lamb blew out more air again. "Yeah, right. The guy's a complete quack. He's the poster boy for the paranormal. If you'd ask him who the real Santa Claus is, I'd almost guarantee he'd tell you it was E.T. or Casper the Friendly Ghost."

Reynolds gave Lamb a slight nod, then stared down at his iPad.

"Speaking of quacks, when are we going to deal with Hamilton? You probably don't care since he's been bustin' your ass?"

Reynolds nodded again, took a long sip from his cup. "I need to meet with him in the next two days. I need to get these loose ends tied up first." His eyes narrowed. "Just a few more loose ends."

ESPN—The NBA has added another gaming partner in the expanding US sports betting market. On Tuesday, the NBA announced a multi-year partnership with international gaming operator The Stars Group, which runs the BetStars online sportsbook.

The NBA will promote The Stars Group across the league's digital assets, including NBA TV, NBA.com, the NBA App and NBA social media platforms. In turn, The Stars Group will promote the NBA across its gaming platforms, including popular online poker site PokerStars.

Chapter 70

Jason finished his glass of skim milk during the pre-game meal in the middle of Carver-Hawkeye Arena. Linen table cloths, china dinnerware, Italian glassware scattered on tables. The walls crowded with photos of university athletes, lined up perfectly like cemetery plots. Tyreke Jackson, Tony 'the Tiger' Robinson, and Jason sat at a round table watching Sports Center on one of the five large screen

TVs. When coaches were around, most of the players made an attempt to look as if they liked Jason. Carson pushed his third empty plate to the center of the table. He noticed that his plates were the only ones empty, others were left with food half eaten. How could people leave uneaten food on their plates, he asked himself? He folded his hands behind his head and sat back in his chair. Because he wasn't paying for the food, he tended to overeat. It was as if he forgot about his pregame nausea. Lately he seemed to keep paying for his mistakes. He sat still for a moment as he mentally prepared, drumming his fingers on the edge of the table, oblivious to his surroundings, concentrating. He'd poured in twenty-four points in his first game against the Spartans and pulled down eleven rebounds. Tonight's rematch was being showcased on ESPN's Prime Time, Jason was ready to put on a show, entertain the masses, wow the NBA scouts.

"Later," Robinson said curtly as the two players left the room.

Jason kept debating with himself whether his meeting with the FBI could actually be true. The offer to snitch on Ricardo Perez. They wanted him to testify in a deposition, whatever that was. But they told him if he followed directions, he'd be cleared. He'd be cleared and his name would be kept out of the public because of some act or something. His mind and head had taken a beating the last few weeks, the line of conscience and subconscious seemed melded together. What kind of things would happen if he stood up to Perez? It scared the hell out of him. The FBI agents hadn't discussed this with him, not yet. Jason stood, plodded through the arena. He wanted his dorm pal back again. Someone he could talk to other than Krista. He wanted to get 'ridonkulous' again with Brandon, but then again, that old pal had ended up taking too many 'sick days' in a row. Mostly, he needed to talk to his mother. He fished into his pocket and pulled out his phone. He started to press speed dial number one and suddenly his phone buzzed back at him. The number displayed on the screen was "private." He had seen that number before. He debated whether he should answer, or just let it go for now. It buzzed again. Sooner or later, he'd have to reply. But if he ignored the call, it might bring more attention to the situation, an alert that something was wrong. It buzzed a third time. It took him a long time to pull his eyes from the phone. He pressed the answer button, moved the phone to his right ear. He held his breath, waited for the voice.

He heard breathing, then, "Hola, Jason."

Jason didn't respond, seized by a feeling of anger, guilt. His tongue imitating sandpaper.

"Am I interrupting anything, Señor?"

"Um, kinda." He looked back and forth and saw no one.

"Maybe you're with that cute blonde ball-player friend of yours, and you can't talk right now…that it Jason," he whispered, accent hard.

He didn't know how to say it was none of his damn business. How did he know about Krista anyway? Was he always watching him? "No. I'm just finishing up with pre-game stuff, Ricardo," Jason snapped.

Jameel Johnson jogged past him, didn't even look up as if Jason wasn't even there. Johnson was one of the four guys that hated Jason; he was a starter last year but Jason had taken his place.

Jason rubbed the back of his neck with his fingers, looked back and spotted a couple of maintenance men with ESPN jackets running wire in the ceiling. "Can't really talk right now."

"Fine," Ricardo said." Then you can listen…I want to talk about Saturday's game." After the silence went a bit too long, "that game shouldn't be very close."

Jason didn't reply

"The spread on that game has moved up to twelve points now."

"I don't watch that stuff, Ricardo."

"Well, well. That's why I'm here to help you. We can work something out, no?"

Jason wanted to squeeze this voice of fear out of his hand. The confidence he had moments ago was so flimsy, so weak, that he couldn't hold on to it any longer. His lip began to tremble. What did the FBI want him to do here? "When is this going to stop Ricardo...when does it all end?"

"Jason, Jason. We have a nice agreement here. We have a special relationship. We lent you a large amount of money."

Jason's jaw muscles tightened, he glanced around the tunnel. "I need to worry about school, not this extra crap."

"Important that you keep your side of the bargain, make people happy, no?"

Rage started to seep in. "Listen Ricardo, I'll be paying you back soon. You wait and see." He said trying to bring his confidence back again.

Ricardo seemed as if he didn't know what to make of that. There was a long pause. "As long as you listen to what we tell you, no one gets hurt." There was a slight pause again. "I will call tomorrow with instructions," he snapped, and the phone went dead.

Chapter 71

The two story beach house stood eighty feet from the Gulf of Mexico on Sanibel Island, Florida. The white sandy beach held a seventy-five foot metal pier that rested on the gulf's water and a thirty-five foot Crisscraft floated in the water as the sun perched over the horizon. Seagulls glided over the shoreline looking for crabs or fish that were left from the morning's high tide. A brown pelican drifted across the water as if the water itself was lifting the wings of the bird in suspended animation. Ricardo Perez teetered down the driveway in his bare feet in a royal blue silk robe to pick up the morning Miami Herald. Perez' lower back ached as he reached for his newspaper. No signs of life today, Perez noticed. He loved the quiet, the solitude. But this morning his head was bloated from last night's tequila and cocaine. Paying the price for a late night on his boat with a girlfriend he had found three weeks ago on one of his trips to Las Vegas. Tricia was still sleeping and probably wasn't going to be up before noon.

Inside the house a man with a Miami Dolphin's hat and sunglasses moved on the Italian marble floor without making a sound. The six-foot seven man plodded down the hallway with a small limp and peered into the master bedroom. He stalked into the bedroom and onto the white carpeting without making much of a sound. He looked to the bed and saw Tricia sprawled face down wearing only a pair of red laced panties. The only noise was a man's voice from a television in the kitchen. A stream of light from a window on the ceiling crossed over the back of her tanned body. The man crept toward the bed. His distorted shadow loomed over her. He stood gazing at her body; her back moving up, then down deep in sleep. He seemed to be waiting for a response. He reached into the pocket of his hooded sweatshirt, withdrew a needle the length of his hand and pulled off the plastic cover. As she breathed in, he could hear a slight sigh coming from her. He turned his head slowly and saw himself in a full-length mirror on the side of the bed. He moved closer and reached out his hands, covered with latex gloves. He bent over the bed and raised the needle to the edge of her naked leg. He lowered his hand like a surgeon and pierced the copper skin of the girl in the back of the leg. Her body suddenly flinched, and she began to raise her head, blonde strands tumbling over the pillow. He grabbed her head and drove it into the pillow. Her legs kicked, but his body craned down on top of her back. His hand pushed harder muffling her screams into the pillow. Her arms tried to reach for him but they were no match for his strength. The muffled screams stopped and her body went motionless. Seconds later, the man capped the needle and placed it into his pocket. He covered her body with the navy silk sheet and turned and made his way to the garage.

Meanwhile, Ricardo Perez unrolled the newspaper as he wandered up the driveway. He stepped off the concrete and onto the sodden, callous grass. A gecko scampered away from his left foot and ran under a bush. He scanned the front page as he reached into his robe pocket, fingering the two Cubans that he hadn't smoked the night before. He spit into the lawn. He pulled out one of the cigars and thought about smoking it as Tricia slept. From the back deck he could read the newspaper, drink his Colombian coffee and look at the ocean; waiting for instructions from Mexico City. He stepped toward the door on the side of his garage and reached for the handle. He heard a screech from a seagull and looked toward the ocean. He smiled to himself. He pushed open the door as he heard a sound from inside the house. Tricia wouldn't be awake this early, not after a long night? Maybe she was up getting something for her head and then back to bed he told himself. He moved to the kitchen door, opened it and felt the cool marble on his feet. He reached for the brass door knob and began to close it. A hand reached from behind the door and grabbed his wrist. He turned his head and saw a man with a Miami Heat ball cap and sunglasses, now pressing cold steel against the side of his neck. Ricardo's robe slid off his shoulder as he tried to think. He looked around without moving his head and saw no one else. He felt his heart accelerate, pushing his sludgy blood through his veins. He smiled. "My wallet is in the laundry room drawer," he said as his breathing quickened.

The man lowered his head next to his ear. Whiskers bristled his neck.

"Don't want money, Perez," he growled.

Perez didn't move. The stench of cheap cigars and rotten eggs moved into his lungs. The man straightened and threw Ricardo's head against the door.

"Let's talk," he said as he patted Ricardo's pockets, found the cigars and tossed them on the granite counter. Perez felt the gun in his lower back. The man's other hand clamped onto his neck with incredible strength and shoved him forward. He stumbled into the great room and onto his knees. Sweat broke out on his arms and neck. He spotted another man wearing a Miami Dolphin's cap standing next to his couch holding something.

The man standing next to the couch was twitching. His eyes glistened with rage, surprise and bewilderment. He stared at him with purple, pulsating eyes. "Sit your ass down, Perez," he wailed.

The first man squeezed his neck again. He propelled him toward the couch and kicked him in the lower back. Perez flew head first into the pillows. He immediately felt a fist to the side of his head and his neck jerked to the side, pain slicing through his skull.

"Mierda…what da hells dis all about," he screamed.

The man charged a palm to his throat without waiting for another sound. "We want names, Perez," the newest man said, then pulled handcuffs from his back pocket, slapped them over his wrists.

He shook his head, "Don't know anything; you're hurting me."

The man with the Dolphin hat lifted what he had been holding. It was silver and long, a weird skinny knife. Perez couldn't let his eyes off it. It wasn't a knife, it looked like it was made of steel, arrow like, pointed. It was an ice pick for god's sakes.

"Time to start talking Perez." The man lifted the pick, wiggled it in the air and in one move jabbed it into his shoulder making a popping sound. Ricardo howled. Blood squirted and splashed onto the white couch. His jaw flapped, chewing at the air instead of breathing. Blood slid down the side of his face.

"You're not listening, you bastard," the man shouted with lips now blue as if he was chewing raspberries. His face was white as death now. "No more games, Perez. We want every name of every player, coach, trainer, bat boy…any association of yours and we want it now."

Who are these guys? His mind racing. Where was Tricia? Did she know where he kept the gun?' "Un momento, por favor."

"Let's start with English, asshole," the man screamed as he raised the pick in front of his face, looked at it for a second and slammed it down into his left thigh. Perez wailed, then coughing, then wailing again. He gasped for air as tears exploded from his eyes, blood erupted from his leg like a geyser. His head swelling, he felt he was going to faint. A hand gripped the bottom of his jaw and swung it around, two eyes that looked like coffins staring at him. His shoulder ached, his thigh was on fire.

"Bien, bien, OK OK, I'm talking," he cried as his chest was collapsing, looking for air. His heart pounded against his ribcage. The first giant man threw a recorder in front of his face. He tried to take a breath, the agony was flipping his stomach like a cement mixer now. "Ahora," Can't remember…the names right now," he gasped for more air, his mouth moving. "There are too many."

The man wiped the bloody pick across Ricardo's chest. "Give us each person's sport. We also want to know all the names of the Diablos. You leave someone out, and we start cutting off pieces of your face. First, your nose, then your ears." The man with the Dolphin's cap slid the ice pick under his nose. He could smell his own blood, he coughed again. "Then we cut off each ear for every person you don't tell us about, and we've got a long list already, so don't get forgetful here hotshot."

Why were they after him? He felt the end of the ice pick slowly ripping down the side of his left cheek as his eyes watched the hand move in front of him. He lifted his cuffed hands to his face, touched his cheek, looked at his palm and tried to take a breath. "Please quit," he said as more of a gargle. The air seemed like syrup, like trying to breath underwater. The names are in a file…In the safe."

"Where is it Perez? If you lie, you're a dead man."

His leg was throbbing like a hot poker, burning. "The safe is behind the picture on the mantel," he cried as tears rolled down his face.

The man with the Dolphins hat grunted, "Good Perez…you need a little payback," he said showing his teeth. The gash in his arm and in his leg were beating in rhythm. The giant with the Heat hat swung the painting away from the wall. A black faced safe with white numbers sat behind it. "What's the code, dickhead?"

He tried to swallow, tasted blood seeping from the corner of his mouth. "7272," he gasped.

"What about the artwork. How do we find it all?"

How did they know? He wanted to be careful now but the pit in his stomach told him to cooperate. "The directions are all in the safe, too."

The man pressed the numerals. The safe popped open. His gloved reached in, pulled out a watch and a necklace. He reached in again and pulled out a black notebook. He threw it open and scanned the pages. Nodding, running through the names. "Looks like this is it." The man raised his head. "How many more?"

Perez swung his head from side to side. "Dat's all."

A hand slapped the side of his face. Blood projected through the air. His nose crunched.

"Just returning the favor. All those poor bastards you Mexicanos have murdered over the years," the man whispered as his face moved inches from Ricardo's bloody nose. "Remember last year you hammered a few nails into a player's back…just because they weren't able to give you what you wanted. Who else did you leave out from the list?"

The giant howled as he jammed two fingers into his nostrils.

Ricardo's eyes pulsated in his head, temples vibrating. Gagging. The man pulled his fingers from his nose, wiped them on the front of his robe. The giant nodded to his partner who walked over to Ricardo, lowered his body and pulled the pistol from his sweatshirt. He watched in delicious shock as the hand moved in slow motion to the bottom of his chin. The giant hand rammed the silencer into his mouth. He began to gag again, he couldn't breathe, his eyes blurred from tears. He tried to shake his head from side to side but without success. He could taste the carbon from the gun, biting on it, trying to stop it from moving further into the back of his throat. His front tooth cracked. He wanted to close his eyes, but his brain was telling him to watch. He needed air. Got to get air. There was a tornado inside his head scrambling his brain. Only one thing he was trying to focus on— stay alive. Could he somehow stay alive. The man jerked off his glasses and stared at him with a smile that was sinister and utterly evil. He was looking for some ray of hope in those eyes; any kind of hope. The eyes stared at him, looking. The eyes started to go small and the smile suddenly extinguished from the man's face. The man pulled back, lowered his jaw, jammed the gun another inch down his throat and squeezed the trigger.

Chapter 72

At 7:20AM the following morning, Reynolds marched down the long hallway of the FBI's Marines Corps Base Lab in Quantico, Virginia.

He spoke with Paul Forester yesterday who told him he may have some information for him. Forester had helped him with the DNA information regarding Agent Henderson's murder months ago in Phoenix. The flooring in the hallway was an unblemished vanilla and squeaked as his feet marched upon it. The lighting was exactly as he remembered, bright and invading. Forester was waiting for him at the end of the hallway. The two exchanged hellos and did not shake as normal. Moving into a small room, Reynolds was handed a starched white lab coat which he put on and buttoned, then rolled up the sleeves to fit. The two men put on white elastic gloves, white hats and hard cased safety goggles. They moved into a lab room of glass, slides, Petri dishes, beakers, metallic tools, and shelves, to a row of oversized microscopes. Computer screens hung above each microscope displaying what was on the slide below. Forester turned his head as his gray braided pony tail flipped over his shoulder. He reached over and handed Reynolds a box.

Reynolds could wait no longer. "What did you find for me?"

Forester stared at him with eyes that looked fatigued and disturbed at the same time. He shook his head. "I've been working on this all night. I needed to make sure."

They sat down on cold steel stools. Forester leaned towards the microscope. "I have had our Trace Evidence Unit identify all of DNA from the Sanderson death on Chesapeake Island and the death of Ricardo Perez in Florida. We hadn't any success for days. We ran all evidence through our Combined DNA Index System with no results until we received a hit on a microscopic hair analysis comparison. There are thousands upon thousands of items and this is where we got a bit lucky." Forester picked up forceps and placed a slide under a microscope. The photo of the slide appeared on the screen above the scope. "We found two strands of hair through non-probative association which gives us a ninety six percent accuracy rate. Please take a look."

Reynolds bent over and peered into the microscope. The light around the object blinded him for a moment as he waited for his pupil to adjust.

"We first identify animal versus human, then the type of scales, and look at cuticles, cortex and identify resemblances. Take a look at this," he said as he slid off the stool and waited for Reynolds to look through the scope again. "Can you tell?"

"Looks like the same to me."

"As to me as well."

Reynolds was fidgety. "What does it mean?'

"We have identified an exact match of hair. The hair's locus and DNA ascertains the type of mammal, racial character, place of body where the hair was found, whether it was normally or forcibly removed, etc.

"One found at Sanderson's murder sight, the other at Perez's? Forester raised his chin a bit and squinted. "I stayed here last night because I wanted to test the match that we found in Phoenix?"

For a moment this caught Reynolds by surprise. He was talking about the death of Agent Hamilton. "OK"

"I was able to get a protein coding gene from the Mexican match that was presumably left behind. A partial profile but a match with the match," he said with a smile.

This was coming at Reynolds too fast. He walked in a circle around the room and then looked up. Exact matches?"

"Correct."

"Were the two hairs from Sanderson and Perez both forcibly removed?"

He laughs a sudden startling laugh. "Correct again."

Reynolds took a deep breath and smelled the lab's immaculate crisp air. His eye began to twitch. "And you can identify race?"

"Yes, in all three." His face is fierce with belief.

Restlessness surged through him. He straightened to his full height. "Did the hair come from a Hispanic?"

Forester looked at him for a moment. "Agent Reynolds, it did not. It came from a man of western European descent. A typical Anglo Saxon white male."

Even before he was seated in the Cessna, Reynolds placed his cell phone next to his ear to answer the call from NSA Chief Keith Anderson.

"Thanks for your help with this," Reynolds said.

Keith Anderson began, "this has happened to us too many times lately. Assholes are getting too sophisticated."

Reynolds was confused. He sat in his seat and leaned forward. He needed to know if McMurray was telling the truth about his phone calls to someone he said he didn't know. "Did you find any callers? I need to know if this guy is telling the truth."

"We only have the calls from Perez. You have the transcripts of those, but we couldn't find anything else."

"So McMurray is lying to us?"

There was a moment of silence. "Not necessarily agent. In fact, as I said earlier there's a chance that others can cover their calls with a device that supersedes our IMSI Stingrays. It's a GSMK Crypto Phone which can detect the detectors. They can detect our Stingray interceptors and we have no ability to intercept comm or data."

Reynolds bit a nail on his left hand, then one on his right, then back to his left. When they first began to interrogate McMurray, the truth seemed to ooze out of him like a faucet. He had an answer that seemed to line up with every accusation. But he just knew something wasn't right. Was he trying to protect Perez? His temples pulsed. "So he may be telling us the truth?"

"We looked for any calls made after he spoke to Perez and found none, but—"

"But what."

"They could disguise any call made by McMurray if they used a Crypto Phone. Russian spies have been using them for years."

"So maybe he is telling me the truth?"

Anderson waited a moment. "I wish I could be more help to you Agent Reynolds."

NEW YORK—Major League Baseball became the largest US sports league to partner with a gaming operator, with commissioner Rob Manfred announcing a multi-year deal Tuesday with MGM Resorts International.

MGM sportsbooks will begin to utilize baseball's official statistics feed and have access to enhanced stats on an exclusive basis. MLB intellectual property, like league and team logos, will appear in MGM advertising and at the company's sportbooks.

Financial terms were not disclosed.

Chapter 73

Reynolds was perched in his Steelcase Neutral Posture Lap chair in the office of his home at 11:45PM while his wife slept. He hadn't slept properly the last three nights and he could feel it now in every movement he made.

He heard the single chime from the grandfather clock in the dining room that he had built close to twenty years ago. He had been reading from his Macbook for the last four and a half hours. The laptop that he kept in his office, never leaving the house, untraceable. His head was teetering on that small pain that normally signaled the bigger pain soon to arrive. He twirled a pencil over his thumb. Forge ahead, he kept telling himself. He pulled out a key from his pocket and unlocked the bottom drawer on his desk. He reached in and pulled out a small wooden box he had made in high school shop class and placed it in front of him. He dialed in his four digit combination, opened the lid and pulled out two memory sticks. He slid one of the sticks into the tablet, then typed a password for a software file. Reynolds had trained himself years ago to always keep extra files at home. He vehemently tried to prepare for every situation that could occur. In the last four and a half years, he had expanded his file base by tenfold. While most married men in America spent their evenings watching television with their wives or watching their kids play some sport, or dance in some rank dance hall, Reynolds poured over research documents pertaining to his current case. And that information was bugging the hell out of him right now. At times throughout his career he had inklings that someone was watching him, tracking his movements, looking over his shoulder, downright spying on him. He remembered what his Boy Scout leader always used to tell him when he was having trouble earning a new scout badge: "things don't always appear as they seem."

He rubbed his eyes with the heels of his hands, took a drink from a glass of water, then tapped his feet on his wooden foot stool. His wife hadn't spoken much to him since he returned home at 7:30 that evening, but that was the new norm the last few months, or was it years, he really didn't care much now.

Ever since his only girlfriend Mary Rowenski hadn't come back to him his private life was a complete mess. His life at the Bureau was the only thing that kept him away from her. He chewed on two of his nails as he looked at the screen with a small desk lamp the size of a silver. He pulled out a cheap Samsung phone from the back of his drawer, studied it. Dialed his trusted ally, Ron Lamb; knowing full well that he would be in one of his surly moods, especially after being awakened. After the fourth ring, Lamb answered. "This better be good," he hissed.

Reynolds aimed for his gentlest voice. "Who do you think killed Perez?"

"Is this the 'Double Jeopardy' answer of the day?"

Reynolds ignored the question. "Strange how we don't have any idea? Assumptions, but nothing substantial." He drew a sharp breath, "how did Tim McMurray know we were watching him?"

"Dr. Spock from Star Trek told him," Lamb said in a mocking voice.

Reynolds sat there and pondered, heard the heater turn on, tapped his knees with his fingers.

"I've been keeping track of the money that's being exchanged. Money that has been rolling into Vegas on games and it's in the billions. Even the ownership changes in some of the casinos seems odd."

"We've been over this, Scott."

"There's been dozens of athletes and coaches, maybe hundreds that we're still trying to nail."

Lamb sighs. "Can't this wait till morning?"

"What about the Carson kid's roommate? Suicide? Who's hacking the communications?"

"Job security for the both of us," Lamb answered with a voice barely audible.

"It all comes back to Vegas…everything runs through Las Vegas."

"And I love the showgirls too. Best built bodies money can buy… plastic surgeon's windfall, buddy."

"Cut the B.S. Ron. I can't figure out what happens now that Perez is dead."

"We know he probably was the front man for the Diablos and he had dozens of contacts."

"But who wanted him dead?"

"Probably someone that didn't get paid. That's the way it usually works."

"Maybe."

"I also got word tonight that our informant, Gregory Scarpa is missing. We haven't been able to contact him for three days."

"Maybe the Diablos put a bullet in his head. Asshole deserved it. Should be in jail for his day trading scam."

"But he risked his life being an informant for us. He's the one that found Perez and the Cartel," Reynolds responded. "I actually hope he's OK"

"If he's dead maybe I can have his Lamborghini? OK, Let's talk in the morning or is it morning already? So glad we had this chance to catch-up," Lamb said sarcastically.

Reynolds knew he wouldn't be getting much sleep. "OK We'll talk tomorrow."

Scott Reynolds and Ron Lamb waited to be seated at Carmine's DC on 7th Street. A few tables were empty but the hostess didn't seem to be in much of a hurry. Reynolds pointed to a booth in the rear.

"Can we take that booth?" he asked. The black-haired hostess with hoop earrings large enough to jump through, jaw tight, lips hard, peered in back. "Guess it will be fine," she sniffed through her nose. The two slid into the booth, Lamb snickering. "I told you we should have gone to Capital Bistro."

Reynolds signaling with his eyes. "That place is crawling with legislators."

"Have it your way, always do anyway."

Normally Reynolds would charge back to that kind of statement but today was different. He sneered and nodded. He waived to the waiter two tables away. "Can we get a couple of menus here?"

"Why can't we do this in the office?" Lamb asked.

Reynolds' eyes scanned the room. "Someone might be listening."

"In the office?"

He shrugged.

The waiter gave him a wave and ran back into the kitchen. A minute later he delivered a menu to Ron Lamb and then he suspended Reynolds' menu in front of him, peeked inside and finally handed it to him.

"What the hell was that," Lamb sputtered.

But Reynolds also noticed that the waiter kept watching him as he moved around the restaurant. He opened the menu, a white printed 8 X 10 sheet was taped inside. Reynolds tilted it toward him and read.

"REYNOLDS@@@@ FOR YOUR EYES ONLY@@@. YOU WILL NOT DISCLOSE OR YOU WILL DIE.@@@ YOU WILL COME TO GRAND CENTRAL STATION TOMORROW NIGHT AT 9:00PM.. GO TO THE MEN'S BATHROOM ON MAIN FLOOR. YOU WILL NOT TELL ANYONE. NO ONE IS TO COME WITH YOU. NO FBI……FOLLOW DIRECTIONS OR YOU ARE DEAD@.

Ron Lamb set down his water glass, peered over his menu. "Already know what I want. I know you like to take ten minutes to find exactly what wets your appetite." He took another slurp of water. "Don't think you'll like anything here, though. No Gluten free, lactose free, sugar free, hell with all that free stuff you shouldn't even have to pay," he laughed.

A new waitress came to the table, cheery with a whiny voice. "You loves know what you want?"

Lamb grinned. "Want you to keep calling me that. My friend here usually takes half the day to decide."

Reynolds put the message in his pocket, closed the menu and stood. "I need to check on something. Don't know when I'll be back."

Ron Lamb replaced his smile with a stunned look. "I'll have the meat loaf, extra gravy please."

Chapter 74

Scott Reynolds had never mastered the art of waiting around, but the hours between 7:00 to 8:50PM were excruciating. And despite the fact, he tried to keep figuring out how these people knew where he was. Guessing, hoping, willing himself to understand had brought him miserable dread. Reynolds continued to anguish over everything. He squinted at his watch again, eyes inflamed: 8:54. He moved inside the station. Even at this time of night, Grand Central Station was active. A small roar echoed in Reynolds' ears, diesel exhaust scratching his corneas. His hand gripped the handrail, balancing each step. After searching the blue prints of the station earlier in the afternoon, he knew exactly where he was to go, and approximately how many steps it would take. A skinny kid with plastered black hair flashed in front of him on roller blades almost knocking him over. Didn't these kids have parents? As he approached he could see a sign in front of the men's bathroom: TEMPORARILY UNDER MAINTENANCE. He bent below the rope and entered the men's bathroom. Lights on, rows of sinks positioned in front of him. And for some reason all of the sinks were turned on; water spilling out, storming. Another sign hung from the door of the closet toilet; GO OPEN BOX.

Scott opened the door. A black box rested on the top of the toilet. He bent over, placed an ear next to the box. No sound. He reached into his pocket, pulled out a pair of Nitrile surgical gloves and stretched them over his trembling hands. He reached down and forced himself to pick up the box. He turned it over with the care of a human organ. He opened the box. He waited, looked inside and instantly recognized the hand held GPS device. As he pressed the ON button he thought he heard the sound of footsteps. He stopped. He jerked as the GPS buzzed in his hand. He listened, there was only the sound of running water. Then he heard one of the stall door's close. How far away was it? Had he checked all the stalls when he came in? He picked at his face. The GPS flashed. He tried to move it into his pocket but his hand kept shaking. Finally he slid it inside, then pulled out his Glock. He reached into his other pocket, no silencer. He had forgotten it. He never forgot, never. Reynolds bit down on his lip, finally let out a breath. Would the Cartel actually kill him here? The door squeaked as he opened it. He studied himself in the mirror. He looked smaller, barely recognizing himself. The room felt as if it was vibrating. The splashing running water unsettling him. Be in control here. He took two steps forward. Nothing. He stepped to the side, trying to stay balanced, then another step. The door to his left flew open. No one came out. Without thinking, Reynolds jumped in front of the door his gun wobbling in his hand. There was a grunt and then he turned. An old man with a gray-beard down to his chest was reaching for a torn back pack on the floor. He wore green tennis shoes with holes, laces untied, stained jeans and a rust colored sweatshirt that was torn at both sleeves. The man frowned at Reynolds as he shouldered on the back pack. "Got a few bucks for a guy down on his luck, pal?" he asked.

"You shouldn't be in here, friend."

The old man smiled with tiny teeth. "Look who's talkin'."

Reynolds stepped back. The blare of the water was now manic. He went for the exit, looked out into the station, no one was paying any attention. He pulled out the GPS again, there was a text message on the screen: "Press start and follow path. Make sure NO ONE FOLLOWS." He forced himself to be calm and pressed start. A general odor of waste seeping through a sewer grate found him as he turned onto East 43rd Street. Taxis cried in rhythm, Reynolds heartbeat quickened with his cadence. He cantered one block to Madison Ave and turned right. His map told him to walk seven blocks. Cars charging down the streets, but the sidewalks were almost empty. What absorbed him was the feeling that he was all alone. This was his game. Stopping each time he glanced at the GPS a bit dizzy from his lack of sleep. His fingers cold and coiled, he stopped to take off the latex gloves, blew into his fists. The map told him to walk another half block and soon he found himself in front of St. Patrick's Cathedral. Reynolds raised his head to admire the edifice. Clustered columns turned into spires, long and lean and almost alive as if they were ascending into the heavens. A garbage truck steamed, muffler growling. He could use some water but no time now. The GPS pinged. "Go inside church, side door." He treaded up the stairs and stood in front of the door. Sign in front read; Hours 9:00 to 8:30 daily. His watch read 9:13. For a long time he stood in front of the door trying to absorb it. Should he really be doing this alone? He had rationalized over the last few weeks there was no one he could trust. He pulled the handle and pushed the door. Damn thing seemed to weigh half a ton. He stepped inside; gloominess surrounded his body like a dark suit. As his eyes adjusted he could see the flickering of candles from the front entrance. He moved to the Nave. He grabbed onto a wooden pew and looked up. A small light illuminated the ceiling of the church, the altar glowing, dazzling as it wallowed in the twinkling candles. He could have used some spiritual guidance here, but it had been at least a year since his last confession. The GPS bloomed with light and told him to head down the nave and to the front entrance. Toward 5th Ave he told himself. As he made his way to the front, the GPS chirped: "Walk to the Baptistery, go behind, pick up flashlight, walk up stairs to top." No way was he going to the top in here. The place was designed to evoke shades of heaven, but it was dark as hell, then again, that was life wasn't it, he reasoned. A multitude of sin?

He found the flashlight but no back entrance as instructed. He examined the walls—hands feeling, eyes searching from the ceiling to the floor, nothing. He did find a patch of brick and his instinct told him something was different. He pushed on it and it moved two inches. He pushed harder and the wall crept open allowing a two foot wide space to pass through. As he slid inside, he turned on the flashlight. He could see only a few steps that wrapped around the small wall like a labyrinth. He stepped onto the first circular step. He reached for the handrail but found frigid concrete instead. Everything was curved, no way to keep your direction. He leaned against the dewy cold wall, the light pulsing from the flashlight in front of him. He took three more steps but his head languid, feet unsteady, yet he continued to march upward. How much more, how much higher? Finally he clutched the handrail with both hands, the flashlight under one of his arms, and hoisting himself up, one step after another. Reeling from each step, he was convinced the journey up would never end. He stopped to breathe for a moment and his head began clearing. Seven steps later he had arrived.

The GPS had chimed twice while he climbed, he finally reached for it. The darkness was stimulating him now. He moved down a narrow path listening to horns on the streets below, a train whistle blowing in the distance. He worked his way down the entire length of the church and found himself overlooking the choir loft and part of the glowing alter. The beam of the flashlight revealing the cathedral's jagged organ pipes. Two stained glass windows stood beside his head. He waited and listened.

"Shut off the light, Mr. Reynolds," came from a voice around the corner, intense.

Reynolds responded, legs weary now, fingers cold and feeling brittle.

"This is a very special place Agent Reynolds. These are the Secret Rose windows of St. Patrick's Cathedral." The voice was bitter. "These windows cannot be seen from anywhere except where you are standing… Not from the street…not the main floor.

Reynolds stirred for a moment. "Who are you?"

Arising out of the darkness as if a Supreme Being, annunciating, "Someone that cannot be seen but is always there…such as these Rose windows."

An inkling of understanding was blooming inside of Reynolds.

"Much is at stake." The cloister voice was hollow. "Your investigation is now complete."

Reynolds' temples began to pound. "Who are you?" His voice echoed. "What do you want?"

"We demand this to end. No…more…looking."

He swallowed, a thin wake of smoke swimming up from below. "But the games. They're all corrupt. Billions of dollars bet every year. The lives lost."

He waited for a beat. "Go on."

"Every sport, maybe every game, everything that's bet in Vegas," he was short of breath, "everything bet off shore…much of it," his voice echoed. "Corrupt."

There was a long pause. "Keep your country safe…Exterminate the goddamn cartels, Agent Reynolds…as soon as you flush them…your job is done."

The root of the situation was germinating in his head. "The cartels were moving into a landscape that has already been growing," he protested.

"Well done, Agent Reynolds. The cartels were growing and beginning to sprout, but we made sure not to root."

"So the prostitution and contamination of the games will continue."

The Voice was hollow and hungry. "Precisely. "You will now quit since the cartel has been terminated."

"I don't think so. I don't bargain."

"Oh yes Agent Reynolds. And you're the one to help us. The scent of the hunt has captured the fox and we need you to keep the scent away from us."

"This will stop. Stop through legislation, the NCAA, the owners for god's sakes. It will stop."

A biting shout: "You are naïve, Agent Reynolds. Millions have been contributed to lobbyists, special PAC donations to every candidate." The voice now merciful. "The American Gaming Association and subsidiaries own Washington. Money flows into lawmaker's pockets."

Reynolds knew politicians resisted the gaming issue more than any other. "Maybe."

"Bullshit," he bellowed. "Every politician resists bringing gambling legislation to the floor. Does your research show this, Agent Reynolds?"

The voice was right. He looked around for some sort of light but everything still had the reflection of gray. His thoughts from last night lingered. "What about Scarpa? Is he a part of this?" No need to stop there. "And the communication system. Did you hack that? And Ransomware, how long has…."

There was a shout from above. "Silence. You will never be able to continue. Your life is in jeopardy, and we are leaving you an option. You're worth more to us alive then dead. You need to call off the hunt." There was a slight pause. "Give immunity to as many as we tell you. They have helped get rid of the Mexicans. You are finished. Let the Bureau know that the situation is resolved. The cartel is gone. Should be a big win for you Agent Reynolds."

He knew before he asked. "And my other option?"

There was a laugh thundered from the rooftop. "You will die, Agent Reynolds. Not just die but tortured. Tortured by watching your wife die first and then we will torture you for weeks until you ask us to kill you."

He didn't respond. He knew they needed to keep him alive to close the case at the Bureau. Where could he go from here? He had no evidence against them.

"And we will reward you in two to three years. We will have an uncle or aunt of yours die and leave you a couple of million dollars. We can do it anyway that works for you. You'll be able to retire in safety and comfort."

He chewed on his thumb. There was no way out. "Do I have time to think about it?"

"Of course. The change in tone and intensity suddenly deceived him. "You are what Martin Luther was to the Catholic church. A martyr. If you do not quit your search—"

"You'll excommunicate me," Reynolds rapped.

"No martyr…no choice. You will follow our doctrine."

"I have more questions."

"You have sinned enough."

He needed to ask one more question. "Was our informant Gregory Scarpa involved?"

"Your confession is now over. If you do not leave immediately with your instructions, I will nail you to the cross…now go."

Chapter 75

Scott Reynolds sat behind the wheel of his Toyota Camry in the Bureau's parking ramp. He stared into his steering wheel. As soon as you were born, torment was right there waiting for you; a fog of disbelief thickened around him. The slam of a trunk from an SUV behind him normally made him jump, but right now he barely noticed. His jaw was heavy. He took breaths from his mouth, waiting for his brain to engage again. Tell him what to do? Where to go? Who to talk to? The world was swimming around him and no one was around to throw him a rope. Could professional and college games actually be fixed? How would anyone even know? How could anyone really tell? His temples vibrated again. He loosened his tie. He reached for his phone, pushed a button and waited.

"Lamb here."

His voice was strengthless, he could barely hear himself. "Just checking in Ron."

"You OK short stuff?"

"Yeah."

"Where've you been?"

Reynolds didn't answer.

"You there, buddy?"

He hesitated. "We'll go over all of it tomorrow in our briefing," he said looking into his rearview mirror; perhaps expecting someone to be watching him. "Just felt like checking in," he continued, and glad Lamb wasn't able to see the doubt in face. He looked around the ceiling of the car, ran a hand over the sun visor in front of him. He surveyed the coin holder. Could be anywhere he thought to himself. Someone had to be listening now. He wanted to believe, trust in the system again but he knew things weren't ever going to be the same. He didn't know where to look. He listened into the dead silence of the phone as he waited, but it wasn't dead silence. There was a slight hiss on the other end. He bit down on his forefinger, crushing the only shard of nail he had left. He was underground but the Defense Special Astronautics Center could pick up a signal from his auto antennae and send it to one of their satellites dishes on Observation Island. Could the NSA be using their codeword ZARF on him at this very moment? If his phone was on, he knew it was possible to eavesdrop. He pushed the thought away.

"Everything's just fine," Reynolds voiced, rubbing his eyelids with his finger. He felt like turning on his car and placing his lips around the exhaust pipe, filling his lungs with a garage full of poison and calling it all off. What were his choices now?

Lamb continued. "What'd you want to talk about? You got another hair up your ass again."

Reynolds stuck a finger between his collar and neck, pulled on the shirt. "Just concerned about the communication network… encryption…intelligence security. Also wanted to make sure the Carson kid would be OK. Make sure we were keeping our word."

"With Perez dead, I think the Diablos are done."

"Questions for tomorrow's meeting," Reynolds said, running a hand under his seat.

"Thought this had more to do with waking up my ass last night…had a great dream going as well; pitching for the Red Sox."

Reynolds tried his best to sound regretful. "I thought it would be about me, Ronnie." He paused for a second. "Sometimes things aren't always as they seem."

Chapter 76

For a long time now, Tim McMurray had no idea how he would get out of his situation. He glanced around the Atlanta Marriott bar, glazed faces, big screen TVs fissuring his concentration. Threadbare hopes lingering, he stirred his tonic water and lime juice with his finger. After meeting with the feds, the stars and constellations were lining up his way. A streak of luck was no fluke, it was a kismet design, all in the cards, and he had waited for it. He deserved it. He peeked at his Patek Philippe, 11:10PM. He found out about the death of Ricardo Perez through his Twitter account. It was time to call off the dogs, no need to pay a private eye two grand a week to watch his kids. Men in suits wearing lanyards began to move into the bar. The bartender was suddenly busy with the suits placing ordering, all waiting and watching the screens. A boisterous babble soon belted through the room and Tim wanted out. He peeked over at a couple in a corner table fondling each other with abandon and he thought about the women in his next cities: Toronto, Phoenix, and Sacramento. His phone buzzed.

Wondering who it was he answered. He recognized full well when he heard the voice that he only heard in nightmares: "We're interested in hearing about what you want to tell us," the voice said. That voice he hadn't heard for weeks.

The tone of that voice, the reverberation of its sound echoed into his head. He surveyed the room, sat up in his seat and tried to control his breathing. He opened his mouth, nothing. He tried again. "Who, who's calling?" he snapped.

"Your old friend, business partner, Mr. McMurray. Thought you'd recognize the voice, my friend. Thought you said you had something new to tell us."

His tongue was dry, "You're not who I thought you were."

"I'd like to keep it that way, Mr. McMurray. Probably best for the both of us."

What the hell did that mean? He shook his drink, ice clanking the glass. Wouldn't the FBI have taken care of this by now?

"Haven't heard from you in awhile," he muttered.

"That's why I'm calling." The couple in the corner were now moving out of the booth, still tightly entangled. "The Mexican mob is now out of the picture."

McMurray didn't answer. The Feds guaranteed his depositions would exonerate him if he collaborated. Keep his officiating gig in the NBA secure.

"No more deals with the Diablos. Glad you've helped us get rid of the bastards."

McMurray shook his head. What the hell was happening? "I don't understand," he said.

"Now McMurray, you can deal strictly with us, an exclusive arrangement. A partnership that will make you wealthier and safer than your arrangement ever was with those punks."

And then, suddenly he was confused. "I thought you were the FBI."

"Let's just say we're part of the system." The voice let that sink in. "No, Mr. McMurray, you now work exclusively with us. We'll take care of things much better. More skin in the game if you will."

McMurray's stomach spasmed and he bent forward.

"You'll be paid into accounts off-shore through internet gambling sites. Paid handsomely. You keep shaving a few points here and there and everything will work out. Everyone will remain safe."

McMurray was baffled by this, not grateful at, sickened.

"We'll call you soon McMurray. Get you on the payroll right away 'Zebra'."

The phone instantly went dead.

Chapter 77

Jason had been sitting and studying in the Gerdin Learning Center over four hours. His eyes burned but his intentions were absolute. It was a genuine test for him. Basketball had taught him how to work; you exert through toil and muscle, pain and sweat, a thirst and desire for the prize. Nobody could ever know what drudgery and toil could produce, because if you lost your desire, you'd lost everything.

In basketball, when he would throw the ball out of bounds or take a contested shot when others were open, or when coaches would scream at him, or players shun him, he'd attempt to transport himself to the gentle words his mother would say to him; 'Your faith will get you through anything,"

So today, when he knew he needed a passing grade, he turned to the words of his mother. He took a drink from a paper cup. He read paragraph after paragraph, slowly, his finger trailing the words, moving a bit faster all the time. To his astonishment, the door to the study room opened and Krista moved inside. The aroma of her perfume and the intensity of her smile consumed him.

"Hey big fella. Sorry I'm late. The team project went way too long." She slid into the seat and tapped his forearm. "I can't believe you're still here."

"Drive to strive," he said.

"You didn't return my text messages."

Jason patted his pockets, unzipped his backpack and found his phone. "Sorry. I didn't have it on."

"Wow," and the way she looked at him, puzzled, almost waiting for the joke. "I don't remember you not looking at your phone. Keeping up with scores at least."

He shrugged. "I got work to do."

"I thought you hated studying?"

"It's the new daily grind." He untwisted the top of an aluminum bottle and filled his cup.

"Is that coffee?"

He felt her staring at him, felt she was seeing something he didn't even know himself.

"Since when do you drink that?" she pointed. "Caffeine?"

"I need to keep working."

"Serious, huh?"

"Whatever it takes."

She thought about it for a moment and squinted her powder blue eyes. "I can't get over you studying this long."

"Practice makes the man."

She tilted her head and gave him a look.

"Or the woman. Sorry, didn't mean it that way." He leaned closer.

"Really."

"Better." She smiled. "You're on the right path."

Hopes forged to vague hopes, slight hopes, modest hopes. He turned a page, then rubbed his sore shoulder with his fingertips. He said, "Probably getting a better grade tomorrow than you."

She sat back, laughed. "No change in cockiness I see." She thumbed through his notebook, swatted him with the back of her hand. "Where you getting your performance enhancing drugs?"

Making a fist he thumped his chest. "It's all heart, sis."

"I got to say, kinda proud of you."

It was something his mother had said to him. Something that she'd preached to him, something that he had yearned to hear again "Umm… thanks. Thank you," he said then swallowed.

Her eyes were gentle and satisfied with the force of the moment. She placed her palms on his arm, squeezed. "Think I'd like to spend more time with a guy like this. Guess you're kinda growing on me."

He needed to keep studying but he craved her attention. His appetite had changed. He stared down at the table for a moment then looked at her. "Guess that's what I've been hoping for."

She gave him one of those looks that reminded him of how many times she told him he always got everything he wanted; but there was more of a perplexity in her eyes now. "I thought you only needed a C to pass?"

"I'm looking to boost my grade point."

She gave him another look. "I thought you just wanted to pass?"

"It could help with my cumulative…That's if I stay another year."

She swayed back in her seat. "When did you start thinking about that?"

"I've been wondering what would be best. Best for everyone ya know."

She shook her head wildly. "Everyone. Who's everyone?"

"I've been thinking about what my mother told me. What you've been telling me. Stuff."

"Stuff?"

He shrugged. "All kinds a stuff. Stuff I wanted to talk to you about…. like if I stayed another year. A couple of websites have my chances to move up in the draft if I stay another year. Be number one. That's been the goal."

"It sounds like you have some new goals?"

"Kinda."

"Kind of like major goals."

He shrugged.

"Well now. When were you going to share this stuff, with me?"

He hadn't had too much practice communicating with others. "Now."

She paused, licked her lips and gave him a half smile. "OK, this is something we should spend some time talking about."

He nodded. "I'm just throwing it out there. It could change a lot of things…get to see you more and give me more options."

She stared back.

"In the meantime, let's get back to work here," he said sliding a book in front of her.

She continued to gaze at him as if a shooting star was crossing his face. "OK…back to work."

Chapter 78 [Two years later]

For his whole life Jason had been waiting for situations like this. Wiping his face with a towel he watched his coach draw up the play for him. Music violently drumming from above, he studied the dry erase board; double screen catch behind the three point line, he knew it well. Huddle broken, fans standing twirling Atlanta Hawks' towels above their heads. It was the third time-out in the last 12 seconds and second lead change. Jason checked the game clock again, 2.8 seconds left. Score, Atlanta Hawks 104 Philadelphia Seventy-Sixers 102. This was what he was designed to do. It was time to be the hero and he knew the script better than anyone. He moved to his spot under the basket, photographers gripping their cameras with two hands. Referee handing the ball to the player in front of his bench, the whistle blows. Jason darts through the lane, around two screens and catches the ball, Atlanta guard throws an elbow into his ribs. Jason fakes forward, slight contact, then begins to step back as a whistle blows three times. A referee runs in waving hands, punches his arm forward other arm behind his head, offensive foul—Atlanta's ball with 1.2 remaining. Jason glares over to his bench, his coach yelling. Ball inbounds, game over. Fans screaming, Jason is disgusted, lost. His coach jumps toward a ref. "Piece a shit call McMurray…you're the worst," but McMurray is long gone, already off the floor.

Final Notes

Tim Donaghy was an NBA referee and used his information and position, while betting on the very NBA games he officiated. Donaghy eventually served 15 months in prison and 3 years of probation.

NEW YORK TIMES, May 14, 2018
SUPREME COURT RULING FAVORS SPORTS BETTING
By Adam Liptak and Kevin Draper
Washington—The Supreme Court struck down a 1992 federal law on Monday that effectively banned commercial sports betting in most states, opening the door to legalizing the estimated $150 billion in

illegal wagers on professional and amateur sports that Americans make every year.

The law the decision overturned-the Professional and Amateur Sports Protection Act- prohibited states from authorizing sports gambling. Among its sponsors was Senator Bill Bradley, Democrat of New Jersey and former college and professional basketball star. He said the law was needed to safeguard the integrity of sports.

But the court said the law was unconstitutional.

THE WASHINGTON POST—by Rick Maese

The Supreme Court on Monday ruled in favor of New Jersey in the case that was formerly known as Chris Christie vs. NCAA (Christie's name has been supplanted by Phil Murph, the state's new governor), striking down a 25-year old federal law known as the Professional and Amateur Sports Protection Act (PASPA) that largely outlawed sports betting outside Nevada.

The court's 6-3 decision overruled the Third Circuit Court of Appeals, saying PASPA violates the state's 10th Amendment rights, thereby creating a path for New Jersey and other states to offer sports betting.

"Congress can regulate sports gambling directly, but if it elects not to do so, each State is free to act on its own," wrote Justice Samuel S. Alito Jr., for the majority. "Our job is to interpret the law Congress has enacted and decide whether it is consistent with the Constitution. PASPA is not."

On it goes ...

EPILOGUE for THE GREAT GAMBLE

by Jim Leach

In the last weeks of a thirty year career in Congress I helped manage the passage of a controversial bill called the Unlawful Internet Gambling Enforcement Act. By background, at the turn of the 21st Century I represented several university communities in Eastern Iowa. Based on town meetings, calls and letters from parents of students who had dropped out of school because they had gotten over their heads betting on sports on the Internet, I decided to delve into how foreign Internet casinos could brazenly spurn US law to operate in the American market. While I hesitated to intervene in economic activity where individual choice was so poignantly at issue, the evidence indicated that corrupt foreign based casinos were at the embryonic stage of gambling on steroids. The spectrum of stories about students who gambled away their summertime earnings that had been intended for tuition convinced me of the need to reign in dubiously taxed, sparsely regulated Internet casinos owned by Europeans and Asians operating largely in Caribbean countries. The legislation that I introduced was strongly supported by most of the country's religious communities whose pastors, mullahs, and rabbis had found their pastoral obligations increasingly including work with parishioners who had become victims of gambling addictions. Since the legislation targeted solely corrupt foreign Internet casinos and held harmless individual American bettors, it had the support of all the professional sports leagues and the NCAA.

I had little doubt that the picture I got a dozen years ago of a law-breaking Internet gambling market place would soon be competitively challenged by established American casinos. Gambling forces have a long record of marshalling extensive influence in Congress and the Executive branch on gaming issues whatever political party controls the levers of political power. Today, in the wake of court rulings, Internet gambling has been effectively legalized in the United States, presumably mooting the legislation discussed above. In some ways the change in law dutifully expands the rights of individual citizens to spend their resources as they see fit and properly causes casinos, foreign and domestic, to operate in America within the rule of state and federal laws. In other ways it may hold dangerous social ramifications.

What this thoughtful novel dramatically describes is how athletes can easily be hooked and taken down a path that tempts moral and social codes within families, teams, and the community at large. Few institutions, after all, are more susceptible to criminality than gambling. Casinos operating legally within the US are the big winners but big bettors know that the only way to manage their risk is to cheat—i.e., pay athletes to shave points or otherwise cause a likely winner to lose or win by less than published odds. The upside of citizen betting is that it accentuates involvement in and support of local and state teams. The downside is that all casino gambling is tilted. Even in re-established legal circumstances the bettor is likely in the long term to lose money because the casino always takes a cut and because a tendency of sports betting participants to support local schools could be more emotive than rational.

As for academic institutions and professional leagues, nothing brings greater fear to administrators and coaches than anything that jeopardizes the integrity of sports. Whether it be certain Olympic sports or the football game that we call soccer, sophisticated cheating —the first with drugs; the second principally in Europe and Latin America, with financial incentives and family threatening of players and referees—has been widespread. In Central America the intensity of fan advocacy for national teams is so extreme that it once led El Salvador and Honduras to engage in a 100-day war.

On the prudential side, the professional sports leagues in the US, led by the NFL, spend millions of dollars reviewing, for instance, every referee's role and how he/she reacted on every play in every game. Likewise in basketball, owners, coaches, and players understand that in games of inches and split-second action the teams cannot afford the loss of reputation that would come if episodes of point shaving or an unbalanced calling of fouls were to occur. What the meteoric growth of Internet gambling underscores is the importance of paying enhanced attention to the integrity of the competitive framework. Rules and the manner they are upheld matter greatly to all sports and to our American culture within which competitive team playing is a central ingredient.

As for sports participants, the vulnerability is high for student athletes who come from impoverished circumstances or have family members in need of costly health care. It takes extra character to avoid conflicts. When I entered politics I used to think that campaigns and competitive sports were similar. Each were competitive; each required discipline to understand the challenges competitors pose; each activity has numerical outcomes. But as time passes I came to the conclusion that sports ethics are higher today than political ethics. In sports there are rules that cause flags to drop or fouls to be called; referees err from time to time in a game but seldom with prejudice; coaches teach players to respect their opponents; in politics, on the other hand, campaign managers instruct candidates in close races to go negative; likewise, in politics there are few rules; indeed historical restraints on campaign financing have recently been eviscerated by a 2010 Supreme Court ruling that causes our democratic system to begin what may evolve into a slippery slide toward corporativism. The relevant question today is whether the introduction of massive new betting approaches on the Internet, coupled with the "monetization" of university athletics —i.e., the paying in varying ways of athletes—could spark an analogous weakening of amateur sports values.

The social costs of Internet gambling are not slight. There is nothing about gambling, especially Internet gambling, that grows jobs and causes economic growth. For every individual who may get a job in the casino industry, jobs of far greater magnitude are eliminated in all aspects of retail marketing. In particular jeopardy are enterprises like shoe stores and restaurants that depend on customers controlling adequate levels of disposable dollars. The only polling review on this subject that I recall relates to the Midwest's largest shopping center, Mall of America, in Minneapolis. Years ago it did a survey assessing its market competition in the metropolitan area. Was it the downtown business district, smaller shopping centers, neighborhood shopping districts, or the nearby Indian casino? By a large factor the survey reportedly revealed that the casino proved to be Mall of America's largest competitor for disposable dollars. Today it would not surprise if the biggest competitor for disposable dollars across the country is now on or about the Internet, companies like Amazon, Apple, and Internet casinos.

Community banks, like shopping centers, face a surprisingly large new challenge. Casinos, after all, are financial companies competing directly with deposit taking institutions. Our free market system depends on a banking system that securely attracts deposits that are then made available as loans for automobiles, home ownership, or the growth of companies. When the disposable dollar shrinks, the availability of credit is reduced. And when the savings dollar is eroded by gambling losses, the quality of loans can too easily decline. Just as in state lotteries, the largest relative losers in Internet gambling are addicted gamblers from financially poor backgrounds. The difference between state lotteries and Internet casinos is that the former amount to citizen payment of a voluntary tax and the latter represent the gifting of assets to casino owners.

There is no pot of gold in sports betting for anyone other than casino owners, especially those who may corporately be organized as a nontaxable foreign entity, or fast street talkers who are likely to find themselves at some point behind bars for employing illegal strategies to improve their betting prospects. Everyone in America is aware of Alcoholics Anonymous (AA) that assists through dialogue addicts in efforts to save their lives and their families. The financial counterpart is Gamblers Anonymous (GA) that provides analogous services for gambling addicts. It is astonishing how pervasive Internet gambling has become in such a short time. Gambling is now the fastest growing addiction in America despite its being a financial game that poses a distinct possibility of destroying family life, losing job security, and even contemplating suicide.

All citizens can make their own judgment whether America is better off with or without a pervasive gambling ethic. But as this thought-provoking novel soberly reveals, the Internet has brought the casino into the living rooms and kitchens of American homes, the work stations of American businesses, the dorm rooms of college students, the cars, buses, and even the walking paths of America's parks and forests. Due to the privacy and anonymity of the Internet, electronic devices have become extensions of the hand and mind of underage youth as well as their parents. Mathematical efficiency packed into ever smaller devices has many constructive uses. Propelling "24/7" gambling may not be one.

Fiction is a far more compelling way to reveal social truths than political treatises. David Bluder is uniquely positioned to write this pioneering novel about sports betting. A former banker who is married to one of the most respected coaches in America, Lisa Bluder the 2019 National Coach of the year in Women's Basketball, he understands finance and more importantly, he is well aware of the varied pressures being placed by society on student athletes, their coaches, referees, and league officials.

Jim Leach began a public career as a US Foreign Service Officer at the Department of State. In 1973 he returned to his home town (Davenport, Iowa) and three years later was elected to Congress where he served for thirty years. Upon leaving Congress he was appointed the John L. Weinberg Visiting Professor of Public and International Affairs at the Woodrow Wilson School of Princeton University. Subsequently he was appointed a lecturer and interim Director of the Institute of Politics at the Harvard Kennedy School. President Obama then named Leach the ninth Chair of the National Endowment for the Humanities. Four years later he accepted a dual appointment as The University of Iowa Chair of Public Affairs and Visiting Professor of Law.

Acknowledgments

I am immensely grateful to the team that is required to author a novel. I would like to thank the following people who helped turn my story into a book. Editors: Gordon Mennenga, Eric Goodman and University of Iowa Press Director, Jim McCoy. Thanks to Randy Larson for reading drafts of the story and International Writing Program Director Christopher Merrill at the University of Iowa and Congressman James Leach for their invaluable help and advice. Thanks to Jenny Moy, copyeditor, Amy Margolis, Director of the Iowa Summer Writing Festival and Jan Zenisek and Deb West at Iowa Writers Workshop. I am deeply grateful to friends for their generous support and encouragement.

Finally, I send gratitude and endless love to my wife Lisa and three children for being always by my side.

David L. Bluder holds a degree in business from Northern Iowa University and received his MBA at St. Ambrose University. Before becoming an author, David was a banker, politician, business owner and investor, as well as taught Business Policies at the University of Iowa.

He currently lives with his wife, Lisa Bluder (20 years as University of Iowa Women's Basketball and 2019 Naismith Coach of the Year) and three children.

The Ice Cube Press began publishing in 1991 to focus on how to live with the natural world and to better understand how people can best live together in the communities they share and inhabit. Using the literary arts to explore life and experiences in the heartland of the United States we have been recognized by a number of well-known writers including: Gary Snyder, Gene Logsdon, Wes Jackson, Patricia Hampl, Greg Brown, Jim Harrison, Annie Dillard, Ken Burns, Roz Chast, Jane Hamilton, Daniel Menaker, Kathleen Norris, Janisse Ray, Craig Lesley, Alison Deming, Harriet Lerner, Richard Lynn Stegner, Richard Rhodes, Michael Pollan, David Abram, David Orr, Tom Brokaw, and Barry Lopez. We've published a number of well-known authors including: Mary Swander, Jim Heynen, Mary Pipher, Bill Holm, Connie Mutel, John T. Price, Carol Bly, Marvin Bell, Debra Marquart, Ted Kooser, Stephanie Mills, Bill McKibben, Craig Lesley, Elizabeth McCracken, Derrick Jensen, Dean Bakopoulos, Rick Bass, Linda Hogan, Pam Houston, and Paul Gruchow. Check out Ice Cube Press books on our web site, join our email list, Facebook group, or follow us on Twitter. Visit booksellers, museum shops, or any place you can find good books and support true honest to goodness independent publishing projects so you can discover why we continue striving to "hear the other side."

Ice Cube Press, LLC (Est. 1991)
North Liberty, Iowa, Midwest, USA
steve@icecubepress.com
twitter @icecubepress
www.IceCubePress.com

To Fenna Marie your loving soul
and heart are precious.
To Ingrid, a love I'm so thankful
to have found.

PGIL2020USA